Flag McAndrew

Braid Anderson

Published by YouWriteOn.com, 2011

CHAPTER ONE, DECEMBER 1957

Inglis Knight McAndrew was stunned by the contents of the letter gripped tightly in his hand. Years of hope and ambition had just been shattered by a single sheet of typewritten paper, on Admiralty letterhead. The words blurred before his eyes.
'Their Lordships very much regret......change in Defence Policy......
.....guided missiles only......no more manned fighter
aircraft.......services not now required.............'

He couldn't believe that at this, the eleventh hour of his single-minded purpose, the dream was gone - finished - murdered by a shortsighted, not to mention idiotic, bureaucracy.

In less than three weeks time he was due to report at Devonport to begin Naval officer training - they had told him officially. Now they said just as officially that it was not to be. He was 17 years old, and for as long as he could remember, his sole ambition had been to fly a fighter plane. For years he had spent every available minute watching the planes at the nearby aerodrome. He could remember the Spitfires, Meteors and Vampires; the visiting Sabres and a couple of short-lived Swifts; and more recently the eerie-sounding Javelins, and the eternally beautiful Hunters. The drone of the giant B36 bombers clawing their way across the sky had fascinated him, but a fighter pilot was what he was going to be.

He threw the letter onto the dining room table, ran from the house, and jumped on his pushbike. Half an hour of furious pedaling later, he was at his favourite spot - sitting on the fence above a road cutting, where he could look straight down the main runway of Leuchars fighter base. From the same place he could see the Junction railway station in the opposite direction. There he could indulge both his hobbies at the same time - planes one way, trains the other. But always the planes had taken precedence. There was a magic about flying which held him spellbound.

The steam locomotives of the time were fascinating in their own way, but they were tied forever to the ground in two dimensions.

He'd had some hairy, and scary, experiences sitting on that fence watching the planes and trains go by.

As he watched the 3 o'clock Flyer swoop down the long curve towards the railway station, a real flyer was warming up its jet engine behind him. He glanced round to see a visiting Canadian Sabre taxiing to the far end of the runway. By the time the Flyer cleared the station, the Sabre should be taking off over his head.

He turned round again on hearing the roar as the pilot opened the throttle. The Sabre rolled down the runway towards him, trailing a plume of black smoke as its speed increased. Three quarters of the way along the runway, its wheels left the ground. By the time it crossed the end of the runway, the wheels were already folding into their bays - and the noise stopped. The jet engine had flamed out, and the Sabre came onwards in a silence more deafening than the noise which had preceded it. It was sinking back towards the ground, and Inglis could see the pilot's head through the canopy - as the Sabre headed straight for him. It was going to hit him!

He sat frozen with fear as the realization punched him in the stomach. The plane grew huge, filling the sky; a giant's winged foot about to crush Inglis McAndrew like a beetle.

He knew it was too late as he threw himself backwards over the fence, eyes still locked on the Sabre. His mind was filled with the thrilling horrific fascination of imminent death. Then somehow, it suddenly didn't really matter much anymore, if he couldn't be a pilot himself.

The starboard wing dipped and hit the fence two panels from him. The main body of the plane passed over his head before he even hit the ground. Inglis could FEEL the air whistling beneath the Sabre, over the crack of the fence panel breaking. Time slowed almost to a stop as the plane scraped over him by what seemed a hairbreadth. It seemed huge - much larger than a Sabre had any right to be; and it took forever to pass his wide horrified gaze.

Then, by a seeming miracle, it was past, and began to cartwheel, across the road cutting and into the plowed field beyond. He could smell unburned kerosene, and he could see every detail of the plane's

4

belly. Inglis didn't remember ever hitting the ground - he couldn't tear his eyes away from the Sabre. It plowed into the field and exploded with an earthshaking detonation, stunning him with its force. A ball of flame shot upwards and outwards - away from Inglis. He could see parts of the plane spiraling through the air above the flames, and before the smoke.

It was a scene from a nightmare, and he could hardly believe he was still alive. One wheel of the plane was later found embedded in the platform of the railway station, and the largest identifiable part of the pilot weighed just five pounds.

Inglis was scared and shaken. Twenty minutes later, when the whole area was crawling with RAF men, he was still in the same place. He had started trembling, and couldn't stop. They wrapped him in a blanket, gave him hot drinks, and asked him questions he couldn't answer until later.

He just wanted to be alone. He didn't want to talk to anyone. Into his head came a picture of the Minister for War, Mr. Duncan Sandys - with Inglis' hands round his neck, squeezing. He felt as if his whole life had been for nothing. Even the last part was no good now. The preliminary questionnaires, followed by a week of intensive testing at RAF Hornchurch. Eyesight tests, hearing tests, coordination and balance tests. Intelligence tests and fitness tests; testing under stress and disorientation. Tests from before dawn until long after dusk. All designed to establish whether you were good enough to be a pilot in the RAF.

Then more interviews and tests at HMS Sultan for another four days. Which was the Navy's way of saying that good enough for the Air Force didn't necessarily mean you were good enough to fly *their* jet fighters. And at the end of it all, four of them out of the original fifty having their photographs taken together, flushed with success, and a feeling of being different from the rest of the world.

Inglis was going to fly the naval version of the Saunders Roe SR54. It was canceled at about the same time as he was, in spite of strong interest from the Germans. Along with half the British aircraft industry - which could not have been more effectively sabotaged by the

Russians than it was by the good old British politicians.

He decided he would join the Merchant Navy and run away to sea - the farther the better.

CHAPTER 2

The Forth Tanker Company accepted Inglis so quickly it almost took his breath away. He posted his application to them on 21st December, and joined his ship at Smith's Dry Dock on the Tyne less than three weeks later as Senior Cadet - in spite of Christmas and New Year holidays.

The Security man pointed him in the right direction, and he lugged his suitcases through the busy shipyard towards *MV Forth Venturer*. She lay high and dry in the dock, the flash of welding here and there, her sides a patchwork of different colors and scars. She was five years old, but when Inglis first saw her she looked as if she had already been through a war or two. Dock workers and their tools littered the decks, among the planks, pipes and sheets of metal. To his ignorant eye the scene was one of utter chaos. So much so that he doubted she would ever sail - and wondered what on earth he had got himself into. But as McAndrew Senior was wont to say - Fools and children should never see a job half done.

Gradually over the next two weeks she became a ship again, while Inglis set about getting to know her. She was built in Belfast, which to him meant second best to Clydebank. But he forgave her that for now. Sitting in the dock the ship gave the impression of a stranded whale, with extra humps on its back. At the front end was the smallest hump called the forecastle. This was raised much higher than the main deck, and was flared out at the sides - enabling the ship to break and surmount the waves without becoming a submarine. It also provided a place to put anchors and winches and things where you could see them - and get to them at sea without being swept overboard.

The middle hump was much larger, containing the bridge and wheelhouse. This was the nerve centre from which the ship was controlled at sea. Behind and beneath the bridge are the cabins where the ship's officers live. On the next deck down are their dining and recreation rooms. Finally, right down at deck level there are storage rooms, with watertight doors sealing off that level from the outside deck. A couple of lifeboats swing from davits on the level below the bridge - just in case she does become a submarine!

Right up on the top of the wheelhouse is a place called the Monkey Island, which is a very apt description. You almost have to be a monkey to climb the narrow vertical steel ladder leading up there; flat against the bulkhead so you can't get your instep on the rungs, and use only your toes.

At the blunt end of the ship - which is really the wrong end for a whale - is another hump, almost as big as the middle one but not as high. This contains the rest of the crew members, together with their eating and playing facilities - and another two lifeboats. Down below them is the main engine, a huge four cylinder diesel. Inglis never thought a four cylinder engine of any kind could be so huge. It was two stories high, and each cylinder could accommodate a man with room to spare.

Mounted on top of the rear hump is the massive funnel, which is really mostly for show. The outer casing surrounds an inner dummy casing, with a ducted air space between for ventilation, and to supply some of the air needed by the engine. Inside the funnel is an exhaust pipe as big as a battleship's main gun.

Forth Venturer was a 'spirit ship', which meant she carried only refined petroleum products. This was much better in Inglis' eyes than being sent to a crude oil carrier. Spirit ships are like tramp steamers, going anywhere in the world that can accommodate them; whereas crude carriers ply only between the oil wells and the refineries.

Inglis presented himself on board in his brand new doeskin officer's uniform, convinced he was God's gift to the Merchant Marine. The uniform had appealed to his vanity in the choice of company. Unlike other Merchant officers, those employed by Forth Tanker wore a uniform almost identical to that of the Royal Navy. To anyone who really knew what he was looking at, the difference lay in the oval background to the anchor in the cap badge. But not too many people looked that close, and Inglis had already been saluted by one young policeman. That had made him feel ten feet tall! The other side of the coin was that the government owned 51% of the company. It could therefore call on Forth Tanker at a moment's notice to supplement the Naval Fleet Auxiliary in times of emergency. As far as Inglis was concerned this only added to the spice of the job, and he was dumb enough then to hope an emergency would come along especially for his benefit!

The First Mate wasn't at all what he'd expected, though he wasn't sure what he *had* expected. The Mate was six feet tall, with a broken nose and longish curly dark hair. But contrary to his appearance he was a most gentle, patient and well-educated man, whose abiding passion was classical music, and above all the opera.

Inglis quickly came to like and respect him as he patiently answered all of his questions. The Mate showed Inglis where his cabin was, before taking him on a short tour of the ship, explaining the purpose of each piece of equipment they passed. The layout of the tanks and their valves was clearly outlined, without a hint of condescension or impatience. The Mate took all of it in his stride, though he was by far the busiest man on the ship right then. He could easily have excused himself the task of showing a completely ignorant junior around.

Inglis' cabin was on the boat deck amidships. One storey down from the bridge, between the Third Mate and the Chief Steward. He shared it with the junior cadet, a small dark haired gnome from darkest Glasgow. Jimmy was sixteen years old, and had already attended Merchant Navy College. His knowledge of ships and the sea was therefore considerably greater than Inglis' - which was not saying a great deal. But because of quirks of age and education, Inglis had been appointed Senior Cadet - not only of the ship, but of the company.

The largest tanker company in the country at that time had been split into three companies. Forth Tanker was the junior of the three, being less than two months old as a separate entity. All of the company's cadets were new, and as the oldest with the highest formal education, Inglis had been appointed instant Senior before even setting foot on board ship. Didn't that make him feel important! The rumor was that the splitting down of the main company was a tax dodge by the private shareholders to save paying for the upkeep of a couple of extra destroyers. The name of the ship was only now being changed from *English Venturer*, while other painters changed the funnel colors.

Being early January it was cold and slippery on deck, and more than once in the first few days Inglis finished up on his backside. The Mate had inspected his footwear, and told him he should get some more suitable shoes as soon as possible. Soft soles of rubber, rope or canvas were the best. But on no account was he to wear shoes with metal objects of any kind in their soles. This averted the risk of a spark igniting petroleum fumes from the cargo. It also put paid to Inglis' best pairs of shoes, which had leather soles with metal brads. But the Chief Steward issued him with a pair of rope-soled boots, and canvas shoes. These were free, but replacements would have to be paid for.

The Mate told Inglis and Jimmy that they would have a week in which to find their way around the ship before starting serious work. They wandered round for hours, poking their noses into every corner of the hull, with Jimmy explaining what he could to Inglis. What he didn't know was explained to them by whoever was handy, and it wasn't long before they learned to be more careful about whom they asked.

The Second Engineer caught Inglis with a good one when he was alone on the very first day. Straight faced he told Inglis that any ceiling on the ship was called a bulkhead. This was because a lot of ceilings on the older ships were very low, and you had to stoop to avoid banging your head, and making it more 'bulky' as a result! It was days before Inglis found out he was being taken for a ride. A bulkhead is a wall, the ceiling being the deck head.

Then of course the ship's carpenter asked them to hand him his left-handed hammer, and the Third Engineer sent Inglis to ask the Chief for a tin of elbow grease. One of the seamen had him almost convinced that a marlin spike was something you put on the end of a long pole for landing big game fish. It's actually used for rope splicing. Inglis was on his way to fetch a sheepshank from the cook for the Steward when Jimmy chased him to say it was a knot. When the cook asked him to bring him a Turk's head he dug his toes in - that was another knot.

By the end of their first week on board, the honeymoon was over, and the two Cadets reported to the Second Mate for their first serious work. He grinned at them and said
"Today you are going to get cold and dirty, and covered in grease

10

and muck."

He seemed to be enjoying the prospect as he continued

"First you have to go and find the Donkeyman and tell him I sent you
to help him with the Donkey pumps. He'll take it from there, and I'm
sure you'll have a great time. Off you go."

They hurried below to the main deck, where Inglis grabbed Jimmy's
arm and asked him "What the hell's a Donkeyman, Jimmy?"

"Don't ask me" he shrugged "I never heard of him."

"That's what I thought" says Inglis, "The buggers are having a go at
us again, aren't they?"

"Looks like it Inglis. But what to do?"

"I'll tell you what we'll do" he answered. "We'll go to the recreation
saloon, play a game of cards and listen to a record."

The Officers' Recreation Saloon was empty, so they grabbed a pack
of cards and played pontoon. There wasn't much choice of records, and
they finished up with the White Horse Inn scratching tinnily on the
record player - which someone must have picked up at a jumble sale; it
was an ancient wind-up model.

They lived it up for half an hour, maximum stake one penny. Even
then Jimmy had taken Inglis for a couple of bob by the time the
Second Mate burst in the door. Then all hell broke loose. He glared at
them and started shouting.

"What the hell do you think you're doing? I told you to report to the
Donkeyman, and here you are playing cards - and gambling into the
bargain. Shit, you're in bloody trouble now, the pair of you."

They both jumped up from the table, scared and confused.

"But sir...." Inglis started.

"Don't bloody but me, and shut up and listen!" he shouted. "I've
been at sea a long time, and nobody ever did this to me. I'm taking you
to the Mate right now, and he can decide what to do with you. When
the Skipper comes on board you'll be lucky if you lose only your first
month's wages before you've even bloody earned them!"

"Sir" Inglis said again, determined to be heard. "I'm responsible.
Jimmy only came along at my suggestion. I thought you were just
pulling our leg, like everybody else has been doing. We never heard of

11

anyone being called a Donkeyman. We've been sent for tins of elbow grease, raw sheepshank, Turk's heads, and God only knows what else. I thought this was another one, honestly sir. There's no way we would have done it if we'd thought you were serious. I'm sorry sir, but that's the honest truth, whether you believe it or not."

The Second Mate glared for a moment longer, then burst out laughing. It took him a moment or two to straighten his face again and recommence shouting.
"Right! One time you get away with it, and once only. The Donkeyman's waiting for you in the after pump room. And in future you'd better remember that when I tell you to do something you do it like NOW! When I say jump, you take just long enough to ask how high. If I tell you to jump over the bloody side that's what you'll do. Now bloody move yourselves, before I turn your arses black and blue with my boot!"

Bang went Inglis' concept of an officer and gentleman. They ran from the saloon, and kept running until they reached the after pump room - at least they knew where that was. It was like a small steel cabin on the main deck. That's what it looked like from the outside. When they poked their heads in the door, the whole scene changed dramatically.

Inside the door was a platform with a rail round it. A steel ladder descended from the edge of the platform, down into the gloom below. Inglis peered over the edge and saw another platform ten or twelve feet beneath - with one more ladder leading from it to yet another platform farther down. There was at least one more silhouetted against the dim light from the bottom of the well. Inglis leaned over the rail and called out.
"Hello, is there anybody down there?" After the first word the echoes mixed in, and the rest of the sentence reverberated around in triplicate. Two words came back from far below.
"Come down."

Inglis looked at Jimmy, shrugged, and felt gingerly with his foot for the first rung of the ladder. *Just don't look down and you'll be okay*, he told himself. Jimmy followed him down and trod on his fingers. "Shit! Watch it Jimmy. That was my bloody fingers you just stood on."

The words echoed from the bulkheads, tripping over each other again.

On the first platform they agreed Inglis should go first and call okay when he reached the next one. Then Jimmy would come down and join him. That way his fingers lasted all the way down to the bottom.

Awaiting them was the mysterious Donkeyman. He was a gnarled, hunchbacked little man, who looked as if he had been born in the bowels of the earth, and was never meant to see daylight. His gray skin was almost the same colour as his dirty overalls, and lengths of cotton waste and rags sprouted from every pocket. He moved around like a big gray crab, and had the unnerving habit of cackling away to himself every now and then, like some mad scientist.

The cadets were shown a pile of metal parts and told to clean them in an open drum of kerosene. When each part was clean enough to pass inspection, the Donkeyman would put it back in the pumps. The pump room was dimly lit by a shaded electric bulb encased in airtight armor glass. Water ran constantly down the walls (bulkheads!). Where it came from Inglis hadn't a clue, since they were in DRY dock. More greasy stagnant water sloshed underfoot, and strange sounds reverberated through the bulkheads. It was as if they had been banished to an ancient dungeon, with the Donkeyman as Chief Torturer.

After most of the day down there, they felt like convicts on release day as they re-emerged into the fresh air. Daylight was fading and a thirty knot wind blew wet snow across the deck. Lights glimmered through the snow as they shivered their way back to the cabin. After dinner they had to start their journals. In these they were to enter the events of days at sea - and in port - for the remainder of their time on board.

Next day they reported to the Bosun for work on deck. Anything was welcome after the dungeon. The bosun issued them with chipping hammers, paint scrapers and sandpaper. Then he gave them a section of boat deck railing each on which to practice using them.

It took them two days to get the first ten feet done completely to his satisfaction. Each time they reported finished he would find a speck of old paint they had missed, or a tiny patch of rust, or a slight stain of some kind on the woodwork.

He was an ancient Swede with a walrus mustache, stained brown from decades of smoking his pipe and sniffing snuff. His English was quaint but adequate, with the Swedish lilt adding flavor to his old fashioned manner of speech straight out of a pirate story.

On the morning of the third day he poked and peered, stroked his mustache, and finally shook his head again. The metalwork was now okay, but there was still something not quite right about the woodwork. Then, as if a sudden inspiration had hit him, he snapped his fingers and told them the missing ingredient was the elbow grease he'd forgotten to give them. He told Inglis to go and fetch a tin from the ship's carpenter. Inglis looked him straight in the eye and told him that one had already been tried on them, so what now?

Chuckling away to himself, the bosun fetched some red lead paint and linseed oil, and told the cadets to apply them liberally, after one final quick going over with the fine sandpaper.

That evening the Mate intercepted them at the cabin door to inform them they would be allowed ashore until 11pm tonight; *and* from midday until 11pm the next day, which was Saturday. They hadn't been ashore since joining the ship, and had begun to watch with envy as others came and went on the gangplank to the outside world.

For the first week it hadn't seemed to matter. They had been finding their way round the ship, with everything new and interesting. But now they could hardly wait to set foot on tarmac instead of steel for a while. The Second Mate was to act as their chaperon, much to Inglis' disgust. It was company policy to keep new cadets under close watch for their first few weeks. But after the first trip afloat you came under normal ship's discipline. In other words at the first port of call they would theoretically be out from under Mother's wing. But no doubt someone would be asked to keep a discreet eye on them even then.

CHAPTER 3

The Dun Cow was a typical boisterous Tyneside pub not far from the shipyard gates at Wallsend. There seemed to be railway lines here there and everywhere. Smoke from them and the forest of factory chimneys mingled with the snow, which was heavy now that the wind had died. The atmosphere inside the pub was a fug of smoke and steam much the same as outside, but much warmer. A roaring fire cheered the place up from behind its strong fire guard in one wall. The noise and jostling were new to Inglis, coming as he did from one of the quieter byways of semi rural Scotland, but he soon adjusted, and even began to enjoy it.

This was where the Industrial Revolution had really got a grip, and the railways had earned their keep very early in their history. The home of the original militant railway workers, with Railway Institute and Mechanics Institute which were the envy of all others at the end of the previous century. Thousands of steel machines had been put together in this part of England, from ships to railway locomotives. Bridges and towers had been fabricated here for erection in the area and far beyond. Tanks and guns had gone to battle in their thousands from Tyneside. And most of the men who made them met in pubs like this at the end of the working day. While the Moneylenders grew fat in their clubs in London.

They pushed their way to the bar and ordered drinks. Inglis had no trouble getting a lager - he didn't trust English beer - since he looked more like twenty than seventeen. But poor wee Jimmy, who looked even younger than he was, had to settle for a soft drink. It was hard to believe there was actually less than a year between them in age.

The Second Mate found half a table, and they settled back to enjoy the bustle. Conversation was not too easy above the din, so they finished the first couple of drinks without much talk. The crowd thinned out around 8 o'clock as men became hungry for their dinners. A piano struck up near the fire, and soon everyone was singing the old favorites.

Two girls sat down at their table, chattering away as if determined to use up every word at their command as quickly as possible. They had no drinks, and after a few minutes one of them looked straight at Inglis and asked

"Well, aren't you going to buy a lady a drink then?"

For a moment he didn't know what to do or say. He'd never been in this situation before. The Second Mate was looking at him with a grin on his face. Inglis raised his eyebrows at him, but he refused to be drawn.

"Well then, cat got your tongue?" asked the girl.

"Yes, I mean no, sure. What would you like?"

"Double gin and tonic, and a double scotch for Doreen. I'm Mary, what's your name?"

Inglis gave his name, and introduced Jimmy and the Second - whose grin now threatened to split his face. The girls' drinks cost an arm and a leg, and Inglis returned to the table shell-shocked, walking wounded. Christ, what was he doing? They looked like nice girls, but he couldn't afford many more of what they were drinking. And he was due back on board the ship in a couple of hours. Maybe he could chat one of them up and meet her somewhere tomorrow afternoon - he was free then until Sunday night.

The girls flirted and chatted, with Mary concentrating on Inglis, and Doreen sounding out the Second Mate. He didn't seem to be too interested, so she started competing with Mary for Inglis' charms. Jimmy got an occasional smile, but he seemed to have gone into his shell.

When the glasses were empty Inglis looked hopefully at the Second Mate. He grinned again and shook his head slightly. It looked as if Inglis was left carrying the can, and the whole field was open to him. He decided he would buy one more round, but that would be it. His wallet looked pathetic after he shelled out for the drinks. This had best lead to something.

The girls now concentrated all their attention and charms on Inglis. He felt flattered, and soon the money didn't seem so important after all. Mary really was quite nice, and he couldn't understand why the Second wasn't interested in Doreen. The next round took most of his remaining money; but it would be closing time in half an hour anyway,

16

so what the hell - in for a penny in for a pound - or two, or three.

Inglis was trying hard to sound out Mary on the chances of a date tomorrow. But every time he got to the point, the conversation switched to something else - and he was becoming extremely frustrated. Surely she would enjoy dating a good looking bloke like him - with an officer's uniform thrown in for free.

Ten minutes before closing time the boyfriends showed up. For a few minutes Inglis didn't realize what was happening. Two men in their twenties came to the table, and were greeted cordially by the girls - who picked up their handbags, and rose from their chairs. Mary gave Inglis a charming smile.

"Well, thanks for the drinks Inglis. See you later."

He was dumbstruck. Christ, he had spent nearly all the money in his wallet on them, and now they were leaving.

"Hey, wait a minute. What's wrong? What's happening? I wanted to ask you something."

One of the blokes looked at him hard and asked

"Yeah, what's the problem sailor boy - wha'd'ya wanna ask?"

Inglis pushed his chair back, but the Second Mate grabbed his arm and held on tight, forcing him down again.

"No problem" said the Second Mate. "Nice meeting you girls I'm sure. Have a good night. Inglis is just a bit under the weather."

The four of them turned and left the pub. Inglis was spitting with anger, and shouted at the Second Mate. "What d'you do that for? You're not my bloody mother!"

The Second Mate still had his hand on Inglis' arm. Now he squeezed hard and glared.

"Sit down and shut up! Who the hell d'you think you're talking to? You were stupid and you got taken for a ride. Why the hell d'you think I didn't buy a round? They picked you as an easy mark, with your swollen head, and your nice new uniform. Wake up son. You're not the answer to every maiden's prayer - not that they were maidens anyway. And the boyfriends would have eaten you for supper if you'd started a fight over it."

17

If he'd wanted to deflate Inglis' ego, he'd done a pretty good job. Now Inglis started to feel foolish. The anger subsided, and was replaced by embarrassed humiliation.

"Sorry, Second," he muttered. "Any chance of a last beer?"

"That's better" he said. "I'll get it. And while I'm doing that, you might now ponder why you're not allowed out in the big bad world on your own, eh?"

He laughed and made for the bar. When Inglis thought about it, he had to admit he'd been suckered pretty good. He was still angry inside - but at himself now, not anyone else. He sat and brooded over his beer, but soon began to see the funny side of the affair, if somewhat ruefully.

The piano player packed up for the night, and the landlord called for last orders. Jimmy did the honors, and soon they were on their way back to the ship.   At least they'd had a night out and a sing along, even if Inglis had made a fool of himself. He was a bit poorer, but hopefully a mite wiser. By the time they reached the ship he was laughing at himself almost as much as the others.

Next morning Inglis had a hangover, and the world didn't look so good again. The Captain arrived on board at exactly midday, and was met at the gangplank by the First Mate. They closeted themselves in the Captain's cabin, while Jimmy and Inglis made themselves scarce ashore with the Second Engineer. Like them, he wanted to do some shopping. They traveled into Newcastle, and Inglis spent most of his remaining money on working clothes and a decent pair of shoes with soft soles. On returning to the ship they were told she would definitely sail on Monday morning's tide, destination unknown for sure, but probably Rotterdam. The snow stopped on Saturday evening, and Sunday dawned cold and clear. Instead of having the day off, the cadets were sent to help the bosun make preparations for putting to sea.

Ropes had to be checked and properly stored. The contents of the paint store were listed. For more than an hour they helped carry fresh meat and vegetables into the cool room and refrigerator. The quantities seemed enormous to Inglis, but the Chief Steward said it was nothing to what he would stock when they went 'deep sea'. Then they would have at least six weeks' rations on board every time they left port. Now he was only stocking up for a fortnight.

They had a long break for lunch, and afterwards they stood at the rail on the main deck, watching the dock workers preparing and checking the massive timber and rubber fenders along the side of the dock. The bosun had smaller versions laid out on the ship's deck, ready for the big moment.

Inglis was fascinated by the height of the hull. At sea a tanker, especially when fully loaded, seems very low. But when you see all of it out of the water in dry dock, it's a long, long way down from the deck to the bottom of the hull. When fully loaded *Forth Venturer* would have the height of a three storey building beneath the surface of the sea.

The Mate came along and gave them permission to inspect the hull from the outside.

"This will be the last chance you get to see how big she really is before she goes back in the water" he said.

They jumped at the chance, following him onto the dock side, then down the ladders to the bottom of the dry dock. The floor of the dock was ankle deep in rust, old paint, and thousands of barnacles, mixed in with rotting weed. All of this had been scraped from the hull before the new paint was applied. The smell curled noses as they took in the scene. A dozen dock workers were digging out the rubbish and loading it into a skip suspended from a small crane on the dock side above.

The ship's hull was sitting in huge steel cradles, mounted on wheels which ran in railway tracks along the bottom of the dock. Massive timber baulks were propped between the hull and the lower corners of the concrete dock. More baulks were jammed between the sides of the ship and the dock walls. Looking up the ship's side from below the midships accommodation was like standing on the pavement outside a ten storey building.

When she was loaded, the volume beneath the water would be far in excess of what could be seen above. It was worth remembering. Inglis didn't want to be the silly bugger who forgot one day, and ran her up on the rocks! He went to bed that night excited by the thought of sailing at last.

CHAPTER 4

Forth Venturer was alive with noise and bustle long before dawn on Monday. Jimmy and Inglis were up at 5.15am, and talked the Steward into giving them some corn flakes for breakfast. He even threw in a pot of tea.

The shipyard workers opened the dock valves just after 6 o'clock. By 7.30 the ship began to gain buoyancy, and baulks of wood and rubbish were floating far below, as the water level crept up. The dock gates swung ponderously open at 8.30. It was high water, and Inglis stood on the forecastle watching everything. That's exactly what the Mate had ordered him to do - watch everything and stay out of everyone's way. Jimmy was at the other end of the ship doing the same thing with the Second Mate. *Forth Venturer* was now a live creature, no longer dependent on the shore installations for succor. She vibrated to the beat of the massive diesel heart buried in the rear of her body.

Lead ropes were run out by launch to a couple of tugs, as the off duty members of the crew lined the side tending the fenders. The bosun and four seamen were following the instructions of the Mate, easing out ropes from the forecastle to the side of the dock. Ideally the ropes should be kept balanced, holding the ship clear of the dock walls, and protecting the new paint work. The tugs at the other end pulled the ship backwards. Slowly and carefully she felt her way stern first from the dock into the river, which was alive with other shipping.

The Captain shouted to the Mate through a loud hailer. The pilot signaled to the tugs by means of the huge steam whistle mounted on the front of the funnel. The tow-ropes were placed on the drum of the stern winch as the tugs came closer. Then one tug gave them back its tow-rope, followed soon by the other. The bow ropes had been cast off by the dockies, and the bosun was urging his men to get them in as fast as they could. *Forth Venturer* was on her own, and the deck reverberated to the thrust of the gigantic propeller under her stern.

At first the ship rode very high in the water. The Donkeyman and the Third Engineer scurried around the deck, opening tank valves and crossover valves. The main sea valves had already been opened, and water was pouring into the bowels of the ship. The purpose of all the activity on deck was to distribute the incoming ballast water so the ship could be trimmed just the way the Skipper wanted her for the voyage. Their destination was Rotterdam, where they would pick up a cargo of refined oil for distribution round Europe.

The weather forecast was not good. Winds of over thirty knots were predicted, accompanied by sleet and snow. Inglis had long since become cold and wet in spite of his 'waterproofed' duffel coat. Visibility was poor, and the radar scanner on the monkey island was revolving to assist the pilot, who would stay on board until the ship cleared the mouth of the river.

Two dockyard men were on board, checking out various pieces of equipment. They made sure the compass was right by checking it against known bearings as they sailed down river. The main engine was cleared and the pumps tested. The winches had already proved they worked okay, and the radar was functioning properly. There were ships of various shapes and sizes all around them, like a busy city street of water. Time after time Inglis was almost sure the ship would collide with one of them, but had at least enough sense to keep his mouth shut. There were skilled and experienced men on the bridge with the knowledge necessary to avoid just that. But still he watched closely as ships on apparent collision course slipped past at what seemed the last moment.

Inglis had to be careful walking from one place to another as the ship moved beneath him. One minute his foot would feel empty air just as he thought it should touch the deck. A moment later it would jar down as the deck moved an inch or two higher than expected. It would take a few days to get his sea legs.

When they reached the mouth of the river Inglis didn't envy the pilot and dockyard men. They had to climb down a rope ladder over the side of the ship and jump onto the bobbing pilot boat as it came alongside. But he needn't have worried - they were old hands at the game. The pilot went first, waiting on the ladder until the boat swooped up to meet him on a wave. Then he calmly stepped across the gap at exactly the right moment, into the arms of two sailors who pulled him inboard. The dockyard men repeated the performance without getting a hair out of place.

21

Now *Forth Venturer* was really on her own, and the ship's head turned southwards. Work on the forecastle was complete, and everything stowed away before Inglis made for the dining saloon and a late second breakfast. The ship was going through a sort of corkscrewing motion, and as Inglis sat down he began to feel slightly queasy. He drank some tomato juice which settled things down a little. But when the Steward brought the scrambled eggs and sausages, his appetite suddenly evaporated. He sat and looked at them as his stomach rebelled. Not wanting to make a fool of himself, he shoveled some of the food into his mouth, swallowing it by sheer will power. But when his stomach received the scrambled eggs, it sent an urgent message straight back up.

Inglis pushed his chair back and made a run for the nearest bathroom, with his mouth filling fast. The scrambled eggs ejected themselves into the toilet bowl - along with some other unidentifiable garbage - in a long pulsating stream. He retched until his stomach muscles were sore; then retched on to exhaustion.

Eventually he staggered upstairs to his cabin and lay down on the bunk. As soon as he lay back, the cabin began to swim around him, and he grabbed the sides of the bunk as he drowned. He sat up again and limped out to the boat deck. His head was aching and he felt sicker than he'd ever felt before in his life. After ten minutes out on deck Inglis discovered that he didn't feel quite so terrible if he kept his face into the bitterly cold wind.

The Second Mate came along and told Inglis he was wanted on the bridge, where the Third Mate would give him his duties for the rest of the day. He reeled up the ladder to the wing of the bridge, slid open the door to the wheelhouse, and reported to the Third Mate. He gave Inglis a bucket, some soap and a scrubbing brush, and told him to fill the bucket at the fire hydrant on the boat deck. Then start scrubbing the deck on the port wing of the bridge.

Inglis scrubbed and retched, and scrubbed and retched, on his knees for the next two hours. Now and again he would refill the bucket from the hydrant, staggering down the stairs and reeling back up. There wasn't much left in his stomach, but every so often a trickle of greenish goo would drop from his lips to the deck. Then he had to wipe it up and scrub that bit once more. He felt more and more miserable; he was cold and wet; and he began to wish he was dead.

The seasickness was continuous for the next two days, all the way to Rotterdam. Inglis got no relief from it. When he lay down it felt even worse, so he couldn't sleep, and spent most of the night on deck or in the bathroom. He wondered what would happen if he kept on being sick like this every time the ship put to sea; and decided he would commit suicide rather than put up with it forever. He could always quit the sea of course - but what would his friends and family think of him then? The big brave hero ran home because he got seasick. The thought of that made suicide a more attractive alternative.

Eventually the ship reached Rotterdam, late in the evening of the second day. As they sailed upriver, the motion of the ship subsided. By the time she was secured alongside the dock, Inglis' seasickness had gone. He went to the cabin, fell into his bunk, and slept until 8 o'clock the next morning. Jimmy woke him and told him he was to report to the Second Mate in his cabin at 9 o'clock. Inglis bathed, shaved, and had a quick breakfast - with second helpings of everything to make up for what he had missed in the past two days. Then he reported to the Second Mate on the dot of 9 o'clock.

He gave Inglis a schematic diagram of the ship's tanks and their valves, and told him to take a walk on deck. He was to identify each valve and its purpose, before meeting the Third Mate in the deck cabin at noon. Inglis would then be standing cargo watch with the Third Mate until 4pm, and from midnight to 4am.

By 11.45 he was convinced he would never learn all of the information on that diagram. There were literally miles of pipes, with scores of valves littering the deck like jungle undergrowth. There were black valves and white valves, red ones, green ones and yellow ones. Main valves, tank valves, crossover and bypass valves. And that was only for the cargo. There were more miles of water and steam pipes with all their valves. Inglis began to think that if all the pipes on the ship were laid end to end, he could walk back to Newcastle on them. He sat in the deck cabin poring over the diagram once more in ever-increasing despair, as he waited for the Third Mate to appear and find out how dumb he was.

When the Third Mate did finally come, he took one look at Inglis' worried expression and laughed out loud. "You're worried sick because you can't learn all that in a couple of hours" he said after the laughter. "Man, it'll take weeks to learn properly. Just start off by remembering that the tank valves are red for the port side, green for starboard, and yellow for the middle ones. We have nine rows of tanks, starting aft of the forecastle with row number one, and finishing this side of the coffer dam ahead of the engine room. That's where the fuel for the engine is kept, and it's like an extra, narrow tank. So the first green valve this side of the forecastle is starboard tank valve number one, and so on. Forget the crossover and bypass valves for now, I'll handle them. Just make sure you open the right tank valve - or shut it - when I tell you. Every valve on the ship turns clockwise to close, anti-clockwise to open - got all that?"

"Yes Third, got it" said Inglis with relief.
"Okay then, but just in case you hadn't noticed, every tank valve has a number painted on the stem. So when I say open number three port, you open the one with the red wheel and the number three painted on it, by turning anti-clockwise. You got it all now for sure? If not, then for Christ's sake say so now, and we'll go over it again, before the loading diagram gets stuffed up."

Inglis got it. Explained his way it couldn't be much easier. Then the Third showed him the wheel spanners kept in the deck cabin, and explained how to use one to open a stiff valve, by hooking onto the wheel and heaving.

"A lot of these valves will be stiff as a result of rust while the ship's been idle, and new paint slapped on by the shipyard men. So you'd better carry a wheel spanner whenever you go out on deck. And don't leave it lying around. You'll notice it's rubberized at the business end, so you don't make sparks. *Always* check the rubber before using it. If there's a hint of bare metal near the hook, *don't* use it - and report it straight away. Meanwhile, you mark it, and bring it back to the deck office, which is what we call this cabin while in port - at sea it becomes the sick bay."

Inglis had wondered why the double bunks were on the starboard bulkhead. He didn't really think they were for dozing in while on watch! The office faced aft, and was in line with the catwalk which ran from the midships island to the after island. The midships section contained the officers' accommodation and facilities, while the after one had more or less the same for the crew.

The catwalk was like a raised footpath about eight feet above the deck, joining the second storey of the two islands. It was very necessary, because when the ship was loaded, the waves crashed over the deck, in anything more than a fair swell.

During Inglis' first watch they switched tanks five times. By the fifth one he was losing his fear of screwing everything up, and could begin to see what the Third Mate was doing, and why. He showed Inglis the inclinometer on the forward bulkhead of the office. This was a pendulum, hung through an arc inscribed in degrees. It told you how far the ship was listing to either side of upright. Third explained how the Captain had instructed him that the list was not to exceed ten degrees. So they would be busier than on some tankers, "especially the lazy buggers who let her go over nearly twenty degrees before switching tanks."

It was also important, though less so, not to let the ship adopt an attitude too far up or down in the head. Therefore, the ship's officers had to work out a loading plan beforehand, and stick to it from watch to watch. A loading log was kept, with the state of each tank marked in at half hourly intervals. On the port bulkhead of the office there were three longitudinal section drawings of the ship showing respectively port, centre and starboard tanks. The state of each tank was constantly upgraded on these by means of colored chinagraph pencils on a clear Perspex overlay. There was a different color for each major product such as gas oil, motor spirit, aviation spirit, bunker oil, etc.

As Inglis learned to understand things, the job became more interesting, and therefore more enjoyable. Every half hour they 'dipped' the tanks being loaded. This was done by means of a long thin, plastic-coated steel tape, with a plumb bob on the end. Above the centre of each tank was a short pipe projecting from the deck, with a hinged lid screwed shut by butterfly nut. The procedure was to open the lid, shine a gas proof torch down through the pipe, then lower the plumb bob. Before it reached the surface of the oil, you had to start it swinging from side to side. When the plumb bob just touched the surface of the oil at the bottom of its swing, the depth could be read off the tape. Together with the time of the reading, this was then noted in the loading log.

In Rotterdam it was possible to simultaneously load three different products into different tanks, which was what they were doing. As a result of this efficiency they would be fully loaded by noon the next day. So if Inglis wanted to see Rotterdam it would have to be tonight.

The Third Mate wanted to stay on board, but the ship's electrician asked Inglis if he would like to go ashore with him for the evening. Jimmy was on watch with the Mate from 8pm till midnight, and had gone ashore with the radio operator. If you ever go to sea in a merchant ship, learn to operate a radio first - you'll have loads of free time in port.

Harry and Inglis went ashore at 6.30, catching a bus from the refinery gate. They drove through miles of docks and wharves before reaching the city. Rotterdam was the biggest port in Europe, and there were hundreds of ships tied up, with just about every kind of cargo you could imagine. Inglis told Harry he didn't have a great deal of money to spend.
"I know cadets never have much money" he said, "unless Daddy's rich. Don't worry about it. You buy every third round of drinks and I'll cover the rest, okay?"
"Okay, and thanks Harry" Inglis answered gratefully.

Harry's idea of seeing the sights was to visit his favorite bars and clubs. At the third one they visited he met a girl he knew, and she was with a girlfriend. To Inglis they were women, not girls - they must have been at least twenty-one. Both of them were dark, well built, and could have been sisters. When Harry introduced them he said they were sisters - non identical twins actually.

They spoke more than passable English, and asked Inglis lots of questions. But Harry was the one they were really interested in, and Inglis was a bit bashful and tongue-tied. Besides which, he didn't fancy a repeat of the episode at the Dun Cow in Wallsend - so he was cautious as well. All of which didn't make him the life and soul of the party. After a while the girls gave up talking to him, and he drank his beer in silence.

A few beers later the perverse side of Inglis' nature got the better of him, and he started trying to make bright conversation, in order to win one of them. The beer helped his confidence. Harry had kept his word, buying two of every three rounds, which Inglis was sure the girls had noticed. But he had left his rally too late. Some of his jokes brought blank stares, and he began to worry if maybe he had B.O. - he couldn't smell it!

In the end the girls invited Harry back to their place, pointedly leaving Inglis out of the invitation. Harry started to protest at leaving him, but Inglis put on a brave face and told him to go ahead, he'd be okay. Who did he think he was kidding? Ten minutes after they left, a woman in her thirties sat down at the table and asked Inglis for a drink. He thought of saying no, but any company was better than none, so he forked out, getting one for himself at the same time. She was a hard looking woman, but quite sexy.

When the drink was nearly finished she told Inglis it would cost him ten gilders to go to bed with her. He told her he didn't have that much to spare, thinking she might bargain. Instead, she emptied her glass and slammed it down on the table, muttering a string of Dutch oaths. Then she made a bee-line for a forty year old man in a crumpled suit, sitting three tables away. He bought her a drink, and minutes later they were both looking at Inglis and laughing.

That was enough for him. He drained his glass and went out to the street. The combination of Inglis and his uniform didn't seem to be working nearly as well as he had expected. He caught a train to the docks, and walked the last half mile to the ship.

Before going on watch, Inglis wondered what had happened to the romance of being a sailor.

CHAPTER 5

Forth Venturer sailed at noon the next day. As soon as the ship was in the open sea, Inglis' seasickness struck again. But thank God it was a short trip to Dunkirk, where they were to unload some of the gas oil and motor spirit. The ship's own pumps had to be used for the unloading, and since this was a slow process they all had a chance to go ashore at their leisure.

The Third Mate and Inglis were on watch together, so Big John decided they would go ashore together - just so Inglis wouldn't get lost and leave him on watch by himself. Also, he reckoned Inglis should see some of the sights of Dunkirk under his guidance. His idea of seeing the sights was much the same as Harry's. They visited bar after bar, downing gallons of beer at a high rate of knots. Which was okay for Big John Soutar, who was the size of half a house. Inglis' handling of it was another matter. He was beginning to have trouble walking between bars after a while.

By the time they reached the strip joint, Inglis was only just aware of the fact that it WAS a strip show. He managed to come round a bit when he realized he was sitting in a front seat right at the stage - where a shapely redhead was taking her clothes off very close to his nose. She was singing the Ertha Kitt song 'Old Fashioned Girl' - in French. Towards the end of the song she came right up to Inglis stark naked, and asked
"Et vous monsieur, etes vous un millionaire?"

As she spoke she leaned forward, and her breasts dangled within inches of his popping eyes. This was almost more than a poor little Baptist boy like Inglis could handle - but he forced himself. Inglis leaned forward with his mouth hanging open in amazement. Just then she drew her chest up and thrust her pelvis forward, and he damn near got a mouthful of her nether regions. He was dazed, enchanted - and drunk.

Soon John dragged him out to the cold dark night. He had to drag Inglis because he didn't want to go. He wanted to date the vision with the red hair on her head, and tawny hair on the other bit! The night air hit Inglis hard, and he had to have a cup of coffee to steady himself.

They entered another bar, where John ordered Inglis a coffee to go with his Nth beer of the night. The coffee was strong hot and black, so he let it cool for a while as he hung grimly onto the swaying bar. It was half as bad as seasickness, with the bar moving around like that.

Finally Big John told Inglis to drink up or they would be late on watch. He grabbed at the coffee - missed - again, and swallowed a mouthful. There was no sugar in it. It was bitter and vile as only French coffee can be, and his gorge rose to eject it. He dashed for the nearby door, and just made it in time for his stomach contents to spread themselves out for inspection on the sidewalk. Peering at what the coffee had brought up with it, he mumbled "Diced carrots, diced bloody carrots."

With his stomach empty Inglis managed to make it back to the ship without John having to actually carry him - not that he couldn't have taken that in his stride. Inglis moaned and sang, and danced and tripped and fell - and got up to start again. John was the organ grinder and Inglis was the monkey. Big John had swallowed gallons of beer without visible effect.

Inglis' watch was a kaleidoscope of half remembered bits and pieces. John took pity on him when he leaned too close to one of the tank pipes with the tape. The blast of air and petrol fumes hit him in the face, making him gag again. Big John let him doze in the office between tank soundings, but warned him - with a huge grin - "This kind o' nonsense better no' happen again laddie."

Drunken sickness was replaced by seasickness within hours, when they once more put to sea. Next port of call Antwerp. More gales, more snow storms and more misery.
"Mind over matter, mind over matter," Inglis muttered to himself, as the matter erupted from the hole just below the mind. The bosun started to teach him rope handling and seamanship, while the Second Mate instilled the basics of navigation. Meanwhile he was allowed to share the Third Mate's watch at sea, from noon till 4pm, but not the midnight to 4am.

Inglis' work started at 7am, with a short breaking of the fast at 8.30. A pattern began to emerge, with chipping and painting from 7 to 8.30, rope work and seamanship - which could include more chipping and painting! - from 9 till noon. 12 till 4 on watch with the Third Mate, during which Inglis sometimes had a go on the steering wheel with the helmsman. Then four till six, still on the bridge doing practical navigation with the Second Mate, whose watch was four till eight. From six till eight was spent in his cabin, going over the theoretical side of navigation, ship handling, signaling, loading problems etc. Before turning in for the night, his journal had to be written up, detailing the events of the day. This had to be left out for inspection by the Second Mate when he came off watch at eight in the morning.

The cabin had to be kept neat and spotless at all times, and was inspected daily by the first Mate. Inglis was seeing Jimmy for only a few hours a day now, as their hours alternated with each other. Jimmy was on the bridge with the Mate from 8 till noon, and did his study while Inglis was on the bridge doing his practical, and so on. Jimmy got an extra hour in bed in the morning, since he had done a lot of the other stuff in Merchant Navy College. So he had a shorter day than Inglis, and he was a real whiz kid with ropes and knots.

The seasickness continued for a few trips, until the 'mind over matter' finally worked. From that day on Inglis was never seasick again. Whenever he started to feel queasy he would tell himself it was a load of old rubbish, and all in his imagination. And it worked, time after time, until he didn't need it any more.

They had a day in Antwerp, and Inglis wasn't sure what to do. His money situation was not good. The Cadet salary of one pound fourteen shillings and ninepence was not designed for gracious living. Thank God for the four and ninepence danger money! Extras like beer and cigarettes were very cheap on board, being duty free. But ashore was a different matter.

Harry's finances were still recovering from his night of debauchery with the twins in Rotterdam, so he suggested Inglis go to the Seamen's Mission with him. At first Inglis thought he was joking, but he insisted it could be fun - and was very, very cheap. That convinced Inglis, and they set off on shanks' pony and tram car for their destination. Inglis wasn't exactly full of joyous anticipation, but at least it was better than staying on board - he hoped.

The Mission looked like a church hall, which it probably was. They were greeted at the glass doors by the Padre himself, complete with dog collar and saintly expression.

"Come in, come in" he said, bathing them in his heavenly smile. "It's good to see you, and we have a little entertainment for you tonight. But first let us say a small prayer for those in danger on the sea." Inglis clasped his hands, bowed his head and closed his eyes as the padre intoned the well known words of the Sailors' Prayer. Inglis' own silent prayer went something like "Oh God, what have I got myself into this time?"

Immediately after the 'amen', the padre became all bustle and business. Inside the entryway was a large refrigerator. Opening its door, he spoke once more.

"Now that's over, I'm sure you boys would like a little bit of fun. Here, grab a carton and follow me. The girls are inside waiting for you, and there aren't many customers yet."

Inglis could hardly believe his senses as Harry winked at him, grabbed a carton of beer, and followed the padre through the door. Inglis even forgot to grab a carton himself, and had to go back for it. Inside the main room their arrival was greeted by a small cheer from the half dozen men already there. About twenty girls were scattered around the room, and half of them came over to say hello. Two of the men were fiddling with the wiring from a record player to a couple of speakers. Inglis called to them.

"Let Harry have a look at that, he's an electrician."

They were instantly popular. Even more so when Harry had the music playing within minutes. Then it was time to dance, and with the girls outnumbering the men by more than two to one, there wasn't a great deal of drinking time in the first hour. More men drifted in and the odds gradually shortened. Harry was having a ball, and after the first few beers Inglis came out of his shell too, starting to chat up the girls. He wasn't much good at this yet, being a bit shy and nervous until the third or fourth beer. He was still only seventeen years old, not twenty seven like Harry.

The beer was free, and Inglis wondered how the place could afford it. Until Harry told him he'd heard on the grapevine that the local brewery had just donated a whole truckload. He hadn't told Inglis earlier in case he 'shot his mouth off', and too many freeloaders turned up. Harry had quite a reputation for being in the know in a dozen different ports around Europe.

The evening went with a swing, and all too soon it was time to return to the ship, and the midnight watch. Inglis made a tentative date with a pert little brunette for 6 o'clock next evening; it was only after arrival back on board that he remembered he wouldn't be here tomorrow evening. No wonder sailors had to be so fast with the girls!

From Antwerp they headed for Hamburg, which according to those in the know, was THE most red hot night spot on the whole Continent. On the way Inglis was introduced to the new Decca Navigator. This worked on the basis of intercepting radio beams, whose transmitting stations were scattered all over coastal areas of Europe. Each beam had its own frequency, and by reading off the various colored dials on the machine, a ship's officer could plot his position to within a few metres. That was the theory - in practice it was early days yet, and there were frequent problems. But Inglis was sure it would become a highly reliable navigation tool in time - for as long as you were on coastal duty around Europe. The trouble was, he wanted to go 'deep sea' and explore the rest of the world.

In the meantime he learned to operate the 'contraption' as the Second Mate called it. He was steeped in more ancient methods of navigation, and resented a machine trying to usurp his function, as he saw it. You could always tell when the Decca was playing up, from the look of malicious glee on his face.

CHAPTER 6

Hamburg was an experience not to be forgotten. As *Forth Venturer* sailed upriver to her berth - which was closer to the city than most other places - she passed a galaxy of shipping stars. Here was the old sail training ship *Passat*, sister to the ill-fated *Pamir*, on which so many German cadets had recently died. Both ships had taken part in the last grain race from Australia to Europe.

Over there was a passenger liner in the shipyard, being altered and fitted out. Her bows were being flared, and a single streamlined funnel replaced the old multiple straight ones. Her new name was *Hanseatic*, but she had started life as *Empress of Japan*, changed to *Empress of Scotland* when the Japs entered the War. Which was a bit of a slap in the face for Scotland if you thought about it. Now she belonged to the nation against which she had ferried so many Allied troops to battle from the Americas. Fair enough Inglis thought, remembering that the largest liner of her day, the *Vaterland*, had sailed from this very city more than forty years ago. When the First World War came along, she was impounded by the Americans, and renamed *Leviathan*. Pride of the American merchant fleet, she had also ferried thousands of Allied troops to battle in that war. Scores of other lesser ships lined both sides of the River Elbe, from passenger liners, through fast cargo liners, to the ubiquitous Dutch Coasters - and of course the tankers, large and small.

From their berth on one side of the river they were able to ride a 'water taxi' across to the nearest pier to 'Sin City'. Some of the crew had told Inglis this was the nickname for the most notorious area of Hamburg, San Pauli. It included the Riperbahn and the Willemstrasse, with their miles of clubs and brothels. This Inglis just had to see - for research purposes of course.

His biggest problem was lack of funds with which to carry out his research. But this could be overcome, with a touch of risk. Inglis hadn't yet started to smoke; but had been advised that one of the best currencies in Hamburg was British cigarettes. On the way from Antwerp he bought 3 cartons of Woodbine Export, duty free from the Chief Steward. The story was that they were worth five times their duty free price once he got them ashore. The catch was, he had to get them past German Customs undetected.

Inglis and Harry dressed very carefully before hailing their water taxi. Harry smoked, and was paid a lot more than Inglis; so he didn't want to sell too many of his cigarettes. But Inglis wanted to sell the lot - all 24 boxes of 25 cigarettes each. It was quite a tricky and lengthy business stashing that lot away, without appearing ungainly.

Inglis wore his dress uniform, with long raincoat over the top. Every pocket contained a box, which took care of the first eight. One box was inside each shirt sleeve, above the cuff, with another inside each sock above the ankle. Three more went inside his underpants. A further eight were spread around his waist, inside the shirt above his belt. The last one went under his cap!

At the pier they lined up for Customs and Immigration. The German officers asking the questions wore bottle green uniforms complete with jackboots and riding breeches, looking like moldy Nazi S.S. men. They were searching every third or fourth person in the queue, and Inglis started to regret the impulse to spend up big in Hamburg. When he reached five places from the front of the queue he was sweating and starting to panic. He turned round to Harry.

"Oh hell Harry, I forgot my money belt." Inglis started to push past Harry in his funk, but Harry grabbed his arm and said loudly "Don't worry Inglis, I've got plenty money. You can pay me back later." He muttered in a much lower voice "Cut it out, they won't search you, I promise. I know the way they think. Here, take some money from me."

Inglis took the money he was holding out for the Germans' benefit, shrugged, and turned to meet his fate. What would they do to him if they found the fags? How did the inside of a German jail look? The 'Nazis' frisked the man five ahead of him, and his heart was in his mouth. *If I go to jail, I'll find you and kill you Harry, if I have to hunt you to the end of the earth.*

Then Inglis remembered his old adage of 'look like you own the place, and chances are they'll think you do.' Just change it a little to suit the circumstances. He psyched himself up by remembering the last time he had used it, in his final term at school. He had bragged that he could walk straight into the fighter base without being stopped. Several boys had been caught scaling the perimeter fence, and now his schoolmates challenged him to put up or shut up.

"I'll do better than that" he'd answered. "Two of you can come with me, and I'll take your photo standing beside a Hawker Hunter jet fighter. The pictures will cost you five bob each."

Nobody wanted to volunteer, but Inglis told them he would guarantee not to get caught.

"Even if we were caught, you just say I told you I was a fighter pilot, and invited you along."

That did it, and he had his volunteers. More important was the ten bob for the photos. Inglis had put on his double breasted blazer and flannels, with a canary yellow Paisley pattern cravat round his neck. This was the 'uniform' of young pilots at the time. Then, with the camera slung negligently over his shoulder, they strolled in past the guard room, past the notices announcing

NO CAMERAS ALLOWED

ALL VISITORS MUST REPORT TO THE GUARD ROOM

Tommy and Wilf were shaking in their shoes, but Inglis just waved casually to the duty RAF policeman, who merely lifted his hand in acknowledgement. They made a bee line for the nearest Hunters, and Inglis placed Tommy and Wilf for their photographs. Then he persuaded Wilf to take one of him with the planes. While Inglis was standing close to the cockpit of one plane, a voice shouted from the other side of the fuselage.

"Hey, what the hell are you doing there?"

Inglis stepped out from behind the Hunter to see a Land Rover on the far side of the low rope fence of the hard standing. An Air Force sergeant had just stepped out of it. When he saw Inglis he said

"Oh......are you in charge there sir?"

"Yes, quite okay thanks sergeant. Everything under control."

The Land Rover drove off, and Wilf gave him back the camera with shaking hands, pleading could they please go now. Inglis said he had a couple of things to do yet, and took a small notebook from the pocket of his blazer. It was a spiral bound type, and on each page was written THIS COULD HAVE BEEN A BOMB

Strolling round as many aircraft as he could, Inglis placed a page in each jet pipe, while Tommy and Wilf pleaded with him to get the hell out of the place. When he was finished they strolled back out past the guard room, where Inglis gave the guard another wave and smile.

There had been quite a fuss at the base later that day.

It was Inglis' turn for the German Customs man, as he returned from memory lane. He looked up and dazzled the man in the green uniform with a smile of pure innocence. The Customs man smiled hesitantly in return, and asked if Inglis had anything to declare. Inglis said no. The Customs man said "Cigarette?" Inglis thought quickly and pulled out the box in his right coat pocket. The Customs man took it from his hand, broke the cellophane seal, and handed it back with another weak smile. Looking at Inglis' shiny officer's cap he said "Pass."

Inglis passed without having to be told a second time. The Customs man waved Harry through without even quizzing him - and then frisked the man behind. Jackpot - he had three half bottles of Scotch, and was promptly marched off to God knows where - a concentration camp maybe? Harry and Inglis made themselves scarce. The nice officer's uniform had FINALLY come in useful.

Hamburg was still in a mess from the fire bombing and multiple conventional bombings it had copped during the War. New buildings were sprouting from the rubble of the old, but it would be a few years yet before the scars were all healed. Hoardings were everywhere, in front of bombed-out lots, and poor people wandered around in ragged overcoats in the freezing cold. Inglis wondered what became of the elderly and helpless among them.

There was a wide main street just before the Riperbahn. At the intersection, what appeared to be cameras were mounted on the corners of the buildings overlooking the junction. The cab driver said they were television cameras used by the police to control traffic - and a few other things, he thought.

When they left the cab Inglis told Harry he had to go for a pee. There was an underground toilet quite near the intersection, so he rushed down the stairs and through the doors, unbuttoning his raincoat as he went. Inside the door he almost bumped into a woman in uniform, with a ticket machine and moneybag round her neck. A bus or tram conductress he thought, as he stammered out his apologies. Obviously he had entered the wrong toilet in his hurry for relief. It would be a lousy laugh if he went to jail for this, in the Land of the Huns, after evading Customs. Very sorry, I could have sworn the sign said Herren, not Dammen.

"Is okay" says she, "To pee is free, cubicle five pfennigs."

Inglis looked past her, and sure enough there were the stalls, with two men relieving themselves, completely oblivious to her presence in the place. Inglis blushed and stammered, and parted with the money for a cubicle. Later he wondered who had the brilliant idea of putting a woman down there to make extra money from bashful foreigners. Meanwhile he remembered the writing on the toilet wall back home.

'Here am I broken hearted - Paid my penny and only farted.'
That was before he learned to open the door with an iceblock stick instead of a penny.

The two adventurers headed for the noise, bustle and lights of the Riperbahn, looking at every window advertising the attractions inside. There seemed to be something for every taste imaginable - and quite a few Inglis had never imagined. They descended a flight of stairs to a basement bar Harry recommended as a one-stop trading post for the smuggled cigarettes. While they had a beer at the counter, Harry had a quiet word with the barman. He fetched a smallish man in a homburg hat, who wouldn't have looked out of place in a James Cagney gangster movie. Behind him hovered a gorilla in evening dress.

The small man spoke urgently to Harry, and waved them farther into the gloom of the bar's interior. The price was soon agreed. Not quite the five times duty free Inglis had been told, but not far off. More than half his month's salary for 600 fags wasn't to be scoffed at.

One more beer and they were back on the street, with Inglis feeling suddenly rich, and ready for anything - he thought. But then, he had not yet seen everything. They decided to have a look in a club advertising lady mud wrestlers. The ladies wrestled in a recessed square in the floor, round which the customers sat at tiny tables, just big enough to hold a few glasses. The wrestlers slipped, slid and slithered around in brief costumes. At least once in every bout, one or other of them would lose some or all of her costume, much to the titillation of the audience - Inglis included.

A brief picture did flit through his mind, of old 'Hellfire and Damnation', the minister at the Baptist church where Inglis had taught bible class not so long ago. He would have closed the place down single-handed, throwing everyone onto the street, and cursing them all with eternal damnation. But he wasn't here, was he? After that brief discomfort, Inglis sat back to enjoy the show and the beer.

The Tabu, the Roxy, and half a dozen others they visited, drinking at each - though Inglis was alternating beer with Coke - and watching strippers with no end to the variations they brought to the business. He had never dreamed there were so many ways just to take your clothes off. One especially attractive stripper in one of the bigger places actually managed to make it seem like an artistic happening, raising it well above the level of the others; and incidentally appealing much more to Inglis' senses. He always liked beautiful things, and when they are marred by scars or crudity - or even just simple dirt - some of the appeal is inevitably lost. This girl was beautiful; her costume was beautiful; and her movements flowed evenly, without jarring discrepancies. In the end, she was only briefly naked, but gave the impression of having revealed more than some of her sisters who had it all off in seconds, and flaunted their nudity as they strutted about the stage like puppets.

At the tender age of seventeen Inglis was already learning something about discretion and discernment - or was it just snobbery? Whichever, it surely worked for him.

In one particularly seamy joint they came across the fraulein with the famous 'cash box'. After stripping naked, she invited the audience to throw coins onto the stage. An assistant stacked the coins, while she psyched herself up to the sound of pseudo Eastern music. Then she squatted over the stack of coins, with her upper body swaying to the music. Her pussy slowly zeroed in on the stack of coins, as the music increased in tempo. Then, a few at a time, the coins were engulfed, as

38

the mouth of her sex gulped them into her body.

For her finale she was given a large fat cigar, which she lit and puffed for a few moments. Squatting again, she placed the cigar in her pussy. The music changed to a more military style, with a distinct beat. Protruding obscenely from between her squatting legs, the cigar glowed and emitted puffs of smoke in time to the music.

Following a raucous round of applause, the cigar was auctioned, the winning bid of twelve marks coming from a fat man at the front. From initial titillation, Inglis' feelings had changed as he watched; first to embarrassment, then to pity for this not-too-pretty woman, reduced to the degradation of a freak live performance, in order to eat. To go on living in order to perform like this, in order to go on living, in a vicious circle, deprived her of all pride and decency.

Inglis suddenly felt sick, and asked Harry to leave - after throwing a banknote onto the stage, which she could pick up like a normal human being. He wanted to cry, or beat someone, or do something to vent his frustration. On the other hand he didn't want to seem peculiar, so he tried to keep his feelings from showing. How many others there felt like him, but pretended in order to be one of the boys? And how many just couldn't care less anyway? God knows. All he knew was that instead of feeling like an adventurous young man on an exciting night out, he was feeling dirty and degraded by association.

Surely this wasn't what sex was about. Did all these men really want such things? Was he so different? Did he need a psychiatrist? NO, he told himself, this CAN't be what it's about. There's a decent side to men; even two or three sides to every man. Take them away from here, and most of them would probably be decent ordinary people - he hoped.

What was he doing here anyway? Only spending money to help perpetuate it all, while looking for cheap thrills. Did that make him any better than anyone else......? Inglis wondered again just how MANY of the men around him felt as he did; but were afraid to show it, as he was, in case they were thought of as freaks. Or was it just that, at seventeen Inglis hadn't yet been exposed to enough of life to be a real Man? He didn't want to believe that, but it nagged at him. If this was what real men did - because they *wanted* to - he didn't think he relished being one after all. But what then? *Aw, hell, cut it out and let's get drunk*! But he couldn't afford to get too drunk, because he was on watch at midnight; which was why he was drinking Coke between beers.

They went for a stroll down Willemstrasse, sauntering casually past the huge notice bearing the legend *OUT OF BOUNDS TO ALL ALLIED PERSONNEL*

Nobody seemed to be enforcing it much, as there were quite a few soldiers, sailors and airmen walking around in uniform. Inglis' education in the ways of the world was being advanced in leaps and bounds as the evening progressed. On each side of the street were rows of what at first glance looked like ordinary houses. A closer look revealed ladies of the night seated or standing in lit windows, smiling and beckoning to passersby outside. Some wore scanty night dresses, while an occasional brave - or desperate - one showed herself completely naked.

Inglis looked at his watch and reminded Harry he would have to start heading back for the ship in a bit over an hour. Harry said he just wanted to say hello to an 'old friend' in one of the houses, and then they would go.

He led Inglis into a house with a yellow glass door, and a red light glowing through partly open curtains - where a woman stood, wearing only brief panties. Inside the door was a small reception area, where Harry was met by a smiling redhead of about thirty, who seemed to know him. He asked her if he could see Greta, and was told she would be available in a few minutes. Then he asked Inglis if he would like a girl for a short time, and Inglis declined with an embarrassed smile. When Greta came to collect Harry, Inglis was told he would probably be more comfortable in the main lounge, where he could have a drink - and maybe join in the fun while he waited. Harry winked and leered when he said the last bit, and Inglis wondered what was coming next.

He didn't have long to wait before finding out. A plump little brunette ushered him through the curtains, brushing him with her exposed breasts as she remained in the doorway. It was just as well they all seemed to have efficient heating systems in the naughtier parts of Hamburg, or he was sure the cases of pneumonia would have outnumbered those of venereal disease - of which Inglis was petrified. Old 'Hellfire and Damnation' had told him that if he consorted with wicked evil fallen women, his pecker would fall off. Inglis still wasn't certain he had only been trying to scare him onto the path of righteousness. The stories he had heard, usually whispered among the boys at school, were pretty gruesome and horrific. One boy even uttered - in *his* bible class! - his blasphemous version of the Garden of Eden.

Adam ate Eve's apple all right
But not the one from the tree
That is why the Lord did smite
Mankind with awful Vee Dee

Inglis had waited for God to strike him down in His wrath, but it must have been one of His busy days. Anyway, the cheeky little brunette with the upstanding breasts showed him to a settee, where she took his order for drinks - one for her and one for him. Hers cost a fortune - naturally - but he wanted some company, and she looked safer than most of the women in the room. Besides which she was nearer his age. It was a large room with a bed near one end, fitted with what looked like light scaffolding at the bottom. Their settee was at the side of the room, against the long wall, and only a few feet clear of the roomward end of the bed. At the opposite end of the room were two curtained doorways, through which men and women went in couples, as though summoned by Noah to the Ark - then later rejected as unsuitable.

The brunette's name was Anna, and she was really quite attractive. She wasn't as plump as Inglis had first thought - more firm and substantial than plump. Her breasts were large and full, which had made him presume the rest of her was bigger than it actually was.

She didn't seem the least embarrassed by her naked breasts; in fact she seemed rather proud of them. Inglis couldn't blame her for that, because the more he looked at them, the prouder he felt about them himself. The looking was quite difficult, as he was trying hard not to stare at them. But his eyes kept being drawn back by some magnetic influence.

41

Finally she laughed, the fourth time his eyes were 'influenced'. She turned her chest to him, cupped a breast in each hand, and said

"They are beautiful, no?"

Inglis glanced furtively round the room before drinking in their magnificence with his eyes, clearing his throat before answering.

"They are beautiful - yes."

She took a thin housecoat from the end of the settee and draped it over her shoulders, still revealing more than concealing. The coat was similar to those worn by the other nine or ten women in the room. She rose from the settee, then kneeled down in front of Inglis, with the housecoat concealing her actions from the rest of the room, but revealing all of her to him.

Her fingers darted out and undid the buttons of his raincoat, followed by the fly buttons of his uniform trousers. Inglis leaned forward, grabbed her wrists, and spoke in an urgent whisper.   "Hey, whoa, what the hell are you doing?"

She just grinned cheekily up at him, carefully pulled the front of the raincoat open, and sat down in his lap.   "Now we watch" she said.

There was a great deal of activity on the other side of the room, with men clustered around two of the women who wore more clothes than the rest. Inglis asked Anna what was going on, and she painstakingly explained in her quaint English. The women were taking bets from the men for a 'hole in one'. The odds were four to one for a male participant, who had to pay five marks to take part. Spectators could bet on the contestants at odds of two to one, but couldn't bet against them. The money was held by the two women, and a judge was appointed from among the spectators.

The judge was not allowed to bet on the outcome, but received five marks for his services. The 'hole in one' had to be scored within five seconds of the word GO from the referee or judge. Inglis said yes, yes, but what the hell IS a 'hole in one?'

"You wait, you see. Now give Anna ten marks for little special?" Inglis asked her what the hell is a 'little special', but again she would only say "You give ten marks, then you see."

He laughed and gave her the money.

"Okay, I give, I see, right?" Ten marks was only the price of a few drinks anyway, and he had more than fifty left.

"Right!" says she, leaning over to put the money in a handbag on the settee beside them. Then she swiveled on his lap and stood up. Turning to face him she quickly removed the housecoat and put it on back to front. She sat down in his lap with her back to him, and the long coat now screening most of them from the rest of the room. Her hands came round behind her and she undid his belt, and slipped the trousers down over his thighs, with the help of a wiggle from him - might as well give in gracefully! What the hell was he doing?

His raincoat was already open, and he noticed with a jolt of surprise that her panties had disappeared. Under the housecoat she was completely naked, and her bare back looked surprisingly sensuous. Inglis had never thought of a back being sexy before - his education was surely being rounded out tonight. And in spite of all his previous good intentions, there was a little man struggling to get out of his underpants. Anna could feel him too, and released him, only to recapture him immediately between her thighs; as she moved up and back to sit on his stomach, knocking a gasp of air from him. Inglis slid down and forward on the settee - *we must all suffer at some time for the sake of a well rounded education*, he thought; and everything in sight right now *was* well rounded.

"Now we watch game" she said.

"How the hell can I watch anything from here?" he demanded - staring at her back from close range, and mentally qualifying the question at sight of the cleavage between her buttocks. His soldier was now standing rigidly to attention, and he hoped like hell nobody could see - though Anna seemed to have the situation well covered. She moved her head and shoulders to the right, and her legs to the left, with his penis still hopelessly caught between her upper thighs.   "Now can see?" she asked.

Inglis said yes in a slightly strangled voice. Then his brain registered what his eyes were seeing not ten feet away. One of the women who had taken the bets was lying naked on the bed, while the other betting woman tied her legs over the light scaffold. Her legs were pulled wide apart, up and back, with her buttocks and pubis

43

projecting ahead of them over the end of the bed.

The second woman moved aside and was replaced by the referee, who moved forward until the crotch of his trousers was against the naked pubis. He signaled to the woman, who then made some minor adjustments; which resulted in the projecting private parts being lowered slightly. The referee then stood off to one side and called "Ready?"

"Ready!" came the answer from the far end of the room.

Inglis couldn't see that end past Anna since she moved. She was massaging his impatient penis by slowly moving her thighs in opposite directions. It shed a small tear of ecstasy at this treatment. The referee had a stopwatch in his hand, which he pressed as he shouted "GO!"

There was the sound of running feet advancing down the room. Into Inglis' line of vision came a skinny man wearing only a vest. As he ran, his right hand was clasped round the base of his erect penis, holding it down and out; a miniature spear thrusting ahead of a skinny white Zulu. Inglis' mouth dropped open in disbelief as he aimed at the projecting pussy of the woman on the bed. Instantly Inglis now understood the significance of a hole in one as the range quickly closed. The racing penis was bobbing and weaving as Skinny Zulu ran. Just at the last second he thrust forward, and the two opposing projections amalgamated. Inglis could see clearly that he'd scored a bull's-eye - on the wrong target!

The woman on the bed let out a yelp, while Skinny Zulu collapsed on the floor, clutching his fast-diminishing spear, which hadn't been up to the shock of impact - up for, but not to! The referee called "Miss!" before stooping to assist the wounded warrior from the arena, showered with confetti from the torn up tickets of the losing bettors. There was a smattering of applause and a few good natured jeers as the vanquished contestant was led away.

The woman on the bed was unstrapped and swapped places with the second one. The latter was inches taller than Inglis, with huge breasts and thickish thighs. When she removed her panties she was completely naked, including her pubis which had been shaved.

The bed was lowered on its corner posts, until the mattress was only eighteen inches above the floor. This had Inglis puzzled until the woman turned her back, spread her legs, and leaned forward onto the bed. A harness was brought forward from the bed head and placed around her chest, above the huge breasts and under the arms. She put her feet close into the bed and leaned backwards, buttocks projecting to the rear, head down with the harness taking the strain.

A burly six and a half foot man moved close behind her to gauge the height. The referee and the first woman brought wooden blocks which they placed under the feet of the jackknifed Amazon, until the burly man was satisfied. He removed his clothes and disappeared to the far end of the room, blocked once more by Anna. The referee came forward to inspect the target, which looked large and swollen, as if gorged with blood. He parted the lips of the Amazon's vulva, exposing the dark tunnel beyond. Anna leaned back and whispered to Inglis.

"This one hole in one you win, okay?"

Inglis agreed, not really knowing what she meant; but what the hell, it was a bit late to back out now. He was efficiently trapped in any case, whether he liked it or not. And he honestly couldn't make up his mind. He felt fascinated and ashamed; excited and embarrassed; liberated and trapped. The participants in this obscene contest were obviously willing volunteers. What's more, everyone seemed to be having fun, laughing with each other and exchanging jokes, with not a hint of nastiness or violence.

But what they were doing was still obscene by all the rules Inglis knew. Yet the atmosphere was more like Ascot on race day, than Soho on an orgy day. Most confusing and upsetting. More than that, it was downright world-turned-upside-downing, if there was ever such a thing. Anna gyrated gently, squeezing with her thighs, just as the referee called loudly.

"Ready?"
"Ready!"

"GO!" shouted the referee, and the floorboards shook as the bull charged. This bull didn't miss either. The massive penis was swallowed whole by the Amazon's gaping pubic maw. The referee called out "Hole in one, hole in one!"

The Bull was in no hurry to disengage; and neither by the look of things was the Amazon, who was straining backwards to remain impaled. The referee asked the Bull "Forfeit?"

The Bull nodded urgently, grunting "Yeah!"

Soon it became apparent that another contest was underway - a trial of strength between the sexes. The Amazon signaled to the first woman, who released the restraining cord to the harness. Now her whole (sorry) weight was against the Bull, who thrust forward to take the strain, as the Amazon swayed sideways, calling "Ole!" The Bull thrust, and thrust again. Placing his hands on the Amazon's buttocks, he withdrew three quarters of the length of his massive cock, then lunged explosively forward, burying it to the hilt. The Amazon wasn't at all intimidated, lunging backwards in return, and shouting "Ole! Torro!"

The crowd took up the chant, clapping in unison and calling "Oleeeeeeee" as the Bull withdrew, and "TORRO!" as they crashed together again, watching wide-eyed the Clash of the Titans. Gradually the rhythm speeded up. The Bull and the Amazon were both now dripping sweat, slippery with it, bathing the floor with it. But still neither was willing to submit. Anna leaned back and whispered hoarsely "You win, okay?"

"Okay, okay" Inglis grunted in reply.

She parted her thighs, lifted her hips, and swallowed his rigid member deep within her hot wet pussy, as smooth as velvet - more exciting than anything this seventeen year old pilgrim had ever experienced. Inglis shuddered with pleasure as she arched her back and leaned forward. Then she started slowly gyrating and lifting at the same time, while the crowd chanted their encouragement to the Titans, on the long-drawn "Oleeeeeeeee," which seemed to last forever. When the crowd changed suddenly to "Torro!" Anna lunged down and back, burying his shaft to the hilt; and even then it wanted to explore deeper yet, lost in the heat of the moment; thrusting of its own volition towards the hot mysterious Eldorado.

The chant picked up speed, becoming almost frantic, with the "Oleeee" shortening and sharpening. The Titans were straining and grunting, thrusting and moaning. Inglis grabbed Anna's breasts and rolled them in his hands; squeezed them separately, then together;

46

pushed them forward, sliding his hands out and along, until the nipples were between fingers and thumbs. Then as the breasts receded, gripping the nipples and holding them forward. Anna let out a small yelp, and Inglis let go.

"No, no, is good" she gasped. He cupped them again, squeezing and rubbing the nipples together, one on the other, little Eskimoses rubbing noses. Anna moaned again.

"Is good, is good", revolving her hips in a circular motion, pressing down with her weight as Inglis rose to meet her.

The Bull and the Amazon were almost spent, the floor now slippery beneath their feet. The Amazon let out a blood curdling whoop of triumph as the Bull made one last desperate thrust, face contorted; then lighting up with pleasure as the Amazon moaned and collapsed forward on the bed. They were still locked together, both bodies shuddering. It was declared a draw!

The crowd cheered and clapped, and Anna rose quickly from Inglis' lap, changed her housecoat the right way round in a flash, and squatted down again facing him. Her hot wet pussy engulfed his towering inferno once more. She cupped her breasts and thrust them in his face. Gathering the nipples together Inglis took them both in his mouth, sucking hard with his lips, and rolling his tongue across and back, up and down, round in a circle, and across again. Anna moaned, ground her crotch into his, and the world exploded just as she shouted out loud "Aaaaa.....yeah.....!" She collapsed against him as the shudder ran through both their bodies, exhausting and draining them. Now she was trembling, and Inglis couldn't help trembling also.

"Oooh, was Goooood" she whispered, burying her face in his neck. Oh, wow, Inglis thought, if that's a 'little special', what the hell's a big one like? If this is what sex is all about, no wonder God wanted to keep it all for himself! Then, and only then, Inglis realized the crowd had still been chanting, and had just finished up with one final "Torro!"

He glanced up over Anna's head, and promptly buried his face back in her hair - it smelled nice. The crowd had been watching them! Oh my God, what the hell was he going to do now? Please settee, swallow

47

me up and spit me out somewhere else. He could feel the fire of abject shame and embarrassment burning his face. Anna burrowed closer and hung onto him, as if to keep them there on display forever. A hand descended on Inglis' shoulder, then Harry's voice sounded in his ear.

"Come on Inglis, you horny young bugger. You're going to be late on watch if we don't leave soon."

"Harry, thank God. Lend us your raincoat for Christ's sake. Throw it over my head and get us out of here. Grab my cap too - please Harry!" Harry laughed raucously.

"Okay Inglis, if that's what you want. But don't you think it's a bit late to be bashful now? That was quite a show you and the little lady were giving. 'Just a shy boy from the country' he says. Here you are then", and his coat was over Inglis' head. The errant cadet did up his trousers before lifting Anna to her feet with part of Harry's coat over her head. Then, with one arm round her and the other clasping the coat to his face, he followed Harry to the door, peering through a small gap in front of his eyes.

The crowd parted and cheered, and a few hands patted Inglis' back, to the accompaniment of lewd and embarrassing comments, the edge taken off them by the grinning faces. *So much for the Baptist boy with the high and mighty moral ideas - here comes the alley cat*, Inglis thought shamefaced and mortified.

In the foyer he put his cap on with the peak pulled well down, turned up the coat collar, and gave Harry back his coat. Anna made him promise to come back and see her again. With a cheeky and completely shameless grin, she said "Next time sell tickets!"

Fat chance, Inglis thought - but still.....she is really attractive....? Then he was out on the street with Harry, beating a hasty retreat to the haven of *Forth Venturer*.

"For God's sake Harry, don't tell anybody about tonight."
"What? Can't keep a good story like that to myself!"

Inglis cursed and reviled himself as they walked down the street, calling on God for forgiveness. But even then he wasn't sure he really meant it. It had been fun while it lasted.

Then the terrible thought hit him like a lightning bolt.

Would his pecker really fall off? Please God, don't let it happen, not that. The Spirit's strong, it's just the Flesh that's so damned weak. This time he knew he meant it!

On the way back they stopped for a last beer at the bar where they had sold the cigarettes. They were hardly in the door when the barman signaled to someone farther in, then told them,

"You go quick. Police come, make big trouble."

Just to make sure they got the message, four big men - including the well dressed gorilla - threw them onto the street, before Inglis even knew what hit him. He'd heard of your feet hardly touching the ground; now he'd experienced it.

Harry rose from the sidewalk dusting himself off.

"Shit, we're not going to stand for that, are we Inglis?"

Inglis thought briefly of being a hero, before remembering that discretion is the better part of valor. He was quite good at that, especially when valor meant facing up to vastly superior odds.

"Some other time Harry" he said. "There's only just enough time to get back for my watch as it is. Otherwise we could tear the place apart!"

Harry nodded in agreement, and Inglis heaved a sigh of relief. He wasn't drunk enough to see the point in taking on a mob of professional toughs. What's more, he never did like the thought of his pretty face being bent out of shape. Even more so, now he had discovered Real Sex - as opposed to mucking about with the girls next door.

Cowardie, cowardie custard! Ah well, he could live with it, up to a point; and right now sure as hell wasn't the point. So, off they went back to the ship, faces intact, and fit for further adventures.

CHAPTER 7

From Hamburg the ship sailed a very short distance down the River Elbe to a small tank farm at Stadersand. This served the town of Stade, a few miles from the river. Inglis decided to visit Stade on his own, in order to get his breath back - and maybe see a few real sights. The local bus took him in from the tank farm gates.

Stade was a delightful example of a medium sized German market town, with a pretty little town square containing many trees. Looking stark now in their winter nakedness, they would no doubt be most attractive in summer and autumn.

The town was quiet and clean compared to the dirt and bustle of Hamburg. Like a breath of fresh air after the smog of the big city, which could be seen in the distance. Inglis felt comfortable and almost at home as he looked round at the few people and vehicles dotting the square.

A slim girl with a dark blonde ponytail caught his eye. His heart skipped a beat as he took in the Bardot-like elfin features and graceful walk, with just a touch of alluring sway to the slim hips. Making a sudden brave decision - very brave for him, in spite of recent developments - he approached her and asked if she spoke English. She did, quite well, with a fascinating accent he could have listened to all day.

Inglis came suddenly back to earth with the realization that she was looking at him quizzically, waiting for him to speak. For the life of him he couldn't think of a thing to say, and blushed scarlet as he searched desperately in his blank mind. She seemed amused at his discomfort, a smile on her face, her eyes sparkling with mischief. This disconcerted him even further, until he blurted out that he would be obliged - obliged, mark you - if she could tell him what sights were to be seen in the town. She smiled again, gently hooking her arm through his.

"I walk with you a little. I must go to the shop of my aunt, where I am working. We may talk as we are walking, no?"

They walked and talked. Well, she walked; as Inglis floated in the air beside her. She was so full of vitality, and good to be with. It was still not quite 9am, and she was due at her aunt's shop at nine; but it was her early day, and she would be free after four o'clock. The sound of her speech held him enthralled, as she chattered away.

They passed a cinema on one side of the square. From what Inglis could decipher there was a screening at 4.30 that afternoon. He asked her if she would have tea with him when she finished work, before taking in the movie with him.

She said yes, SHE SAID YES, ooh la la. He almost skipped the rest of the way to her aunt's shop, which sold clothes, linen and drapery. They agreed to meet outside as soon as he could get there after his cargo watch.

For the next two and a half hours Inglis wandered round town, caught up in his own cloud of euphoria. Heidrun was her name. *What a beautiful name - the most beautiful name in the world.* He hummed to himself as he strolled through the park. People gave him peculiar looks, and he felt sorry for them. *They* didn't know his secret - not that he would have minded sharing it with the whole world.

The park was lovely, the birds were singing, and he ended up back on the sidewalk outside the shop of Heidrun's aunt. What a coincidence. Inglis peered in the window and saw Heidrun sorting through a pile of blouses. She looked up and saw him, smiled, and waved. He waved back as a thrill of warmth and excitement flowed through him. He was lighter than air as he glided off along the footpath.

Passersby turned and shook their heads at the foreign looney in the sailor suit, skipping along with a beatific expression on his face - just before Inglis tripped and fell on it!

I don't care, I don't care. Clap hands for the looney everyone. Clap hands for yourselves everyone. Make merry on the merry-go-round, swoop and swoon on the swings. Paradise is still not lost for those with eyes to see. For the young and the young-at-heart, the world is yet a wondrous place.

"Excuse me, are you all right sir?" asked the policeman, frowning at him as he picked himself up from the sidewalk.

"Yes, yes, never been better in my life. Isn't it a wonderful day? Are

51

you in love with your wife? Do you have lots of children? I hope so. Did they get lots of presents for Christmas? I hope it snows again soon."

The policeman tilted his cap and scratched his head as he watched Inglis' erratic departure. How could even a sailor be drunk in this town at this time of the morning, was the unasked question on his puzzled face. Little did he know, poor man, that Inglis' drunkenness was not the result of booze.

He bought a hot dog - a good German hot dog - and dreamed his dreams of romance, walking once more through the park. Drawn back again - and again - to the shop of Heidrun's aunt; where the object of his dreams never failed to notice him and wave. Until it was time to catch the bus back to the ship; and work; and the other world.

On the bus, the conductress told him that in the afternoon the buses would leave the tank farm for town once every hour, on the hour. In the morning they had run every half hour, and this information was catastrophic. How long would it take if he ran all the way? Would he be in time? Would Heidrun wait for him? He was in an instant panic - maybe he would never see her again. How could he get a message to her? Should he go back on this bus and risk the Old Man's wrath? Or could he trust someone from the ship going into town, to take a message to her?

Back at the ship he couldn't wait for his watch to be over. At one stage the Third Mate asked
"What in the name of God has got into you? You act like you lost a sixpence and found a pound note. What the hell have you got to be so happy about all of a sudden?"
Inglis just mumbled and gave nothing away. He kept watching the gangplank for signs of someone going ashore. But everyone going ashore for the day had already gone; and those going ashore for the evening would be leaving after the end of his watch anyway.

Big John must have noticed him checking his watch - like every other minute. Near the end of the watch keeping he asked if Inglis would like to join him and the Third Engineer for a beer after tea. Inglis told him no, thanks all the same, but he had to go ashore again straight away. Big John exploded with mirth and slapped him on the back, knocking the breath from his lungs.

"I thought as much! You've got a girl in town, haven't you? Aren't you the dark horse then."

Inglis mumbled something in embarrassment, and John patted his shoulder.

"Never mind me laddie, I'm just jealous. Best o' luck."

"Well, if it's any consolation I've probably stuffed it up anyway," said Inglis, trying to keep the tremor out of his voice. "I promised to meet her soon after she finishes work at 4 o'clock - and then found out the bloody buses only go once an hour - on the bloody hour!" Inglis looked a picture of abject misery, and Big John looked at his watch, then up again.

"It's only quarter to four now. If you hurry you can still make the 4 o'clock bus. I'll cover for you - what the hell's a few minutes anyway, to stand in the way of true love, eh? Well, don't stand there with your mouth open looking stupid - move yourself, or you'll miss it!"

Inglis began to stutter out his thanks, but Big John just waved a hand and gave him a shove, with a huge grin on his face.

Inglis set a new record between coming off watch and leaving the ship that day. He was sitting on the bus with time to spare, on the way to see his beautiful lady.

At 4.15 he was outside the shop, and there was Heidrun just saying goodbye to her aunt. She saw Inglis coming, and waved him over to introduce him to the pleasant middle aged lady who was her Aunt Tilde. Inglis felt embarrassed by the cool all-over look Aunt Tilde cast his way, reminding him of the woman next door, the time he took her daughter to the school dance. He had been waiting in their parlor while Helen finished preparing herself. She was a year older than him, but they got along well, as she was still a tomboy. He had overheard her mother talking to her.

"You watch yoursel' wi' yon laddie. He has that look aboot him, and I'm never wrong aboot that. Dinna you let him get you alone onywhere. I wouldna' trust him near a warm loaf."

It had taken him a long time to work out what she had meant.

Heidrun and Inglis said their goodbyes to Aunt Tilde and walked to the coffee shop. Heidrun told him that although the picture show was billed for four thirty, the main feature would start after five.

She slipped her arm through his as they walked, and a thrill of excitement surged through him. They didn't eat much; just sat drinking coffee and each other, and talking, talking, talking. There was so much he wanted to know about her. He was jealous of all the people who had known her before they met, and he wanted to catch up with them and get ahead.

Towards the end of the last coffee she leaned across the table and put her small hand over his. It was as though an electric shock passed up his arm. She smiled, and her beautiful green eyes sparkled once more.

"After the movie we may walk for a while. Then would you please to meet my family and eat with us dinner?"

His heart jumped, but he didn't hesitate.

"I'd be delighted Heidrun. I'm sure your family must be nice people, and I'd like to meet them."

This time her whole face lit up and radiated happiness; so much that Inglis thought the other people in the coffee shop must be able to feel it - he certainly could. The words tumbled from her lips.

"That is gut. If you were saying no I was not to be going to the movie mit you. I am happy you are saying yes."

Afterwards, Inglis couldn't remember what the movie was about. He sat watching Heidrun rather than the screen most of the time. Inglis was shy and hesitant; afraid to touch at the risk of being rebuffed; happy just to watch her profile in the light from the screen, and see the sparkle in her eyes when she looked at him instead of the movie. In the end she was the one who put her hand in his, and laid her head on his shoulder.

He put his arm round her and reveled in the fragrance of her hair. Their coats were off, and she felt warm and soft beneath his hand. The magic of the moment entranced him with witchery. Right then he thought he would have done anything she had asked.

For nearly an hour after the movie they walked aimlessly around the town, hugging each other as they walked. In the park they kissed for the first time, hesitantly to begin; then as if two dams had burst, the waters raging together to form a maelstrom of feelings.

Still Inglis kept his hands away from where they might not be welcome; but it didn't seem to matter much anyway. The closeness and warmth, and the exchange of emotion via their lips, seemed enough for now, and Inglis didn't want to spoil it. He wanted it to go on and on forever; for time to be suspended indefinitely; for the joy and comfort never to end, keeping the outside world at bay, just Heidrun and him.

It was 8.30 when they finally reached her house, which came as a bit of a surprise. It was a semi-detached two storey affair almost identical in design to the one Inglis had grown up in, across the sea in Scotland.

Heidrun's father, who drove a steam engine on the railway, was in his early forties, and smoked a pipe that could have come out of Inglis' father's pipe rack. Her mother was a slim good-looking woman, not at all the hausfrau he had half expected. The family was rounded out by Heidrun's young brother, who was in high school.

The family name was Poltrock; Inglis had clean forgotten to ask Heidrun, who didn't seem to need another name - Heidrun was so complete on its own. Everyone was pleasant, and at pains to make him feel welcome. The meal was served soon after their arrival, and could have been dinner at home, except for the sauerkraut. In fact Inglis felt more at home here than he ever felt in his own home, where his stepmother had done her best to make life a misery for him most of the time.

Talk at the table was general, with a few discreet questions about Inglis' duties and ambitions from Mr. Poltrock. Stade was a railway junction, where the line to Bremerhaven left the Hamburg to Cuxhaven line. Inglis had stopped to watch the trains this morning, and noticed a glut of big black 2-10-0s. This was the type Heidrun's father usually drove, and he had been driving one this morning at about the time Inglis was watching.

Was it only this morning he met Heidrun? It couldn't be. He felt he must have known her much longer than that.

There were murmurs of disappointment round the table when he mentioned that his ship would sail in the early hours of the morning, and he had to be back on board by midnight.

Mr. Poltrock and Inglis talked about railway locomotives for a while, followed by a discussion with Albert about aircraft. He wanted to be a fighter pilot, and Inglis wished him the best of luck, with a grim quirk behind his smile. He told them about his abortive attempt to be a fighter pilot. Maybe he should have been German. They were rearming within NATO, and had no intention of giving up manned fighter aircraft in favor of guided missiles.

At 11 o'clock Mr. Poltrock suggested that Heidrun and Inglis might like the parlor to themselves for a while, as he helped his wife to clear up. Albert was sent packing off to bed amid loud protests; and Mr. Poltrock said not to worry, he would drive Inglis back to the ship when it was time to go. Inglis thought that was very nice of him, especially when Heidrun whispered that he started work at 5 o'clock in the morning.

They sat in the parlor, huddled close and holding onto each other as if their lives depended on it. They talked and touched, and touched and talked. In the end she kissed him long and deep, making his head swim, and crushing her slim body against his. Then she whispered in his ear "Touch me", and placed his hand on her breast, which he could feel through her sweater. Fearfully Inglis put his hand inside the sweater. Soon her small firm breast was bare in his hand, and she hugged him close, almost crushing hand and breast together between their bodies. It was pure magic; more than Inglis could have hoped for, and more than he had been prepared to settle for. They kissed with desperation, and Inglis could feel her heart beating beneath his hand.

It was time to leave, and Mr. Poltrock warmed up the engine of the old Volkswagen that was his pride and joy. Inglis said goodbye to Mrs Poltrock, and Albert leaned out of the upstairs window to shout his farewell.

They sat huddled together in the back seat, holding tight and dreading the final goodbye, which came all too soon. They stole one last kiss at the bottom of the gangplank, as Mr. Poltrock discreetly faced the car the other way. They promised to write, and Inglis made his way on board with feet of lead.

He stood at the top of the gangplank and watched the little car until it was out of sight; then stared after it for several more minutes, caught in the sadness of parting.

A large heavy hand descended on his shoulder, and Inglis came out of his reverie to find the Third Mate looking down at him, a bittersweet look on his face.

"She's beautiful son. I hope you see her again before too long. Deck office in ten minutes."

He turned and walked away without another word. Inglis had dreaded the thought of some lewd comment he would have to do something about; but Big John had a heart as big as the rest of him.

Inglis made his way to the cabin, where he changed into working clothes before presenting himself below in the deck office. They had less than half an hour of pumping to do before the ship would sail. When would he see Stade and Heidrun again?

CHAPTER 8

By one o'clock in the morning Inglis was on the forecastle with the first Mate and seamen, ready to cast off and receive a short pull from the local tug. Bow and stern ropes were in, with only the springing lines to go. The lead line for the tow-rope was on the tug, being followed by the tow-rope itself. This was soon made fast; the springing lines were cast off, and the tug started to take up the slack.

As yet Inglis still had no specific duties on the forecastle, his brief being to watch and make sure that when required to take over anything he would know what to do. There had been some slight confusion in the passing of the tow-rope, which seemed well in hand now.

For a minute or two Inglis gazed towards the distant glow of reflected light marking the position of Stade. Heidrun would be in bed now. He wondered if she was asleep, or was she lying awake thinking, as he was, what would become of their feelings for each other? How long would it be before he came back? How long would she wait for him? So beautiful and gay, so full of magic. Some bold German lad would scoop her up for sure, while he was far away. He felt the tears of self-pity prick his eyes, before shaking his head angrily at himself, and returning his attention to what was happening on deck.

As Inglis looked, one of the sailors stepped across the tow-rope, which was still slack, while the tug surged ahead to take up the strain. There was a bight, or loop, in the wire rope between the bollard and the fairlead. Taffy, the Welsh leading hand, put his foot in the bight as he walked to the rail.

Inglis opened his mouth to shout at Taffy. The tug took the strain at that moment, and the rope snapped tight.
Time slowed almost to a halt, as Taffy's leg was severed below the knee. He began to lose balance, a look of surprise on his face, and not a sound from his mouth.
Inglis was moving even before the rope had snapped tight. He fought his way across the deck, as if in slow motion through water. His mind screamed at him to move faster than he could.

Still he got there, after what seemed minutes, in time to cushion

Taffy's fall to the deck, which was turning red from the blood spurting out of the remains of his left leg.

Amazing as it seemed, nobody else had yet seen what had happened. A half strangled cry came from Inglis' throat, the words he knew not what.

Taffy's severed foot and shin lay on the deck beside Inglis, the foot encased in a canvas lace-up boot. Inglis grabbed the gruesome relic and tore a lace from the boot with demented fingers, which slipped on Taffy's blood.

Vaguely he was aware that people were moving towards them as a result of his cry. With his seaman's knife, Inglis slashed Taffy's overalls at the thigh, as Taffy's fresh warm blood gushed over him. Inglis quickly tied the boot lace round Taffy's thigh above the knee, placed his knife above the knot, and tied it again over the knife. Then he started to turn the knife as quickly as he could, tightening the lace to staunch the flow of blood.

Hands began to appear round Inglis, and someone took over the knife when he had it tight. Taffy was lifted and carried away.

A moment, or ten minutes later, who knows, Inglis was aware of hands on his shoulder, and a voice trying to penetrate his consciousness.

He was sitting on the deck, sobbing and trembling. Big John Soutar lifted him gently to his feet, and with his arm round Inglis' shoulders, led him off to the dining saloon.

Inglis felt foolish, and ashamed of his weakness. In the dining saloon he kept his eyes downcast on the table rather than meet anyone's gaze.

Big John put a glass of rum in Inglis' hand.

"Here laddie, drink this and you'll feel better. I saw it all from the bridge. What you did made me feel proud of you. Never mind how you feel now; you did the right thing when it was needed. What you're feeling now is a reaction any decent man would feel; especially the first time, and at your age. What matters now is that Taffy will be okay, thanks in part to what you did. He's on the tug now, and he'll be in hospital in no time."

Inglis looked up at him in gratitude as he downed the rum, which warmed and steadied him almost immediately.

"Now stand up," said Big John "and shake me by the hand MISTER McAndrew."

Suddenly people were patting Inglis on the back, and he didn't feel so foolish any more, though still embarrassed. Somebody took his coat, and the pantry boy brought a bowl of warm water and soap for him to wash some of Taffy's blood from his hands and face.

The Chief Steward arrived to inform them that Taffy was right now being transferred to an ambulance at the pier. He looked at Inglis, shook his head, and muttered
"You're a funny one right enough."
He opened two cans of lager, handed Inglis one and raised his own.
"Here's mud in your eye laddie."

Then he glared at Inglis over his hooked beak, drank the whole can in one hit, put the empty on the table, and strutted from the room without another word. There was a small cheer and Big John grinned at Inglis.
"You don't know how highly honoured you are Inglis. That can of beer was from his private stock; and that's the first time I've ever heard the old bugger say anything like a kind word to anyone. Now we're going to get roaring drunk. Just make sure you're awake in time to lend me your most valuable assistance on the bridge at noon" - Big grin -
"The pilot and the Skipper are in charge for the next few hours."
The beer started to flow and the night gradually faded away. Inglis would never forget Stade.

When he woke at 10.30am they were just entering the Kiel Canal. Jimmy told him they'd had a five-hour wait before entering. The canal pilot was on board in place of the river pilot.

Inglis took two aspirin, brushed his teeth for about five minutes, and swallowed a glass of Andrews Liver Salts. Soon he would feel better, he hoped.
In the Officers' Dining Saloon he ate three slices of dry toast accompanied by three cups of coffee. Gradually he began to feel

human again.

Inglis was on the starboard wing of the bridge well before noon, beginning to enjoy the fresh air as his head cleared. The canal was massively constructed, with concrete or rock walls all the way so far. It looked wide enough to take five ships their size side by side.

Five cables (1,000 yards) ahead of them was a small dirty white passenger ship, while another five cables behind was a fast green banana boat - refrigerated cargo liner! She was not very fast now though, since they were all progressing at the breakneck speed of six knots. At which speed it would be 6pm and well after dark before they reached the Baltic. The Third Mate took over the watch from the first Mate and promptly called Inglis into the wheelhouse.

"McAndrew," he said, sounding very official, "I want you to stay with the radar screen and call out the distance to the ship ahead every five minutes. You will call out clearly 'Radar. Ship ahead five cables', or whatever the distance may be. If neither myself nor the pilot acknowledges your call, you will repeat it after fifteen seconds, and continue to do so until acknowledged. If at any time you notice a quickly changing distance to either the ship ahead or the one astern, you will immediately call 'Warning. Radar warning', followed by a concise explanation of what is happening. Is that all clear?"

"Aye aye sir!" Inglis replied, standing to attention. "Ship ahead distance every five minutes. Increasing change either ship call attention immediately, SIR!"

Big John winked at him as he turned away, and the penny dropped. Inglis had never seen him this way before. But he was Officer of the Watch, and they had a German pilot and their own Skipper on the bridge to impress; and as far as Inglis was concerned, what Big John wanted, Big John would get from him every time.

The radar screen was mounted on a box-like pedestal in the middle of the port side of the wheelhouse. In order to see the screen clearly in daylight, it was necessary to bend forward and place your face against the hood, which was shaped to fit round the eyes, with a notch to accommodate the nose.

The screen could be set on three different ranges, and was currently on short range. That meant the distance from centre to edge of screen represented five nautical miles; with the ten concentric circles engraved on the glass five cables apart. So the ships immediately ahead and astern should both appear on the first ring, if they all kept station. The sweeping green line representing the radar beam took ten seconds for each revolution of the screen.

When Inglis first put his face in the hood he saw what initially looked like an indecipherable mass of green splotches all over it; fading slowly behind the sweep, and disappearing altogether just before it came round again.

On close scrutiny he was able to make out the clearer patch ahead and astern which was the canal, disappearing into the general clutter at about fifteen cables. There, sure enough were the 'blips' of their companion vessels, both bang on the five-cable line. At least Inglis knew what he was looking at, since he had been told how to interpret radar on a visit to the control tower at the fighter base; and the tests for the Air Force at Hornchurch had included a radar screen as part of the co-ordination series.

Inglis found that if he stared into the screen for too long, his eyes played tricks on him; so, every three sweeps he would raise his head and look at the ship ahead to confirm her real position with her radar image. At 12.05, 12.10 and so on he stood erect and called out his piece loud and clear.

At 12.20 he was about to open his mouth again, when he noticed the Skipper and the pilot calling to each other, one in the wheelhouse, the other on the starboard wing. Inglis politely held his tongue for them to finish.
At exactly 12.20.30 the Skipper paused, glanced at his watch and, without turning his head, bawled out with a deafening roar.
"RADAR REPORT!"

Inglis almost jumped out of his skin before calling out   "Radar, ship ahead five cables SIR!"
The helmsman, nicknamed Elvis for his guitar-playing ability, grinned at Inglis like the Cheshire cat, then rolled his eyes skywards.

The Old Man must have had eyes in the back of his head, because the next thing he roared out was

"Helmsman! Eyes on the ship ahead!"

Elvis snapped his eyes down and answered "Aye aye SIR!"

Now it was Inglis' turn to hide a grin. Meanwhile the Skipper resumed his interrupted conversation with the pilot as if nothing had happened.

By 3 o'clock they were passing under the large railway bridge near Rendsburg. During the twenty minutes Inglis could see details on the bridge, it was crossed by four trains. Three freights headed by black 2-10-0s, and one short passenger train hauled by a large unfamiliar tank engine. It looked capable of hauling at least three times the load it had.

Forth Venturer was still carrying 80% load, since she had filled up in Hamburg, and Stadersand had taken only - *Only!* - five thousand tons of fuel. She was therefore drawing twice as much depth as the ships ahead and astern. Half a nautical mile seems a long way when you look at it. But the truth is that, even at only 6 knots they would be hard pushed to come to a dead stop inside that half mile with the engine full astern. There was currently 30,000 tons hanging on *Forth Venturer*'s single propeller - or screw as it was called. Some warships of less than a fifth of her displacement had more than twice the installed horsepower. Even the banana boat astern had about three times as many horsepower per ton as she did. Tankers are not the easiest things to throw around - definitely no wheelies! The difficulty in stopping is probably more easily understood if, instead of 30,000 tons at 6 knots, one imagines stopping 6 tons from 30,000 knots!

The range fluctuated slightly, and Inglis noticed that the pilot preferred to stay a bit over the five cable distance. He acted urgently whenever the gap looked like coming down below that; so he was well aware of their relative clumsiness.

Big John had been studying the well-worn passenger ship ahead. He caught the Skipper's eye and remarked with a chuckle

"The old rust bucket ahead doesn't relish having a loaded tanker breathing down her neck sir. She's had a man on the monkey island since we started, watching us through an old naval range finder."

"I don't blame her Skipper one bloody bit," said Captain Evans. "I've been saying for years that they should give loaded tankers at least an extra three cables through here. But no bugger listens. No bugger ever listens until it's too bloody late for some poor sod!"

He stalked out to the wing of the bridge, hands clasped behind his back, like a miniature version of the Duke of Edinburgh. John winked at Inglis. He obviously knew some of the Skipper's hobby horses. The atmosphere in the wheelhouse became less tense. It was no fun having the Skipper stalking around in there all the time. Maybe that's what John had intended to achieve. He was big, but he wasn't stupid.

Inglis thought the pair of them felt uncomfortable when they were too close. The giant Third Mate towering over the pint size Skipper. There was a rumor going around that Captain Evans would be the shortest man in the company without his built-up shoes! Inglis wasn't much over average size at 5'10" and 147 pounds, and he felt big beside the Skipper. He could imagine how Captain Evans felt when Big John blocked out his sunlight.

By the time Inglis finished his practical navigation with the Second Mate, they were passing the myriad lights and busy shipping of Kiel. Their next stop was to be Fredericia, a town on the mainland of Denmark; opposite the island of Fyn, on which Odense was located.

Once clear of Kieler Forde and into Kiel Bay, they would have to go the long way round Fyn. To the south of Fredericia the narrows are spanned by road and rail bridges, under which *Forth Venturer* could not pass. Her course would therefore take her between the islands of Langeland and Lolland, then between Fyn and the main island of Sjaelland, on the far side of which lies Copenhagen. They would actually approach Fredericia from the north-east, though their current position put them just east of due south.

Fredericia was a clean fresh looking town of which Inglis saw very little. From there they headed for Copenhagen, just twelve hours after arrival - which was why Inglis didn't see much of it.

While making their way round the north of Sjaelland in the Kattegat, they received orders to call at Helsingborg in Sweden to unload a couple of thousand tons of motor spirit. Helsingborg was another attractive town, with a busy ferry service across the narrows to Helsingor in Denmark. This latter being of course the famous Elsinore of Shakespeare's Hamlet.

As the tugs fussed round them in the harbor they passed close to a Shell tanker in the next berth. One of her seamen cupped his hands to mouth and bellowed.

"Got any Geordies aboard?"

Back on the instant came the equally loud reply from *Forth Venturer*'s deck.

"Naaaaa.....we've jist been fumigated!"

This little exchange led to a brawl ashore later, in which Inglis was thankfully not involved. He was busy on a cultural expedition at the time. Helsingborg had no opera house, so the Mate decided Jimmy and Inglis should accompany him on the hydrofoil to Helsingor, in order that their broader education be not neglected. For this purpose Inglis was excused cargo watch, and since the Mate was paying for the trip Inglis thought it wasn't a bad deal. Jimmy on the other hand was heard to mutter

"Bloody Shakespeare for Chrissakes, whit next?"

Later he approached Inglis with a worried expression on his little screwed-up face and asked

"D'ye think this is the thin end o' the wedge Inglis? He might try and force us tae go tae yon operry stuff next. I dinna think ah could stand that!"

Inglis laughed at the look of utter despair on his face.

"I doubt it Jimmy," he replied. "The talk is that his wife will be joining him in Copenhagen, and she'll be sailing with us for a while."

Jimmy's gnome-like features lost their worried look.

"Thank God for that. Oh whit a relief. I love her, and I hav'na even met her yet."

Poor Jimmy didn't get away scot free, and would have liked to kill Inglis later on the hydrofoil. Inglis dobbed him in to the Mate with an innocent expression on his face.

"You'd best keep a close eye on your wife when she arrives sir. Jimmy has fallen in love with her already. He sees her as his salvation from the delights of the opera."

The Mate roared with laughter, while Jimmy shot daggers at Inglis from under his bushy little eyebrows.

The hydrofoil was like being on a jet aircraft after so long on a tanker. The sensation of speed was exhilarating, and they were in Helsingor in no time.

Hamlet's castle looked quite impressive under its mantle of snow, but not as big as Inglis had thought it would be. In fact it wasn't much bigger than the local castle back home, and that was built for an archbishop. But it was in ruins, and this one wasn't. Guarding the narrow entrance to the Baltic, it had been used as a 'toll' collection backup in the old days. Inglis had expected something more like a town with a hundred gun ports. It was in fact more like a village with not many gun ports at all.

The Mate was most pleasant, taking them to a coffee shop for a meal after their visit to the castle. While walking round the ramparts he had been rattling off quotes like '2b or knot 2b' and mumbling about a dagger with its handle towards his hand - Inglis just hoped he wouldn't give it to Jimmy right then.

Anyway, the quality of his mercy was unstrained afterwards - like the tea at the coffee shop. What idiot apart from Inglis would order tea in a Danish coffee shop in the first place?

CHAPTER 9

Next day *Forth Venturer* sailed for Copenhagen. There was hardly any wind, and the snow came down in large silent flakes. The temperature had risen to within a few degrees of freezing, instead of being off the bottom of the thermometer.

The falling snow blanketed the sounds of shipping, of which there were plenty. It was only a short four-hour trip, and they should be berthed in time for lunch................until the engine broke down. One minute it was throbbing and thumping beneath Inglis' feet confidently enough. Then there was nothing, as it suddenly stopped without warning.

Inglis could hear the hissing of water along the ship's sides as her massive inertia kept her going. The sounds of other shipping now made themselves heard, in spite of the snow thickening. Soon visibility was down to between two and three hundred yards, and Inglis was called to the bridge to sound the foghorn. Other foghorns could be heard through the snow as he gripped the handle. Being a large power vessel they were required to use the huge steam whistle mounted high on the funnel. The operating handle was located on the starboard bulkhead of the wheelhouse, clear of the door. A wooden handgrip was swivel-mounted to the bottom end of a vertical metal rod which passed through bearings held clear of the bulkhead by brackets. A downward pull operated the whistle. When released, the handle returned to the off position by means of a spring. The whistle continued to blow for just as long as the handle was held down

There was also a clamp for the metal rod, which could be tightened in order to hold the whistle on for long periods. Nobody could tell Inglis how long it would blow before running out of steam, but he was sure it would be a long time. Although *Forth Venturer* was a motor vessel, the auxilliary boilers were of high capacity, being used to operate the unloading pumps, and the Butterworth steam hoses for fire fighting and tank cleaning.

The Mate ordered Inglis to sound the whistle at exactly one minute intervals, blowing one three second blast followed by two of one second. The bridge was getting crowded. Apart from Inglis at the whistle, Jimmy was at the radar, the Skipper was shouting at the Chief

Engineer on the engine room telephone; the Mate prowled around everywhere giving out orders, and more hands were ordered to the bridge for instructions.

Aussie took over the whistle from Inglis after the first four blasts. Elvis was on the wheel, which would soon be useless. Big John arrived and took over the radar from Jimmy, and the two cadets were then posted on the wings of the bridge as lookouts. Inglis scored port while Jimmy was awarded starboard. They had just taken up position when the Third Mate bellowed above all the noise.
"RADAR OUT OF ORDER SIR!"

The Skipper *ran* across to the radar cabinet to see for himself, peered briefly under the hood, and emerged cursing and swearing. Turning to one of the newly arrived seamen he shouted
"Second Mate, electrician, and radio operator to the bridge at the double!"
From the time the engine had stopped, it would take about twenty minutes for the ship to completely lose way through the water - during which time she would travel about two statute miles. As Inglis stood peering into the snow he could still hear the hiss of water along the hull.

They had two Aldis lamps, which are like searchlights with shutters over the lenses for signaling. They were now mounted on the forward outer corners of the bridge wings, the port one being Inglis' responsibility. He was peering so intently for the first ten minutes that his eyes began to smart and play tricks on him again. It became obvious to him that it was better to keep looking around his sector and relax himself just a little. More lookouts had taken up their posts on the forecastle, poop, and monkey island.

Inglis' sector was from the port bow to port quarter, a sweep of ninety degrees. The snow was falling thick and fast, the ship beginning to resemble a huge birthday cake for an avid sailor. The deafening blast of her giant whistle now sounded out at thirty-second intervals; one long, two short - 'I am not under command'

In the wheelhouse meantime, the radio operator had been instructed to transmit a message detailing their situation and position. The

Second Mate was busy with his charts, and the electrician - Harry - busied himself with the wiring on the radar. Apparently the screen still glowed, but the antenna had stopped rotating. Soon Harry was tracing wires and cables through junction boxes, testing with his circuit tester, and other such gobbledygook. So far he seemed to know about as much as the rest of them what had gone wrong.

In the engine room the engineers were hard at work. A bearing had overheated and seized up, starting a small fire, which had been quickly put out. The duty greaser was on Captain's Orders for gross negligence. He'd had a long boozy night and had gone to sleep on duty. The Third Engineer was also in trouble for not having caught him sooner, and for allowing him to come on duty in an unfit state in the first place. Fun and games were due when they reached Copenhagen. The Chief Engineer estimated about two hours to fix things.

A gray patch in the snow. A ship? Yes, and pretty close too.
"Ship bearing four zero degrees on the port bow," Inglis shouted at the top of his voice, repeating "four zero degrees port bow," as he grabbed the handgrip of the Aldis lamp, swung it to point at the gray shape in the snow, and pulled the trigger - one long, two short - pause - one long, two short. A few moments later the blast of *Forth Venturer*'s whistle sent out the same message, to be answered by one long blast from the phantom now taking shape as a Dutch coaster on her port side. Inglis triggered the Aldis again before shouting "Bearing now port six zero degrees."

The bearing to the coaster was changing rapidly, which meant it would pass safely at a range of about a hundred yards. Too close for comfort, but safe. As she came abeam of them, a hooded figure appeared on the wing of her bridge with a loud hailer.
"Can I be of assistance?" boomed the amplified voice across the water. The Mate appeared at Inglis' elbow with his bullhorn to his lips.
"Thank you no. Engine and radar both out, but should be under control soon."
Inglis hoped the Mate was right. He turned to Inglis.

"You're doing a good job son, but you can cut out the bearing and degrees and any other superfluous Royal Navy stuff when you report.

Keep it short and sweet, like 'port 60' - okay?"

"Okay sir, got it. Sorry."

"Yes, something like that," he said with a smile.

Shortly after the coaster disappeared, Big John relieved Inglis, telling him to join the Second Mate in the chart room. The Decca Navigator was working perfectly for once, just at the right time. Inglis was to help the Second Mate by double-checking everything, since "You seem to have an affinity for the contraption," as he put it. True, Inglis enjoyed working with it - when it worked properly. He was always good with figures, and he liked reading off the colored dials to produce a precise latitude and longitude from a set of quick calculations.

Their job was to produce the right answers with no mistakes, so the authorities ashore would know exactly where they were, and could warn other shipping accordingly. The shore radars were having problems with the weather conditions and the density of traffic.

An ocean going tug had been dispatched from Copenhagen and would be with them around noon, just in case they had underestimated their problems. They were causing quite a stir ashore by now. It's no fun having a loaded tanker blind and powerless in the middle of a busy sea lane in heavy snow.

The Second Mate set the red dial and called out the reading, with Inglis looking over his shoulder and calling 'check' as they both wrote down the figures on separate pads. Then the other dials; green, purple and so on. A start time and finish time were noted, and they each did the calculations and compared the end result, before entering the position in the log. The Second Mate did the log entries and Inglis initialed them. Strictly speaking a cadet wasn't supposed to write anything in the log, but this was a special case.

Every five minutes they repeated the process, which kept them very busy, as there wasn't much time to spare for errors. At ten-minute intervals the fix was plotted on a large scale chart on the chart room table. The position was written on a message sheet, signed by the Second, countersigned by Inglis. The sheet was then taken by the junior steward to the radio operator for transmission to the shore. All this made Inglis feel important and part of a team effort. Mind you, the fixes were starting to come on top of each other on the chart, as they were now merely drifting.

At 10.50 Harry burst into the wheelhouse covered in snow.

"Brush burned out on the rotation motor sir. I have spares and should have it going in about ten minutes." Harry disappeared again, trailing snow in his wake. The Second Steward arrived with steaming mugs of thick cocoa - and left within seconds with an empty tray. The Second Mate and Inglis scored one between them, with a promise of more to come.

Before the second mug arrived, Harry crashed into the wheelhouse again, looking even more like the Abominable Snowman. He charged across to the radar screen, poked his head in the hood, and shouted "Radar operational sir!"

This announcement was met by a spontaneous cheer from the less senior personnel present, quickly silenced by a sweeping glare from the Old Man, who said "Very well, and thank you for a quick job. Steward, inform the radio operator our radar is operational."

He turned towards the chart room and bellowed "McAndrew, if you please", pointing at the radar cabinet. His instructions were short and precise.

"Report bearing and distance any ship within ten cables."

"Aye aye sir," Inglis replied, shooting across to the radar screen and scrutinizing the green electronic world within - he was in big demand today. At least they were no longer blind - and he was the one with the X-ray vision, just like Superman!

There were three ships within ten cables, all of which Inglis reported. One was heading away, and the other two would pass well clear. For half an hour nothing came closer than six cables, which was quite close enough really. But there was plenty to report just the same.

At 11.30 Inglis picked up a blip at 20 cables on the starboard quarter, still well outside his brief, and with another seven or eight on the screen at the same time. For the next ten sweeps of the beam the bearing to this ship remained constant, while the range steadily decreased. It was now showing at under seventeen cables, and if it maintained present course and speed, would be in danger of hitting *Forth Venturer* in nine or ten minutes time. Inglis watched it for another two sweeps, while carefully checking his calculations, before deciding to open his mouth.

"Ship approaching on collision course. Range sixteen plus cables, bearing relative one two zero degrees, speed eleven knots!"
There was a sudden flurry of movement in the wheelhouse. The Mate shot across and shoved Inglis unceremoniously aside before peering into the radar hood. As he did so Inglis told him
"Bearing has remained constant for two minutes sir. Range reduced by just under four cables in that time. I know it's more than ten cables sir, but..."
"Don't ever apologize for doing the right thing lad," answered the Mate, with his eyes still glued to the screen. A few moments later he raised his head and called to the Skipper.
"Collision course confirmed sir."

Turning to the Second Mate he rattled off bearing, distance and speed of the other ship, and instructed him to give its position and course to Sparks for urgent transmission to the shore, with the time of the plot. The Old Man spoke.
"Man the starboard Aldis and train one two zero degrees. Mister Vickers stand fast on the radar. McAndrew report any change in the ship's head. Bosun take over the whistle and sound the collision alert at twenty second intervals. Fowler relieve the Third Mate on the port wing. Mister Soutar prepare the rocket apparatus for immediate use. Red stars, ON MY ORDER ONLY!"

This latter was the distress signal, and strictly speaking was against the rules in their present situation. But Captain Evans was obviously intent on protecting his ship with every means at his disposal - and answer for his methods later. Their whistle blasts changed to two shorts and a long, as Inglis stood behind the wheel watching the lubber's line on the compass repeater, in case the ship should begin to swing.

Big John fetched the rocket gear from its locker in the chart room, and the Mate called out a distance and bearing to the invisible approaching vessel. It was still heading straight for them, and there was absolutely nothing they could do to get out of its way. Sparks was in constant contact with the shore, who were unable to contact - or even identify - the oncoming ship.

By 11.38 they were three minutes away from a collision. *Forth Venturer*'s head had by this time gradually swung ten degrees to starboard - so the relative bearing to the mystery ship was now 110 degrees. The two ships seemed to be attracting each other like magnets.

Tension on the bridge had built up to an almost unbearable pitch, and the Captain was pacing back and forth, hands behind his back. Once more he shouted instructions.

"Bosun two shorts and one long, continuous. Mister Soutar, I want rockets launched *at that ship*, and I want you to aim as if you are trying to hit her with mortar shells. Maybe that'll wake the bastards up!"

"Aye aye SIR!" came the enthusiastic reply from Big John, followed a few seconds later by "Ready to fire rockets sir."

Captain Evans came right back.

"Fire away, and keep firing until I say stop."

Immediately there was the zzzzziiiiiiiifffffff of a rocket leaving the starboard wing, followed ten seconds later by another - and another. *Forth Venturer*'s whistle continued to blast out over the noise of the rockets. The Mate called distance and bearing. Inglis called another degree of swing. Altogether the bridge was a cacophony of noise; a replay of Bedlam, or shout-as-you-please day at the looney bin. Above it all the Skipper's voice boomed out again, like the roar of a bull from the body of a terrier.

"Munro, commence flashing two shorts and a long. Keep at it, and don't stop for anything son."

The clack of the Aldis added to the general din. Inglis didn't know how everyone else's nerves were holding out, but his were just about screaming. They were now about ninety seconds from being rammed, and the phantom ship still came on - heading straight for the tanker's 20,000 plus tons of highly explosive cargo. Any moment now she should become visible through the snow. Just as the thought passed through Inglis' mind, Jimmy shouted from the Aldis.

"Ship in sight one one zero degrees, bow on!" There was a tremor in his voice, for which Inglis didn't blame him one little bit.

"Man the port side lifeboats!" screamed the Skipper, grabbing the bullhorn on his way to the starboard wing. The off-duty engineering and deck staff were already on deck - all six of them. Three each headed for the two lifeboats. The ship carried only four boats, two on each side. The whole crew could fit in two boats if necessary, as their total complement was 52 officers and men. Captain Evans raised the bullhorn and screamed at the oncoming vessel - a cargo ship of about 6,000 gross tons.

"Get away from my ship you bastard. Turn - Jesus God, turn, you blind son of a bitch!"

Inglis couldn't see the other ship from where he stood, and he desperately wanted to have a look; but his vision was restricted to about one zero zero degrees, just ahead of the menacing hull bearing down on them. By now it must be less than two hundred yards away, and already nearly too late to miss them. The Skipper ordered the engine room evacuated.

"She's turning!" cried Big John exultantly. "Christ, I damn near hit her bridge with the last one!" Another rocket sped off.

"Belay the rockets, and well done Mister Soutar," shouted the Captain. "Now, start praying like you never prayed before. Mister Vickers stand fast. The rest of you - all of you - man the port side lifeboat."

Inglis' normal abandon ship position was at the starboard midships lifeboat. The port one was the Second Mate's responsibility, with his crew of four men. By the time Inglis got there the cover was off, and the davits already swung out. Once on the boat deck abaft the boat, Inglis could see the gray and white shape of the other ship - it seemed to be almost looming over him now. She must hit them -mustn't she?.....she wasn't exactly bow on now. As Inglis looked, the foremast was in line with the starboard side of her wheelhouse. A moment later it was heading out along the wing of her bridge. She *was* turning, but still it looked too late.

Inglis felt he could almost reach out and touch her, and he was scared. Heart-in-the-mouth scared, not frozen panic scared, but scared nevertheless. Soon she was starting to run almost parallel to their side, her hull plates less than a hundred feet from *Forth Venturer*'s, and her bridge coming up level with theirs. A bearded man stood on the wing of her bridge with a bullhorn. The words came loud and clear.

"You try to shoot my ship you crazy man. Nearly you start the fire with your rockets - imbecile!"

The tanker Skipper's reply was a barrage of curses and insults to the other Skipper's parentage and competence, while the 'bastard' shouted an order over his shoulder to the wheelhouse.

The greatest danger now was from the stern of the other ship, which was still swinging towards them as the bows started to run parallel. Inglis could see her helmsman spinning the wheel - but he knew that if she was as slow to answer as *Forth Venturer*, it was already much too late.

Her bows remained at the same distance from them, but the stern was moving inexorably closer to their hull, second by second, as it drew level with their bridge. The rudder was hard over to port, but still her stern swung the wrong way. By the time it reached half way between the tanker's bridge and forecastle, the gap was down to less than thirty feet - it had narrowed by 70% in half the distance.

Her bow wave had already smashed onto their foredeck. Now the trapped waves of water boiled between the two hulls; and still her prop threshed through the water.
Forth Venturer had rolled to port in response to the other ship's bow wave. Now she rolled back to starboard to meet the cargo ship's wake - which surged across her main deck, swirling round the tank tops, and racing beneath the catwalk to smash into the scuppers on the port side, rising in a vertical sheet of water as they met.

Unless the cargo ship stopped swinging in the next two seconds, her poop would strike the rise of the tanker's forecastle at the forward end of the foredeck, which was just completing its roll to starboard.

Inglis held his breath, unable to tear his eyes away, as thousands of tons of steel came closer and closer. Now there was no discernible gap from where Inglis stood. A man could jump from her poop onto their deck.

The flare of the cargo ship's poop seemed to overhang the tanker's forecastle, just as she started to roll back to port......and she was past.......she had missed.........by a hairbreadth.

Inglis saw the name painted in large letters on her stern before she disappeared into the enveloping snow ahead.

PARTHENOPE

PANAMA

Someone had a peculiar sense of humor. She'd almost lured them to their deaths all right, but certainly not by singing to them.

Fifteen minutes later the engine room telegraph rang, and the pointer moved to 'Stand By'. The Chief Engineer was on the phone informing the Skipper that repairs were complete, but he would appreciate running the engine at no more than half speed until he was sure the new bearing was okay. They could feel the deck vibrate beneath their feet as the engine came to life - it was a good feeling. A smoke ring came from the funnel during the first few rough revolutions, then the engine settled down to an even rhythm.

The Skipper rang down 'Half Ahead', and gradually *Forth Venturer* picked up speed, until eventually she was doing eight knots. The seagoing tug from Copenhagen arrived shortly after they got underway, and she stood by to accompany them for the rest of the trip. They saw her only briefly when she first arrived, as the snow was still falling thick and silent. Once on station five hundred yards off their starboard quarter, she was invisible behind the curtain of white.

Forth Venturer's whistle continued to blast out its warning every minute, and Inglis was allocated to the radar screen, since he was now officially on watch with the Third Mate. Elvis was back on the wheel, and one of the seamen replaced the bosun on the whistle handle.

By 1.30 the snow was thinning out and they could see the tug most of the time, nudging the sea aside with its blunt aggressive snout. The extra lookouts were stood down, and soon there was no further need for the whistle.

Everyone began to relax and smile, and crack nervous jokes. It had been a very close call indeed. Captain Evans was demanding an enquiry, and had sent the cargo ship's name and other details to the shore by radio.

"Bloody Panama registry - should be outlawed," he muttered.

CHAPTER 10

Visibility was about a mile when they arrived off Copenhagen to pick up the harbor pilot. The deep water channel was marked in a right hand curve, and looked quite sharp for a ship of their size. Just within the range of visibility Inglis could make out the Little Mermaid, sitting alone on her rock off to starboard.

The pilot took over the con and they nosed into the outer end of the channel. Inglis went to the forecastle to join the first Mate and his men, who were making ready to receive the harbor tugs. His job now was to take the place of poor old Taffy, who had lost part of his leg in Stadersand. His replacement should join the ship in Copenhagen when they berthed.

Today they were using the thick heavy manila ropes instead of the steel cables that Inglis hated to handle. On more than one occasion men had lost fingers and more to the steel ropes, when a frayed wire grabbed a glove feeding the cable onto the drum of a winch.

The manilas were big and heavy, and difficult to handle because of their size and weight. But at least they were more forgiving of men's little mistakes and weaknesses, where the heartless steel ones seemed always ready to pounce and bite at the slightest opportunity. Inglis thought maybe the Mate hated them too, which was why he opted for the manila ropes more and more. They had used them only once before Stadersand, but constantly since. On the other hand, maybe the Mate was an amateur psychologist, using the manila in deference to the superstitions and fears for which sailors were renowned. In either case, Inglis for one was grateful as he grunted and heaved on the forecastle - working up a sweat in spite of the cold bleak weather conditions.

Once everything was ready in position they had time to look around and take in the view. The Little Mermaid was much closer now, her shape quite clear to the naked eye. Inglis hadn't expected her to be so close because of the bend in the channel. Looking around more, he noticed they weren't in fact following the marked channel at all. Instead, they were cutting across it, their course analogous to the string of a bow, with the channel as the bow itself. Inglis pointed this out to the Mate.

78

"Why would the pilot do that sir?"

"I don't really know son, I've been trying to figure it out myself for the last few minutes. Maybe they've been dredging a new channel that's not yet marked. I hope the pilot knows what he's doing - that's what he gets paid for after all. But Captain Evans doesn't look too happy about things."

Inglis looked up at the bridge and saw what he meant. Their Captain was striding quickly back and forth on the starboard wing. He stopped beside the pilot, waved his arm towards the marked channel, shook his head and continued his agitated pacing.

The Little Mermaid was now so close it was possible to make out her features. Their forward motion created the effect of relative movement behind her, from right to left, or as though she was gliding slowly backwards on her rock from left to right. As Inglis watched she slowed down, and he felt a sensation of rising, like a slow elevator. The Mermaid's progress across the seascape was slowly arrested as the tanker ran aground.

Inglis felt himself being drawn towards the bows, and took a couple of paces to steady himself. The ship had stopped moving forward, and the bows had risen several feet in the water. It had all been so smooth and gentle as to be almost unnoticeable. Inglis had never dreamed that running aground in a dirty great tanker could seem such a genteel event.

Just before bedlam erupted he looked once more at the Little Mermaid, and he could have sworn she smiled at him - a hint of a wink even?

The seagoing tug that had accompanied them was just entering the harbor, having preceded them as they picked up the pilot. Now she was summoned to their assistance, and did an about turn. From the forecastle they could quite clearly hear the Skipper cursing and swearing, his voice filling the air without need of artificial amplification. The pilot was embarrassed to say the least, as the Skipper stopped barely short of sitting him in the corner of the wheelhouse with a dunce's cap on his head.

The ship began to vibrate, the Skipper having insisted on 'Full Astern', and the hell with the new bearing - bathe it in oil, Chief! It was half an hour before high tide; so if the ship didn't refloat within the next hour or so, she could be in big trouble - and so could Copenhagen. Tankers are built to carry liquid cargoes while themselves immersed in liquid, with weights and pressures inside acting against those outside. Try lifting a loaded tanker out of the water, and she was more than a little inclined to break her back and drop her bundle.

If there was a ledge under her, rather than say a gentle sand bank, there could be really serious problems, depending on the position of the ledge. When the tide dropped, relinquishing its support, the resultant stresses could quite conceivably break her back. Rather like taking a long thin-walled cardboard box, filling it to 70% with water, then hanging one end over the edge of a table. Not quite, but it gives some idea of the consequences; and nobody - but *nobody* - relishes the idea of twenty thousand tons of unrestrained oil messing up the neighborhood.

The Skipper and the authorities were immediately caught in a dilemma. They had two main choices. Either they could throw every available tug into the job of pulling the tanker off whatever had stopped her; or they could start pumping her cargo into smaller tankers as soon as possible - provided there were enough available right now.

The first option was the more attractive, provided she didn't spring a leak, of which there was no sign as yet. The second option was not so attractive, for the simple reason that the ship's pumps were quite incapable of pumping out even a fifth of the 20,000 tons of oil still in the tanks within the next four hours. That was how long they had before the tide would be low enough to cause serious consequences.

In the end Captain Evans opted for what they all thought was the best possible combination. This was to go for the tugs, while at the same time transferring weight aft. Fortunately, for once they had a single product cargo, made up entirely of motor spirit. Therefore they could transfer oil from any tank to any other.

The plan was to fill the after tanks to the brim with the oil from the forward ones; starting with the number nine tanks being filled from the number ones, and working from there. This was not quite as easy as it sounds, but still only a matter of manpower and proper co-ordination.

The Skipper sent for the Mate to take charge of this important operation, with the Donkeyman and off-duty engine room staff to assist. This left Inglis suddenly in charge of the forecastle party, but with two extra hands to assist. Everybody on board was now employed in some capacity or other, Inglis' extra hands being the junior steward and the pantry boy.

The cooks were being similarly pressed into service on the poop, under the Second Mate. Soon they would all be very busy. The massive screw under the tanker's stern was threshing the water at full revolutions astern, and water was foaming and boiling forward along the ship's sides. Inglis looked over and noticed the water was yellowish brown in color, which was a good sign. At least there was mud and sand under them, whether or not rocks were present.

Inglis raised his eyes to meet those of the Little Mermaid; which seemed to express disdainful amusement as she watched the foolish antics of these humans, from the security of her rock.
The seagoing tug arrived, and a line was soon passed to her from the poop. Two harbor tugs could be seen in the distance, on their way to help the stupid stranded whale.

The Mate had things under control on deck very quickly, and pumping was underway before the seagoing tug took the strain. The sea boiled under her stern, the tow-rope rose from the water and began to sing, but *Forth Venturer* would not budge. The Skipper ordered Inglis, via his bullhorn, to make ready a second tow-rope on the forecastle, and prepare to pass one each side to the harbor tugs. They were to make the ropes fast to the forward twin bollards and pass them out through the after fairleads of the forecastle.

The harbor tugs arrived soon after their preparations were complete, and for the next fifteen minutes they were very busy. They passed the port rope first, then immediately set about passing the starboard one. Both ropes were turned once on their respective bollards, then led onto one drum of the main winch. The ship's carpenter joined them, and was in charge of the winch as they eased out first one rope, then the other. The idea was for the harbor tugs to nuzzle the tanker's side just forward of the after accommodation, facing in the opposite direction to *Forth Venturer*. Then take the strain, pulling her backwards from the front; which isn't quite as Irish as it sounds, even if she was built in Belfast.

Meanwhile another two harbor tugs had left their berths and were on their way to join the party. Inglis had both the tow-ropes made fast to the bollards with extra turns, and still passed twice round the winch drums. If any of the tow-ropes gave way it wasn't going to be his. Facing the bridge, he held one arm out to each side, then crossed them above his head to signify that both ropes were secure. Moments later the tugs took up the strain, and now a total of seven screws threshed the water into a boiling brown maelstrom.

The discolored water raced along the tanker's sides and curved away ahead of her, taken by the tide, which was now on the ebb. The sea was soon stained for a distance of half a mile, and increasing.

Almost imperceptibly *Forth Venturer* began to move, creeping slowly astern, being dragged from the bank. There was no grinding or squealing of tortured metal, so hopefully the bottom was soft after all. The ship moved about ten feet before stopping once more, held fast by the clutching seabed. Their hopes plunged again.

A coastal tanker arrived, and stood off three hundred yards from their port bow. She had hoses and a 'vacuum cleaner' rigged to the jib of her foremast - just in case they sprang a leak.

The two extra harbor tugs nudged in and took tow-ropes from the poop, where the Second Mate and his gang now had their hands full, with three tugs to tend. The whole ship trembled as eleven screws and God knows how many horsepower strained to pull the stranded tanker from her ignominious perch. She moved slowly again, another ten feet; then once more she stuck, stubbornly refusing to go any farther. Ropes sang with the strain, water squeezing from their tortured strands. The pumps continued to thump in the bowels of the ship, transferring more weight aft in a race against the receding tide. The Skipper darted around on the bridge, bawling orders through his bullhorn; while the pilot relayed his instructions to the tugs via blasts of the ship's whistle.

Another two harbor tugs came on the scene, and Inglis wondered where the hell he was going to tie them on - there wasn't much room left! But the Skipper had different ideas, and didn't want them tied on at all. Instead, he ordered one to each side, and stopped his own screw, which would have interfered with his plans.

His idea was to 'wiggle' the ship out of her predicament. The fresh tugs nosed into the flanking harbor tugs. The starboard tug pushed inwards first, while the port one rested, and the three tugs pulling from the stern swung to their starboard. Slowly the ship's stern swung to port in answer to the balance of forces exerted on her. When she would swing no farther, the Skipper ordered everything changed round the opposite way. Now the new tug on the port side pushed inwards while the starboard one rested. The seagoing tug and her two companions swung the other way. *Forth Venturer*'s stern moved the opposite way through its arc, until once more it would go no farther. Still she wouldn't come off the bank, and the procedure was reversed yet again.

This time, just as the stern passed through its original position, she started to move astern. The whistle blasted its message to the fresh tugs, which pulled away from her sides as her own screw began to churn the water once more. She kept moving astern this time, and now they could feel her floating free, by the change under their feet; difficult to explain, but quite definite.

A huge cheer swept through the ship as Inglis leaned over the bow, looking for the tell-tale spread of oil on the surface. There was none. The Skipper had just earned his pay. What they had witnessed was a brilliant piece of improvised seamanship and ship handling, which only a great depth of experience could have conceived and acted on with confidence.

On the forecastle they became busy again, taking in the starboard rope and coiling it. Then they had to take in the port rope, before passing it back out through the forward fairlead, and transferring its anchor point to the after bollards, ready for the berthing tug.

They sailed into Copenhagen via the marked channel this time, after Inglis waved goodbye to the Little Mermaid. One of the crew watching him raised his eyebrows.

"Who the hell are you waving to Inglis?"

"The Little Mermaid of course!" he replied. "She's been laughing her tail off at our antics!"

The seaman raised his eyebrows further, and looked sideways at Inglis.

"I always said you were nuts - now I know for sure."

The rest of the forecastle grinned and nodded agreement.

"Well, I'm not alone then," Inglis retorted. "I'm not the silly bugger who ran us aground - he's nuttier than me!"

There was a murmur of agreement as they all looked up at the bridge; where the pilot stood leaning on the rail, head in his hands. The bill for the squadron of tugs would be hefty indeed, and they all knew where Captain Evans would be sending it!

CHAPTER 11

Forth Venturer tied up at 4.45, with darkness already upon them. More important to Inglis was the fact that the Skipper had changed the cargo watches. From now on while they were in port, Inglis would be doing an eight-hour watch from 8am until 4pm, assisted by the Donkeyman and one seaman. He therefore had a whole night in which to enjoy his new-found freedom of movement. While in port, one eight-hour watch was much better than two four-hour ones.

Apparently the Mate considered Inglis competent enough to take over a watch in his own right - with the Donkeyman there just in case he made a mess of it! On the other hand, his taking over a watch left the Mate free of a fixed cargo watch in port, which probably had something to do with his decision. The three watches in port were now the responsibility of the Second Mate, Third Mate, and Inglis. Unlike some of her sister ships the tanker had no Fourth Mate, so it looked as if Inglis was elected - acting, unpaid, of course. But he wasn't about to complain. He felt important. They surely knew how to appeal to his ego - maybe the first Mate was a *professional* psychologist.

Poor Big John Soutar was the worst affected. He had the 4pm to midnight, which meant no evenings ashore - unless he could swap with one of the others. Inglis kept well out of his way until he was ready to go ashore with Harry, who had volunteered to show him the 'sights' of Copenhagen.

Inglis and Harry headed quietly for the gangplank - and ran smack into Big John hiding in ambush. Before he could open his mouth, Inglis said
"No, please John, not tonight, maybe tomorrow."
"Okay - done!" said Big John. "You've got my watch tomorrow and I've got yours. Thanks Inglis, I'll let the Mate know."

He turned and strode off with a huge grin on his face. *Me and my big mouth*, thought Inglis. He had volunteered to stay on board tomorrow evening while Big John went ashore - and John didn't even have to ask. Harry looked askance at Inglis.
"Bit quick on the draw weren't you? Are you sick or something? What happened to that much vaunted bloody brain of yours?"

"Aw, shut up Harry," Inglis answered. "Can I help it if a higher education made me dumb? Anyway, I owe Big John one."

Still, he couldn't help laughing at himself for being suckered, as they strode off along the dock. When John had said "Done!" he wasn't kidding; Inglis had been - like a dinner!

Harry had the evening's entertainment mapped out ahead, and was busy filling Inglis in on the gory details. What was he letting himself in for this time? First port of call was a bar near the docks - naturally. Fortified by a couple of beers they took a bus into the city, where Harry knew a cinema which showed movies that 'will really blow your mind.'

The weather couldn't make up its mind what to do, so in the meantime a few stray snowflakes drifted down in the almost still air. They had another beer in a bar near the cinema, where the show was due to start at 8.30. Harry said it would 'open your eyes', but Inglis wasn't so sure, and started feeling uncomfortable about it. By show time the beer had helped allay his reservations, and his natural curiosity would probably have got the better of him in any case. There was a certain fascination about the seamier side of life after all.

Harry bought the tickets at the booth, which didn't seem too busy. Three hefty doormen stood around the foyer scrutinizing the small flow of patrons, who were nearly all men. On the wall were some lurid pictures, depicting couples copulating in living technicolor, and in various positions - some of them extremely athletic-looking.

The lights were dim when they entered the cinema, which was quite small, even intimate. It contained less than a quarter of its capacity of customers as they were shown to their seats. The usherette wore a short white skirt and black stockings, topped by a red blouse, buttoned down the front. She didn't appear to be wearing a bra, and the place seemed to employ a great deal more usherettes than were required. All similarly dressed, except that some wore black skirts instead of white. They were all shapely and attractive to a greater or lesser extent.

Harry insisted on sitting at the rear, where the seats were most unlike the ones in the cinemas in Scotland. In fact they looked more like double divans than cinema seats, with solid padded arms between.

Each row of seats was noticeably higher than the one in front, with greater spacing between rows than Inglis was used to. There was no balcony, the rear seats being almost as high as a normal balcony would have been. The gap between the rear rows of seats was wide enough to walk comfortably along while the seats were in the down position - they didn't look like they folded up anyway. The cinema was warm, and the usherette took their coats in return for a cloakroom ticket. Harry sat down on one divan and waved Inglis into the adjacent one. It was soft and comfortable, so if the movie was a bore he could go to sleep on it. He had noticed that the admission price was very steep, but Harry had insisted on paying.

"Any extras you pay for yourself though," he added.

Inglis looked around before the lights went out. Above the wide padded arms of the divans were curtains, cinched in by tapes tied to rings set in the rear wall. The curtains hung from a rail six feet above the floor. This rail was continuous and passed in front of the divan, before curving in to the wall at each end. Obviously the curtains could be drawn to provide some privacy for the occupants of each divan. Inglis conjured up some reasons for the curtains to be drawn, and began fidgeting uneasily.

The screen lit up and the lights went out. After ten minutes of advertising - mostly sex books, movies and 'aids', plus a few sex clubs - the main feature got underway. As far as plot line was concerned, there wasn't a great deal. An over sexed school teacher, with a larger than average (Inglis hoped!) penis was employed to teach biology at a girls' school; and started off well by seducing the games mistress on the floor of the locker room. This was graphically depicted on the wide screen, with the actors going to great pains not to block the camera's view of the proceedings.

At one stage a closeup filled the whole screen with a gigantic twenty feet long penis pistoning in and out of an equally large vulva - which looked more like a fleshy cavern surrounded by bushes. Why the camera didn't become entangled in the action Inglis couldn't fathom. It seemed to be suspended from one of the hairy bushes.

A few schoolgirls spied on the seduction scene, and each of them decided to stage a similar scene of her own over the next few days. For his first week at the school, the new biology teacher was kept very busy; in the locker room, the domestic science room, and of course his own biology room.

It was quite remarkable how well developed most of the schoolgirls were - Inglis couldn't remember that many voluptuous bodies at his school. One girl in particular must have been in her fourth year in the fourth form. She had paid very careful attention to her biology lessons, which didn't stop her from being kept behind after class. The teacher had no need to seduce this one. Before he could say Jack Robinson - or the Danish equivalent - she lay on the table, wearing only stockings and suspender belt. Legs wide apart in open invitation while airing her pussy.

Once he was sufficiently aroused and ready to couple, she pushed the teacher away and sat down on the floor. Then she took his rigid member in her mouth and began to suck; drawing it in farther and farther, until Inglis was sure she must choke. She played with his balls with her right hand, while the left one massaged her own pussy.

The action speeded up until the teacher reached his climax, pulsating penis still in her mouth. White goo dribbled from her lips around the swollen shaft, running down her chin onto her chest, where she rubbed it over her breasts, massaging them with both hands. Then she swallowed as he withdrew. Inglis thought yuck! How the hell can she do that?

The lights went up and it was intermission time. Inglis looked for Harry and couldn't find him. The curtains were drawn round his divan, and now Inglis could hear grunting and panting from within. He sat back, feeling embarrassed and lonely, and not sure where to look.

The usherette who had shown them to their seats came and asked if Inglis would like anything, looking at Harry's drawn curtains with a smile. He said yes please - a Coca Cola and a bag of sweets! She took some money and returned a few minutes later with his order and change, which he told her to keep - last of the big spenders! She sat down beside him and started talking.

"You like if I sit down for intermission okay?"

Inglis said okay and offered her one of the sweets - they were licorice allsorts. She was attractive in a healthy sort of way. Straw colored hair above dark blue eyes, a short nose and freckles. She laughed as she talked, offered her name - Ulven - and asked what ship Inglis was from.

The lights went down, and the stage was lit - at first dimly, then more brightly as a tango tune came over the speakers. A man appeared from the right side of the stage, dressed in a leopard skin jerkin and loincloth. From the left came a woman similarly clad, advancing towards the man, until they met and began to dance. The front lights cut and the couple were backlit as they danced gracefully to the music. The woman spun away from the man, to the limit of his extended arm, clasping his hand to hers as she leaned outwards and removed her jerkin with the other hand. Holding the garment at arm's length, she then tossed it to the side of the stage; then rolled in along their joined arms until they were close again. Undoing his jerkin she tossed it over beside her own, before pressing her body to his, and slowly sliding down to a sitting position.

The tango continued as the man took both her hands, swung one leg over her head, and pulled her through between his legs, raising her back to her feet. They continued to dance, undoing each other's loincloths as they went, and finishing naked, still backlit and in silhouette. The man was visibly aroused, but for minutes they danced on as if fully clothed.

Then the footlights began to brighten, and their flesh tones could be made out. The music changed to a ballet, and the woman rose on her points, gliding around the man - who reached for her, missed, reached again and captured her. He lifted her to his shoulders and spun. She clasped her knees around his neck and fell backwards and outwards as they spun slowly round.

Her crotch was at his face. Placing his hands under her buttocks, he lifted and pulled, his tongue extended towards her vulva. Still they spun as his tongue reached its mark and began probing in time to the music. Now she had her hands on his shoulders, and was pulling herself onto his tongue, then retreating before pulling again. For a few more minutes they continued this way. Then he stopped spinning and lowered her until her hands touched the floor. Quickly she reversed her position, facing inwards instead of out. The music changed to a quickstep and the man lifted the tall slim woman until his face was buried between her thighs, which were bent forward over his shoulders. As the man danced, the woman took his burgeoning penis in her mouth, drawing it in and out to the beat of the music, as his tongue massaged her pussy to the same beat.

Twice round the stage they went, sucking and probing. Inglis was fascinated in spite of himself, and couldn't drag his eyes away from this musical sex fantasy. He found it hard to believe this was all happening on a stage in front of him. Once more the music changed to ballet. The woman returned to her feet, and together they flowed gracefully round the stage, twining and separating, gliding and twirling.

The woman made her escape, flitting round the stage pursued by the man. Each time he caught her she slipped back out of his grasp. Until finally, inevitably, he caught her from behind, and this time she couldn't escape. Arms outstretched to the sides, fingers interwoven, he forced her to her knees, lowering himself behind her. She leaned forward, arching her back, breasts straining outward and upward; as his throbbing member thrust forward unerringly, to become submerged in her body.

She writhed from side to side in time to the music, but he would not be denied. The tempo of the music had slowed as the two dancers began to sway back and forth, first together, then apart, the dark rod between them appearing and disappearing, gliding in and out of her body.

Gradually the tempo increased, approaching a climax. Kettledrums banged out and cymbals clashed. The woman strained rearward, back arched and arms outstretched, as the man made one last desperate lunge forward, releasing her hands. She dropped them to the floor as the man bowed forward over her, hugging her breasts tightly with his hands as she bowed her head also.
The lights went out and the curtains closed across the stage.

Inglis could hardly believe what he had seen, despite the fact that

the Danes were renowned for their 'free' sexual thinking. The show had disturbed him, and appealed to him more than he cared to admit to himself. Much more than the movie with its wall-to-wall sex in various combinations. Inglis was glad of the tunic jacket masking the bulge in his pants, and more than a little aware of Ulven still sitting beside him. She had her blouse partly unbuttoned, and was in the process of sticking two licorice allsorts in the gap. Aware of his stare, she looked up and grinned, thrusting her chest forward before saying
"You want sweet, you eat, no?"

Inglis looked, was tempted, and decided to resist for once - she looked very young, and shouldn't be working here, he thought.
"No thank you Ulven. No offense, you're a very pretty girl, and I like you, but I really have to go."

Inglis leaned over and took the sweets from her cleavage, putting one in his mouth, and one in hers. Then he gently buttoned her blouse, and put the first two fingers of his right hand to his lips, then to hers.
"Maybe next time, when I'm in the mood," he told her, knowing full well there would be no next time. "Meanwhile, could you please tell my friend Harry for me that I'll be in the bar along the street when he's finished?"

He had no stomach for the second part of the movie programme. She pouted for a moment, then relaxed and smiled at him.
"You are nice man. I tell your friend message."
"Thanks," he said. "This is for you, and keep the sweets."
He handed her five crowns, which brought a look of pleasant surprise to her face. She fetched his coat and hat.
"Goodbye" she said. "I see you later."

Inglis doubted it somehow, but nodded agreement anyway as he turned to leave. The bar was only a short walk down the street. The weather had made up its mind at last, and fat snowflakes drifted down all round, staying underfoot without melting. The fresh snow squeaked beneath his shoes as he headed for the bar. Neon lights glowed and flashed, tinting the falling snowflakes with their colors. Vehicles drove slowly and carefully along the street, sliding now and then on the fresh fall.

Inglis stopped outside the bar for a while to soak in the sights and sounds of this winter fairyland, softened and rounded by the magic of the snow. This was worth at least as much as any sex movie, and didn't cost a penny.

He must have stood there for a long time, just letting the sights and the muffled sounds soak into his brain. A hand pulled lightly at his elbow. He looked round to see a young woman standing beside him, wrapped in furs. It was Ulven. She smiled up at him from under her hood.

"I tell your friend message. But I say maybe you no go back tonight. You buy for me one drink and we talk?"

"Yes, why not. Let's go inside where it's warm."

She held his arm as they entered the bar, steering him to a small booth in the left corner of the room. There were about thirty people in the bar, mostly couples, and groups of three or four men. Dark wood paneling, stained glass windows, and coaching lamps made the place cozy and cheerful. The booth was U shaped, with a comfortable padded bench surrounding a small table. They sat together on the inside end of the booth, and Inglis ordered a couple of drinks.

Ulven told him she had asked her boss if she could go home, because there were not many customers at the cinema. He had agreed, provided she accepted a two hour cut in her pay.

"You can walk with me home after?" she asked him. "I have nice flat not far, and I cook for you one omelette, okay?"

Inglis thought for a moment. He was free until 4pm tomorrow, with nothing much else to do in the meantime. What the hell, why not? Nothing ventured nothing gained, and he would be a fool to say no to an offer like this.

"Okay," he said, "I'd like that. I didn't realize it until now, but I'm really quite hungry. Shall I buy a bottle of wine to go with the omelette?"

She clapped her hands like a little girl - she still didn't look old enough to be working in that cinema - and a delighted grin lit up her freckled face.

"Oh, yes please," she said. "I make extra special omelette. Put good Danish bacon in. We go now?"

Inglis ordered two bottles of moselle, which arrived as they finished their drinks. Ulven's flat was only two streets away, so they walked arm-in-arm through the fairyland of snow. It was a centrally heated block, and her apartment was cozy and warm when they arrived.

She seemed suddenly nervous and shy as she made her preparations for the meal; flitting here and there with fleeting glances in his direction. Inglis found the crockery and set the table, opening one of the bottles of wine, and placing a glass at her elbow in the small kitchen. There was a dummy fireplace in the lounge/dining room, complete with mantelshelf containing two candlesticks. The candles in them were real, so he placed them on the table and lit them. He still didn't smoke, but always carried a box of matches.

Ulven made a giant bacon omelette that she divided in two, placing the larger part on his plate. He switched off the light and they sat down to eat and drink in the candle-light.

In the soft light of the candles her eyes looked larger and even darker, almost indigo. Her sudden smiles were infectious as they chatted between mouthfuls of omelette, washed down by the pleasant moselle. Ulven was six months older than Inglis, but he kept thinking of her as younger, with her freckles and her little-girl freshness. He asked her what on earth she was doing working in such a place - how many times must that question have been asked around the world? She explained that she really was an usherette, and was not supposed to 'entertain'. The entertaining girls wore black miniskirts, whereas the usherettes wore white ones. Inglis had noticed the difference, but hadn't realized the significance.

Ulven had fetched one of the black-skirted girls for Harry while his attention was elsewhere. The rule was that only those girls were permitted to close the curtains round the divans. The white-skirted girls had to stay in sight at all times, and were allowed to 'tease' a little, but not indulge. The world was a much more complicated place than Inglis had thought only a couple of months ago!

"The pay very good, and I like be independent," added Ulven.

She asked if he would like a hot bath after the meal, which sounded really good to Inglis. They had baths and showers on the ship of course, but the bathroom was freezing cold most of the time; which rather spoiled things, especially as the walls and floor were of steel.

They chatted away while the bath was running. Inglis opened the second bottle, which was half gone by the time the bath was ready. Ulven explained that she shared the flat with a girlfriend who was away for a week. She felt scared sometimes being in the flat alone at night. Could Inglis possibly stay the night? No strings, no conditions. He could sleep in her friend's room if he liked.

Inglis told her he had no duty until four o'clock next afternoon. She too was free until six, and she promised to show him some of the real sights of Copenhagen in the morning. So that settled his plans for tomorrow. By this time Inglis was luxuriating in the bath, bigger than most, and he was able to stretch out full length in it. Ulven passed a warm bathrobe through the doorway. It was very gay and fluffy, and too short, but who was going to notice? From behind the half open door she asked hesitantly.
"Please, you like I wash your behind?"

Inglis burst out laughing, and almost choked. Her voice came again, sounding anxious and puzzled this time.   "Please.....I say wrong? Why you laugh?"
Inglis tried to explain, but couldn't find the words between chuckles.
"Come in and I show you why I laugh."

She peered timidly round the door prior to venturing across to the bath. He made sure his back was towards her, so neither of them would be embarrassed too much. He put his hand over his shoulder and patted below the neck, saying "This is back." Then he put his hand under the water to his buttocks, "This is behind."

Inglis turned his head in time to see her covering her blushing face with her hands. Then she began to laugh, opening her hands slightly to peep out at him. She was dressed in a bathrobe similar to the one she had fetched for him. No competition - she looked much better in it than he ever would.

Inglis laughed again and handed her the soap. The water in the bath was by now soapy and opaque, so his crotch was well screened. She lathered his back, then rinsed it, using a large enamel mug to dip in the bath water and pour over him. He felt her hair on the nape of his neck as she lightly kissed his back, bringing goose bumps to his skin.

"That was nice Ulven. You want me to wash your behind?"

She covered her face and laughed again.

"Oh no, cannot. Too shy with you."

Inglis made an offer he hoped she wouldn't refuse.

"Why don't you get in the bath? I'll cover my eyes, and you can switch off the light and leave the door open if you like."

She hesitated for only a moment then, without another word, she switched off the light. Inglis covered his eyes with his hands as she removed the bathrobe and stepped into the bath. As she did so he couldn't resist having a peek - she was beautiful! So much more so without her clothes than with them. Already he had begun to discover that with most women it was the other way round.

The light from the kitchen streamed through the half open door, its reflections bathing her body in softer indirect light; accentuating the delicate curves of her figure. As she stood with one foot on the floor and the other in the bath, he just had to speak.

"You are really beautiful Ulven. Much more than I thought you were."

With a squeal she shot down into the bath, splashing water all over the floor - and Inglis - in her haste.

"You promise you hide your eyes," she hissed vehemently.

"Yes, but I didn't say for how long," quipped Inglis, wiping his eyes with the towel. When he opened them again she was kneeling in the bath facing him, hands covering her breasts, a small scowl on her face. Inglis rubbed his fingers under her chin.

"Koochee, koochee, pussycat angry - smile please."

He placed his hands as if taking a photograph. The tension evaporated. She laughed and turned her back, passing the soap.

"Now you please to wash my BACK!" She laughed again.

Inglis' legs were bent around her waist as she presented her back for washing. He worked up a good lather with the soap, stroking and rubbing her smooth skin, then splashing with water from the enamel mug. She leaned back slightly, and he put his hands under her arms and around her breasts, lathering them before dropping the soap in the water.

They were firm and rounded, not heavy, but substantial enough. His hands glided over them, lubricated by the soap, and they felt deliciously smooth and slippery. He could feel her nipples swelling to his touch as she leaned on his chest, no longer objecting. At the same time his penis was swelling, and beginning to search for more room, trapped as it was between their bodies. He squirmed his buttocks, trying to find a way out - or in - for it. Ulven could feel the pole at her buttocks, and said.

"No, please, we dry and go my room, okay?"

Inglis nibbled the lobe of her ear before saying okay, and splashing water on her breasts. Then he rose from the bath behind her, embarrassed by the flagpole projecting in front of him. Briefly he wondered how it would look with a small Union Jack hanging from it, before grabbing a towel for camouflage. He dried quickly and wrapped the bathrobe round himself. Then he took the other large bath towel and held it up for Ulven as she stepped from the bath. This time she didn't hide her breasts, but kept one hand screening the area between her thighs until the towel was round her.

Seeing that she was still a little bashful, Inglis went through to the kitchen and poured the last of the wine into the glasses. When she came through in her bathrobe he placed one glass in her hand and said "Skol."

Half the contents of his glass went down in one gulp, while Ulven just sipped at hers, huge dark eyes staring at him from above the wine.

"Come, you must drink," he said, "or I'll be offended."

She took a larger sip, then another, followed by a third, leaving the glass less than half full. Inglis placed his glass on the kitchen bench, took hers to place beside it, then gently put his arms round her, pulling her close. A thrill went through his body as he realized she had put no clothes back on under the robe. She went up on tiptoe as he bent to kiss her, long and full, warmth on warmth, tongues swimming one around the other.

He lifted her in his arms and carried her through to the bedroom she had pointed out earlier. She was even lighter than he expected, and he felt he could carry her all night without tiring. Inglis sat her on the bottom of the single bed while he pulled the covers down, and returned to kiss again. They held each other for a long time before Inglis slowly untied the sash of her robe and toppled onto the bed, still holding her close. He wasn't sure what to do next - really! - letting his right hand gradually work round to her left breast.

Suddenly she drew back, and Inglis thought she had changed her mind. But instead, she quickly shrugged off the bathrobe and dived under the bed sheet, turning to hold her arms out to him. He joined her under the sheet, after pulling off his own robe and dropping it over the edge of the bed. Then they lay face to face, holding tight, touching from their mouths to their feet.

She was trembling, and he realized he was too, as he felt her breasts warm against his chest. He ran his hand slowly down her back, and shivered. So warm and soft and silky, her back delighted his hand, which encountered the smoothly rounded hillocks of her buttocks. Oh wow - backs are sexy, bums are sexy, where was there a part that wasn't sexy? Life was beautiful to hold such secrets, waiting to be discovered anew by every generation.

Inglis brought his hand back up to touch her face, her mouth, her ears and neck, her beautiful shoulders; and those priceless golden freckled breasts, with their almost invisible soft down of tiny hairs. Her breasts were triple crowns, rising one upon the other. First the main swelling, golden and freckled on top, creamy white below. Then the smallish pink aureoles, standing proud from the main body, hillocks in their own right, atop the symmetry of the rounded hills. The smallest crowns of all, her nipples, swelling upward and outward, promising nourishment, not only to a generation as yet unborn, but to lovers as yet unknown - and to Inglis. Buds, ready and willing to burst into full flower at the touch of his fingers, as he ran his knuckles lightly across them.

Inglis stared, rapt in wonder at the magic beneath his fingers. And he shivered with delight, before leaning forward again to kiss her eyes,

97

then her nose, and finally once more, her warm sweet mouth.

Inglis wondered at himself, and the feelings coursing through his body. His desire was not only to touch her, but to *taste* her as well. Was he peculiar? The whole world was opening up to him; a new world fresh to his experience after more than seventeen years in the old one.

Tentatively Inglis worked his mouth down to one of her breasts, kissing the freckles, and licking her skin, so soft and smooth, yet somehow vaguely furry. His tongue licked the pink nipple, which sprang out at him, expanding as he took the swollen aureole in his mouth, sucking gently. Ulven was pressing on his back with the palms of her hands, then running her fingers up and down his spine, before gently massaging his neck.

"Is nice English," she murmured.
Inglis removed his mouth from her breast.
"Inglis, not English, ING-GULZ."

They kissed again, while he ran his hand down between her thighs, and rubbed gently. She put her hand on his, increasing the pressure as her thighs parted. His heart was thumping in his chest, and his organ was rigid. Was now the time? He felt dampness on his fingers - wasn't that supposed to be a good sign?

She pulled him onto her, and he nestled between her thighs, his penis probing for entry to her pussy. Where was it? He put his hand down between their crotches and groped around. Where the hell was the hole? Oh Jesus, he couldn't find it! He tried again, but it wasn't there, and he panicked. In his panic and frustration, his penis was dying, fading away.

Christ, this couldn't be happening. What had gone wrong? It was supposed to be easy, so how come he couldn't *find* it?
Inglis rolled off her, and lay back on the bed, almost crying with frustration. Then he started to think the whole thing through. And suddenly it was pathetically funny, like some way-out farce. Inglis started to laugh, and Ulven spoke urgently.
"What is wrong - why you laugh?"

98

He stopped laughing long enough to blurt out.

"I missed, I bloody missed - couldn't find the hole!"

Then the laughter came again, and this time he couldn't stop. Ulven beat his chest with her fists, and cried out.

"You.....you.....not funny! Why you do this?"

She picked up her pillow and slammed it in his face. Inglis started to cough with the laughter, and the pillow wasn't hard enough for her purpose. She leaned over for one of her slippers, and began beating his chest with that instead. It stung - she was getting serious. She shouted as tears ran down her face.   "You are bad.....get out........GET OUT!"

Inglis rolled out of bed, with arms round his ears as protection from her slipper. Where the hell were his clothes? He remembered, and made a run for the bathroom; tail well and truly between his legs, and not much left of it either. Something hit the wall near his head - an Ulven missile! Grabbing his underpants, Inglis hopped around getting them on. Ulven appeared at the door in her bathrobe. He looked around for an escape route, but there wasn't one.

"You sleep other room, please," she said quietly with tears in her eyes. Inglis started to make his excuses, but she was gone. Her bedroom door slammed shut with a bang, and he heard the bolt clicking home. He slunk through to the other bedroom with his clothes in his hand.

After slipping into bed, Inglis lay awake for hours, thinking what an ass he'd made of himself. But what else could he have done? She might at least have helped him find it! If anybody found out about this he'd be a laughing stock, so he sure as hell wasn't about to tell. Would Ulven tell anyone? Christ, he hoped not. He would have to be nice and apologetic to her in the morning. Maybe she would let him try again?

Inglis dozed off to sleep, and had a nasty dream about driving a car into the face of a cliff instead of through the tunnel.

CHAPTER 12

In the morning they moved cautiously round each other, like boxers sizing up their opponents. Finally they both began to talk at the same time; then went silent again, each waiting for the other. Inglis broke the silence first.

"I'm sorry about last night Ulven. I wasn't laughing at you. I was laughing at myself. Believe it or not, I never went to bed with a girl before, and I didn't know what to do. I feel so stupid and hopeless now. I'm sorry."

"Is okay now Inglis. I not do before either, not in the bed. We make breakfast now?"

She kissed him lightly on the cheek, and he washed the dishes from last night. Ulven cooked breakfast while Inglis reset the table and made a pot of tea. She wasn't going to let him back in her bed this morning, he could see that. So he'd better just make the best of things one way or another. It was just that he felt so damned stupid and incompetent; he could probably crawl under the carpet without leaving a bulge.

Breakfast was eaten in almost total silence, while Inglis wondered if he should volunteer to get lost. But he didn't want to let go while there was any chance of redeeming himself in her eyes - and his own. He was nothing if not an optimist.

They cleared away the dishes and washed up together, while the tension relaxed a shade. Then it was time to bathe and dress before venturing forth to view the sights of Copenhagen. Inglis didn't really want to any more, but she insisted, and he wasn't about to upset her again.

They left her flat to begin their sightseeing tour on foot. Ulven lived only ten minutes walk from the Radhuspladsen, or Town Hall Square. Here they climbed the steps inside the town hall tower, to the viewing platform. From there they could see for miles across the city. The snow had stopped some time during the night, and the air was clear and sparkling, the sun reflecting everywhere from the snow covered roofs, spires, towers and domes of Copenhagen.

The tension between them soon evaporated, and they began to laugh again, and enjoy each other's company. They walked hand-in-hand along Vesterbrogade to the Tivoli Gardens, where they rode on a couple of amusement rides which were open for business, before having coffee in one of the restaurants within the gardens. They walked across the frozen interlocked pools, among the empty flower beds. Inglis thought he would like to see them in the summer, when they would be a riot of color from the thousands of flowers and shrubs.

Soon they walked back the way they had come, and across the square to Stroget, the narrow winding street which twists and turns through the heart of the old city. In a small shop Inglis bought a souvenir pennant for himself, and a matching brooch and earrings for Ulven, featuring the Little Mermaid. He told her that no matter what happened now, he would always remember her as his Little Mermaid of Copenhagen; and they had their photographs taken together at a booth.

The photos would be ready in two hours, so they wandered round some more streets, finishing up in Kongens Nytorf Square, looking at the Charlottenborg Palace. By two o'clock they were back to pick up the pictures, one each. Inglis reminded Ulven that he had to be on board ship by 4 o'clock, and suddenly there wasn't enough time left in the world. Big John had told him they might leave Copenhagen in the early hours of the morning, depending on the report of the divers inspecting the ship's hull for damage.

They hurried back to the flat to be alone. Suddenly Ulven was no longer worried about being shy, though she did ask him to wait outside the bedroom until she called. When he entered the room at her summons, she lay naked on the bed - with ornaments. She still had the licorice allsorts he'd given her at the movie theater. Now five of them adorned her body. One at the base of her throat, one on each nipple, another in her navel, and the last one on the fuzzy mound between her thighs; his course was laid out for him. She looked at him with a trace of the old shyness.

"You not think I silly and naughty?"

"No, Ulven," Inglis replied, removing his clothes awkwardly. "I think right now you're the cleverest and most gorgeous girl in the world - the whole universe even."

After the slow and delightful task of tracking down all the sweets, they made urgent and desperate love; and this time she made sure he didn't miss! But with all the tension, and the nagging doubts, he blew it again. No sooner was he home than he ejaculated; and felt he had cheated them both.

Ulven was sympathetic and understanding, but she sure as hell couldn't have been satisfied. Inglis wanted to try again, but there just wasn't time. What a bloody mess he'd made of things; it was a wonder she didn't just throw him out. But she seemed to genuinely understand, and kissed him long and hard - at least he could still do that right!

It was time to take a taxi to the docks. She insisted on coming with him, and as things turned out they reached the ship with time to spare. The taxi waited for her as they kissed at the bottom of the gangplank, to the accompaniment of wolf whistles from the deck. Inglis gave Ulven the telephone number that would put her through to the deck office, so he could let her know when they would be sailing. Then he turned and walked up the gangplank, his face flushed with more than the weather. Big John met him on deck.

"This is getting to be a habit laddie. What have you got that I don't?"
"Youth and beauty, John," Inglis retorted. "Youth and beauty, and a hell of a lot of luck, by the look of things."
Little did Big John know the real facts, thank God. He punched Inglis lightly on the arm - nearly knocking him over sideways.
"See you in the deck office in twenty minutes, Casanova."

Inglis changed in his cabin and was back on deck in fifteen minutes. A quick glance at the loading chart and log told him all he needed to know, and he told John he could knock off.
"Listen to you!" said Big John. "You're getting pretty sure of yourself Inglis. A long way from the shy cadet who walked up that gangplank two months ago. You'll be wanting to be Skipper next year at this rate!"

"Go on, get lost, you big mullock heap," Inglis answered with a grin. But he was right in a way. Inglis was much more confident on board now. He'd worked hard at learning all he could about the ship, and felt he really knew her. Nautical terms no longer baffled him, to be met with panic. The layout of pipes and valves was imprinted on his memory in three dimensions, and he knew every nook and cranny, every secret place on board.

When they were loading, he knew instinctively the point at which the ship was nearing maximum allowable list, without having to run and consult the inclinometer all the time. While on cargo watch he knew exactly the state and contents of every tank at any given time, and the soundings were almost routine.

His recent experiences with the opposite sex had probably helped his outlook too, in spite of the setbacks and disappointments - or maybe even because of them. Before leaving home he'd had only a couple of hole-in-the-wall encounters with the girls next door - when he didn't even know what he was supposed to do, and they didn't know much more either. Plus a romance with a girl at school a year and a half younger than him - both of them scared to go past kissing.

The bragging of other boys had made him feel left out, and he'd thought maybe girls had a special reason for not liking him. So, rather than be rebuffed, he'd spent most of his time getting into mischief, looking for adventure, and chasing planes and trains.

While other boys were chasing girls, Inglis was helping Andy Bridges and Willie Moffat put the French master's Baby Austin car on the roof of the old air raid shelter; stringing the caretaker's bike between the Twin Towers of the ruined cathedral. Hiding in the ramparts of the old city wall, complete with white sheet and glowing turnip lantern, to scare the hell out of the lovers as they walked in the dim gaslight between the wall and the cliff tops. And more than once the boyfriend ran off faster than the girlfriend!

Sometimes they would soak scraps of newspaper in sodium chlorate solution, stuff it in an old bicycle pump, and see how big a hole they could blow in the railway bridge. Inglis sprained his ankle jumping from the viaduct with a home made parachute that worked, more or less - thank God. Or standing in the middle of the road with an air rifle; with the task of shooting out both headlights of an approaching lorry, between the time it passed the second lamp post and the time it ran over you - including reloading. And many other such boyhood pursuits. They didn't call themselves the Three Musketeers for nothing. It was all a long way behind him now.

Ulven rang at 10 o'clock, and Inglis had to tell her they were sailing at 2am. The divers had found no damage worth worrying about, and nothing which couldn't wait until the ship's next inspection. They talked until it was time for his next round of the deck. Inglis would not be allowed to leave the ship between coming off watch and sailing, and she finished work at 1 o'clock, so it was goodbye until next time. He checked his pocket watch - a gift from his father with his name engraved on it - and it was time to sound the tanks again.

For the next two hours he was busy, checking that all of the tanks already pumped out were as empty as possible. Then he had to tell the bosun on which tanks he could start opening the main covers and installing windsails for ventilation. The Donkeyman helped Inglis with the sea valves, and they began flooding some of the empty tanks with seawater, while still pumping the last of the cargo ashore.

The Skipper wanted all three number one tanks cleaned on the way to Goteborg, where they should arrive shortly after noon the next day. Ballast was to be carried in numbers two, five and eight tanks, with just enough to give reasonable stability, and keep the screw more or less submerged. The more ballast they took on, the more they had to pump out again when they arrived in Goteborg ten hours later. They were to load a full cargo of diesel (gas oil) in Goteborg for delivery to Malmo and Stockholm.

When Inglis came off watch at midnight there was no sense trying to get any sleep, as he would have to be back on deck by 1.30 preparing to leave port. So he had a shower, and persuaded the Second Steward to rustle him up some bacon and eggs in the dining saloon. The weather was changing, with a gusty wind plucking at the windsails over the tank tops when he went back on deck at 1.30am. He looked at the sky and could still see groups of stars, but with clouds scudding across them at speed. They were in for some dirty stuff before long.

Inglis asked the Mate if he knew the weather forecast, and he said there was a force ten gale in the North Sea, the edge of which was heading their way. They laid out the tow-rope ready for the tug, took in the springing lines, and transferred the head rope to the winch drum. The Mate told Inglis he was in charge of the head rope while he looked after the tug; which took the tow-rope at the first attempt, in a nice display of seamanship and co-ordination.

The pilot was taking her out stern-first, swinging the ship on Inglis' head rope, while the forward tug bided her time. It looked as if the Mate was throwing Inglis in at the deep end to see how he would handle it. He watched the rope stretch tight as he signaled to Paddy on the winch drum. He had a hundred feet of rope laid out on deck, ready to feed via the winch to the bollards on the dockside, where two dockies stood by, ready to release the bight. As Inglis looked down a woman appeared behind them, waving a handkerchief. He looked closely at her, and his heart gave a thump; it was Ulven. Hell, he couldn't have been that much of a failure after all. Or maybe, like him, she didn't know the difference. Taking off his cap, he waved it at her and called out.
"Bye Ulven. See you soon, I hope."

Inglis didn't know if she had heard above the rising wind, and he had to put his cap back on to signal Paddy to ease the rope out a bit more. He looked quickly around for a rag, and couldn't find one. The sailor beside him had a lump of cotton waste sticking from his pocket. Patting him on the back, Inglis grabbed the waste, wrapped it round his pocket watch, and tied his hanky round the small bundle. He waved his hat to attract Ulven's attention, then leaned back before throwing the bundle as hard as he could, across the widening gap between ship and dock.

For a heart-stopping moment he thought he had left it too late, and it would fall short into the water. But one of the dockies leaned out and caught it with one hand, and passed it to Ulven, giving Inglis a wave and a grin. There was a cheer from the sailors on the forecastle, and he signaled Paddy to ease out a little more rope. Right in the middle of a short lull in the wind, a woman's voice sounded clearly.

"Come back soon Inglis!"
There was another ironic cheer from the deck, and he tried hard not

to look at anyone - especially the Mate - as he signaled once again for more rope. Then the Skipper's voice came over the bullhorn. "Let go forrard!"

Paddy quickly ran the winch drum forward, releasing enough rope for the dockies to heave the other end off the bollard and down into the water at Inglis' signal. Paddy reversed the winch, and wound in as quickly as possible. Inglis ran across to help the two seamen on the tailrope, and they laid it out on deck, heaving and running. Meanwhile the Mate was busy with the other two seamen attending to the tug, which had only a few minutes' work to do before they would have to winch that rope in as well.

The ship's carpenter was in the rope store, and Paddy joined him while the other two seamen fed the wet rope down to them for hanging in the relative warmth down there. If wet ropes were left on deck in this weather they would freeze in no time.

Inglis looked shorewards from his position near the winch, and could still make out the small figure of Ulven waving her handkerchief. He waved again with his cap at arms length, describing a large arc above his head. Moments later she was lost to view as the first snow squall descended on them.

As soon as the ropes were stowed Inglis went to the cabin, washed and tumbled into bed for a few hours sleep. He was due to report to the Mate on the bridge at eight in the morning, so he booked a call with the Second Mate for seven. That left him four hours in which to get some sleep.

The wind was still rising, and the ship began to rock and roll in the rough seas overlying the rising swell. It was more than a week since Inglis had finally conquered his seasickness; now it threatened to return. Putting on denims and duffelcoat over his pajamas, he went out on the boat deck, where he stood for ten minutes, letting the wind whip at his face. The queasiness was soon gone, and fifteen minutes later he was fast asleep.

CHAPTER 13

In the morning Inglis was awakened by one of the seamen shaking his shoulder.

"Seven o'clock mister McAndrew. Second Mate said to call you. I thought you were never going to wake up."

"Thank you," Inglis said groggily, swinging his feet over the edge of the bunk so he wouldn't go back to sleep. The seaman left, just as Inglis realized he'd picked a bad moment to swing his legs - too late! His body followed his feet from the bunk, catapulted across the cabin as the ship rolled heavily to starboard. He smacked into the bulkhead at a fair rate of knots, taking most of the impact on his hands at the last moment. He looked out of the porthole - since he was already there - to see white-capped waves racing past in the darkness of predawn. He staggered around in the process of dressing, losing his balance half a dozen times before he had all of his clothes on.

Making his way below for breakfast was no easy task either, and he remembered the old adage 'one hand for the ship and one for yourself.' In this case Inglis was using both hands for himself. The Kattegat was living up to its nasty reputation.

Breakfast was cold cuts of meat, cheese and salad, with coffee. The galley was in a bit of a shambles, and the pantry boy had lost the tray of eggs over the catwalk rail - the galley being on the poop. The Chief Steward promptly ordered no more hot food from the galley to the Officers' Dining Saloon, except what could be carried in billycans and buckets. That meant soup and/or stew for lunch, unless the weather suddenly died down. Sounded pretty good to Inglis anyway, since he always liked soups and stews in cold weather.

At five to eight he was in the wheelhouse being briefed by the Mate. He wanted Inglis to keep an eye on the radar, while at the same time watching how Paddy handled the ship with the steering wheel. From ten till twelve he was to take over steering under the tutelage of Elvis, who was the best helmsman on board.

Inglis had already done a few turns on the wheel, but only when the sea was not too rough. Now he was to learn how to handle her in heavy weather and a high wind. The Clearview screens were spinning in the forward wheelhouse windows, one for the helmsman, the other for the officer of the watch.

These comprised a large circle of glass set into the window. At the centre of the circle was an electric motor which spun the glass, via its drive shaft, at high speed. As soon as water or snow hit the spinning glass, it was immediately thrown off by centrifugal force, thereby giving a clear view at all times - hence the name.

Outside, the sea was raging in the early light, with whitecaps all around whipped up by the wind - which was now registering 8 on the Beaufort Scale. This put it just into the category of a gale, with average speed about 44 miles per hour, and still rising. The cup anemometer on the monkey island had already registered a gust of 55 miles an hour, and the average speed would soon pass into Force 9 category if it continued to rise.

In the past hour two distress calls had been sent out by trawlers in the North Sea, where the gale had briefly reached Force 11. Fortunately it was not expected to go beyond 9 in the Kattegat, where they were now. Nevertheless it was the roughest sea Inglis had yet seen, and they had encountered a few rough ones. By now most of the coasters, trawlers and smaller craft had run for shelter, and the radar screen was host to the blips of only the big league members like themselves.

The main underlying swell was from the north-west, coming at them from about forty five degrees on the port bow. This was one of the worst kinds of sea for steering and stability, causing the ship to roll as well as plunge, and resulting in a nasty corkscrewing action. The steering was made more difficult by the fact that the wind was blowing from the port beam, as the centre of the storm moved southwards over in the North Sea.

This was having the effect of a giant hand constantly trying to push *Forth Venturer* sideways. She was riding much lower in the water than Inglis had expected, and shipping quite a few waves. The Mate explained that the Skipper had rousted out the donkeyman and duty hands to take on more ballast during the Second Mate's watch. He had

108

tried to strike a balance between the amount of side area she presented to the wind, and the amount of water shipped on deck. Apparently the ship had been heeling badly from the wind by 5.30, when the Second Mate had called the Skipper for instructions. It would now take an extra four hours to pump out the ballast when they arrived in Goteborg, about which Captain Evans was not at all happy.

Adding to his timetable problems was the fact that their effective speed through the water was down by a quarter on optimum. So they would be about seven hours behind schedule, and the company didn't like Captains who ran behind schedule. Coming on top of an engine failure and a running aground, all within a week, Captain Evans' cup was certainly running over. Inglis could see it would be wise to stay on the right side of him over the next few days - preferably so far on the right side as to be completely out of sight.

He watched Paddy at the wheel, between bouts of crystal ball gazing under the hood of the radar set. It was most unlike steering his father's Austin van, in which he had taught Inglis to drive. In a motor car you drive round the bends when you come to them. On a tanker you have to steer round imaginary bends before you come to them - which takes a certain amount of inspired anticipation.

Paddy's anticipation was not always sufficiently inspired - though he was a qualified helmsman - with the result that the bows were consistently swinging back and forth through an arc of up to twenty degrees. Fortunately the Decca Navigator was functioning impeccably - for the second time in a recent crisis - so the navigation did not present the problem it would have if they'd had to rely on dead reckoning.

The sky was 100% overcast, though the thin snow was coming in short squalls, driven almost horizontal by the wind. They had no problems with other shipping, those ships which did show up on radar keeping well clear of them. But due to the weather the Skipper had given up all thought of tank cleaning, for which the seamen were most grateful. The windsails had long since been gathered in, and the tank tops closed and sealed. The Skipper didn't want any more blots on his copybook right now, like sinking his ship in the Kattegat.

At 9.30 there was a distress call from a fishing boat to the south, but their assistance was not required. Two Swedish ships closer than them went to the rescue. Why the fishing boat was out in this weather God only knows, as there had been plenty of warnings over the past seven hours. Maybe she was smuggling Cherry Heering to the Swedes, or ball bearings to the Danes, they would never know.

At ten o'clock Paddy was relieved on the wheel by Elvis. Inglis took up position at his elbow, watching and listening for the first ten minutes before he was invited to take over. The secret seemed to be to ignore the short waves and whitecaps raised by the wind, and concentrate on picking out the pattern of the underlying swell. This was not as easy as it sounds, because the wind was whipping up what sometimes appeared as a false swell at forty-five degrees to the main one.

Having established the pattern of the main swell, you weren't even half way there yet. You then had to begin to anticipate it by nearly twenty seconds. This was approximately the time it took for the ship to answer the helm after you put the wheel over, depending again on the sea conditions and loaded state of the ship. Twenty seconds sounds like a very short time, but it can be a very long time when you're holding the wheel over in what appears to be the wrong direction, while wondering if you're doing the right thing after all. Then, twenty seconds becomes exactly twenty long separate seconds, as you watch the lubbers line to see how far out you are this time.

For the first ten minutes Inglis had the bows swinging through anything up to fifteen degrees either side of their mean course - a total of thirty degrees - in spite of Elvis' coaching. He could see the worried look on the Mate's face, which didn't help his confidence one little bit. And less than an hour ago he was the one who thought Paddy was a lousy helmsman.

Inglis started to sense the rhythm, and his anticipation came closer to the slot; more at odds with what he was seeing, but more akin to what Elvis was saying. It was also a little reminiscent of one of the tests at RAF Hornchurch, where you steered a pointer on a winding path round a rotating drum, with a built in delay between steering wheel and pointer.

By ten to eleven he had the arc down to no more than twenty-four degrees. Then suddenly it all clicked, and he could see in his mind what was happening, and feel it through his feet. At the same time he could see the small flash from the radar beam as it passed a chink in the hood - exactly once every ten seconds. Inglis still counted to himself, but the radar told him if his count was accurate, so he could adjust if necessary.

Between counting, watching the swell, and catching the flash of the radar in the corner of his eye, he was too busy to hear what Elvis was saying. Which might have spelled disaster if he'd got it wrong - but he had it right! He did it again, and again, and again. By eleven twenty Inglis had the swing down to a maximum of eight degrees either side of their main course, and the Mate was smiling. Between then and noon the bows didn't once swing more than that eight degrees off course. Inglis was elated; he was steering better than Paddy, and nearly as well as Elvis. Roll up everybody and see the star helmsman!

At noon they were relieved by Aussie, and Inglis turned to leave the wheelhouse. The Mate handed over the watch to Big John and caught up with Inglis outside the spare stateroom, as he was about to descend the inside stairway to his cabin.
"You just won a dozen cans of lager son," said the Mate.
Inglis raised his eyebrows in surprise as he continued.

"The Third Mate bet me you would have the swing down to under ten degrees each way before the end of your trick. If you didn't he paid me a dozen, and if you did, I paid you the dozen. Well done son, and happy to pay up. You'll be doing a two-hour trick on the wheel every day from now on while we are at sea; and no more chipping and painting. Happy?"
"Yes SIR!" Inglis answered. "Thanks very much sir."

He slid down the stairs without using his feet. Only when he was in the cabin did he realize how exhausted he felt after two hours of unremitting concentration and effort. No wonder the helmsman did only two hours at a time, reduced to only one hour in gale conditions; which were already on them. Aussie would be relieved by Paddy at one o'clock. Inglis hadn't appreciated till now just how much it could take out of you.

As he sat down in the dining saloon it dawned on him that he was feeling not the slightest trace of seasickness. In fact he couldn't wait to get stuck into the thick stew on his plate; which he trapped on the thick lip of the table with his left hand while using a spoon to scoop it up with his right.

The salt and pepper shakers were broad based, and wouldn't topple over. It was quite interesting to speculate on where they would stop sliding or hit the edge of the table, as the ship corkscrewed through the sea. Sometimes they would slide straight, at others their course was curved as the ship plunged fore and aft and rolled sideways, both at the same time.

The wind was still causing the ship to roll farther to starboard than port, and his seat was on the starboard side of the table; so he didn't let go of his bowl of stew for a second. He exchanged the empty bowl for a cup of coffee, which he refrained from placing on the table at all. Even then he nearly spilled it - oh, for a life on the ocean wave.

It was just after three o'clock in the afternoon when they took on the Goteborg pilot in the relative shelter of the river mouth. By the time they berthed and began pumping ballast Inglis' watch was already over, and he was free until eight o'clock next morning. He couldn't make up his mind whether to go ashore in the abominable weather conditions, so he had a couple of beers with the Third Engineer - compliments of the Mate and Big Johns' bet. Finally he was talked into going ashore for a look round with the Fourth Engineer, who had never been to Goteborg either.

They fought their way along the docks to the ferry just upstream of their berth. The main part of the city lay on the other side of the river, and the ferry was in danger of being canceled because of the weather. They debated whether they should take the risk of being stranded on the other side, and having to make a long detour to get back. The vote was to stay on this side and visit the nearest pub.

Inglis noticed the name of the ferry was David Carnegie, and the hotel on the other side of the river was the Carnegie Hotel. He

112

wondered if this Carnegie was a relative of the great Andrew Carnegie, Scottish American industrialist and philanthropist from his home county. What Inglis did know was that many Scots had settled and done business in Goteborg more than a century ago, and made a lot of money; while the Dutch built canals there, and the Germans got into steel and shipbuilding. So it was a very cosmopolitan city, of which he was not about to see much tonight.

At nine o clock they decided to call it quits, and fought their way back to the ship through the wind and snow. They would be pumping ballast until at least midnight, due to the new regulations the Swedes had introduced.

All ballast from incoming tankers now had to be pumped ashore for cleaning, whereas until recently it had been customary to pump it into the sea on your way in. Worse still from the company's point of view, was the fact they were not allowed to start loading until ballast pumping was completed, and the tanks inspected. In a lot of ports then it was quite usual to pump ballast over the side while loading into tanks which were empty; but not in Sweden.

This was okay by Inglis, since it meant they wouldn't complete loading until the early hours of Saturday morning, at the earliest. As it was still only Thursday night, he would therefore have one more opportunity to see Goteborg on Friday evening.

Inglis was asleep in his bunk by eleven o'clock.

CHAPTER 14

When Inglis woke in the morning the worst of the storm was over. Stray flakes of snow were being blown around by a wind from which most of the ferocity had gone. They were taking on a full cargo of gas oil for Malmo and Stockholm, so there were no problems with the loading plan. As a consequence the day dragged rather slowly. If the loading rate was maintained they would sail about four o'clock Saturday morning. The ship seemed to be acquiring a distressing taste for leaving port in the wee small hours.

Inglis went ashore on his own in the evening. The Carnegie ferry took only ten minutes to deliver him to the far side of the river, where he inspected the Carnegie hotel. It was quite nice, but nothing special. He asked directions from the hotel staff, and was soon standing at the tram stop in a wide main street, where he intended catching a tram into the city centre.

Using his superior powers of deduction, he knew from the sign that he was at the right stop, even though he spoke not a word of the language. When the tram came it was a 'double', comprising driving tram and trailer. Inglis boarded and confidently asked for a ticket to Centralst please. The conductor raised his eyebrows with a puzzled look, so he repeated it with more of a French 'r'. The conductor scratched his head.   "Centralst.....Centralst.....oh, Central Station?"
Inglis nodded dumbly, holding out a handful of change as his face overheated. So much for his superior powers of deduction!

Unlike most countries in Europe, the Swedes still drove on the left side of the road, but there were plans afoot to change over to the right. The Yanks had a lot to answer for in 'proving' their independence. At Central Station Inglis decided to check out the trains, since he was here anyway. Unfortunately he knew that the Swedes, having no large coal deposits of their own, had given up steam traction earlier than most, in favor of electricity. But it was worth a look in any case.

As Inglis entered the station his pulse quickened to the familiar smell of coal smoke, steam and oil. There at the buffer stops stood a beautiful little 4-6-0 locomotive, a trace of smoke wafting from her chimney, and a wisp of steam at the cylinders.

He purchased a platform ticket and walked over to the steam engine. She had outside Walschaerts valve gear, and driving wheels not much under six feet in diameter. The driver spoke reasonable English, like most Swedes. He told Inglis that many of the country's steam engines had been put into storage in working order, rather than scrapped. This created a reserve of traction power for use in case of national emergency. Typical of the Swedes to think of that, instead of merely scrapping machinery because it was 'old fashioned'. This particular locomotive was on its annual workout, and was to haul a passenger train on the first leg of its journey to Stockholm tonight.

Inglis stooped to examine the valve gear more closely for a few moments, before stepping back for a wider view. He'd been taking no notice of other people, and as he stepped back, someone ran into him.

Knocked almost off balance, he turned round to see a young woman land on her backside on the platform beside him. He stooped quickly to help her back to her feet as she berated him volubly in Swedish. The little bells began ringing in his head as he looked at her. Angry or not, she was truly beautiful.

Almost platinum blonde hair - even blonder than his - peeked out from under the fur hood she wore. Her eyes were bright blue, her nose straight and even, and her mouth neither too large nor too small, above a smoothly curved chin. Under the expensive-looking suede coat she wore, the rest appeared to leave nothing to be desired either. Altogether a breathtaking sight to behold so unexpectedly.

She punched him lightly on the chest with both fists - he presumed it was lightly, because he couldn't feel a thing in his daze - and continued to rattle off what sounded like highly uncomplimentary Swedish. Inglis shrugged, holding his arms out to the sides in surrender, before relocating his voice.
"I'm terribly sorry, really I am. I didn't see you. My fault completely," he stammered. The tattoo on his chest came to an abrupt halt, and a beautiful voice spoke.

"Are you English?"
"Scottish actually, but no matter for now. A lot of people don't seem to know the difference."

"Oh, but I know the difference. We have many people from Scotland here," she replied. "My grandmother came from Dundee in Scotland. Where do you come from?"

Now she was smiling, the anger gone as quickly as it had come. She smiled beautifully, and Inglis grabbed his chance.

"I'm from St.Andrews, just twelve miles from Dundee across the River Tay. Can I buy you a coffee or something at the buffet, and apologize for my clumsiness?"

"Sorry Mac," she said in a pseudo-American accent, and his heart hit his boots before she continued.

"It might cost you more than that, but coffee first."

She hooked her arm through his, and led him off to the station buffet, his spirits soaring; wondering at his luck, and at a loss over what she had said. But he didn't care what else it cost him, she was still with him. He ordered the largest pot of coffee available, in the hope of keeping her around for as long as possible. The buffet was very warm, so they took off their coats and put them on a spare seat. Under the coat she wore a plain black dress, shaped like a million dollars. Perfectly tailored, high at the front and low at the back, it was set off by a single strand of pearls at the neck. She looked as if she had just stepped straight out of the pages of a glossy fashion magazine. Inglis was stunned once more; trying hard not to stare as he sat down, but unable to tear his eyes from her. She laughed at the look on his face.

"What's the matter Mac?" she asked. "Haven't you seen a good looking girl before?"

Her English was almost flawless, with a neutral American accent overlying the faint Swedish lilt. Inglis wondered how to answer her, until eventually managing to stammer out.

"Yes, but.....you're *really* beautiful. I've never been with anyone quite so beautiful......I don't know what else to say."

She laughed as she replied.

"So drink some coffee and say nothing for a few minutes while I do the talking."

The American accent had gone, replaced by a vaguely uppercrust Scottish gentry one. What an amazingly unfathomable girl. She proceeded to tell him about herself, almost as if reading from an

116

autobiography. Her name was Kerstin Larsen, she was 'nearly eighteen', and she was in her first year at Goteborg University. Her father owned a machine company in Malmo, and she had intended traveling home by car tonight for the weekend. But, because of the road conditions, and the fact that the forecasters were predicting clear weather to settle in during the night, her father had suggested she stay in Goteborg overnight. He would send his plane to pick her up in the morning. Inglis never knew anyone who owned his own aeroplane before!

Kerstin had driven one of her friends to the station to catch the overnight train to Stockholm, and now she had a problem - about which she would tell Inglis after he had given her his name and background. He started rather hesitantly, but before he finished he'd told her more than he had intended, such was the effect she had on him.

She told him her problem, and what a beautiful one it turned out to be. Having originally intended returning to Malmo tonight, she had refused invitations to attend a dance at the university. Now she wanted to go to the dance, rather than just go home early, and all the men worth going with already had partners. In desperation she had been just about to ring a boy she wouldn't normally be seen dead with.

"Now you have dropped from the sky," she said, "so you must take me to the dance instead, to make up for your unforgivable clumsiness in assaulting a lady - right?"
Oh, Lady Luck, I love you. Look at a steam engine, and finish up escorting the most beautiful girl in town.
"I will make the other girls jealous," added Kerstin. "You look so handsome and dashing in your uniform."

Inglis looked at her in genuine amazement. *Who, me?* He had just started to think he was the only one left in the world who thought he looked handsome and dashing in his uniform! Wait till he told Jimmy Shand and his band there's a new dance called the Dashing White McAndrew! Kerstin was staring at him, her question still hanging in the air between them. His answer came out in not quite the smooth, urbane, dashing and handsome manner he would have liked.

117

"Yes......yes. The least I can do....I mean, I'd be delighted.........oh, wow....surely......for certain, yes."

She laughed at him, the sound of it music in his ears.

"Okay," she said, "the dancing starts at eight thirty, but there are drinks and snacks from seven o'clock at the Students' Union. It is now after seven, so why don't we go? My car is parked just outside."

Kerstin had a new SAAB car - a present from her father! She was a skilled driver, and the slippery sections of the road seemed to hold no fears for her. Inglis had not realized how many canals there were in Goteborg, which was almost like another Venice of the North.

They soon arrived at the university, and it was quite easy to pick out the students' union. There were lights and bustle, and cars parked outside. It certainly looked as if Kerstin was by no means the only Swedish varsity student with her own set of wheels, though not many were as new as hers.

He had been told before that Sweden was an affluent country, where nobody went hungry or without a roof over his head. Come to think of it, Goteborg was the first port in which he had not yet seen any down and out people in the streets; so maybe it was true.

Inglis' father had worked hard for twenty years to get a company car, and still had no car of his own. He had served his apprenticeship as a joiner and cabinetmaker, and was now head agent for a large building company in Dundee. During the War he had been in a reserved occupation, but had still managed to go to sea in the *Prince of Wales* battleship when she chased down the Bismark. He said they were still doing the final touches on board when the battle began, and he went to war with his hammer, chisel and saw! 'Never forget son,' he'd said. 'That's what happens when you take half an hour to be five minutes!'

It had taken Inglis more than five minutes to work that one out the first time. But here in Goteborg, it looked more like he'd fallen into a situation, in not much more than five minutes, which he couldn't have engineered deliberately in half a century.

They walked arm-in-arm up the steps to the front door of the

Union, where they left their hats and coats. They even had a cloakroom attendant, it was that sort of place.

For the first half hour he felt a bit out of *his* place, as people greeted Kerstin and made a fuss of her. They looked and acted like an elite, and Inglis was taken aback by the veiled suggestions by some of the girls - young ladies - which he was not accustomed to parrying. He could see his sophistication needed some urgent polishing before he would be able to keep his end up among this lot. But at least he was wearing the right clothes, which is one really good thing about an officer's uniform - it's in place any place.

Most of them spoke excellent English - better than most migrants he knew in Scotland, who had lived there since the War; which had been over for more than twelve years now.

All Inglis could remember about the war was bits and pieces. Like being thrown under the dining table when the bombs came down; watching the houses in the next street burning; playing in the huge crater where two German bombers had fallen, locked together, their full bomb loads still on board. After the war, the Council made the crater into an outdoor skating rink for winter, and a sports ground in summer. It's an ill wind..

This country he was in now had been neutral for a very long time, and it seemed they had reaped the benefits very nicely thank you. It didn't really worry him much; not if worrying about it might chase Kerstin away. After a few Tuborg lagers he was more relaxed, and better able to join in the conversation. They sat down at a table with three of Kerstin's friends and their escorts. At one stage, while Kerstin was at the ladies' room, her 'friend' on Inglis' left put her hand on his thigh, moving it slowly upward to rub his crotch, while apparently leaning forward in casual conversation across the table. He sat petrified, not knowing what to say or do, or even where to look. Fortunately (?) Kerstin came to the rescue. She had returned unnoticed from the ladies' room behind them.

The first Inglis knew of her arrival was when the girl with the wandering hand sat bolt upright with a loud "OH!" This was followed immediately by the sound of Kerstin's voice.

"Oops! I'm so sorry Gerda; how silly of me to spill."

119

She sounded about as sorry as a hungry tiger feels for the deer it has just killed. Placing a half empty glass on the table, she began to fuss solicitously over Gerda, who was looking daggers at her while saying

"An accident Kerstin. I'm sure it couldn't be helped."
It sounded as if what she really meant to say was
"Let's not scratch in front of the children. I'll kill you later."
Inglis handed Kerstin his large handkerchief for her ministrations to Gerda, while suppressing a grin with difficulty. Humanitarian supplies only - this was one war in which it was Scotland that would remain neutral.

Soon the band appeared, and the dancing began, mostly quicksteps, with a few tangos, sambas etc thrown in. Inglis could quickstep with the best, and enjoyed dancing with Kerstin, who was light and graceful on her feet. A tall, good looking blond man in his early twenties tapped Inglis on the shoulder and took her away from him! He was devastated, and returned slowly to the table to lick his wounds, feeling suddenly lonely and abandoned. What chance did he stand against this bloke? Before he could sit down again, Gerda jumped up and grabbed his arm.

"Come and dance with me. I am a good dancer, even better than her, you will see."
Who was Inglis, a mere jilted male, to argue with this dark haired enchantress? Gerda was right, she was an excellent dancer. She glided in his arms, following every move as if hooked into his brain. She moved with a sensual suppleness that made him marvel - and sweat. She was also very, very close. Unlike most of the girls, she was wearing loose-legged culottes, and at every opportunity she was quite deliberately maneuvering him so that his right leg would lead between her thighs. She would then move close and kiss his thigh with her crotch, which was most upsetting to his nervous system.

Each time Inglis tried to move away a little, she would come close, pressing her breasts into the front of his jacket, and throwing a cheeky look at him. She really was very sexy, almost overwhelmingly so.

Inglis looked around for Kerstin, and caught her eye just a few yards away, still dancing with the tall blond man. They looked like the perfect couple from a Hollywood magazine, and his heart was in his boots. Well, Inglis thought, I *was* a last ditch resort for her to attend the dance in the first place.

Kerstin looked up at her partner, and said something that caused him to look over and smile. Inglis smiled back - *damn you*, he thought, *may you rot in hell, you handsome bastard*. A few couples came between them, and Inglis lost sight of them as he turned in the dance, locked in mortal combat with Gerda. Inglis was starting to fear - fear? - that Gerda intended eating him for supper. What was worse, he wasn't sure any more that he didn't want to be eaten. He'd never been eaten by a siren before. Was it a terrible death, or merely a new experience? He couldn't make up his mind, like a rabbit mesmerized by a snake.

Someone tapped him on the shoulder, and he looked round to see Kerstin's dancing partner smiling at him, then at Gerda. As Inglis moved slightly back from Gerda, Kerstin slipped neatly between them, and whisked him away - what was he, a ping-pong ball? Talk about a slick operation; she was in his arms and dancing before he had time to think about it. Kerstin looked up at him and asked
"You really want that bitch Gerda?"

Inglis started to answer "Well, ah...", and she pressed herself close to him, whispering throatily in his ear "Or you want me Mac? I like you, she only wants to hang your scalp on her suspender belt."
That took his breath away. He was not accustomed to girls saying things like that. He answered.
"No, Kerstin....I mean yes......I mean, I want to dance with you", knowing, or more than suspecting that wasn't all she meant, and tingling all over from the thought. She continued.
"Two months ago I borrowed her current boyfriend for one evening only, no big deal. Ever since then she tries to steal my boyfriends, in spite of the fact she changes men with her underwear."

Inglis was shocked again. He would *have* to forget his Baptist upbringing around this neck of the woods, or he would be in danger of sinking without trace. Kerstin continued talking.
"Promise you won't go with her, and I'll call you when your ship

gets to Malmo tomorrow. Tonight is already too late for us to know each other well, if you must be back by three o'clock. Now it's nearly midnight, and the band will go home soon. But there's music for another hour from the record player. You want me to call you tomorrow?"

"Oh yes," Inglis blurted out. "Yes please, I'd love that. I think I love you already. I don't even want to look at Gerda if I can be with you. I just thought you looked so good with your blond partner, you wouldn't bother any more with me."

She looked seriously at him before bursting into laughter.

"You silly man, you were jealous, weren't you? I think you are a little in love with me after all, and I like it. Don't look so crestfallen. That tall, blond, and *very* handsome man" - his heart fell again - "is my big brother Bjorne. I'll introduce you to him before we leave."

Inglis could have wept with joy. Kerstin saw the look in his eyes.
"You really have got it bad! I'm so happy, because I think maybe it's just possible I might be able to get it bad for you too. Let's sit down and have a drink."

Did she really say that? Yes, she did. Joy of joys, life is truly marvelous. They sat down, leaning on each other, and holding hands under the table. Nevertheless, Inglis didn't quite manage to keep his promise about not looking at Gerda again, though she had moved to another table. The band packed up and was replaced by rock and roll records. Soon the Elvis tunes began booming out. Inglis was looking into Kerstin's eyes when there was a cheer, and people started clapping to the music. Kerstin looked past him and hissed.
"There goes Miss Hot Pants doing her stuff."

He looked at the stage, and there was Gerda, moving her hips to the music; and for his money doing it much better than Elvis ever did. After a few moments it became apparent she was doing a striptease. Inglis tried not to look too long, but it was very tempting. When he turned back to Kerstin she said
"Go on, look all you like. She just loves showing herself off to the whole world." Then she cocked an eyebrow. "I'm more particular who I show myself off to."

That one nearly floored him again, with its obvious implications. But still he managed to drag his eyes back to Gerda's striptease. Already she had her bra off, and was twirling it round her head as she moved to the music. No wonder she liked to show herself off. Her breasts were high, wide and handsome, and she was obviously very proud of them; and who could blame her.

Tossing the bra behind her, she lightly cupped a breast in each hand, stilling her upper body as her hips continued to sway to the beat. She ran her hands outwards to the nipples, then down over her stomach. Next thing she was stepping out of the culottes and kicking them behind her. She thrust her hips forward and back, then swiveled them in a circular motion, clad only in a pair of flimsy white panties Inglis could almost see through.

Turning her back on the crowd, she bent forward with hands on buttocks, wiggling them at the audience. Then she ran her hands down the edges of the panties, gathering them into the cleft of her buttocks. Standing upright again her hands disappeared briefly in front of her before she turned to face the audience once more. She was stretching the panties upwards, and had gathered them into the slit of her sex, hardly thicker then a piece of twine. A darker area of flesh bulged out round the sides of the 'twine', lightly sprinkled with dark hair. The show was a hit with the audience. If Gerda flunked her exams at uni she would have no trouble earning a living as a stripper!

Kerstin tugged violently at Inglis' arm."That's enough, we have to go now." Just as the crowd started to chant what Inglis presumed was Swedish for "Take 'em off!"
Inglis was sure nobody noticed their departure, and he had not yet been introduced to brother Bjorne either. He was at the forefront of the crowd, right next to the stage, and not about to be interrupted.

They collected their coats and hats and were soon driving to the ship. It was a forty-five minute drive, because the ferry would have made its last crossing from this side of the river half an hour ago; so they had to go the long way round. Inglis told Kerstin he could catch a taxi, but she wouldn't hear of it, thank goodness.

She was very quiet for the first ten minutes. The car was warm, and they hadn't put their coats on before starting off. Occasionally the car skidded on a slippery patch, but Kerstin handled it like an expert. She told him her father had started teaching her to drive when she was twelve, and she had driven a long way since then. The side windows were misted up from condensation, but the efficient demister kept the windscreen clear.

Suddenly Kerstin spoke.
"Do you like Gerda? Would you rather be with her?"
For a moment Inglis thought she must be psychic. He'd been thinking about Gerda's striptease when she spoke; but only thinking about it, that was all. He looked at her in surprise.
"No way Kerstin. Sure, Gerda's good looking and has a sensational figure, but I'd much rather be with you."

She said nothing, but slowed the car and pulled over to stop at the side of the road. Leaning forward in her seat, she put her hand behind her back before switching on the interior light. She shrugged her shoulders and was bare to the waist! Inglis goggled as she glared at him and spoke vehemently.
"My figure is as good as hers - see!"

She thrust her chest out, and Inglis had to admit she had a point - two of them as a matter of fact. Her breasts were every bit as gorgeous as Gerda's, only smaller. They say good things come in small packages, and here was the proof. Inglis glanced furtively through the windscreen.
"Christ Kerstin. You can't do that here in the street. Somebody will come along and see in a minute, then what?"

She laughed as she shrugged the dress on again.
"You British are so prim and proper. Here in Sweden nobody worries about such a thing. But now you can think about me instead of Gerda, or I'll scratch your eyes out and eat them!"
Inglis thought about that one for a moment, and wondered if he'd caught a tiger by the......well, anyway, she switched off the interior light and pulled onto the street, changing gear as if nothing much had happened. But she was right about one thing - he wasn't thinking about Gerda any more.

124

Maybe all the stories Inglis had heard were true after all, and Sweden really was the Land of Free Love. It was surely a thought for this seventeen-year-old pilgrim to conjure with as they drove through the night streets. The snow gangs had been busy, and most of the streets were cleared or sanded. There was very little traffic around in any case, so Inglis wasn't the least bit worried. Especially with the confident way Kerstin handled the car.

"You are very British, Inglis," she said, taking his hand and placing it on her warm thigh. "If you are to stay warm in Sweden you must learn to become a little more Swedish."

Inglis was trying hard, but his education in the ways of the world had been progressing at breakneck speed recently - so was it any wonder if he flunked the tests sometimes? Maybe he should have been a Catholic, so he could confess and start all over again. Now there was a thought. A boy back home had once told him that Catholic priests knew a lot more than Baptist ministers, because 'the silly buggers tell them everything'.   Mind you, Inglis wasn't sure he really wanted to go to heaven any more. He remembered one little girl asking old 'Hellfire and Damnation'
"Please minister, if I go to Heaven, d'you think God might let me out to play with the little devils sometimes?" It wasn't such a bad idea. Inglis wondered what *she* was doing now?

They parked outside the dock gates. Inglis didn't want Kerstin too close to the ship, giving some of the crew ammunition for their jokes and jibes. For a while they sat and talked about their families and backgrounds; before she squeezed between the front seats into the rear of the car, which was a two door.

When Inglis looked, she had the convertible top of her dress down again, and her firm breasts glowed in the light from the docks. She looked straight at him before speaking.
"Come Inglis. You mustn't think I let you look only in order to tease, then don't let you touch."

Inglis almost did himself a serious injury on the hand brake in his anxious scramble to reach the back seat. There wasn't a great deal of room back there, but that didn't worry him in the least. Her breasts were beautiful, and she enjoyed having him play with them, fondle and kiss them. But she told him tonight was touch only, not all the way - as if he'd asked.

"There is not enough time Inglis. I want you to make love to me, but not now, not here. We will have more time tomorrow - today - in Malmo. Now you should go to your ship, and think about me as you sail south. I must go and sleep."

Oh boy, Inglis would think about her all right. How could he not. They kissed for a long time before he extricated himself from the car and donned his coat and hat - it was bloody cold outside. Kerstin laughed out loud at his surreptitious attempt to adjust the front of his trousers - brazen hussy!

But still she seemed to have the knack of keeping things from getting too serious. To her, sex was something to have fun with. And Inglis was starting to understand that point of view, after years of thinking about it as dark and unmentionable, serious and without joy. It seemed to him that he'd been conned for too long. He was going to learn how to enjoy the fun of sex. It wouldn't be easy or quick, but he was always a good student with things he wanted to learn - and did he want to learn that!

He wandered back to *Forth Venturer*, his floating home and university, with his thoughts vaguely wandering around in dreamland.

Then the thought hit him - what if he missed again? That brought him up with a jolt, and he started sweating and worrying. What if Kerstin was only leading him on? What if she had just said things for kicks? What if she didn't bother to ring him in Malmo? What if....what if....?

CHAPTER 15

Forth Venturer cast off at four o'clock in the morning, and ten minutes later the tugs were dispensed with. Another fifteen minutes and the pilot left. They were on their way in the dark of night once more. Inglis was restless and didn't want to sleep yet, so he stood leaning on the forward rail of the boat deck ahead of his cabin. The wind had eased to a steady twenty knots, and the sky was overcast and heavy, but there was no snow falling.

If anything, the swell was even higher and steeper than when they had arrived, which seemed unusual. But the storms in the North Sea had continued, and this swell was the result. It was just that the highest winds hadn't quite reached them again. He watched the flash of foam as the swell crashed onto the foredeck below him, rushing beneath the catwalk, swirling round the tank tops, pipes and valves as the water sought hungrily for something to snatch up in its powerful grasp. Ten feet ahead of him on the deck below, the ship had less than eight feet of freeboard with her current load, so the waves had no trouble heaving themselves inboard without an invitation card.

The rolling motion of a loaded tanker is unlike that of any other vessel. When she rolls to one side, the liquid in the tanks surges across to that side, causing a secondary after-roll, which holds her over for moments, before the external forces acting on her begin to bring her upright again. Slowly she starts to come back over, gathering speed as the liquid cargo shifts again, then whipping quickly through the upright position, over to the other side; the cargo following in a rush, to push her over the opposite way, where she teeters for moments before starting the whole process over again.

This laggardly action presents some golden opportunities for large waves to roll inboard; opportunities made so much easier by the puny distance between the deck and the mean level of the surrounding sea. Of all the ships afloat, a loaded tanker brings her sailors closest to the realities of the sea's brutal power; to its serenity; its ever-changing moods; its merciful and merciless expressions; its mysteries, and its blatant exhibitionism.

Recently Inglis' elder stepbrother had been serving on board an aircraft carrier – *HMS Indefatigable* - one of the final designs of the war, with a specially strengthened and armored flight deck - when a car ferry sank in the Irish Sea. Rushing in response to the Mayday call, the carrier's flight deck - inches thick steel armor plate - was peeled back like the lid of a sardine can, by the ferocity and awesome power of the waves. So she was not as Indefatigable as her name might suggest. Now he was due for a posting to a submarine - almost, he'd made it early.

At the dock in Goteborg when they had tied up, right in front of his face, carved into the wood of the dock, was the legend J. DONALDSON M.V. THAMES ASPIDISTRA 3/9/57. Inglis' other stepbrother had been here less than six months ahead of him. Inglis carved his details immediately below his stepbrother's with his seaman's knife.

The last letter from home had informed him that his younger brother was about to sign on as galley boy on a tramp steamer bound for Africa. Did they all have salt water in their veins? Or was it just a case of follow the leader? They had grown up with the sea, mucking about in boats whenever the opportunity presented.

Summer holidays had been spent on the west coast of Scotland. One holiday house in particular, when Inglis was nine years old, was pure magic. On the beach at Kilmun on the Holy Loch, it was possible to dive from the back window into the water at high spring tides. Now they were planning to turn the whole loch into a submarine base. Where the rows of ships awaiting scrapping had huddled together, soon there would be submarine mother ships suckling their lethal offspring. Merchant seamen *hate* submarines.

More than once Inglis had almost given his father a heart attack, out on the loch in his rowing boat in the middle of a storm, thrilling to the sight of the huge waves - they looked huge to him then - as he pitted himself against the elements. On one occasion, when the ferries had been suspended because of rough weather, the lifeboat was launched to rescue him out in the middle of the loch. When they arrived, there he was, rolling about in the boat, still trying to catch some more fish.

For the rest of that holiday his boat was confiscated, and he was forced to turn to other things for amusement. Like swinging on a thick rope suspended from a giant tree - on top of a 300ft precipice. On the outward end of each swing he could look almost straight down on the tiny 'puffer' tied up at the jetty. His rope was confiscated, and the offending branch cut off, in case someone else got the same idea. That had led to games of 'chicken' on top of the famous local waterfall up on the mountain; until Inglis came within a hairbreadth of becoming a dead chicken. He'd been hanging over the edge for twenty minutes by the time he was rescued, and his arms felt as if they'd stretched to about ten feet long. Next holiday he got his boat back.

Now he stood watching as the sea clutched at *Forth Venturer*. The swell was still from the north-west, but now it was on her port quarter, the opposite 'corner' to where it had been on her way north. Inglis was trying to catch the rhythm of the swell, because he would be helmsman - on his own - from ten until noon today. The swell was moving not a great deal faster than the ship, which prolonged the agony of each movement. First it would gather under the stern, lifting and trying to push her to port, while the top crashed over the rails of the main deck. Then, as it moved farther forward, the ship would begin to stagger upright, gaining speed as the front edge of the swell approached the midships accommodation. Just before she was upright, the swell would bulge around the midships island and burst onto the foredeck, surging across the deck as the ship began to heel to port, stern now high as she made a half hearted attempt to surf on the swell; before plunging downwards to meet the next wave, as the bows rose in the air, the ship still teetering to port. Then she began to tip back over to starboard, gaining speed until the next swell met her stern, as the previous one still pushed the bows upwards.

The ship was like a tortured beast, being constantly twisted and baited by the sea, which could go on twisting and baiting indefinitely, waiting and watching for the first sign of weakness, so it could move in for the kill. But the Irishmen who built her knew the sea's tricks, and had allowed for most of them. So the contest went on and on, neither side winning, neither contestant weakening.

Inglis had to stop the poetry and start the mathematics as he pictured what he would be doing at the wheel if he was there now, mentally putting the helm over and then counting to see how close he was as the swells pushed, pulled, rolled and lifted. Big John opened the porthole of his cabin and called out.

"What the hell are you doing out there Inglis? If you can't sleep, come and have a beer with us. Harry's here."

He joined them for a beer, and endured Harry's embellished version of how Inglis had disappeared in Copenhagen with the 'sexiest little usherette in the place - who wasn't supposed to disappear with anybody.'

"That was her on the dock when we left, John," he said. "You know, the one the Student Prince here threw his watch to? The same one who shouted out for everyone to hear 'come back soon' - that's her. Now the young bugger's onto something else already, no thought for the poor lonely girl he left behind. Sparks reckons he was necking with a blonde in the back seat of a SAAB at the dock gates tonight, just before we sailed. Where the hell does he dig them up from, eh?"

Inglis felt uncomfortable, especially over what he had said about tonight. Christ, there were eyes and ears everywhere - Inglis hadn't even seen Sparks. But then, he had been concentrating on what was going on inside the car, not looking outside. He felt himself go hot and cold as he wondered how much Sparks had seen. The windows *were* misted up, weren't they? To have seen anything he would have had to look in the bloody windscreen - maybe he did!

"Sit down laddie," said Big John, forcing Inglis gently back into his seat with a giant hand as he got up to leave. "Never mind Harry, he just doesn't like anybody else muscling in on his reputation. With you around he's in danger of becoming a wallflower any time now."

"Bullshit!" shouted Harry. "I'd just forgotten how some of the women are attracted like magnetism to some stumbling young bums like him sometimes." He flashed a grin at Inglis' shocked look.

"Only kidding for Christ's sake. And to prove it, you can visit my girls in Stockholm."

Inglis held up his hand, but Harry continued.

"Not a bloody night club or anything this time. I've got a real girlfriend in Stockholm, and she shares a flat with another girl. Your job is to keep the other one out of my hair, okay?"

He watched as Inglis tried to make up his mind; then before Inglis could answer he went on.

"What have you got on in Malmo, anything?"

"None of your business!" Inglis shot back before thinking.

"Only asking in case I could help out," he added, as Big John slapped his knee and guffawed.

"I told you Harry. He's getting to be a better organizer than you. Next thing he'll have a chauffeur driven limousine with a beautiful blonde in the back seat picking him up from the ship in every port!"

Harry was waiting for an answer to his original question.

"Okay Harry," Inglis told him. "Tell you what I'll do for you. Give me a pound spending money in Stockholm, and I'll devote one whole evening of my valuable shore leave to keeping the ugly sister out of your hair - how's that?"

"Bloody hell, I didn't say I'd *pay* you for it for chrissake! Anyway, who said she's ugly? She's a doll. I might even go for her myself if my girlfriend wasn't there."

"Says you!" Inglis retorted. "Sorry Harry. No pay, no work. As far as I know she could have three eyes, a hare lip, and her brains in her bum."

Big John roared and slapped his knee again. Inglis could have sworn the whole ship shook.

"He's got you there Harry, you have to admit. Unless you've got a photo of this lovely, beautiful....?"

"Her name's Linda. She's cute.....no, I don't have a bloody photograph.....but she *is* quite beautiful.......ten bob Inglis."

"Fifteen bob - final offer!"

"Done," said Harry. "Let's have a beer....*pay* him....shit!"

"Why don't you get in on the act John?" Inglis asked. Big John Soutar shrugged with an embarrassed look.

"Aw, he's too bloody big - gives them nightmares. They're all scared of him, and run away," answered Harry with a laugh. Inglis saw the hurt look flit across John's face an instant before he joined in the laughter at himself. It hadn't occurred to Inglis before how the average girl would feel about dating him. Now, as he thought about it, he could see John's problem. He wasn't just big, but *big* - seven feet four inches in his bare feet, with the build to go with it. Inglis would just have to ask Kerstin if she knew of any big attractive and witty girls anywhere, who would like to date a giant with a heart of gold. That was the least Inglis could do for Big John after all John had done for him. He would make a point of it - Project Number One. Who would have thought little old he might be able to help out this, to him, magnificent big human being. If Kerstin rang. If she turned up. If Inglis ever saw her again.....

Inglis finally got to sleep about an hour before it was time to get up again - which was worse than not sleeping at all. His work pattern at sea was now following a different course, more akin to the one in port. From eight till twelve he was on the bridge with the Mate, doing his steering trick usually for the second half of the watch, and a variety of things during the other half. Then from twelve till four he was still on the bridge for Big John's watch. John wasn't too hot on maths, so it was becoming customary for Inglis to do most of the calculations from the Decca Navigator. Which wasn't really proper, but what Authority didn't know about, Authority didn't grieve about either. Inglis did it, and John signed it, which kept the books straight.

Inglis was becoming very good on the Decca, and probably more familiar with it than anyone else on board, except the Mate. The Decca was a new tool, and nobody else on board had previous experience of using it at sea. So Inglis had started on an even footing with the rest, and was now ahead of all but the Mate.

The Mate was highly proficient at everything he did, making the rest of them look like rank amateurs in most things. The sea was his life, apart from the opera, and he was master of every task his job entailed. Since it now required a knowledge of the Decca, he had spent hours and hours of his spare time getting to know it thoroughly. He had just joined the company from Caltex, where he had been a Skipper, and was serving his obligatory three months as a Mate before getting his own command. Anyone serving on board the ship he commanded would be fortunate indeed, and Inglis' biggest worry was his replacement on *Forth Venturer* next month when his time was up.

Sometimes, for an hour or two on either watch, Inglis would be called on to carry out more mundane tasks on deck, assisting the bosun or carpenter. Just to remind him that he was still only a cadet, not a qualified watchkeeping officer. Poor wee Jimmy was left in no doubt, still doing his minimum two hours manual labour on deck in lieu of

Inglis' trick on the wheel. He had tried his hand at steering, and just couldn't get the hang of it. The first time he tried, the ship had described almost a quarter circle before the Second Mate had managed to bring her head back the other way. Jimmy reckoned he didn't know what happened.

"Ah jist kinna froze, ah didna' ken whit tae do!' he'd said.

Inglis took a stroll along the catwalk before breakfast, in order to wake himself up. Standing on the catwalk was like being on a pedestrian bridge over a raging river, except that this bridge didn't stay still. The swell was very heavy, sending cataracts of water cascading across the deck. That, and the cold wind, woke him up pretty smartly. The galley was now better organized, and Inglis asked the cook if he wanted anything taken forward. The cook promptly presented him with a tray of eggs that the pantry boy was scared to take, because of his previous accident.

It was no easy task balancing the tray on one gloved hand, while trying to maintain his balance. He progressed in stops and starts, with his left hand gripping the rail and his feet wide apart whenever the ship heeled too far over. Then a quick dart forward as she swung through the vertical, stop and hang on once more. But he made it to the pantry eventually, where the Second Steward welcomed him with open arms - just as he tripped over the high coaming at the door.

The tray flew from his hand, narrowly missing the Steward, and spreading eggs all over the floor. The Second Steward looked at Inglis, then at the egg-patterned deck. Picking up a utensil, he scooped two of the eggs from the floor, put them on a plate and held it out.

"Here's your breakfast Inglis," he said.

"Funny, funny," said Inglis. Okay for him to act smart now. He had been on the point of having to go for the eggs himself. He obviously didn't fancy the job, or they would not have still been in the galley when Inglis got there. It was one thing to make fun of the poor pantry boy for screwing up, and another one altogether to take the risk of screwing up yourself just to prove you could do it!

At eight o'clock Inglis was on the bridge, ready for whatever the Mate might hand him today. He had taken a fancy to handing him unexpected things to do at a moment's notice of late, and it was quite interesting to speculate on what would be next. At first he had thought the Mate was just trying to catch him out. But he knew Mr.Vickers was a bigger man than that, and realized now that he was trying to teach him, and find out what he could handle.

The weather was still overcast, with clear patches, and visibility had improved considerably. Which was just as well, because the Decca Navigator was having a bout of indigestion. Probably a reaction to having functioned perfectly during two consecutive emergencies. If it went on doing that sort of thing it would be in danger of losing its poor reputation.

The Mate handed Inglis his personal hand chronometer - on pain of death if he harmed it - and the local manual of navigation, which listed all lights and markers in the Kattegat. Inglis was to take Jimmy with him up to the monkey island, and get whatever bearings he could, as the opportunity presented itself.

Inglis armed himself with details of their current compass deviation and local magnetic variation, and they climbed up to the highest deck of the ship. The monkey island was in fact the roof of the wheelhouse, and it was quite scary up there in rough weather. The handrail round the back and sides comprised two strands of wire rope hooked through metal stanchions, the top rope being at only mid thigh height.

So, if you lost your balance and ran across the deck, there was nothing much to stop you from diving over the edge, and into the sea sixty feet below. The secret therefore was, if you *do* lose your balance, do *not* try to regain it; just go down on the deck, then get up and start again.

On this platform called the monkey island were the compass binnacle, the radar aerial, lockers for distress apparatus, and the halyards from which they flew various flags. These latter were looped onto cleats on the only solid piece of rail, at the forward edge of the platform. From there they rose up to the main fore and aft stay, which was a heavy steel cable strung high between the mainmast and foremast of the ship. From one of these halyards they flew the blood red 'B' flag almost constantly, announcing to other shipping that they carried dangerous cargo.

Jimmy sat down on the flare locker with the chronometer and notepad, while Inglis scanned the horizon to port, with the manual in his hand. Inglis' job was to spot and identify any flashing lights, then take bearings to them - preferably when at least two of them were simultaneously visible. Jimmy's part was to note down the bearings and times. Then they would work together to apply the deviation and variation, before reversing the bearings to provide data for a fix. The Mate would then plot the fix on the chart in the chartroom, together with the time. A series of fixes joined together would then show their progress on the chart.

But first you have to find and identify your lights. Every light has a different pattern of flashes which is noted in the manual. If you notice a light flashing, the first thing is to note the pattern, maybe two short, then one long, followed by another short, with an equal period of darkness between flashes.
Then there will be a pause before the pattern is repeated, and the length of the pause should be noted also for safety. Reference to the manual will then tell you what light you are looking at (hope you're not bored). Next, you look desperately round for another light to identify.

Presuming you are lucky enough to spot one straight away, you then take bearings to both lights as quickly as possible. This is done by looking through what looks like a simple gun sight mounted on the compass, which can be swung right round the horizon. As you line up the light in the sight, you can glance at the bearing, which is reflected up almost into your line of sight by a mirror.
Voila, you just did your first compass bearing. If you got it right, go to the top of the class; where you can then do the rest of the job - thought you were finished, didn't you?

By ten o'clock they had six good fixes and two doubtful ones, and it was time for Inglis' trick on the wheel. He was confident he could handle it, even though he had never steered her with a heavy sea on the quarter. For the first ten minutes he was slightly astray, then he got the hang of it and dropped into the slot. He was feeling very proud of himself. Life on the ocean wave was turning out to be a bit of a breeze after all. Then the Mate had to spoil it again. He came storming out of the chartroom, and abused the hell out of Inglis.

"You silly young bugger. Every one of those bearings you did is wrong. I've got plots all over the place, and it's taken me ages to figure out what the hell you did to them. You've only applied the variation the wrong bloody way round, that's all. Not just on one or two, but on the whole damned lot of them. According to the last plot, we're a mile inland, in the middle of a bloody forest! What the hell got into you?"

Inglis' world was falling to bits again. It seemed like every time he built up a tower from confidence in his ability, some bloody thing came along to knock it down again. Oh, hell, how could he have been so bloody dumb? *Hi there, you at the top of the class - can you see me down here at the bottom?*

"I'm sorry sir," he muttered. "I don't know how it happened."

"Sorry!" he shouted. "You'll be sorry enough all right. Soon as you come off the wheel, you get down on your hands and knees and start scrubbing the wheelhouse floor. And you keep on scrubbing till we get to Malmo - clear?"

"Aye aye sir," said Inglis, feeling about an inch tall, just as the ship's stern lurched to port. He had lost his concentration while the Mate was dressing him down. Now he looked back out at the waves - and his heart stopped. Tearing his eyes round to look out to starboard, his worst fears were realized. The next wave, which was already lifting the stern of the ship - that's what had caused the lurch - was a monstrous double. Inglis probably would have managed it if he had seen it in time. Now he had no chance, as he spun the wheel desperately hard over to port, knowing he was already at least five seconds too late, maybe ten.

The Mate had seen it all straight away, and ran to the engine room telephone. The ship's stern kept rising, and was being pushed to port. The bows were starting to swing to starboard, and soon she would be broadside to the massive swell. And still it would be seconds yet before she answered the helm. The Mate was shouting into the engine room telephone.

"Give her all you've got. Squeeze out every revolution. And hang onto something - we're about to broach to!"

Oh Jesus, the pits of hell. Inglis nearly wept with frustration as she continued to swing the wrong way, with the wheel hard over in the opposite direction. The Mate ran to the whistle handle and sounded a series of short blasts - that was the best he could do to warn everyone belowdecks to hang on. Even as he reached for the handle he was having to climb. The deck was tilting further and further. The whole ship began to vibrate in answer to the extra revolutions, as the engine strove to drive the huge screw faster, deep below the crest of the giant double wave.

Inglis' hands were shaking and he looked down at them. They were shaking because the whole wheel was juddering - and creeping back round in a clockwise direction. Inglis threw all his strength against it, but it kept vibrating back the wrong way. He stood on one of the spokes on the port side of the wheel - and it lifted him slowly upwards, rattling his teeth as it went. He shouted to the Mate.
"Sir! I can't hold her sir! Oh Jesus, I can't hold her!"

He realized he was screaming at the top of his voice, and promptly shut his mouth. Then he stepped down to the next spoke below, with his heart thumping, but absolutely determined not to let go of the wheel. The whole of the rudder was submerged, at fifty degrees to the force of the ship's speed through the water, plus the extra pressure from her screw on maximum revolutions. The hydraulics just couldn't handle it. Any moment now something might give, and Inglis would end up either flat on the deck, or with a dent in the top of his head - he didn't know which. He just knew he was scared stiff. He also knew that, no matter what happened, he was *not* going to abandon the wheel, come hell or high water - a most appropriate saying, given the circumstances.

The tilt of the deck was getting steeper all the time, and the Mate slid down the slope to join Inglis. Things were crashing and smashing in the ship below them, thrown from their places by the steepness of the heel to port. The Mate grabbed hold of a couple of spokes of the wheel and shouted to Inglis.
"Jump off and let go for a second - then watch what I do and lend a hand."
Inglis jumped off his spoke - and slid down the deck towards the port bulkhead! His hand touched the after bulkhead, and he got a grip with his fingertips just as his rubber soles found a purchase on the

deck. He scrabbled back up beside the Mate.

The Mate was not trying to heave steadily against the wheel with all his strength as Inglis had been doing. Instead, he let it ease just a shade clockwise before jerking hard back the other way with all his might. Then he did the same again, and again. Each time he did it, the wheel was a little further round in the right direction. Inglis suddenly understood why he was doing it. Every time he eased off and jerked back, the hydraulics gave an extra surge of power. Inglis grabbed a couple of spokes and joined in with his rhythm.

They were winning, but if something blew out now, then just too bad, they were finished. The ship had stopped swinging, but still she teetered sharply over, with the port rails of the foredeck completely submerged below the first crest, as the second passed beneath her.

Slowly, agonizingly, the bows started to swing back to port. They had done it. Just in the nick of time, but they'd done it! They had to fight two more swells, but the worst was over.

When the ship was back on course the Mate gave Inglis back the wheel. Then he spoke in a quiet level voice.

"I'm sorry son. But don't ever take your eyes off the sea when you're steering in these conditions, lad. Not if I tell you to, and not even if I spit on you. I give you my full permission now to tell me to go to hell if I ever do. But well done for sticking with it as you did. You've got the makings of a damn fine sailor in you, if you'll just stop getting too cocky every now and again. Now you make sure you handle her right to the end of your trick - you *will* be okay, won't you?"

"Aye aye sir!" Inglis shouted, getting control of his nerves.

"Good man," he added. "But don't forget you still have some deck scrubbing to do when you finish - reduced to half an hour in the circumstances."

Damn, Inglis thought he might have been let off with it altogether. But half an hour was a lot better than forever. The Mate smiled and went towards the chartroom, where he almost bumped into the Old Man, come to see what the hell had happened. They both went inside, and left Inglis on his own; feeling shaken, and yet at the same time elated. They had beaten the sea together.

The swell gradually decreased as they made their way south, and by the time Inglis finished his trick at noon was noticeably smaller than it had been at eight o'clock. They passed through the narrows between Helsinborg and Helsingor half an hour later, and it was like passing from the sea into a lake. The heavy swell of the Kattegat was replaced by the much smaller chop of the Oresund, and they docked in Malmo just after three o'clock in the afternoon. There was just time for Inglis to open the first valves and begin pumping before he handed over the deck watch to Big John.

CHAPTER 16

Inglis scrubbed himself squeaky clean in the bathroom, before ironing the clothes he intended wearing this evening - his best uniform of course. Even the white plastic cover of his hat was removed and cleaned until it sparkled. Inglis didn't know when Kerstin would call, but he had made sure the telephone was connected before he came off watch.

She WILL call, won't she? Yes, of course she will, he told himself, trying to feel confident about it; and the more he thought about it, the less confident he became. He was going to look a bit silly if she didn't, after his stand in Big John's cabin this morning. *Of course she'll ring - she promised, didn't she?*

By five fifteen it was already dark, and Inglis sat in the dining saloon, picking away at his ice cream - in this weather! - and sipping slowly on his third cup of coffee. Oh God, why hadn't she rung? What had he done wrong? Please let her ring. It was nearly too late now. Maybe he should just go to the cabin and hide under the deck lining?

Big John burst into the saloon, ducking his head as he entered - he had to duck for everything.
"There's a lady outside to see you, Inglis. No, no, don't get up, Your Lordship. I was just checking to make sure you were here. I'll show Her in - she can have my seat, and I'll treasure it forever after."

Just as he was leaving, he turned at the door.
"Christ, I was only joking about the chauffeur-driven limousine you know. You didn't have to *prove* it. Harry's having kittens; wouldn't be surprised if he shoots himself or something."

Then he was gone as Inglis wondered what the hell he was gabbling on about. Inglis walked to the door to greet his guest, followed by the curious stares of the Second Mate, and the Second and Fourth Engineers. As Inglis looked into the corridor, Big John appeared at the far end, shepherding Kerstin ahead of him, John beaming and Kerstin looking radiant. She smiled and ran forward.
"Inglis, surprise, surprise, I'm here!"

She kissed him! Right there, in the doorway of the Officers' Dining Saloon, she kissed him full on the mouth. Oh wow, this one he would never hear the end of. But there was more to come. Inglis sat her in John's seat at the table he shared with him and Jimmy, introducing her to John as he did so.

"Coffee miss?" asked the Second Steward, almost falling in her lap.

"Yes please," answered Kerstin, flashing him a smile that made him her instant slave. Then she turned to Inglis.

"I mustn't stay long, Inglis. Martin is outside with the car, and my parents are expecting us for drinks before dinner."

"Who's Martin?" Inglis asked suspiciously. She smiled beautifully as she replied.

"Martin is Daddy's chauffeur. I left my car in Goteborg, remember?"

Inglis almost missed the last bit as he choked on his coffee, narrowly avoiding spraying it all over the table. He coughed and spluttered before finally managing to blurt out

"Chauffeur? You mean you've got a chauffeur-driven car waiting on the dock - beside the ship?"

"Yes of course, Inglis. I told you Daddy owns the company."

Of course, of course. He *owns* his own plane for God's sake - why wouldn't he send his daughter to pick up her boyfriend in a chauffeur driven car? Oh my God. For a few moments Inglis was at a loss, before starting to chuckle, increasing to a belly laugh, and finally to uproarious laughter.

"What's so funny?" asked Kerstin, sipping at her coffee, while the Second Steward hovered at her elbow, ignoring everyone else in the saloon - the peasants could starve, the lot of them!

"I'll tell you in the car," Inglis spluttered, between laughs. "Drink up your coffee and let's go, before there are too many cases of serious eyestrain around here."

But it wasn't quite that easy. By the time they left the saloon Kerstin had been introduced to just about every officer on the ship, most of whom just happened to pop in while she was there. About the only one she missed out on was the Skipper himself. There had been three officers in the saloon when she arrived, and eleven when she left.

141

Even Harry had turned up for his introduction, a look of reluctant admiration on his face. Inglis felt like a king with his queen. When they stepped out on deck, a group of sailors just happened to be hanging around the gangplank; including Elvis, Aussie and Paddy, the three leading hands. There were a few good natured comments and suggestions, but all very genteel - for sailors. Until Inglis heard Paddy say quietly and quite viciously   "Bloody smartarse young fancy bastard."

He had a scowl on his face when he said it, and Inglis wondered what the hell he'd done to Paddy. But now was not the time to find out, so he ignored it, and helped Kerstin down the gangplank.

There had been no kidding about the car either. A glossy black long wheelbase Mercedes stood at the bottom of the gangplank, complete with uniformed driver, who held the rear door open for them as they stepped onto the dock. The whistles and catcalls came from the deck only after they were safely in the car and underway. Inglis decided to get his own back, and waved his hand lazily against the tinted glass window - just like the Queen!

There was enough room between the back seat of the car and the partition to dance on - if you like dancing on your knees. Under the partition was a cabinet of some sort, flanked by two foldup seats. Kerstin opened the door of the cabinet, took out two cans of Tuborg, and said

"Welcome to Malmo, Inglis. You don't mind meeting my parents do you? I've told them about you, and this is the only evening of the week they are both home for dinner together."

Dinner at home with her parents was not exactly how Inglis had envisaged spending the evening, but quite frankly he would have spent it in a rowing boat with her if she asked. He had never met anyone quite like Kerstin before, and she had swept him right off his feet. She had charm, wit, intelligence, confidence and poise; as well as the beautiful face and figure God had blessed her with. Who wouldn't have been swept off his feet?

All that, and a limousine, and a plane, and goodness knows what else still to come. What on earth did she see in him? Inglis began to genuinely worry about meeting her parents, and having dinner with them. If things continued to follow the current trend, they probably lived in a fairy castle.

How many funny-shaped forks and things did you use to eat food you didn't recognize and couldn't spell the name of? Did you give your coat and hat to the butler or the footman - or to someone else, the name of whose function you didn't even know? Was there such a thing as a coat-taker? Where and when did you wipe your feet? Or did some lackey come along behind, erasing your footprints, so they could deny you were ever there, if you made too many faux pas? What the hell was the plural of faux pas anyway? Faux pases, fauxes pas, faux pax? Inglis was working up a nervous sweat just thinking about it, and needed another beer already.

Who said dating a beautiful woman was heaven? He was fast raising a complete funk. Almost ready to dive out of the door of the limousine - moving or not - when he heard Kerstin speak.

"Inglis, did you hear what I said?" She nudged his shoulder.

"What....pardon? Sorry, I was worrying about meeting your parents, and maybe making a bloody fool of myself. Okay for you - you already met them." *funny, funny.* "You live in a different world from the one I grew up in Kerstin, and I'm not sure I can handle it. Or, to put it another way, I'm scared stiff - help!"

To his surprise she didn't laugh at him this time. Instead, she took his left hand in both of hers and squeezed gently, looking wistfully into his eyes. Then she leaned over to kiss him on the cheek.

"Don't be scared," she said."I'll look after you and keep you out of trouble. Daddy and Mummy are really very nice, and I'm sure you'll like each other. But I have had other friends who were scared to meet them, and I know what you mean - I really do. I won't let you down - trust me?"

She lifted his arm round her shoulders, and leaned her head on his chest. Inglis thought it was just about the nicest thing she had yet said or done. She wasn't all sunshine glamour and glitter; she had perception also. Was there no end to the talents of this girl? Inglis' worries were melting away, and a little of his confidence was returning. He didn't know what he would have done if she'd made fun of his fears. But she hadn't, and now he was certain he'd fallen in love

143

with this wonderful versatile young woman, who had brains and sensitivity as well as her looks and wit. An absolutely devastating combination.

But how was it he could be so lucky? She must have men queuing up for the chance to take her out. Why was she bothering with him? In the end he decided 'mine not to wonder why', and left it at that for now. But the niggling thought at the back of his mind was - how could he ever measure up to her?

They drove into the grounds of a large house. That's all it was. Not a castle, but a modern house in mock Tudor style, barely big enough to be classed as a mansion. But bigger than your average two-family semi detached, attached, if you know what that means. It was certainly big enough to impress Inglis, with its boundary wall and gate, and the curving driveway. Parked near the house was a Bentley limousine next to another Mercedes - normal length - and a black Volvo.

Kerstin had informed Inglis there were a few other dinner guests; three couples associated with the business, and brother Bjorne with partner. At least he wouldn't be the focus of her parents' undivided attention all evening. There was no butler or footman either. The household supported a housekeeper, maid, and Martin - who doubled as handyman in addition to being the chauffeur. Their coats were taken by the maid, who informed Kerstin that everyone was in the library, where they made their own way. No grandiose entrance announcements - was Inglis disappointed? - just a quiet entrance and introduction to Kerstin's parents, who were in their late forties.

Mr. Larsen was just under six feet tall, heavily built without being fat, and with a full head of light brown hair going gray at the edges. His handshake was firm but not overbearing, and he gave off an aura of competence and quiet authority. His wife was quite obviously Kerstin's mother. A little under average height, she was slim, blonde, elegant, and would still turn men's heads at any gathering. She had Kerstin's features, but with a fuller jaw, giving the impression of a strong will beneath the beauty and charm.

Mr. Larsen introduced Inglis to the other guests. There was the company's banker, a fat bald man in his fifties, with a small timid

144

looking wife. Then there was one of the directors of the company, who was also a director of Kockum, and looked like an ex-boxer; with a charming brunette wife, who gave the impression of having just been taken out of her gift-wrapping. The third man was the general manager of Mr. Larsen's company, a fit looking man in his early forties, with an overdressed wife who seemed accustomed to having her own way.

Finally there was big brother Bjorne, tall blond and handsome, with his very attractive dark haired companion. She reminded Inglis vaguely of a slightly slimmer and more elegant version of Gerda; so he knew which way Bjorne's taste in women leaned. She also happened to be the daughter of the Kockum director - keeping things in the family?

The general manager and wife held Inglis and Kerstin in conversation for ten minutes, during which Inglis received the impression of being minutely examined and dissected by the wife. He became more relaxed once they formed a small discussion group with Bjorne and his partner Senta (senta what to where?). They talked about Inglis' duties on board ship, then about soccer. When Kerstin told Senta how they had 'bumped' into each other at the station, Bjorne declared an interest in steam engines, about which they yarned for a while.

Then he told Inglis about some of the exciting developments at the SAAB factory, aimed at giving Sweden the most modern jet aircraft in Europe. He explained that Sweden's neutrality was to be maintained from a position of military strength and efficiency, not merely by statements of policy.

"That way our potential enemies must think twice on the possibility of receiving at least a bloody nose, and not just a verbal smack on the hand from the United Nations" he said. It sounded like a reasonable point of view to Inglis.

Although Sweden's standing armed forces were not large by most European standards of the time, the Reserves were substantial, and were kept up to date in their training and preparedness. Furthermore, stockpiles of arms and ammunition were distributed around the nation for emergency use by local reserve units, rather than piled up in some central store.

Plans were afoot to build special strengthened lengths of motorway around the country, on which the next generation of jet fighters would be able to land and take off, with underground supplies of fuel and armaments.

Inglis was impressed by what Bjorne told him, having read none of this in his magazines back home. Sweden did have a well-established armaments industry, of which Inglis was well aware. And SAAB had produced the 'flying barrel' jet fighter. But according to Bjorne, research and development were currently well underway for the production of Swedish guided missiles, both ground and air launched. This Inglis had not known.

Mrs. Larsen called them to take their places for dinner in the dining room; which was a large airy room, with a high clerestorey ceiling, through which the moon could be seen. Inglis had never seen such a thing in a house before, and thought it a marvelous idea. The dining table was rectangular mahogany, with room to seat fourteen people, six along each side, and one at each end.

Kerstin whispered to Inglis that his place was opposite hers, at her father's end of the table - the senior Larsens sat at opposite ends, facing along the table. On Inglis' right was Bjorne's girlfriend Senta, with male and female alternating along each side, facing their respective partners. Inglis thought it was a very civilized arrangement.

The meal was sumptuous, but most of the details later escaped him, except for the beautiful fresh smoked salmon. When it came to fresh salmon he was an expert, having poached enough in his time. On the few occasions he was unsure which utensil to use, a quick glance across the table was sufficient for Kerstin to discreetly touch the right one, almost as if by accident. She was marvelous, and at no time did anyone suspect Inglis was a lost pilgrim. He could have kissed her each time she helped him. But then, he could have kissed her for no reason at all, if it came to that.

When the wine came, Inglis took the one she 'recommended' in such a way as to suggest he was accustomed to drinking various wines. He knew a few types, but the names were beyond him, never mind vintages or sub types. The one she put him onto was a light moselle from Australia; until that moment he hadn't even known they produced wine in Australia! It was delicious and refreshing, and from then onwards he developed a preference for Australian wines, regardless of the mighty European names and reputations.

Mr. Larsen engaged him in conversation for a great deal of the time, discussing a wide range of topics, including world affairs and politics. He discovered that Inglis had rather strong views on the Suez Crisis, and the Soviet rape of Hungary, both of which were a year and a half old. Inglis' opinions on Communism, business ethics, work motivation and goodness knows what else, were all prised out of him by this skillfully persuasive man before the end of the lengthy meal; which kept them at the table for an hour and a half, including coffee and port. Back in Scotland dinner had taken less than half an hour, after which Inglis was required to do the washing up!

After dinner the older men had a business discussion to take care of in the library, while the rest of them sat and stood in the large lounge, which opened onto a sun room facing the back garden - it looked more like a park to Inglis.

He was feeling drowsy as a result of beer, wine and port on top of a sleepless previous night. Kerstin took his arm and suggested they walk in the garden for a while - which Inglis thought was quite mad, considering the temperature outside. But he hadn't the courage or will to say so. Which was just as well, because a closet beside the door of the sun room contained warm cloaks for just such an occasion - he should have guessed.

Donning a suitable cloak each, they wandered slowly round the extensive grounds, arms round each other's waists, occasionally tripping as they gazed at each other instead of watching where they were going. The sky was clearing, the wind had died down to a light breeze, and a half moon reflected from the snow. They strolled, lost in each other, through a small group of silver birches, raising their ghostly arms to the heavens in the moonlight; their feet solidly planted in the snow; as if wanting to fly, but afraid to leave the ground; their trunks preferring the security of their present position, over the desire of the branches to be free on the breeze.

They kissed beside a bare pergola near an empty pool, warming each other with their closeness. Kerstin put her hands on his face, and looked in his eyes.

"You must be very tired Inglis. It's time for you to go to bed and sleep."

His heart sank. Tired as he was, he didn't want to go back to the ship yet, leaving this beautiful girl here for who knows how long before he would see her again.

"Yes, I am very sleepy, but I'd like to stay a while longer, if that's all right. We'll be sailing about ten o'clock in the morning, and I don't know when I'll see you again. I want to spend as much time with you as I can, please?"

"Silly boy! You don't think I'm sending you back to your ship tonight do you? Everything is already arranged for you to spend the night here. Daddy and Mummy will be very upset if you don't stay - not to mention me. Martin will have you back on the ship before eight o'clock in the morning."

He opened his mouth to protest - weakly, and without his heart in it - but she kissed him again before he could say anything.

"Don't be awkward or say anything silly. You're sleeping here tonight, and that's that!"

She took his hand and led him back to the house. The business guests were just leaving, and they said their goodbyes before Kerstin informed her parents Inglis was tired and going to bed. They said goodnight and the lovers climbed the stairs to the upper storey. A long wide corridor led from the top of the stairs, wide enough to drive a car along, and lit by concealed lighting in the top corners.

They entered a beautiful bedroom, bigger than Inglis' father's living room, with a huge bed floating beneath a deep pink quilt. There was a dressing table in brass and smoked glass, containing a woman's makeup. One whole wall was made of mirrors, forming the doors of a vast wardrobe. The floor was lost beneath a fluffy light green carpet, which felt like soft grass underfoot. The ceiling was midnight blue, speckled with constellations of stars. Inglis looked again, and saw that the light in the room was coming from the stars. He was flabbergasted - this place was something from a Hollywood film set, not the sort of bedroom ordinary people slept in.

Kerstin touched his arm and pointed to the ceiling, while her other hand turned a knob on the wall. The light from the stars faded, until they were faintly twinkling in the darkened room. The effect was breathtaking, and Kerstin asked hesitantly.

"Do you like it? This was all my idea. I even supervised the workmen, so it would be just as I pictured it - wait! There's more yet."

She hit a switch above the knob, and the wall opposite the mirrors glowed. A deep red flush spread across the wall, like the afterglow of sunset. Silhouetted against the glow were the outlines of a host of trees in Spring bud, the upper branches of the closest ones brushing the ceiling. The whole effect was like nothing Inglis had ever experienced; as if suddenly he had wandered into a clearing in a small wood at dusk. He put his arm round her shoulders as she looked up at him for approval in the dim light.

"Well?" she asked, "do you like it?"

"Like it!" Inglis gasped. "I'm almost lost for words, Kerstin. This is like something you dream about, without ever expecting the dream to come true; the concept of an artist brought to reality."

"Oh, I love you!" she said excitedly. "Sometimes you say exactly the right thing, and I know you mean it, and feel it. Believe it or not, some people think this is all just silly and ostentatious, but I love it. Even Mummy said it was a bit silly and childish, but Daddy said I should have it - wait till I tell him what you said. It makes me feel I've created something beautiful."

"I think you have, Kerstin - in fact, I know you have", he said, looking round in wonder. If this was silly and childish, then long may there be a host of silly children around, with him among them.

Kerstin wrapped her arms round him, kissing him fiercely and possessively, her body pressed firmly to his. Inglis was breathless from the intensity of feeling she managed to transmit to him, and he was becoming uncomfortably aroused. He reached over her and turned the knob to lighten the room.

"Hey, girl", he smiled, trying to keep it light hearted. "This could get out of hand. You'd better show me where I sleep now, before you get us both in trouble."

She looked at him with a slightly puzzled expression.

"But you sleep here of course."

"I can't take your bedroom Kerstin," he said. "Where would you sleep? There must be a spare bedroom for me in a house this size, surely to God."

"Oh boy!" she exploded, stamping her foot. "You are so British. I told you not to be so British! This is Sweden, and I am going to sleep with you in my beautiful bed, in my beautiful room. Sometimes you are so exasperating, and you make simple things so difficult!"

Inglis stared at her in disbelief. Not only the room was straight out of Hollywood, but the script was written there too! He was shocked - yes, truly shocked to the core, was the little Puritan, hiding inside his recent man-of-the-world facade.

"But what about your parents for God's sake? This is their house after all. I'd be abusing their hospitality in the worst possible way - it would be like stealing!" Inglis was rattled, and worried, and confused. This was all just too much for him to grasp in one go.

Kerstin's eyes were blazing, and for a moment Inglis thought she was going to hit him, she looked so angry. *Oh God, what have I done or said now*, he wondered. Her words were almost a hiss.

"Do you think for one moment I would do such a thing to my parents if it was wrong, the way you think it is? My parents know I am sleeping with you tonight. I have told them I love you. Now, if you refuse to stay, you will shame both them and me. In Sweden we do not hide behind hedges, or in dark corners, with hearts full of guilt. When two people love each other, they make love to each other; and their friends and families are happy for them. Can't you understand this? Are you so bigoted that you think of sex only as dirty? So twisted that you really don't know the beauty and joy of giving your love to someone without rules and regulations? Do I have to beg you to do what we both want to do? Oh, I *pity* you!"

She ran to the bed and buried her head in her arms, as she lay face down on the quilt, shoulders heaving in soundless sobs. Inglis was mortified - hurt - confused. A lost soul wandering in a land he didn't understand. But most of all he was agonizingly sorry, and in love. If what she said was true - and he was sure now that it was - then he was the despicable one; the seller of dirty postcards; twisted slave of a twisted attitude, in a tormented culture, which set its novices on the course of life, already primed for partial self-destruction. Inglis walked to the bed, lay down beside Kerstin, and took her in his arms.

"Please forgive me for what I am," he begged. "For what my upbringing has made me. I'm so sorry for what I said. I can't say how sorry I am. Please try to understand the shock I felt. I know what you are saying is right - *really* right. Just give me a little time for the rest of me to catch up with what my brain tells me. I love you Kerstin, and I wish I could have been struck dumb, rather than say what I did. But the really awful thing is that if I didn't love and respect you, I wouldn't even have bothered to say it. Can you please, please, try to understand that?"

He held her tight, rocking gently as the tears ran down his face. He couldn't remember the last time he had cried. For years his stepmother had tried hard and sadistically to make him cry, and he had made it a point of honor never to let her see his tears. But this situation with Kerstin was a completely different matter. For the first time he was not ashamed to cry - somewhat embarrassed yes, but not ashamed. It was too important that she understand how he felt; so desperately important, that he didn't care what it might take for her to know.

Slowly she raised her head from his chest, as he quickly wiped the tears from his face with the back of his hand. But she had seen, and ran her fingers lightly over where the tears had been. She murmured throatily as she stroked his face.

"You really are a good man underneath. Daddy said you're a good man before we came upstairs. If he hadn't thought so, or if he thought you were here only for kicks, we might have had to go somewhere else. But he says you are in love with me, whether you know it or not, and he's very clever with people."

"I do know it, Kerstin," Inglis answered, "and I want to be with you here. If I feel a bit guilty, it's only because of what I've been taught. But bear with me for a while - I can learn new things, new ways of thinking. I do have a brain you know. It's just that some things become deeper ingrained than others. The last thing in the world I want to do is hurt you."

They held each other tight for a few minutes, feeling one another's hearts beat, until Kerstin suddenly jumped up.

"Some hostess I am! The bathroom is through that door. You go first. You'll find a bathrobe behind the door - the red one is yours. And there's an electric shaver above the hand basin, though it feels as if you already shaved."

She leaned over to kiss him briefly.

151

"Go! And don't take too long in the shower. I want to cuddle my big teddy bear in my nice comfortable bed."

Inglis started to look at the bed before it dawned on him that he was the teddy bear - dummy! Then he laughed and headed for the bathroom, the tension dropping from him with his clothes, which he hung on one of the hooks behind the door.

The shower had an adjustable head that would give anything from a soft deluge to a skin prickling high pressure jet, and Inglis played with it until he had just what he wanted. He shampooed his hair, lathered his body with perfumed soap, and reveled in the luxury of pampering himself in the hot downpour.

His face was nicely lathered up when something bit him on the bum! He yelped and opened his eyes, only to have them fill with soapy water. It stung, and his eyes closed again in self defence; but not before Inglis caught a glimpse of a nude Kerstin giggling at him, and pinching finger and thumb together in preparation for another assault on his person.

"Foul!" cried Inglis. "I've got soap in my eyes!"

He shoved his face under the shower, washing the soap from it, and trying to flush out his eyes, but they kept stinging.

"Now I've got you!" cried Kerstin, rubbing her hands on his chest, then down his sides and across his stomach. "Stand still for goodness' sake, or you'll do yourself an injury," she shouted, laughing as she cupped his balls in her hand, encouraging instant growth - talk about a green thumb!

Inglis grabbed for her with his eyes still closed, his hands meeting empty air. Then he realized she was kneeling in front of him as he touched her hair, covered with a shower cap. She was lathering his penis as it grew; soon it felt like a tree, as she massaged it gently, rinsing the soap off. Inglis was still trying desperately to rinse the soap out of his eyes.

He felt embarrassed as she ran her tongue along the projecting part of his anatomy, then took the tip in her mouth, teasing with tongue and teeth. No, Inglis told himself, *I'm Swedish, think free, FEEL free - feel......oh wow*! He couldn't stand it (*Take, not stand - there's enough standing here already*) any more. He put his hands under her armpits, pulling her up as the worst of the soap was gone from his eyes at last, and Inglis could see her. She was literally a sight for sore eyes.

Without her clothes she looked small boned, almost frail. Slim and graceful, her breasts seemed almost - but not quite - too heavy for her delicate frame, in spite of the fact that they were by no means big. Somehow, with her clothes on, Inglis had thought of her as bigger - or less small - than she really was. Instinctively, he wanted to smother her, hold her close and protect her - from what, he didn't know. He drew her to him, his arms wrapped round the fine shoulders, as the hot water cascaded over them both. Then gently, he put his arms in front of hers, stooping to run his hands down her flanks to her buttocks, and lifting her face up to his.

His rigid member was making its presence felt between them. Kerstin wrapped her legs over his hips, and popped it down with one hand, to rest between her buttocks, a narrow seat to sit on! She lowered her legs down the outside of his hips, then slowly glided her buttocks in and out, rubbing her sex on his as they kissed hungrily. The combination of water and kissing made breathing quite difficult, and they both had to come up for air.
"I love you Inglis," she whispered in his ear, as he stepped to the side, taking their heads out of the spray.
"And I love you, Kerstin....oh, I love you!"

Inglis squeezed her buttocks, not too hard, and they kissed again, tongues probing and searching. Then she sealed her lips round his tongue and sucked gently. Inglis moved his tongue forward and back, discovering a new erotic sensation. Then she probed with hers, and the tables were turned in the most delightful fashion.
She took one hand from behind his neck, after raising her knees to his waist. Moving her hips, she guided his rampant sex into her pussy, so warm and cozy, smooth and silken; yielding while enveloping, like a warm lubricated glove around his throbbing finger of sex, probing blindly ahead.

The sensation electrified him - not just his skin, but his very being tingled, and flushed with a radiance transmitted via deep contact. Inglis felt an almost unbearable swelling of tangled emotions. Love, tenderness, elation, and a desire for all of him to be in Kerstin; a part

153

of her, and she a part of him; their living cells mingled and interwoven, so fused as to be inseparable.

And it was too much to be contained, bursting forth from his body as he felt the overwhelming need erupt deep within her; a searing surge of sensation, soaring skywards to oblivion......to dissipation and darkness; and an insidious weakness; a trembling of the knees, a spreading ague of the tissues, as he leaned on the wall; still clutching and supporting this winsome woman who had overwhelmed him, drained him - and bewitched him.

"Oh my God!" Inglis gasped. "Too quick.......I'm sorry.....couldn't help it......I love you..........Witch of the North."   He was on the point of collapse, his legs trembling beneath them both, threatening to give way at any moment.

"Wonderful, Inglis," she whispered hoarsely. "Me too.........couldn't help.........either."

It was then he noticed she too was trembling. Gently he lowered her to the floor, and they rinsed themselves under the still-running shower. His blood was singing and he was happy. He'd made it! And it had seemed so natural, and so easy, after all his worrying and fretting.

Slowly and playfully they dried each other. Inglis told Kerstin that with the shower cap on, she looked almost like a boy from behind.

"Oh yeah?" she asked, bending forward away from him.

"Well.....uh.....not exactly...not like that!" he answered, placing his hand between her thighs, waving it at her, and saying "Hi there girl, what's this? I think you sprang a leak!"

He drew his hand back, and gently poked his thumb in her pussy. She promptly straightened up and blurted   "Oh, you......*now* you are Swedish!"

They collapsed laughing into each other's arms, holding tight, and fondling, and caring not a damn for anything or anyone else. They didn't even bother to put the bathrobes on. Instead, Inglis gave her a piggyback ride to the bed - his strength was returning - where she suddenly called out

"Whoa horse! Turn round and go back to the door. We forgot to turn off the daylight. Giddyup!"

She smacked him on the buttock, and he yelped.

"Hey! Watch it! That stung. Any more of that, and I'm a bucking bronco!"

He trotted back to the door, where she hesitated before touching the switches. Poking her head beneath his armpit, she asked "Hey, horse, what's that sticking out front?"

She giggled, and operated the switches before he could think of a suitable reply - she'd caught him with his pants down!

"Back to the stables horse," she added, squeezing his waist with her knees. He cantered towards the bed in the afterglow of sunset, stars twinkling faintly in the ceiling. Everything in the room was tinted red or pink from the glowing wall as his eyes adjusted to the gloom. Just before they reached the bed, she smacked his buttock again.

"Giddup, you lazy horse!"

"You were warned," he said, starting to jump and twist and turn. She hung on for a minute or so as he lurched and cavorted around, letting go of her legs, which she clamped round his waist. Then her legs began to slip as he spun in a tight turn. Grabbing her knees just in time, Inglis collapsed onto the high wide bed, laughing and gasping for breath. They hugged each other, shaking with laughter, until the laughter died down, and they smiled into one another's eyes. And Inglis had thought he was tired!

He was aroused once more, and Kerstin asked him to stand beside the bed, while she kneeled on it and cuddled him. With her kneeling on the bed and him standing beside it on the floor, her eyes were a few inches above his. He stooped to kiss her breasts, massaging them and pushing them together. They were not big in actual size, but big enough for the rest of her slim proportions, and just perfect as far as he was concerned.

She pulled his buttocks towards her, and placed his penis between her thighs, where it nestled comfortably as she swayed gently to and fro. She pulled his ears, drawing his head up from her breasts. With a smile, and a sparkle in her eyes, she said hoarsely (horsely?)

"You haven't finished yet, Mister Horse. You know what boy horses are supposed to do to girl horses, don't you?"

She drew back and turned round, then leaned on him again, drawing his cock once more between her thighs, and holding it up against the smooth warm groove of her pussy with one hand. She began to bounce lightly on the bed, still holding his sex against hers, and Inglis grasped her breasts from behind.

"Giddup horsey!" she said again.

They trotted, then they cantered, and finally they went all out up the home straight. She pushed her buttocks hard back against him as he thrust forward, reaching, reaching. Inglis felt the muscles of her vagina contract round his striving penis as it exploded, having pulled the pin on the grenade of its own destruction. The shockwave of the explosion shook both their bodies, and they collapsed onto the bed locked together, and turning sideways. Even exhausted, Inglis managed to avoid collapsing on top of her, he was so afraid of crushing her fine slim body beneath him.

They lay side by side for a long time, neither of them speaking, her back to him, their bodies molded together as he hugged her, with her hands on his. Eventually they crawled under the sheet and lay face to face, comfortable and safe in each other's company. Kerstin spoke first.

"When we talked about ourselves before, you told me a lot about yourself, your father and your brother, and your home town and school; but you didn't talk about your mother. Is there something wrong with her? Or is it something you don't want to talk about?"

For a few minutes he said nothing, trying to make up his mind whether or not to go into detail. When she went to speak again, he put his hand lightly over her mouth.

"Wait, let me think a minute more."

Inglis hadn't discussed his life with his stepmother with anyone, not even his closest relatives. What she did to him was done mostly in secret, when no witnesses were around to support anything he said; and he was too wary to expect anyone to believe his word against hers. When he had tried to tell his father once, he had beaten the hell out of Inglis for 'lying'.

But something made him want to tell this girl in a foreign land all about it; the secrets he had kept. Finally he had someone who would let him get it off his chest at last..........

CHAPTER 17

Inglis started to tell Kerstin the secret story of his childhood...

"My mother left when I was two and a half years old. I can only vaguely remember her as a beautiful loving woman, and picture her on the last day I ever saw her. That was the day she left, with my father throwing clothes after her - that I remember. I was on hands and knees, peering through the living room door. It was during the War, and my father was rarely home. This time he had found her talking to a refugee land worker, and accusations had flown.

For a couple of years afterwards we had a procession of mediocre or just plain lousy housekeepers, most of whom couldn't care less. I can remember wandering round the streets in winter, when I was about three and a half, freezing cold and crying, wearing nothing but a torn vest. Another time one of the housekeepers stole everything of value she could carry, and disappeared while my father was away. It was days before the neighbors realized something was wrong, by which time my young brother and I were cold and hungry, dirty and frightened. I had been stealing milk from the nearest houses, but I couldn't leave my brother alone for long, because he was only a baby.

Often we went for days, or even weeks, without decent food, because the current housekeeper was stealing or misusing the food ration coupons. At times like these a mug of gruel was a treat. This comprised rough oatmeal - used for feeding the chickens - mixed with salt and water. I would gulp it down as if it was the best and last meal I would ever see. But it was crude stuff, and gave me worms - and that scared me too. I would go to the toilet, and watch all these squirming worms that had come from inside my body, and I would cry.

Then, just after the War, when I was five and a half years old, we got a housekeeper who was good, and we called her Auntie Jean. Things got better, and it was almost like having a mother, like most of the other kids. For nearly two years life was good, and I was happy. I had decent food and proper clothes - even if they were second hand - and the other kids didn't call me Ragbag any more.

Then one day my father married a widow, when I was seven years old. Her husband had been killed on a submarine during the war, and she had two sons, both older than me. Our good housekeeper was replaced by this big strong woman, who immediately began laying down the law. My father was now working on the opposite coast of Scotland as a foreman joiner, and was home only twice a month. On the day he was due home I would walk for miles along the road he used, until I met him coming the other way. He would scold me for it, but next time I would do it again anyway, walking for hours in the country, glad to be away from the terrible woman he had married.

Oh, she fed us well enough, which was one thing to be grateful for. But she set her heart on breaking my spirit, because I refused to bow to her bullying tactics. I would be beaten for the things I'd done, and for things I didn't do. At times I would make it worse for myself by taking the blame for things my younger brother did. He was eighteen months younger than me. He was different, and couldn't take her bullying. In the end he was put in a home for the mentally ill, because he couldn't take it any more. He's out again now, and the last I heard he was about to join the merchant navy too. In the meantime I tried to protect him from the worst she could do, and defied her to break me.

The more I would grin and bear it, the harder and more determined she became, but at least it focussed her nastiness on me, and away from my brother. Sometimes she came close to breaking me, but she never once saw me cry. She would beat me with her special belt - from a railway carriage window - until the blood ran down my back. Tie my hands and feet and lock me in a dark cupboard for hours on end. Once she tried to make me kiss her feet, and I spat on them instead, so she beat me nearly senseless once more. Another time she split my head open with a frying pan, and told the doctor I fell off a wall. Then I was badly scalded with boiling water" - Inglis showed Kerstin the scar - "an *accident* with the cooker. I developed boils and carbuncles, and she would put hot kaolin poultices on - deliberately too hot - and I would scream. When the poultices were taken off I would have burn blisters as well as the boils. She would sometimes hold my head under the water in the bath until I nearly drowned. At other times she would empty the bath in winter, and leave me standing there wet and freezing, and refuse to give me a towel.

One day, when I was ten years old, she caught me looking at a Blighty magazine my eldest stepbrother had brought home. In it was a photograph of a woman in a see through top. She tore the picture out and pinned it to the wall of my bedroom. Then she tied my hands behind my back with string, pulled my pants down, and clamped a clothes peg on my willy. She locked me in like that for hours, and it was nearly the death of my poor wee willy. She told the doctor I'd been playing with rubber bands, and I was too scared and humiliated to contradict her. When I slashed my elbow on a broken bottle, she 'tended' the gaping wound before taking me to the doctor - by scraping the bone with a kitchen knife. I nearly fainted from the pain. One time, when she was really angry, she picked me up and threw me into the wall - I told you she was a big strong woman. I hit the wall sideways, nearer the ceiling than the floor, and that time I *really* thought I was going to die.

I began to have nightmares, and would wake up screaming with terror in the middle of the night - and she would beat me for waking her. The nightmares lasted for years, at the rate of three or four times a week, sometimes every night for weeks on end; leaving me tired and shaken, and scared deep down inside. I wet the bed until I was eleven years old; and I was beaten for it, again and again. Time after time I ran away from home, sleeping in the council depot among the piles of waste paper, or on a bed of pine needles in the woods. And time after time the police would drag me back again.

Until one day the police inspector came to the house, and warned my step mother that his men were making enquiries about what went on between her and me. Our family doctor had finally summoned up the courage to lodge a report with the police that I was having far too many 'accidents', and my body was covered with bruises, boils and scars. The inspector made me take off all my clothes except my underpants, and looked at my body. It was the first time I ever saw a grown man crying, and he lifted me gently in his arms and cuddled me, like my father should have, but never did. Then he cursed and swore at my step mother, long and low; not loud, but strong and serious; and threatened to take me away. He asked me what had happened to me, but I was too frightened and ashamed to tell him anything, and I didn't want to be taken away to a strange place or an orphanage.

After that, things improved a little. She still abused me, but now she was more careful not to leave obvious marks. My uncles and aunts would make excuses for using me to do odd jobs at weekends, just to get me away from her. They had their own suspicions about what was going on, but never cross questioned me too much about it. Thinking back on it now, I think that maybe the police inspector had a talk with them, but I don't know for sure. They just tried to make me feel that at least somebody cared for me. I took my baby cousin for long walks in his pram, and even at the age of eleven I was an expert nappy changer.

On Sundays I would cut the grass at the hotel owned by another uncle, who had no children of his own. Sometimes he would let me watch television in the hotel lounge for a while. That was really something, because there weren't many televisions around then. And always, his oldest housemaid would pamper me with biscuits, and a hug and a kiss. She was quite old, and she usually smelled of sweat, but I loved it when she cuddled me, and told me how she would love to have a son like me. The same uncle let me 'credit' payment for the grass cutting, until I had enough money to buy his old bicycle, at a special price, when I was thirteen. That led to the best holiday of my life. For the whole of the school summer holidays, I cycled right round Scotland, with my tiny tent and frying pan. I snared rabbits, found pheasants' eggs, and caught fish to eat, and drank beautiful sweet clear water from mountain streams.

As I grew older, things weren't helped by the fact that I did better at school than my stepbrothers, in spite of the fact I was a lazy student. My English master once told me I reminded him of Thackery, which I thought a great compliment, until he continued - 'he was a lazy clever dick too!' But I was determined to get out of that house as soon as I could - and here I am. Not that she's hit me much in the past couple of years - she wouldn't dare any more.

I still occasionally have the old nightmares, but now I'm a free man, and I can sort out my own problems. There's more to the story, but that's the condensed version, and you're the first person I've ever told."

Inglis looked at Kerstin, and there were tears running down her cheeks. She hugged him close and hissed

"I could kill her! She is terrible, and should be punished."

"It's all over now Kerstin, thank God," Inglis said. "But I still can't bear to be around big strong domineering women. Which reminds me of something I meant to ask you. Do you remember the big officer who showed you to the dining saloon on the ship - Big John?"

"How could I forget such a giant of a man!" she answered.

"Well, that's the point Kerstin. He's so big that most girls are afraid to date him. And he's really a great man - kind and considerate, and even gentle in his own way. He has helped me a lot, and I would like to help him. I don't suppose you happen to know a really nice girl, who's big enough to put off most men, but would like to date Big John?"

She sat bolt upright in bed, and clapped her hands.

"I do!" she cried. "At the university in Goteborg I know a really nice girl called Hannah. She is good fun to be with, but she is even taller than Bjorne, and the men are scared to date her. But she is really good looking too, if you forget how big she is. Hannah is the girl I drove to the station on Friday. She is spending the weekend in Stockholm with her parents. When will you be in Stockholm? I must ring her in the morning!"

Kerstin looked happy at the prospect, and once more Inglis had that vague feeling of having seen her before somewhere, which he had already experienced a few times. He hated to disappoint her and spoil her plans.

"I'm sorry darling. But if things go according to plan, we'll arrive in Stockholm early on Monday evening, by which time your friend Hannah will be well and truly back in Goteborg. But it's almost certain the ship will sail back to Goteborg for another load after Stockholm, and that would mean being in Goteborg for next weekend. Then I can see you again. I didn't tell you before, because it's not definite, but that's what the Mate reckons, and he's usually right."

"Of course, I wasn't thinking right," she said. "What a pity. But never mind, we'll organize it for Goteborg next weekend. You'll be there, I just know you will. Now, my big teddy bear, let me be nice to you, and make up for that horrible nasty step mother of yours."

She put her head on his chest, as he lay back admiring the stars in the ceiling. They weren't just scattered randomly; Inglis could see a few constellations he recognized - damned clever. Then he looked at the trees silhouetted on the wall. What a marvelous bedroom to sleep

in. Slowly they made love, tender and complete, before they drifted off
to sleep, Kerstin's beautiful head nestling in his shoulder.

Inglis woke with a start to the sound of an animal. There was a deer
barking very close to him. The stars were dim, and a rosy glow was
showing through the trees, where the deer had barked.

"What the hell?" he shouted, sitting up in the clearing.

"Hi, Teddy bear," said Kerstin's voice in the bed beside him, and he
lay back chuckling as she asked "How do you like my alarm clock,
kind sir?"

"You're incredible, you know that?" Inglis replied, kissing her
forehead. "What time is it?"

"Six fifteen I'm afraid. No time for nice goodies. Breakfast will be
ready in fifteen minutes, and you will have to leave by seven fifteen to
get back to the ship in time. Just one cuddle before we get up?"

They hugged and kissed, and Inglis showed signs of arousal.

"Naughty boy," said Kerstin, throwing back the bed sheet and
kissing the 'naughty boy'.

"Enough!" she shouted. "Out, out! Come on, let's get ready for
breakfast. Last one in the shower's a rotten egg!"

In the shower Inglis looked at her beautiful small figure and perfect
features, and that feeling of having seen her before came back again.
Daft, unreal, he couldn't possibly have seen her, but there it was, and
the feeling was so convincing.

They bathed and dressed, and Inglis used the electric shaver as
Kerstin put on a touch of makeup. Why is it that women who don't
need makeup use it, and others who need it don't? A puzzle no mere
male could understand. They kissed before going downstairs to eat.
The maid had a table set, in a smaller room near the kitchen, not the
dining room where they had eaten the previous evening. The aroma of
cooking bacon and sausages made Inglis' mouth water as they sat
down. He had three rashers of bacon, a Swedish sausage and two eggs,
with toast and butter.

At least they were eating alone, though four more places were set at
the table. Inglis wasn't sure if he could look Kerstin's parents in the eye
right now, whatever she said. Still, this was Sweden, and he must try
to think Swedish.

No sooner had he thought this, than Mr. Larsen strode into the room, wearing a blue silk dressing gown. Inglis stood up, nearly knocking over the chair in his haste, and feeling his face flush as all his old fears and inhibitions flooded back to swamp his Swedish ambitions.

"Good morning," said Mr. Larsen cheerfully enough. "Sit down, sit down, and finish your breakfast. I just wanted a quick word with you before you leave. Did you sleep well?'

The blood rushed back to Inglis' face, as he tried desperately to think of what to say, and where to look. But his mind was a hopeless, numb blank.

"Sorry, that was a tactless question," added Mr. Larsen, his eyes actually twinkling. "I forgot for a moment you're not one of us. With your looks, and your opinions on other matters, you are more Swedish than a lot of Swedes. Which brings me to the point I wished to discuss. Coffee?"

"Yes please, sir," said Inglis, after clearing his throat twice.

"No need to call me sir, unless of course you feel more comfortable doing so. Though I must admit it's a great deal nicer than some of the things people call me." He smiled, openly and genuinely, and Inglis relaxed just a fraction as he stirred his coffee.

"You know, Inglis," continued Mr.Larsen, "you're an intelligent and presentable young man. You take the trouble to exercise your brain, and I'm surprised you're not at university, instead of sailing around in that ship of yours. But no doubt you have your reasons - and good ones too, if I'm not mistaken?" He raised his eyebrows, and Inglis nodded his head.

"Yes sir, I do, but they're rather lengthy."

"No matter for now," he said. "I'm sure they're good enough. But what I want to do is offer you a proposition. It's not easy for me to find the right kind of promising management trainees these days, for one reason and another. I would like you to think seriously about the opportunities my company could offer a young man like yourself. I don't expect you to give me any sort of an answer at the moment, or for a few months even. There's a prospectus in the car, describing the company and its products, employment opportunities etcetera. I would like you to take it with you on your ship and give it some thought.

Kerstin can fill you in on any other details. I'll leave you two together now. Have a safe trip, and come and see us again soon." He stood up, shaking Inglis' hand as he too jumped up.

"Thank you sir; and thank you for your hospitality."

"Good manners too. You'll do lad. It was a pleasure having you. Look after yourself, and call me whenever you like."

He turned abruptly and left the room. Inglis sat down in a daze, trying to catch up with all he had said. Kerstin leaned across the table, putting her hand on his.

"You really have made a good impression on Daddy. Almost as good as the one you've made on me, I'd say. He has never made an offer like that before, as far as I'm aware. Grandfather founded the company you know, and Daddy has carried on where he left off. They tell me he can be a hard boss if you do the wrong thing, but he rewards those who work well and help the company. Some of the bonuses he pays are legendary."

Inglis looked at his watch - nearly seven o'clock.

"Could we leave now, Kerstin?" he asked, "and maybe get Martin to drive slowly, or take a long way round, so we get to the ship about seven forty five?"

"Good idea!" she cried, kissing him before rushing off to tell Martin to get ready straight away. The car was available within five minutes. They snuggled together in the rear seat as Martin drove sedately towards the docks. Inglis glanced through Mr. Larsen's prospectus - very impressive, and a lot more paper than he had expected. Multo Machine Company of Malmo. He had heard of them. They made calculators and copying machines, and other office equipment. No wonder they were in a chauffeur-driven limousine; Multo was big and famous, and here was Inglis with the owner's daughter. Now the world was really turned upside down.

When they arrived at the docks, Kerstin insisted on coming out of the car to kiss him at the bottom of the gangplank, in spite of his pleas to the contrary.

"Don't take any notice of jealous people, Inglis," she laughed. "You worry too much. Let me worry instead." She gave him a long hungry kiss, and there wasn't a sound from the deck of the ship!

He turned at the top of the gangplank to wave goodbye as she climbed into the Mercedes, assisted by Martin. From the boat deck above Inglis came a shout.

"Goodbye Miss Larsen - hope we see you again."

Big John stood up there at the rail, waving his hat and smiling. Kerstin waved back to him, then blew a kiss in Inglis' direction.

"Hey Inglis, quick! Before you go on watch I've got something to show you. Come on up here at the double!"

He hurried up to his cabin, where John was waiting, with a copy of LIFE magazine looking tiny in his huge hand.

"Remember you mumbled something to me in the dining saloon about having seen Kerstin before?" asked John. "Well, of course you had - and so had I, *and* most of the rest of the crew, not to mention the rest of the bloody world. Tada, dadum!"

He held up the magazine in front of Inglis' face, folded open at a full-page advertisement. The ad was for the Multo Machine Company of Malmo, and was entitled 'Swedish Gymnastics'. There, two-thirds the height of the page, was Kerstin, dressed in a black leotard, posing with a large black ball in her hand. Inglis had seen the picture dozens of times, and thought how beautiful the model looked - and, thick as a brick, the penny hadn't dropped. It was now so obvious, Inglis wondered how on earth he could have been so stupid. The advert was so eye-catching in its impact and simplicity, and he had looked at it so many times, wondering what it would be like to meet such a girl - he *had*!

"Oh my God, how could I have missed it?" he muttered.

"Don't worry about it Inglis. You're only about the last man on the ship to recognize your own girlfriend. But they always did say love is blind. Now I know what they mean - and how!"

Inglis had wanted a picture of Kerstin. Now he had a bundle. Jimmy grinned from his seat at the desk they shared.

"It's okay Inglis, I've got them all here." He put his hand on a pile of LIFE magazines, and all three of them started to laugh, as Inglis struggled into his working uniform.

For the next two hours his mind was only half on his job, and he mucked up the final sounding as they finished pumping ashore. He just managed to get the donkeyman to shut off the pumps - against which Inglis had already closed the valve - in the nick of time. That earned him another lecture from the Mate, about paying attention to what he was doing, instead of dreaming about his girlfriend. Just so he wouldn't forget, he collected another two hours of scrubbing the deck in the wheelhouse. At this rate it would be the cleanest in the whole company. Inglis' tower had another dent in it.

They cast off at ten fifteen, and were soon on their way to Stockholm. The weather was now clear and dry - and very cold. As soon as they were in the open sea, Inglis took over the wheel, steering easily in the almost calm conditions of the Oresund.

Shortly before his trick ended, they encountered the first ice floes, as the ship rounded the southern tip of Sweden, and entered the Baltic Sea. They were to head south east for the rest of the afternoon, and pass round the south side of the Danish island of Bornholm. Here they would pick up the Baltic pilot, before entering the shipping channel through the frozen sea, kept open by icebreakers.

For two hours after coming off the wheel, Inglis did his penance on the wheelhouse deck, scrubbing away on his hands and knees. Much more and he thought he would make a good Moslem - whereaway Mecca?

He was on the monkey island for the balance of the afternoon, taking what bearings he could. He guessed Big John put him up there just so he could enjoy the view. The sun was remarkably bright, reflecting from the sea, and an increasing number of ice floes. In the distant north east he could make out the edge of the ice sheet closer to the Swedish shore.

By four o'clock the sun was starting to play some fantastic tricks, as it fell towards the western horizon. Through his binoculars he could see the armed guards in their watch towers along the coast of Rugen, in Communist East Germany - more than fifty miles away! The watch towers floated in mid air above the horizon, thrown there by a mirage effect. Inglis had heard all about mirages in the desert, but nobody had told him they happened in places like this. He could actually make out the shape of the guards, and the weapons in their hands, as they stood in their towers.

Not long before sunset they picked up the pilots and turned north east, steering for the edge of the vast ice sheet, now turning pink in the light of the setting sun. The pilots - there were two of them - would be with them for the next twenty-eight hours or so, until they reached Stockholm, guiding and advising as the ship made its way through the ice. They would use the spare stateroom behind the chartroom, standing the same watches as the ship's own officers, and alternating between the two of them - four hours on and four off.

When Inglis turned in for the night they had not yet reached the edge of the main ice sheet, though the sea was by now more ice than water, with the floes covering more than half the surface.

CHAPTER 18

At first light in the morning Inglis was out on the boat deck gazing at the ice. They were now well and truly in amongst it, and following the broken lane left by the icebreakers, between thick solid sheets stretching from horizon to horizon. He had a quick breakfast before returning to his spot at the rail, where he was joined by Jimmy - who seemed even more impressed by the scene than Inglis was. They looked and talked for half an hour prior to his first watch on the bridge.

When he reported to the Mate, he was told to go up on the monkey island for an hour, and just keep an eye open all round. The front windows of the wheelhouse were clouded over. One of the seamen, while hosing down the superstructure, had sprayed the windows, and a film of ice had formed on them before the water could run off again. The pilot and Mate could see the channel okay, but they couldn't see much farther; and they didn't want to stand on the wing of the bridge all the time. Even the Clearviews had a film of ice, since they had been stationary when the spray hit - no need for them to be going in bright clear weather. Finally, just before nine o'clock, the Mate called him down from his perch.

"For God's sake McAndrew, go and get a bucket and cloth, and see what you can do about cleaning the ice off these damned windows."

Inglis went in search of the bosun, and found him sitting in the paint store - smoking his pipe! Inglis shouted - the bosun was a bit deaf.

"For the love of God, bosun! What the hell are you trying to do - blow the bloody lot of us to kingdom come?"

He hadn't seen or heard Inglis' approach, and jumped as if stung by a hornet.

"Is okay, I know what I do," he answered, tapping the perforated metal lid on the bowl of his pipe, his head framed against the notice on the bulkhead behind him:-

SMOKING STRICTLY PROHIBITED

"Come on bosun, play the game," said Inglis.

"It's not okay. You know bloody fine you shouldn't be smoking in here. I don't want to make a fuss, but if the Old Man found out I didn't report you, and you went on smoking, it's my guts he'd have for garters, as well as yours. Put it out now, and the next time I catch you I *will* report you."

"Okay, sorry, I put out. You don't report. I getting old - don't get no more job if you report."

He walked to the fire hydrant, cracked the valve a fraction, and dribbled some water into the bowl of his pipe. It sizzled as the embers were extinguished, and he put it in his pocket.

"I won't say anything this time bosun, but don't make a habit of it. Because I mean it, I will report you next time, old and jobless or not, so don't try any old sweat bullshit on me. I'm not going to be blown to smithereens on your account, and you're bloody well old enough to know better. You're not too popular with the Mate as it is. One of your sailors sprayed the wheelhouse windows with the hose this morning. Now I've got to do my high wire act and get the bloody ice off them - got any bright suggestions?"

"That is dumb bloody Irishman do that. Paddy, he all the time one dumb senior hand. On my ship he don't get no senior hand. I make him junior asshole. Always he make for me the trouble. He steer, make you dizzy. Now you steer, he make trouble for you, so you watch out him, I telling you."

So that was what had been bugging Paddy the other evening. Now Inglis got the message - if he did something well, it made somebody else look not so good. *Tough shit Paddy*, thought Inglis, *I'm not going to stop doing my best just because it might put your nose out of joint - or anybody else's come to that. I've got enough problems as it is, with the things I'm NOT so good at.* The bosun looked at him shrewdly, and made an offer.

"You help me, I helping you. Something you needing - tomorrow, one month maybe, no matter - you come see me, okay?"

"Okay bosun," Inglis answered. "But right now I need to get the bloody ice off the wheelhouse windows for the Mate, remember?"

The bosun fitted him out, told him what to do, and how to do it. Inglis took the gear he was given - bucket, squeegee and rope - and went aft to the galley; where he persuaded the cook to part with a mug full of cooking salt, which Inglis dumped into the bucket. He then went back midships and half filled the bucket with hot water from the bathroom.

After that he mounted the internal staircase to the chartroom, through the wheelhouse, and out to the wing of the bridge. Once there he climbed cautiously over the rail next to the wheelhouse door, and onto the end of the narrow plank which ran along the front of the wheelhouse, three feet below window level - and forty feet above the deck.

He looked down once, and immediately regretted the impulse. Better to look sideways or upwards - it suddenly looked like a long, long way down to the foredeck. The plank was slippery with ice, having also received a soaking from Paddy's hose. This was *not* funny any more! He climbed back over the rail and put his feet firmly on the deck of the bridge wing. The Mate raised his eyebrows before Inglis stripped off his jacket and sweater, and rolled up his sleeves. Although the temperature was freezing cold, the sun gave an illusion of warmth in the clear dry air, and Inglis didn't feel too cold.

All along the front of the wheelhouse there were painted steel loops projecting from between the windows to act as handholds. He leaned over the rail and tied his short rope to the nearest hold, with the bucket balanced precariously on the rail, the other end of the rope tied round its handle. Then he carefully leaned out with the bucket in his hand, until it was suspended beneath the handhold.

Climbing over the rail, he balanced on the slippery plank, holding tight with his left hand, squeegee in the right. Once more it was one hand for the ship and one for yourself. The squeegee comprised a double-sided head about eight inches long, mounted at right angles to a short handle. One long edge of the head contained short stiff bristles, the opposite edge comprising a hard rubber blade. Inglis dipped this contraption in the hot salted water, and quickly ran the bristles up and down the height of the first window. Then he reversed it and scraped the resultant soft ice from the glass with the hard rubber edge. The first time he wasn't quite quick enough, and the ice hardened before he finished. He speeded up the action and got it right the second time.

His feet slipped, his heart jumped, and he grabbed for the next handhold with his right hand; letting go of the squeegee, which plummeted forty feet to the deck below. He looked down - and wished again that he hadn't, as his head swam. Young Jimmy was peering up at him from the forward rail of the boat deck, a worried expression on his face.

"Do me a favor Jimmy. Nip down and get my squeegee for me, would you please?'

"Okay Inglis," yelled Jimmy, with a wave of his hand before his head disappeared. While waiting for Jimmy to arrive, he climbed over the rail onto the bridge, leaned back over, and cut two feet off the free end of the bucket rope.

When Jimmy appeared, Inglis tied the squeegee to his own right wrist, allowing nine inches of slack - he was learning! Back onto the slippery plank he ventured, feeling that he must have offended Blackbeard the Pirate to suffer this. It took him more than half an hour to get rid of most of the ice from the windows - enough to please the Mate. Before he finished he was actually sweating in the sun, despite the fact that the air temperature was a long way below freezing.

He heaved a sigh of relief as he finished the last window. Untying the bucket from the handgrip, he turned towards the port side of the wheelhouse, being the nearer side - and he slipped! He grabbed for the handgrip and missed. His right foot was in mid air, and the left one slipped off the plank to join it as he overbalanced. His arms flailed around, his heart skipped a beat, and he was gone, heading for the steel deck forty feet below.

Oh shit, this is it he thought, trying to remember if his underpants were clean - and stopped dead, just as his head passed the plank. His right arm was almost wrenched from its socket. The squeegee, still tied to his right wrist, had jammed behind the plank as he flailed his arms. He looked down, and was giddy. He looked up, and saw the head of the squeegee already bending away from the handle. *Oh my God, isn't there anywhere else I can look?*

Inglis' right hand wouldn't move to get a grip on the plank - it was under too much pressure. He swung his left arm up, and got his hand over the outside edge of the plank. But his fingers slipped, and the squeegee wasn't going to hold out much longer. The head was coming away from the handle before his eyes. He swung his left arm up again

171

in desperation as the squeegee began to come apart. This time he aimed for the handle of the squeegee, between the plank and the front of the wheelhouse.

His hand closed round it, where the rope was tied on; and the head of the squeegee broke off, tumbling down past him to the deck far below. His eyes followed its dive, until his brain screamed DON'T DO THAT!

Now Inglis had his left hand gripped round the squeegee handle on the inside of the plank, and his right wrist tied to the other end of the short rope which passed over the plank between them. But there was no way he could climb onto the plank from this position. If he let go with either hand he was a goner. The Mate leaned round the corner of the wheelhouse.

"Hang on! There'll be a rope down from the monkey island in a couple of minutes."

Okay for you to say hang on, thought Inglis. *What the hell else do you expect me to do - let go?* Which was exactly what he would be doing soon, whether he wanted to or not. It was a very, very long two minutes, with his right wrist on fire, and both lots of fingers going numb. His recent life seemed to be cluttered with long minutes and short days.

Inglis closed his mind to everything except the absolutely imperative need to keep his left hand clutched round that handle. The rope ladder nudged his hip, and he stuck his right foot out. It found a rung, and he took some of the weight off his arms. But the rope ladder swung outwards under his foot. He couldn't let go his handgrip, or he would still fall to the deck.
Oh God, give me strength; let me hang on a little longer.
Moments later Aussie was on the rope ladder above him. He grabbed Inglis' right arm and shouted at him.

"Let go your left hand, and swing it over to the ladder - I've got you!"
Inglis was terrified to let go now. What if Aussie lost his grip? His hand stayed clamped round the squeegee handle as he looked down at the deck a long way below - and froze again.

172

"For Christ's sake Inglis," shouted Aussie again, "I've got you. I won't let you fall, God help me. Now LET GO!"

Inglis closed his eyes and released his grip - which he couldn't hold much longer anyway. For a heart-stopping moment he thought he was going down after all - a moment that lasted forever, as he seemed to float in the air. But Aussie had a good hold, and Inglis felt the rope ladder against his arm.

He opened his eyes and grabbed the side of the ladder, with both feet on a rung. He couldn't feel a thing in the hand gripping the ladder. Aussie grinned - he looked almost beautiful in Inglis' eyes right then - and shouted.
"Gotcha! Now up we go. Take your time, there's no hurry now. Move only one hand or foot at a time, and go right on up to the top, okay?"
"Okay Aussie," Inglis croaked.

Aussie stepped up onto the plank, and waited for Inglis to climb past him. Then he followed Inglis up the ladder to the monkey island. Every time Inglis gripped the ladder with his right hand, he had to look at it to make sure it was gripping, because he could feel nothing with it. Ginger pulled him over the rail of the monkey island, and cut the rope off his wrist. Some of the feeling began to return, and Inglis wiggled his fingers - all there and working!

The Mate was on the wing of the bridge when Inglis climbed down the steel ladder. He examined Inglis' wrist, and asked
"Are you okay? Can you still manage your trick on the wheel?"
Just try and stop me, Inglis thought. He was shivering from the reaction and the cold, but he answered straight away, before he could waver.
"Yes sir, I can manage."
"Okay, good man. Now off you go and get ready."

A sense of relief flooded through Inglis, and he felt lightheaded. He made a beeline for his cabin to change his shirt, on which the sweat was starting to freeze. He skipped down the outside steps to the boat deck, putting his hands on the rails, and vaulting the last few steps, just like a paratrooper. While still in the air he felt his right hand sticking

173

to the rail, then rip free before his feet hit the deck. There was a slight
tingling in his hand as he brought it up for inspection. He couldn't
believe his eyes! A strip of skin more than an inch wide and three
inches long was missing from the palm of his hand, and already the
blood was oozing out, mixed with a clear liquid like you get in a
blister. There was no real pain - yet.

"Shit!" he cursed "Just not my bloody day."
   He rushed to the cabin, where he smothered his palm with talcum
powder and tied a handkerchief round it. He changed his shirt and put
on a pair of gloves. There was no way he was going to miss his trick
on the wheel today - or any other day. In this weather he could steer
with one hand anyway.

He was on the wheel for ten minutes before the throbbing in his
hand reached its most painful, and it was all he could do just to keep
his face straight. Worse still, he could feel the blood building up and
soaking the glove. Every so often, when nobody was looking, he lifted
the hand across his chest to try and relieve the pain, while steering
with his left hand. But he had reckoned without the Mate's instinct for
knowing what was going on around him. At ten fifteen he strode
across, and without preamble demanded
   "Give me the wheel, then take off your right glove. I want to see
what the hell's wrong with that hand."

   "It'll be okay sir, honest. There's just a little bit of skin off it, and it's
smarting, that's all."
   "Don't argue with ME! Do as I tell you - NOW!" His voice was
like thunder, and Inglis jumped back from the wheel, answering "Aye
aye sir."
   Inglis took the left glove off with his teeth, before plucking
ineffectually at the right one, trying to drag it off slowly. But it was
sticking, and hurt like hell.
   "McAndrew, go below to the Chief Steward, and get that hand seen
to straight away," said the Mate.
   "I can steer with one hand, really I can sir, I'll be all right, I
promise."

Inglis almost wept with frustration, and he was worried the Mate
might think he was a wimp. Whatever else happened on this ship, he

wasn't going to give up steering without a damned good fight. The Mate might take him off it for good.

"DON"T ARGUE!" shouted the Mate. "Go and see the Steward right now, and get that bloody hand fixed. THEN come back and steer with one hand, if it means so much to you. I KNOW you can do it - RIGHT?"

"Right, sir....I mean, aye aye sir! Thank you sir."

Inglis ran off through the chartroom, where Jimmy was sorting out the flags in the locker, crouched on the deck, like a small Scrooge counting his money, flags strewn around him.

"Don't ARGUE!" hissed Jimmy in a stage whisper as Inglis passed.

"You'll keep," said Inglis, heading down the stairs to the Chief Steward's lair, which was next to his own; but with its door facing the stairs, whereas Inglis' was behind them.

When he got there, the Chief asked him first how he had done it, then picked up a pair of sharp scissors, and began cutting open the palm of Inglis' best glove.

"I hope you have another pair of good gloves laddie. But if not, I'm sure I can sell you a pair at a reasonable price."

"Okay Chief, but could you make it quick please? The Mate's on the wheel, and I don't want him asking the bosun for a replacement to take over my trick."

"I'll be as quick as I can," said the Steward, looking up at Inglis and adding "I said you were a funny one, and I was right. Or maybe daft would be a better description. I know plenty of men - on this ship - who would be asking me to get them off duty for half what you've done to yoursel' the day."

But he was as good as his word and washed, disinfected - *shit, that hurt!* - dressed and bandaged the hand in less than five minutes. Meanwhile he got Inglis to describe more exactly how he had done it. Inglis took pleasure in giving it to him in minute detail - complete with an artistic account of his gliding effortlessly through the air, like a bird on the wing.

"Okay, okay, enough!" shouted the Steward. "But you'd better tell the Mate how you did it - and I suggest you cut out the fancy bits, or he might send you back to me for some funny pills. These rails should have been lagged by now. Looks like the bosun's losing his grip. I think the old bugger's going soft in the head. He's been talking to himself a lot lately. Or maybe it's just that he's in his own country, and the tax man's looking for him. There's a lot of Swedes like that at sea. Now, off you go laddie, and be careful wi' that hand."

"Thanks Chief," said Inglis, scooting off to the bridge, where he told the Mate about the rails. He told Jimmy to take the bucket to the bosun - Inglis had forgotten all about it - and tell him to put a couple of seamen onto lagging the rails, before someone else lost some skin.

For the next hour and a half Inglis steered with one hand, the bandaged one stuck into the front of his jacket - just like Napoleon. Mind you he'd heard some lewd suggestions as to what Napoleon was doing with that hand!

The ice was no trouble at all. Occasionally a bigger and more solid floe would get in the way, hidden among the smaller ones. But the ship just brushed them aside contemptuously with the faintest tremor, which you could feel only if you were waiting for it.

It was much more fun to stand on the forecastle, looking over the bows as they plowed through the broken ice. Then you got the impression of power, and plenty of noise. The noise was continuous up there, as the thick chunks of ice ground against each other, crowding and pushing to get out of the way.

After his spell on the wheel Inglis did a couple of plots from the Decca for Big John, before climbing to the monkey island for a good look round. Far off above the horizon was a passenger ship heading south, sailing serenely through the air, upside down. The mirage gremlin was at work with a vengeance.

Spring would be coming soon, so the icebreakers were no longer flat out, most of the channels being kept open by the passage of the ships using them. Inglis didn't get to see an icebreaker doing her stuff on solid ice, unfortunately.

Before the end of his watch he went down to the chartroom to do another fix from the Decca. They were making better time than allowed for, and should be in Stockholm nearly three hours ahead of schedule at this rate. Maybe now the Old Man would start smiling again, instead of sending everyone running for cover when he appeared anywhere.

When Inglis left the bridge the ship was already entering the Stockholm Archipelago. Islands began appearing here, there and everywhere, looking for all the world like frosted ornaments on the icing of a huge cake. He just had time for a quick meal before his presence was required on the forecastle to prepare for the tug. They were approaching a cleft in a massive formation of igneous (He read that in a book!) rock, which rose about two hundred feet from the sea. After passing the line to the tug, they sailed through this cleft into a long fjord, where they berthed at a narrow dock projecting from the northern side of the fjord, backed by a small level area beneath the cliffs.

This was Kvarnholmen, and their cargo was being delivered to the Swedish Navy. On the way in they had passed huge caves in the cliffs, filled with the sea. The Mate told Inglis they were underground bases for submarines and patrol boats. He couldn't wait to get ashore and have a look for himself, and was soon on the dock in his good uniform.

He was told by an armed sentry that he was not allowed to visit the cave bases. However, he could go and look at the fuel storage tanks if he liked. Which was another thing he had noticed - there was a dock and a pipeline, but not a storage tank in sight.

The sentry directed Inglis to follow the pipeline - which made sense. There were two pipes, which disappeared into a cave at the foot of the cliff. Inside the cave was a reservoir tank into which tankers pumped their cargo. Massive shore pumps were connected to this reservoir, and they lifted the oil up along the face of the cliff on a narrow ledge. Inglis followed the ledge on its slope up the cliff face, being careful not to slip - he'd had enough of that for a while. The ledge was as narrow as three feet in places, which didn't leave much room for walking outside the pipes. But at least there was a substantial handrail.

At a height of about eighty feet above water level, the ledge widened, and there was the entrance to a huge cavern. Inside were the tops of the giant storage tanks, protected by fifty feet or so of rock roof. From these the fuel could be fed by gravity to the patrol boats and submarines in their caves. So, even if there was a complete power failure, the ships could still be refueled for as long as there was fuel in the tanks.

Inglis was impressed as he wandered round the vast cathedral in the living rock - and this was only the top; the bulk of the tanks was buried out of sight beneath his feet. It reminded him of the Ben Cruachan hydro-electric scheme in Scotland, where the main turbines were buried in the heart of the mountain. Now he could better understand what Bjorne meant about an aggressor receiving at least a bloody nose.

On the way out he stood for a moment on the ledge outside the entrance, looking down at the fjord. *Forth Venturer* didn't look quite so big from up here, though her masts still reached up above his eye level. The tug that had assisted her was now steaming up and down the fjord in the fading light, making sure the ice was broken. It looked like a toy boat afloat in a bubble bath.

It was time for Inglis to join Harry on the dock and keep his promise. Inglis was anything but keen to entertain the girlfriend's girlfriend, but a deal is a deal, so he would just have to grin and bear it. He'd told Harry the deal covered no later than one o'clock in the morning, and was for one night only. Big John had persuaded Inglis to do his watch as well as his own tomorrow, which meant Inglis would be on duty from eight in the morning right through until midnight - a sixteen hour stretch. John would then do both watches on Wednesday, and they should be ready to sail late on Wednesday evening.

When Inglis got to the ship, Harry was still on the telephone in the deck office. He hung up just as Inglis entered, and turned round rubbing his hands.

"Everything's set. The girls are at home and I've rung for a taxi to pick us up at the dock gate. We have a drink at the flat, then you take Linda to the movies or a club, while I stay home like a good little boy and entertain Ingga. And please don't bring Linda home before midnight. Okay - ready to go?"

They left the ship and walked up the steep road, which had been built to service the dock. It was wide enough for only one lorry to use, and rose very sharply up the cliff face, to the lowest part of the top. Inglis wouldn't care to be a lorry driver coming down it with a load, in the snow on a dark night.

The security gate was less than a hundred yards from the top of the ramp, and the taxi was waiting. It was about ten miles into the city, and Inglis was glad Harry was paying the fare. He held out his hand for the Swedish equivalent of fifteen shillings.

"I was hoping you'd forgotten about the money," said Harry. "You should really be paying me for this you know. Introducing you to a beautiful girl, providing transport, a bed for the night, even if you don't want it - and who knows, you might change your mind about that yet. Some blokes would pay a week's wages for all that, instead of wanting to *be* paid!"

"Not this bloke," says Inglis. "Pay up, or I find my own Linda, and you can get one of those blokes who are just dying to pay you a week's wages, Flash Harry!"

Harry put the money in his hand with a shrug and a grin.

"Can't blame me for trying though, eh? How's the hand?"

"I'll live," said Inglis, who was wearing the brand new gloves supplied by the Chief Steward - for a price.

Darkness had fallen when they arrived at the girls' flat - a two-bedroom affair on the fifth floor of a centrally heated block not far from the city. It was near the Sodermalm, on the southern mainland, most of the older part of the city being located on large islands.

Harry's girlfriend Ingga welcomed him with open arms, while the other girl and Inglis stood looking at each other. Harry introduced Inglis to both of them before they fetched some beer from the refrigerator. Ingga was very blonde, with even features, and a figure on the heavy side for Inglis' taste, but just right for Harry's. Linda on the other hand was slim, almost thin, with light brown hair, hazel eyes, and a slightly hooked nose; which was bigger than most people would have liked to live with. Nevertheless, there was something attractive about the way it all went together, and she certainly couldn't be called horrible. Her personality came through as cheerful and humorous, with an underlying sincerity. But the worst thing from Inglis' point of view

179

was that she was positively old – twenty-two or even twenty-three!

Inglis took Linda to a nightclub about a mile from the flat, where they swapped yarns. She was a nice woman, with a gentle sense of humor, and a lack of pretension. They danced once, though Inglis was a bit stiff and formal, conscious of the huge (!) differential in their ages and experience. She kept her distance in the dance too, almost as if she didn't like it, though she didn't say so. Inglis even managed to stand on her foot once, and broke some of the ice by apologizing.

"Sorry, I washed my feet today, and now I just *can't* do a *thing* with them!"

He was rewarded with a genuine enough laugh, but they didn't dance again. As the evening wore on Inglis became more comfortable and relaxed in her company. She didn't talk down to him or poke fun at his opinions. It wasn't that she appeared to descend to his level - he would have found that insulting. Rather, she drew him up to hers, imperceptibly coming to meet him on the way. Her father was a politician, and more than a little of the tact required for that profession seemed to have rubbed off on the daughter. More probably it was just an inherent part of her nature, passed on with the genes.

Whatever it was, by late evening she had him feeling they were contemporaries; discussing aspects of human behavior and relations Inglis had never really bothered much about before. He was being drawn out of himself in the most subtle manner. Oh, he'd had some long philosophical discussions with some of his masters at school. But they were mostly to do with subjects of study; logical progressions on abstract theories, taken to the limit of his cerebral capacity; frightening sometimes in their conclusions - or non-conclusions. Logic becoming illogical, lost in the impossibility of infinity, and the equally-impossible lack of it.

The whys and wherefores touched on by Linda were almost intangible, but nonetheless real. She played the game of guessing what people were thinking and feeling; what they did for a living; the things they might do next, and the way in which they might do them. Not just a vague wondering, the way she played, it was a game based partly on instinct, partly on experience, and the rest on good solid reasoning and appearances. The latter being split into outer and inner appearance -

apparent and veiled.

For a couple of hours they sat and discussed other people in the club - complete strangers unaware of their scrutiny - and the motivations with which they credited them. By attributing fictional life styles to their unsuspecting subjects, together with stated reasons, they probably found out more about one another's thinking and opinions than by discussing them directly.

The evening wore on, and all too soon it was time to take Linda home. What had started out as a drudge had turned into a pleasant and stimulating evening. Now Inglis had to 'dump' her, which would be difficult. It was never in his nature to hurt people who had been nice to him - he would just have to play it by ear. At the flat they stood outside the door finishing their discussion. Plucking up courage, Inglis moved to kiss her goodnight. She turned her face quickly away from his. Christ, was he that bad?

"Please," she whispered. "Don't do that."
"I'm sorry, I thought you liked me - my mistake."
"Don't take offense," she answered. "I do like you, and I enjoyed your company this evening. I don't often go out with men. It's not you, I just don't like men....that way. I can't stand to have a man touch me....or kiss me. It's just the way I am....sorry. But if a man ever does get to me, I suspect he'll be more like you than not...... goodnight."

She turned quickly, and was gone inside the flat, leaving Inglis face to face with the closed door. Christ, he hadn't come on that heavy - had he? No, bloody right he hadn't, so what got into her?

On the way back to the ship Inglis turned it all over in his mind, and in the end decided she was a lesbian. He wasn't really sure what a lesbian actually was, but he had a rough idea. What a shame; what a bloody awful wasteful shame, was his automatic chauvinist reaction. And she was so nice too, such good company. It surely was a funny old world, and Inglis seemed to be getting more than his share of its peculiarities lately. His reactions were in any case perverse. If she *had* asked him in, he would have said no as diplomatically as possible, because of his feelings for Kerstin. *We're a funny lot, us humans, right enough,* he thought.

But if Linda's a lesbian, how come she shares a flat with Ingga? Surprise, surprise, Harry!

Inglis was in his bunk before two o'clock, thinking about Kerstin, who seemed to be on his mind more and more - especially when he was licking his wounds or nursing his pride.

Tuesday was a very long day, after Inglis managed to drag himself out of bed at seven in the morning. With their slow but steady pumping rate, it would be about eleven o'clock Wednesday evening by the time they finished discharging the last of the cargo and cast off. The Mate confirmed they would be calling at Goteborg for another load, destined for Oslo, Bergen and Trondheim. Inglis waited until he was out of sight before going into a dance of joy.

Meanwhile there wasn't a great deal to do on watch, except check the soundings every half hour, and change tanks occasionally. Most of the time Inglis spent in the deck office, boning up on his Admiralty Manual of Seamanship, Volume 2. By the time he came off watch at midnight he was well and truly ready for his bunk.

On Wednesday he enjoyed the luxury of lying in until eight thirty. After a leisurely breakfast he caught up with his laundry and general housekeeping. Then he had an early lunch before going into the city at one o'clock. There was a bus service to Sodermalm, and he waited fifteen minutes for the next bus. As he waited, the snow began to fall; big fluffy flakes, becoming a heavy fall within minutes, swirling on a fidgety breeze.

Outside the dock gate were the modern Navy Quarters, blocks of apartments ten storeys high. There was quite a bit of activity, and four other people joined him at the stop before the bus arrived.

At Sodermalm - which was actually the name of an escarpment in the city - Inglis walked around in the snow, and was soon happily lost. The 150ft high rock face ran through this part of the city. He saw a garage built into the rock, reminiscent of the tanks at Kvarnholmen. From the top of the sheer wall of the cliff, a footbridge spanned the road far below, to the roof of a huge multi storey block of buildings. The roof of this vast block was laid out like a park, with walkways and empty flowerbeds.

On one corner of the block there was an outside elevator, which Inglis took to the street below; fascinating, especially as the sides of the elevator were made of glass from waist height up. He wandered around in the snow for another half hour, before catching a tram to the city proper. There seemed to be bridges and tunnels everywhere. This was the real Venice of the North, and he enjoyed the tram trip, which was more like a metro, as it dived underground every so often.

Inglis left the tram near the Royal Palace, with its modern guards carrying sub machine guns, and flapping their arms to keep warm. He walked for hours in the heavy snow, looking at the old buildings, including St. Nicholas Cathedral - built in the thirteenth century, not long before the one back home in St. Andrews. Actually, the Swedish one was started nearly a century later, and finished sooner. The Swedes must have had more money to spend in a hurry. Standing on higher ground Inglis could see the ships, boats and ferries on the very busy waterways and lakes, where the ice was given no chance to form a solid sheet.

After dark he found a pub, where he enjoyed a few beers, while idly watching the people, and thinking of Kerstin. Smoking - he'd just started yesterday - and thinking of Kerstin. He had really fallen head-over-heels in love with that beautiful, clever, fascinating young lady.

A man in his thirties struck up a conversation with him, in almost flawless English. He was a ferry Captain, having a beer after his shift. They bought each other a couple of rounds as the pub filled up. After the third round Inglis had bought, his new friend excused himself for a visit to the toilet. Ten minutes later he hadn't returned. His beer was less than half drunk, but Inglis' was finished, so he ordered one for himself. When the waiter brought it, Inglis put his hand in his pocket - his wallet was gone! Inglis searched around the padded bench seat and under the table, as the waiter watched, but there was no sign of it.

He told the waiter what had happened, and the waiter took him over to the corner of the bar, where the manager quizzed him. As they spoke, an elderly man came up and interrupted them. In his hand was Inglis' wallet, which he had found in the toilet. Inglis took it from him with thanks, and searched frantically through it. Everything was still there - except his money, not one note of which was left. The manager told him to drink the beer he'd ordered, compliments of the house, while he called the police.

The time was already nine o'clock, and Inglis should start making his way to the ship soon. But the manager assured him the police would arrive within minutes. It was actually about twenty minutes before they turned up. They then questioned Inglis for ten minutes in the manager's office, before asking him to accompany them to the police station. From the description Inglis had given them, they had a fair idea of the thief's identity. They said he was usually much more careful, but had probably thought that, since Inglis was a foreign sailor about to leave, he would just give up and go away, especially as he'd left everything else where it would be found soon. Therefore Inglis wouldn't bother to report the theft, because of the inconvenience of police statements and so on. Inglis told the policemen they weren't far wrong, as he already regretted their arrival.

"I'm sorry" he said, "But if I don't leave soon I'll miss my ship, and I can't afford to let that happen."
"Don't worry," the larger one replied. "We will ensure you get back to your ship before it sails."
Why did Inglis always worry as soon as someone said 'don't worry'?

Their patrol car was outside, and it took only five minutes to reach the police station, in a narrow street near the Palace. It was now ten o'clock, and Inglis explained to the sergeant about the imminent departure of his ship. He took the particulars, and rang the dock while Inglis went through some large books of photographs, looking for his 'friend' from the pub.

The sergeant told him it would take less than half an hour to drive him to the dock, and the policemen who had brought him would deliver him there after he had looked through the 'photo albums'. Meanwhile one of the patrol car men was typing and asking him occasional questions. After a while the pictures all started to look alike, and Inglis was sure he had forgotten what the man at the pub looked like. This was annoying the hell out of him, so he spoke to the taller policeman.

"I thought you said you knew who the thief is? I've looked at hundreds of pictures and I can't see him. Where's the one who did it - or did you think wrong?"

"You must be patient for just a little longer Mr. McAndrew. That is not the way it is done. We cannot show you a picture and say 'is that him?' You must find the picture and tell us."

He had an amused expression on his face as he said this, and Inglis very soon found out why. No sooner did he turn back to the book, than the thief's face leaped out at him from the very next page he turned.

"That's him!" Inglis shouted, pointing at the picture.

"Are you sure?" asked the sergeant.

"Positive! If I had any doubts, the mole on his nose confirms it as far as I'm concerned. Now, could you please get me back to my ship, before it sails without me? There's only half an hour left, and I doubt if it's possible to make it in that time."

"Okay," said the sergeant. "But maybe you'd like to see the name your driver wrote on a piece of paper in his pocket?"

The shorter of the two policemen produced the scrap of paper. On it was written the name under the picture Inglis had just picked out. Inglis glared at the policeman angrily.

"You mean you let me look through two whole books of pictures to find this one, when you knew all the time where it was?"

"Don't be annoyed. That is the way we have to do it I'm afraid. Now, if you'll just sign this statement, as soon as the man's name is typed in. He's a known pickpocket and purse snatcher. But this is the first positive identification we've had on him in at least ten robberies we know he carried out."

The patrol car man finished his typing, and gave Inglis the statement to sign. He didn't bother trying to read it, as he was in too much of a hurry to get going - and anyway, it was in Swedish!

The trip to the docks was the most hair-raising ride Inglis had ever had in any type of vehicle. They slipped and slithered away from the police station, light flashing and two-tone siren screaming ahead of them. The police Volvo had snow studs in the tyres, but still it skidded at every intersection, as the driver seemed to actually enjoy dicing with death. The snow was falling thick all around, almost clogging the powerful windscreen wipers. The lights of other vehicles flashed by -

on both sides of them - as the police driver used all of the road; forcing oncoming traffic to the side more than once.

At one intersection the car started to spin. Instead of fighting it, the driver just let her go all the way round before catching it, and tearing off again, cool as a cucumber. His Mate in the front passenger seat didn't seem to be the least bit worried either. On he went, swerving from side to side of the road, weaving in and out of the traffic, which thankfully was thinning out as they cleared the city. At one stage he made a broadside turn onto a bridge, the car sliding sideways for so long, Inglis was sure they were going over the edge into the water. But he had it under control at the last second, and they screamed across the bridge - on the wrong side of the road! Inglis hung on for dear life in the rear seat, wondering if he should just close his eyes. But he couldn't close them, staring about him as one near-accident followed another, his heart in his mouth. The dock gate was open when they arrived, and the police car sped through without even slowing, flashing light and siren announcing its arrival.

Then the police driver broadsided the car again, onto the top of the steep ramp leading down to the dock. This time Inglis thought they were finished for sure. He could have sworn his heart gave up beating in disgust as he stared in horror, the edge of the 150ft vertical drop coming closer and closer. There was no way the flimsy fence would stop them from skidding over the edge. A moment before the car would have gone sideways through the fence and flying into space, the right wheels hit a raised kerb at the side of the road, hidden by the snow. The car lurched to the right, its left wheels lifting from the road as it tipped over. Then they slammed down again, and the car was hurtling down the ramp - the same ramp Inglis had thought earlier he would hate to drive down in the dark and snow. Now he *knew* he hated it.

Inglis could see *Forth Venturer*, floodlit below them through the snow, ropes already singled up fore and aft; two sailors standing by the gangplank, and the tug in the process of taking the tow-rope from the poop. The police car shot down the ramp, and he wondered how the hell Boy Wonder was going to stop in time at the bottom. But when nearly there, the driver turned the steering wheel once more, and they skidded sideways towards the gangplank, stopping a few feet short, as

186

Aussie dived for cover. Never again would Inglis hitch a lift in a Swedish police patrol car. He ran up the gangplank, then helped the sailors pull it inboard. Unlike some ships, they used their own gangplank most of the time, rather than shore ones. Before the end was inboard, the Skipper called through his bullhorn from the bridge wing.

"Let go aft!"

Moments later the ship's side moved away from the dock. A two-tone blast came from the police car's siren, and two gloved hands waved from the front windows. Inglis waved back, muttering "Thanks - I think!"

CHAPTER 19

Once the gangplank was secured, Aussie told Inglis he was to report to the Skipper on the bridge. Aussie then went to the poop to lend a hand there, while the second sailor made tracks for the forecastle, where Big John had taken Inglis' place.

Inglis stood on the port wing of the bridge, staying out of everyone's way, and watching what went on. This was his first time up here while entering or leaving port, being normally on duty on the forecastle. The Skipper passed his orders by bullhorn, while the pilot signaled his instructions to the tug via their huge steam whistle.

Inglis was particularly interested in watching the actions of the helmsman Elvis, who was being instructed by the pilot. The Skipper had told Inglis to stay out of the way until they released the tug, then see him in his day cabin behind the chartroom.

At 11.30pm Inglis knocked tentatively on the Captain's door. The tug was gone, and he'd waited a couple of minutes after Captain Evans left the bridge before following him.

"Enter!" boomed the big voice from the small body. When Inglis walked in he was sitting at his big office desk, beside which Inglis stood up straight before saying

"Reporting to you as ordered sir."

"Okay McAndrew. Take off your hat and sit down for a minute. Then tell me, as briefly as possible, what happened to you tonight, and why you were late reporting back on board."

Inglis sat down opposite him and went quickly through the salient points of his misadventure, leaving out the smaller details.

"Yes, that's more or less what the police said on the telephone," said Captain Evans, closing the Captain's Log on his table. For a while Inglis had thought he was going to make an official entry about him being late. He'd probably just finished entering their departure time.

"Well, it's getting bloody late, so I'll keep this short and sweet. The Mate tells me you're making good progress in most areas of your training and studies, and are already as proficient in many things as most cadets your age who have been at sea for more than a year. I just wanted you to know that's the basis of his monthly report on you. But I don't want it going to your head. I want you to keep it up. Don't slack off and relax because you think you're getting ahead. The Mate will be leaving us soon for his own command, but I'll be watching you. The Mate has also recommended that you stand both watches at sea with the Third Mate, doing a two-hour trick on the wheel during each watch. This is a little unusual for a cadet who has been at sea for such a short time. But the Mate tells me you have a natural bent for steering. What's more, one of the ship's regular helmsmen seems to have no aptitude at all. However, the choice is yours. You want to take it on?"

Inglis didn't hesitate for even a moment.
"Yes sir, I'd be more than happy to sir."
"Okay, that's fixed then. But remember I'll be watching you. Start backsliding, and I'll have you scrubbing decks, and chipping and painting before you know what's hit you. Your trick on the wheel tonight is from two until four. That's all."
He waved his hand in dismissal, and Inglis stood up.
"Thank you sir. I'll keep trying my best. Good night sir."
"Good night - and close the door behind you!"

Inglis went to his cabin, relieved and elated at the outcome of his interview - which he had originally thought might be for a reprimand. It was the longest conversation he'd had with the Skipper since setting foot on board. He started going over the details, and it dawned on him that the man he would be replacing on the wheel was almost bound to be Paddy. He was a senior hand, and as such he was a watchkeeper. There were three watchkeeping senior hands - Paddy, Aussie and Elvis. If Inglis replaced Paddy on the wheel, he would be put on day work; which meant he would be in charge of a party of sailors doing all the normal cleaning, painting, scrubbing etc which went on incessantly on a ship at sea. He would *not* be happy.

By the time Inglis took over the wheel at 2am they were clear of the Stockholm Archipelago, and in the south-bound channel through the ice, which curved to the east of the north-bound one. There was very little ice in the channel itself. The night was moonlit and silent, almost eerie as they glided between banks of white. The reflection of the moon's light from the ice and snow made the night like anemic half day. Sounds were muffled, even their own engine seeming unusually

189

quiet. On the bridge they were almost tempted to whisper.

The yacht was in the wrong channel, and therefore going the wrong way. For some reason it was showing no lights. It was also painted white, with white sails, making it almost invisible against the ice and snow. If it had been bigger it might have shown up on the radar screen during one of the periodic checks. It appeared from nowhere - a phantom suddenly become solid in their path. Already too late before Inglis spotted it. A fleeting impression of white moving on white was all he saw, an instant before the reality of collision. The not quite imperceptible impact, as the tanker's bow wave pushed the puny vessel almost clear of her plates - but not far or fast enough.

A swarm of sounds invading the near-silence of the night. The yacht's mast snapping, her rigging becoming entangled in the tanker's foredeck railing, while her hull scraped along the much larger vessel's plates, abandoning ropes and sails to Forth Venturer's *clutches as they were ripped from her. A frightened face looking up at Inglis as it raced past, the yacht heeled far over, rails beneath the water.* Inglis spun the wheel to starboard for five seconds, then back amidships. It just might help to save them, he didn't know for sure - but it was all he could do for them. With a bit of luck the ship's stern - and prop - would side step them. The deflection of her wash by the rudder over to starboard might just push them clear.

Big John rushed over to the engineroom telegraph and rang down STOP ENGINE. Then he ran to the whistle handle, pulling it quickly several times, and the ship began to come alive.
Grabbing the engineroom telephone, John called for a slow buildup to FULL ASTERN, after checking that the yacht was well clear of her screw.
"That was a very smart bit of thinking young man," said the pilot to Inglis. "I think they owe you their lives. Most people would have instinctively put the helm over the other way."

The Skipper appeared in his pajamas, and was quickly on top of the situation, discussing it with the pilot. Elvis arrived to take over the wheel from Inglis just as the Skipper shouted.
"Launch number two lifeboat!"

That was Inglis' boat, and the only one of the four fitted with an engine. Aussie appeared, and between them they scrambled over the boat, stripping off the cover as others arrived to help. The davits were released and tilted outboard, taking the boat clear of the deck. Big John was now in charge, the Skipper having taken over the bridge. John, Inglis and Aussie were in the boat as she started down towards the water. The Third Engineer jumped in after them, his job to look after the engine, which he had going in double quick time. It was running before they were near the water.

Next came the dangerous and tricky bit. The ship was still making about eight knots through the water, and they had to release the boat's cables from the davits at exactly the right moment. If they hung up one end, they'd be swamped in the blink of an eye. All four of them had thrown on their life jackets, but Inglis hadn't yet had time to tie his.

He had his hand on the forward slip, watching Big John like a hawk, and praying he would get it right - they had only practiced this once - while standing still. Aussie stood at the after slip, every bit as tense-looking as Inglis; who wanted to look at the water to see how close they were. But he daren't take his eyes off John for an instant - he even blinked them one at a time! *Please God, don't let it jam.* Inglis pressed lightly and carefully upwards with his thumb - it was okay. He could feel the slight give of the keeper link. John's arm was in the air, as he stared at the water, an occasional ice floe cruising past - don't let one of those hit them either. His hand was circling slowly, signaling to the davit crew. Now Inglis could hear and feel the sea on the bottom of the boat.

Big John's hand chopped downwards. Inglis jammed the keeper hard upwards with the end of his thumb and the back of his forefinger, with his palm clear of the hook. The boat settled in the water, a bow wave appearing before it; the gap widening between it and the ship as the Third Engineer held the tiller a touch to port, with the boat's screw already threshing the water to maintain its speed, and keep the bow up. Bloody perfect! They had just carried out an immaculate lifeboat launching on the move!

John took over the tiller, and curved the boat sharply round to starboard. Inglis heaved a sigh of relief and looked round for the yacht.

Then he grabbed the big torch and handed it to Aussie, for John in case he needed it. They could see the yacht in the moonlight, about three quarters of a mile away, her deck awash, but still - just - afloat.

John passed the torch back to Inglis with a message - stand up in the bows and guide him clear of any big floes. Thankfully there were not many, but twice on the way to the yacht Inglis signaled avoiding turns.

There were three people on the yacht's deck, now only inches above the surface. She wouldn't last much longer, but they were nearly there. Two of the people on her were women - and none of them was wearing a life jacket! As they drew close they could see two young women, with a man not much older than them. The other thing they saw was that the water was now round the yachtsmen's ankles - she was going down at any moment.

They went as close as they dared - it wouldn't help if they got caught up in some of her ruined rigging - and threw the only two life buoys in the boat, retaining the ends of the ropes tied to them. The two girls put the life buoys round their waists, and were pulled to the boat by Aussie and the Third Engineer. Meanwhile the man was panicking as the yacht disappeared beneath his feet. Inglis stripped off his life jacket and hurled it to him as the water passed his knees. It landed just within his reach, and as he slipped it on, Big John threw him a spare line. They had to get the yacht's crew into the boat as quickly as possible. More than a few minutes immersed in that freezing cold water and they would be as good as dead.

The girls were in the boat first, water running off them as *Forth Venturer*'s men stripped their clothes. One of them put up a slight struggle in the name of modesty, but Aussie just ripped the clothes from her back and wrapped her in a blanket, quick as a flash. Then they hauled the man on board, and he was in a bad way, almost frozen. The yacht was gone without trace, and they sped back to the ship at top speed. They had farther to travel now, as the ship was still moving slowly forward, in spite of the engine going full astern.

The ship's screw stopped threshing the water as they drew alongside ten minutes later. The female passengers were shivering, but at least they were talking, and taking some interest in things. The man was almost comatose; pale as death, with a blue edging to his lips, and a glassy look in his eyes. They had put an extra blanket on him, and stood him up, with Aussie and Inglis wrapping their arms round him - like three queers dancing close!

Being in ballast, the ship was riding high in the water, and the quickest way to get everyone on board was to hoist the boat up to its davits. *Forth Venturer* was almost stopped now, and it was no hard task for them to hook the davit lines on in the calm weather. The rest was up to the davit crew, and Inglis was relieved to see the Mate up there - he wouldn't let them be tipped out.

The recovery went without a hitch, and the shipwrecked sailors were soon having a hot shower. The man was put in a bathful of warm water, and by the time he recovered, Inglis' watch was over, and John and he had a beer in John's cabin.

"I've got something serious to tell you, Inglis," said John over the top of his glass. "The Skipper told me to give you a bullocking for removing your life jacket - *and* for not having it tied right in the first place. Consider yourself well and truly bullocked - cheers!"

"Cheers John, and many thanks for the bullocking."

Big John's face split open in a huge grin.

"The only reason he told me to give you the rocket, instead of doing it himself, is that he'd probably have done the same thing himself. And so would I if you hadn't been so quick - *mine* was tied. Cheers again, and screw the rules. They were made to be broken by common sense sometimes. And incidentally, that was bloody quick thinking of you to put the rudder over to starboard when you did. If you hadn't, I think they would have been goners before we could get to them. I told the skipper, and he said to include that in my report - and give you a pat on the back to go with the bullocking. I think we put on a fine show of seamanship all round, though I say it myself – cheers again."

"What I can't understand John, is why the silly bugger was sailing his yacht the wrong way along the channel in the first place - and with no lights!"

"That's easy," was John's reply. "He just wanted to find out what happens when you drive the wrong way up a one-way street - now he knows! Seriously though, I suspect that whatever he was smuggling is

193

now entombed on the bottom. Cheers once more!"

Inglis' thoughts were constantly on Kerstin as Goteborg drew closer. Paddy was becoming a problem. Twice more he had made derogatory remarks in Inglis' hearing, and once on the deck he 'accidentally' barged into him from behind, knocking Inglis to the deck. He wasn't sure how to handle this. Have it out with Paddy and have him claim ignorance? Or ignore him, and hope he would grow tired of the whole thing? For the moment Inglis tried to ignore him, but much more and he might have to ask Big John's advice. They were making good time, and once again they were heading for an early arrival, in spite of the incident with the yacht. Incident to them that is - disaster to the yacht's crew. The survivors had recovered quickly after their warm showers and bath, and had left in the pilot boat at Bornholm.

The original estimate of the ship's arrival time in Goteborg was 11pm Friday, but when they entered the Kattegat it was obvious they would dock not much after eight o'clock - barring further incidents. There was no incident or accident, and they picked up the Goteborg pilot at 7.45. By 8.15 they were pumping ballast, which would take about six hours before they could start loading. Their estimated sailing time was 10 o'clock Sunday morning. Waiting on the dock as they berthed was Kerstin - with a friend. From the size of the friend Inglis guessed she had brought Hannah to meet Big John. How she knew their arrival time was a bit of a puzzle; but with her father being who he was, he could probably find out just about anything.

Inglis waved to them as the ship tied up. As soon as he was finished on the forecastle, he rushed to the deck office to find John. Inglis hadn't told him anything about Hannah yet! He hadn't wanted to be premature, and then have a disappointment. John was studying the loading plan as he entered the deck office - and the bosun had a couple of sailors preparing the gangplank.

"Quick John, listen and don't interrupt. Kerstin's on the dock, and she's brought a friend to meet you. I didn't know if she'd make it until now. Sorry to spring it on you like this. Her name's Hannah, and Kerstin says she's really nice. I'll swap watches with you tomorrow if you like, and you can go ashore with Hannah tomorrow night - okay?"

For a few moments John was nonplused, and at a loss for words. Then he recovered and grinned. "Okay Cupid, I'll go along with that."

Inglis rushed to the gangplank just as the sailors finished placing it. The company's agent was also on the dock, so Inglis waited for him to come aboard before running down the gangplank. Kerstin hugged and kissed him before introducing him to Hannah, who certainly was tall. She wore flat heels, but still she must have been around six feet seven or eight, making Inglis feel once more as if he had suddenly shrunk. Standing beside Kerstin she looked huge - or Kerstin looked tiny.

And yet, as Kerstin had said, if you put Hannah in a swimsuit and took a photograph of her, with nothing to give scale, you would say she was a normal attractive young woman. Her hair was mid brown, with a distinct red reflection in it. The green eyes were set in an oval face, with a straight nose in proportion. When she smiled the effect was quite startling, and had she been a foot shorter she would have had no trouble at all getting plenty of dates.

Inglis ushered the two girls up the gangplank, and led them to the deck office, where they had to wait a few minutes while John spoke to the donkeyman. Hannah and Big John were quite shy with each other for the first few minutes, while Kerstin and Inglis encouraged conversation. But Inglis was sure there was an immediate spark between them - he could sense it as he watched them. And seeing them standing together, it was as if someone had waved a magic wand, and brought them both to average size. Big John was a good eight inches taller than Hannah, and beside him she looked almost petite.

Inglis suggested Kerstin and he have coffee in the dining saloon, and meet the Mate's wife, while John and Hannah got to know each other. The Mate's wife had finally caught up with them in Stockholm, having missed them completely in Copenhagen. She had arrived in Stockholm on Tuesday morning, and accompanied the Mate to the opera the same evening.

Less than a day after joining the ship, she had 'adopted' the two cadets - Jimmy more than Inglis, since he looked much more in need of adoption. But she had heard all about Kerstin from the Mate, and insisted on meeting her. Meanwhile John and Hannah could have a talk by themselves for half an hour or so.

As they entered the corridor Inglis took a quick look round to make sure nobody was in sight, before wrapping his arms round Kerstin.

"What a clever little lady you are. Hannah is beautiful, and they look perfect together. But I should spank you for not telling me about your picture in LIFE magazine. They were all waiting to tell me when I got back to the ship in Malmo."

She laughed briefly before they kissed for long moments, holding each other tight, and warming to one another's closeness. There was a discreet cough behind them, and they flew apart. The Mate and his wife stood in the corridor, the Mate's eyebrows raised, his wife's hand over the lower part of her face, stifling a grin. She was an attractive woman, about ten years younger than him, in her mid thirties.

"Oh, excuse me sir," Inglis said. "I was just bringing Kerstin to meet your wife, when she got something stuck in her mouth!"

That got them both laughing, and he made the introductions before the mood could fade. The Mate condescended to sit with them at Inglis' table, which had four places, only three of which were ever used. The other place was for the Fourth Mate they didn't carry. The Old Man would have had a hairy fit if the Mate had invited Inglis to sit at HIS table! They made small talk for a while, before the Mate's mate said to Kerstin

"I saw your picture in LIFE, and I must say you're even lovelier in real life, which is unusual. Have you ever thought of modeling as a career? I was a fashion model, and still do a little now and then."

That started a long conversation on modeling, during which Kerstin said her father wanted her to stay at university, where she was studying business administration. He would use her as a model for the company, and she was quite happy with that. Then the conversation turned to the subject of Hannah - who was studying Marine Architecture - and how unfortunate it was that men were afraid of her height. At that stage the Mate chipped in.

"What are your plans now, Inglis?"

Inglis said he and Kerstin were going to a dance at the university tonight; and Inglis was swapping duties with Big John so he could have tomorrow evening ashore with Hannah, who was going to the dance with them tonight. The Mate raised his eyebrows across the table and his wife nodded slightly.

"I think we just might be able to do a fair bit better than that - don't you my dear?" he asked his wife.

"I'm quite sure we can darling," she replied.

"You have been doing a good job Inglis, and so has John. I've had an easy passage lately because of your efforts, with most of my time free in port, when I would usually be rushed off my feet. You have no idea what a relief it is to have keen and competent men under you - I know, I've had some beauties in my time, I can tell you. What I propose is that the Second Mate and I divide the cargo watches between us during our stay in Goteborg. He has already told me he has no intention of going ashore. And he's due for his Mate's appointment at the same time as my new command, so I'm taking him with me. Now, I suggest you young people get yourselves organized, while I change into my disused working clothes. I have a feeling it may be a long time before you see Goteborg again Inglis, so make the best of it. Off you go and tell the Third Mate I'll take over the watch in ten minutes."

Inglis stood up from the table, hardly able to believe his ears. This was unprecedented, as far as he knew.

"Thanks sir. I don't know what to say.....how to thank you."

"Just go on trying to do your job to the best of your ability Inglis. That will make me quite happy," answered the Mate, leaving the table. Inglis followed him through the door, after talking to Kerstin.

"I won't be long. I'll change now, and John can change as soon as the Mate takes over. I'll bring Hannah here before I go and get ready."

He skipped along the corridor, rushing to tell Big John the unbelievable news. Unbelievable was right - Inglis had to go over it three times before John would believe he wasn't having his leg pulled. Hannah was overjoyed, which was a good sign. Inglis escorted her to the dining saloon, where he left her in the company of the other ladies, while he sped upstairs to bathe and change into his dress uniform.

John passed him on his way into the bathroom as Inglis came out - he'd been quick. What's more, John entered the saloon just two minutes behind him - he *was* keen. They were in Kerstin's car by nine o'clock, and at the university before nine thirty, having caught the ferry just before it left their side of the river. Hannah drove the car, with Big John beside her. There just wasn't enough room for them in the back, where Kerstin and Inglis snuggled up quite comfortably.

At the Union they met a few of Kerstin's friends Inglis had met before, and some new ones. There was a dance nearly every Friday evening, for those students who were not going away for the weekend.

John was introduced to everyone, and some of Hannah's friends could be seen giving her a little dig, and casting meaningful glances in his direction. It turned out that both John and Hannah had taken top class dance lessons, though neither had found much opportunity to put them into practice. But when they danced together, they clicked immediately, sweeping round the dance floor, their heads showing above the rest, marking their progress.

The band struck up a tango, and the tallest couple in the room stepped into it as if they had been dancing together for years; flowing and pausing, turning and reversing, until the other dancers cleared a space for them, and stood watching. There was a roar of approval when the music finally stopped. John and Hannah came back to the table hand-in-hand, Big John's face flushed and happy, Hannah's like that of a little girl who just found a real live fairy at the bottom of her garden. Before they reached the table Inglis took Kerstin's hand.

"Shake pardner. I think we really got something going here, don't you?"
He kissed her nose as she beamed happily. John sat Hannah in her seat before sitting down next to her, as close as he could get. They held hands under the table as John spoke.
"Hey, Inglis, I don't know how you managed to swing things with the Mate, but thanks a million. As for you Kerstin, where on earth did you find this gorgeous beautiful woman?" - Hannah blushed - "I can't remember when I ever had such a great time at a dance."

"Hell, we haven't even started yet John," said Inglis. "We've got nearly thirty-six hours free and clear ahead of us. Let's make the best of it and enjoy ourselves. Kerstin says we have to see the sights of Goteborg tomorrow in her car; maybe even go for a drive in the country if the weather's okay. What about you - you want to come along don't you?"

"Well, I don't know," answered John, looking at Hannah with a suddenly shy expression.

"I do!" said Hannah, smiling at him. "We're coming, and we're going to have lots of fun." She squeezed his hand, and looked appealingly at him "Aren't we?"

The shy look disappeared from Big John's face.

"We sure as hell are, starting right now - excuse us?"

They went back onto the dance floor, where Inglis watched them for a couple of minutes. It was quite unreal the way they complimented one another, each bringing the other into perfect scale. The dance was a quickstep this time - safe! - so Inglis took Kerstin onto the floor, and once more they glided around, molding their bodies together.

For the rest of the evening they were left almost alone, as Big John and Big Hannah danced on and on, for half an hour at a time. When the band finished at midnight, Kerstin suggested they all have a nightcap at her apartment. She shared it with Bjorne, who had gone home for the weekend.

The apartment was in a luxury block - centrally heated, as most of the blocks seemed to be in Sweden. Kerstin and Bjorne had a suite each, at opposite ends of the large apartment. Between them was a central dining and living area - complete with a spare room for the live-in maid! Mr. Larsen paid the rent and the maid, in return for which his offspring were expected to pass every exam. No pass, no apartment - devastatingly simple. Apparently that was his only rule. Whatever else they did was up to them, without censure, as he trusted their inherent common sense. Just so long as they passed. And he did pay the maid's wages after all, so everyone knew where her loyalties lay.

Hannah's single apartment was on the same floor of the building; which was how the girls had met in the first place. Hannah was already in the final year of her degree course. Her father owned a prosperous shipyard in Stockholm, and operated several coastal vessels.

The table in Kerstin's apartment had been prepared earlier in the evening by the maid, who had retired to her room for the night. Under the cover there were cold cuts of meat, cheeses, and a large bowl of fresh fruits. Kerstin had it all planned before she even left home, the scheming little minx! The fruit must have come expensive at this time of the year, but who were they to worry about it right now?

The latest weather forecast for tomorrow was fine and clear. Kerstin had ordered a picnic hamper, which they would pick up at ten o'clock in the morning. Inglis offered the opinion that her supplier must think she was crazy going on a picnic at this time of year. But Kerstin expressed genuine surprise.

"But it is quite common. There will be many people doing the same thing this weekend. In Sweden, if you picnic only in hot summer weather, then you have wasted most of the year. Anyway, you will enjoy it, just you wait and see."

"Yes, but that's no criterion," Inglis answered. "I'd enjoy a picnic in Hell, if you were there."

"Flattery will get you everywhere, young man," she replied, posing sideways, elbow bent in the air, and her hand bringing some blonde locks forward over one eye. She then winked the other eye, and they all laughed.

They took their time at the table, talking and eating, and polishing off the two bottles of wine Kerstin supplied. Inglis gave himself a mental kick in the pants for that - he should have thought of buying some wine, and it hadn't even occurred to him.

At about 1.15am Kerstin rose from the table and stood beside Inglis' chair, putting her arms round his shoulders.

"I think it's time to tuck my big teddy bear into bed."

Inglis glanced at Big John, who suddenly looked embarrassed. But Hannah had things well under control. Rising to her feet, she pulled John's hand, and spoke quite coolly and matter-of-fact.

"My teddy bear's bigger than yours. Goodnight, and sweet dreams. See you in the morning, but not too early."

Big John was struck dumb, and stumbled to his feet as Hannah led him to the door. Just before they passed through, John looked furtively back at Inglis and mumbled.

"Goodnight. See you." His face was bright cherry red.

Inglis laughed as the door closed, and he hugged Kerstin.

"We should go into partnership as Inglis and Kerstin Introduction Agency - okay, okay, Kerstin and Inglis then, Pussycat!"

"Purrrrrr" chuckled Kerstin. "Pussycat want cream." Then she led him to her suite. "But no hanky-panky in the shower tonight. You first, make it quick. Then get into bed while I prepare your surprise."

Inglis stripped and showered quickly, wondering what his surprise would be. The suite was a contrast to her bedroom in Malmo, probably because it was rented furnished. The whole place was done out in apricot and cream, with simple pinewood furniture. A shaggy off-white cover on the bed looked like it might have kept a polar bear warm in the not-too-distant past.

Inglis slipped under the cover, taking off the bathrobe - which he'd worn for all of twenty seconds - and dropping it on the carpet. A few minutes later the lights dimmed, and speakers beside the bed came alive with soft music. It was Ertha Kitt singing 'Old Fashioned Girl'! Instantly Inglis remembered telling Kerstin about the incident at the strip club in Dunkirk. In fact there wasn't much of his recent life she hadn't got out of him as they lay in bed in Malmo. She could be a very persuasive young lady when she tried.

Now she was moving in time to the music, wearing a housecoat as she moved towards the bottom of the bed, hamming it up. Her movements were exaggerated, and therefore funny as well as sexy. She unbuttoned the front of the housecoat, pausing between buttons, and thrusting a leg each time through the increasing gap.

Finally she pulled off one sleeve of the housecoat, then the other, with her back to Inglis. Holding the coat like a cape, she spun round, doing two complete circles before letting the coat flutter to the floor. Underneath, she was wearing a three-quarter length nightgown, also buttoned up the front. The housecoat performance was repeated with the nightgown, step by step. Underneath that was a shorter nightie. One more time she went through the whole act, as Inglis threatened to burst a blood vessel. She was now wearing brassiere, panties, suspender belt, and stockings. If she kept up the current rate of progress, the record would be finished before she got to the point. But she was slinking round the bed, putting on the style in such a hilarious manner, that he just couldn't complain.

Before taking off the suspender belt, she rolled on the carpet, one leg in the air, then the other. Rising to her knees, and still swaying to the music, she removed her bra and tossed it aside, baring her cheeky breasts. Last of all came the panties, which she pulled down a little on one side, then a little on the opposite side, swinging her hips to the side in question.

She was going to have to be quick now, because Ertha was nearly finished, whether Kerstin was or not. With only a few bars left in the song, her panties flew across the bed, and she leaned forward over his head. Inglis put up his hands to caress her breasts - and she pushed herself up again, withdrawing the beautiful bait! Bringing her hands above her breasts, she then ran them slowly down her body, as Ertha sang the final 'old fashioned millionaire.'

On the last beat of the music, she thrust her pelvis forward over the bed, as her upper body bent backwards - and he kissed the honeypot. She bent forward again, withdrawing that prize, throwing him a smoldering gaze from under lowered eyebrows - and tickled his ribs!

Inglis always was ticklish, and he wriggled on the bed for moments before managing to get a hand out to tickle her. That did it! For the next ten minutes they chased each other on and off and round the bed; first one of them in a ticklish situation, then the other.

The trouble was, Inglis was being careful, because he was scared he might hurt her. Whereas she could afford to go all out with no such inhibitions. So the contest was much closer than might be thought. At last they called a truce, collapsing together onto the bed, laughing in each other's arms, gazing into one another's eyes.

"Kerstin," Inglis said, as the laughter subsided. "I love you.....really love you. I wasn't a hundred percent certain until Malmo. But then it hit me hard. I mucked up the unloading because I was thinking of you instead of the cargo. All the way to Stockholm, in Stockholm, and on the way back, you were on my mind constantly. I don't know what I'll do without you. And yet, right now, I don't know either what on earth to do with you....I didn't mean that!" he blurted out, as she stroked his already swollen member. "I mean I'm not eighteen yet, and I don't have a trade or profession, so what do I do?"

He didn't know what else to say, and what he had said didn't sound quite right somehow. She just smiled, stroked his face, and gave him a quick kiss.

"I'll tell you what to do. You find out more about your job and your ship, so you'll know if that's what you really want to do with your life. If by the end of the year, or the end of your voyage, you decide you would like to take up Daddy's offer, then you telephone, and the rest will be taken care of by Daddy - no, wait, I haven't finished yet," she said, putting her hand on his mouth as he went to speak. "Did you meet any girls in Stockholm?"

His mind changed into panic gear as he tried to think of how to explain what had happened in Stockholm in the best light, so she would understand. He decided to tell it as it was.

"Well...yes," he answered. "But only to keep a bargain I'd already made with Harry, the ship's electrician - to entertain his girlfriend's flatmate while he entertained the girlfriend. Nothing happened - I swear it! I just delivered her home and went back to the ship. I don't want any other girls now I'm in love with you."

She hugged him tight and smiled once more.

"Enough talk. Time for Teddy to find Pussy's honey pot."

"Can you just...…..let me look at you.........all of you, first........can, please?" Inglis pleaded.

Kerstin turned on the second bedside light and threw back the covers as he sat up in bed. She stood on the bed in front of him and slowly turned round, with her arms out to the sides.

She was breathtakingly beautiful; like a fairy princess, small and light, and gracefully rounded. When Inglis first met her he would have sworn she was at least five feet three. In fact, she was barely over five feet. She had at first seemed fairly substantial while wearing warm clothes, yet she weighed only eighty-four pounds. But everything was there, and in perfect proportion. It was just that it was all a little smaller and finer than first appeared.

Her skin was smooth and pale, with just a touch of gold where last year's suntan lingered on. In places her skin was almost transparent, the faint and delicate tracery of veins visible beneath the skin. Inglis gazed, and wondered, and he knew he had found his very own little princess, more precious than any other soul on earth. He pulled her gently forward, kissed her stomach, and hugged her hips.

"Oh, Kerstin, I do love you. So much, I feel I might burst."

Then gently, and almost reverently, they made long and fulfilling love; before drifting off into dreamland, where everything was safe forever; and even eternal youth and happiness was a possibility.

CHAPTER 20

On Saturday they got out of bed at eight o'clock - and back in again at eight fifteen - and out once more at nine o'clock. They then had to rush in order to be ready to leave by nine thirty. The maid had been very discreet, preparing breakfast before knocking lightly on the bedroom door just before nine.

Big John and Hannah joined them for breakfast, already dressed for the day, while Kerstin and Inglis still wore their bathrobes. At one stage, while the girls were in the bedroom swapping exaggerations, John told Inglis urgently that he needed clean underwear if they were going to be away for another night. Inglis had told him on the ship that he should bring some, but he was too bashful. Also, he hadn't wanted to appear as if he was taking anything for granted, which was understanable. That's why Inglis had raided his cabin before the Mate relieved him, and put some of his underwear in a bag!

"No worries John. I knew you were too shy, so I grabbed some of your underwear and brought it along anyway."
John looked surprised, then grinned.
"You sneaky little bugger - thanks! Where is it?"
"In your small grab bag, inside my holdall. You can pick it up any time - always glad to be of service. Is there anything else you require, sir - toothbrush, razor blades - dirty postcards?"
John laughed and slapped him on the back, almost pushing his lungs out through the front of his chest. The girls rejoined them, and Inglis hurried to get dressed.

They collected the picnic hamper, which Inglis insisted on paying for - and didn't that make a hole in his wallet! But he had drawn every cent he had coming, and didn't care if he spent the lot on Kerstin - he could soon earn some more. John insisted on paying for a tank of petrol, and by eleven o'clock they were driving through the countryside, past small frozen lakes and streams.

There wasn't a cloud in the sky, and the air was still and silent. There were farms and forests, all cloaked in white, and reflecting the sunlight. They drove with the river on their left for nearly three quarters of an hour, before turning right off the main road in the outskirts of Vargarda. Ten minutes later they turned off the secondary road.

Kerstin said she had a surprise for them, and gave Hannah directions from the back seat, where she and Inglis were comfortably snuggled up in their own little world. The road became not much more than a track, but it had been cleared of most of its snow recently. The countryside was mostly flat to undulating, so there were no steep hills. But they were now gaining a little height gradually, driving among pine trees.

Suddenly there was a substantial gate across the road, with a sign in Swedish - and a strong padlock and chain! It looked like they had gone about as far as they could go.

"What now, oh Great Navigator?" Inglis asked Kerstin.

"Open the gate of course, oh ye of little faith."

She held out a key to Big John, who jumped out to unlock the padlock, before swinging the gate open. Hannah drove the car through, and John closed and relocked the gate behind it. As they drove on Inglis looked inquisitively at Kerstin.

"I'm getting a funny feeling. Why would I be getting this funny feeling? Where are we?"

"Wait and see," said she. "As for your funny feeling, you could cure that by removing your hands from their present position - only kidding - put them back!" She snuggled even closer to him and spoke to Hannah.

"Just stay on the track. The end is where we're going."

Five minutes later they drove into a clearing on top of a small hill. In the middle of the clearing was a log cabin. Inglis wasn't surprised any more, because he'd begun to suspect something of the sort - he was starting to know something about his little Snow Princess.

"Don't tell me," he said. "This is Daddy's cabin, and it's all ours for the rest of the day. Nobody will disturb us, and if we suddenly get snowed in, the whole Swedish army will come and rescue us. What I don't understand is why it's so far from Malmo."

"Wrong, wrong, wrong!" cried Kerstin, clapping her hands like a little girl. "It belongs to one of Daddy's friends. But he's in Malmo using Daddy's one, so there! We won't be disturbed, though - but how did you know Daddy's friend is a General?"

Inglis started to laugh, almost fit to burst. Getting control, he said "Well I knew it had to be something like that - same difference really."

He told her once more what a clever girl she was, and gave her a long strong kiss. Then they all bundled out of the car, and Kerstin unlocked the door of the cabin. Big John fetched the picnic hamper from the boot of the car, while Inglis stood lazily looking around.

The hill wasn't very high, but most of the surrounding country was less high; so he could see a long way over the tops of the trees. It looked like a Christmas card, painted by an artist who started to paint snowclad trees, then forgot how to stop.

The cabin was quite small, with one main room containing a table and chairs, and two bunks, plus a small kitchen/storeroom. At one end of the main room was a stone fireplace and chimney, with the fire already made up. It required only to be lit - Inglis didn't even have to do his Boy Scout bit! Kerstin got him to light it, while she and Hannah unpacked the picnic hamper and set the table.

"This is really cheating, you know," Inglis told Kerstin. "It's not really a picnic when you do things this way."

"It's a Swedish winter picnic," she answered. "If you want your kind, you're quite welcome to take your plate outside and go sit on a lump of snow. But don't blame me if one of your more important parts freezes up and falls off!"

Big John roared with laughter at that one. He was really starting to loosen up now, and was no longer easily embarrassed by Kerstin's jokes. Inglis asked her for walkies while the cabin warmed up.

"I thought you'd never ask!" She turned to Hannah.

"We'll be gone for about an hour - set your alarm - then we can have lunch. I think we'll work up an appetite. Don't do anything naughty while we're gone - if you insist!"

She grabbed a rolled up groundsheet from one of the bunks and handed it to Inglis.

"You can carry that, darling - for emergency use." She was sparkling with humor and mischief, and couldn't give a damn what anyone thought.

They held hands as they set off into the unknown terrors of the forest - following a path beaten out by previous intrepid explorers. Once out of sight of the cabin, they stopped to hug and kiss and touch, and rub cold noses.

"Oh, Kerstin," Inglis moaned. "I want to make love to you again - and again - aren't I terrible?"

"Me terrible too," she answered. "Come, this way Tarzan. Jane know where."

They ran off the path into the trees. They were smaller and younger here, and in places the trees were so close, they had to duck under the branches and weave between trunks. There were larger areas with no snow, where the trees interlocked and blocked out the sky. At one of these places Kerstin stopped, and spoke urgently.

"Quick, gather up the pine leaves."

She bustled around, raking up the pine needles with her gloved hands, and pulling them in towards the middle of the clear space. Inglis followed suit, digging his hands in, and rolling the needles inwards almost like rolling a carpet. In no time they had a beautiful soft bed, over which Inglis spread the groundsheet. Kerstin hoisted her long skirt without ceremony, and whipped her panties off in one quick movement. Then she kissed him hungrily, fumbling with his trouser buttons. He gave her a hand, and they collapsed on the groundsheet, where they made fierce, feverish love. Within minutes it was all over, and they were both spent, panting in each other's arms. They lay facing one another, Kerstin's coat round Inglis, his round hers. Lying like this, it wasn't cold any more.

"Oh, WOW!" he panted. "You can be a savage little tigress when you try, can't you?"

"It's nice to be a tiger sometimes," she answered. "But now I want to be a pussycat again. In a little while we'll try once more. Only this time long and slow, and tender - purrrrr."

She cuddled close to his chest, and he felt warm all over. They lay like that for what seemed a long time, until finally the hunger returned, creeping through his veins. And they made love again, facing each other on their sides. And it *was* long.......and slow.......and tender.........and complete.

After lunch the four of them sat talking round the table for an hour in the warmth of the cabin. Then John and Hannah went for a walk, while Kerstin and Inglis talked the afternoon away - and availed themselves of one of the bunks.

When John and Hannah returned, the shadows were already lengthening. Inglis couldn't help marveling how the tall couple were getting along with each other. What had started out as an attempt to help a friend have some fun, seemed to have become something much more - and he was glad.

Kerstin produced her camera, and they used a complete roll of film taking pictures outside the cabin. They covered every permutation; Kerstin and Inglis, John and Hannah, then each taking a picture of the other three together. Then a few funnies - Kerstin under one of John's arms, Hannah carrying Inglis in her arms! When they finished laughing and mucking about, it was time to clean up, damp down the fire, and head for home - where they arrived after dark. It was Inglis' most memorable day out, ever.

John and Hannah had dinner with them, and Inglis rang the ship for news. The news was that the ship would definitely be sailing at ten in the morning, and the Mate wanted them on board no later then nine o'clock. It was 8pm when they finished dinner, and Kerstin stood up to make an anannouncement.

"I hope you don't mind, but I want to cuddle my teddy bear. This is our last night together until I don't know when. Will you excuse us please?"

The Big Couple rose to leave, joining hands as they walked towards the door, where Inglis had left John's bag. Just before the door closed, John stooped back through and said

"Thanks, both of you. I'll never forget this, and I love you both."
Then they were gone.

Now there was a thing. The Third Mate telling the Cadet he loved him. Wouldn't the sailors have a ball with that one if it ever got out!

They bathed and went to bed. For hours they talked, and made love, and talked, and made love again; and held each other close, and listened to the sounds of one another's bodies; and explored each other anew, and made love again, and talked.

209

Round about two in the morning, Kerstin's voice trailed off in a mumble, and she was fast asleep in his arms, head nestled in his chest. Inglis didn't want to sleep, even though he was tired. He didn't want to waste a single precious moment; happy to be there, holding her close, knowing she was there. Content to feel the small weight of her body asleep on his; to feel her heart beating, where one breast nestled in the hollow below his ribs. He was at peace with the world, and lay like that for a long, long while. Until, some time in the early hours, he too drifted over the border into that other world, where nothing, and everything, is possible.

In the morning Inglis could hardly drag himself out of bed. He had probably been asleep for about two hours, and stumbled around bumping into things - until Kerstin turned the shower on cold. That woke him up!

They took a while to get dressed, because they kept hugging and kissing. He told her his dark secret just before John and Hannah arrived.

"It's maybe not the right thing to say, Princess, but I'm sore as hell down there!"

"Huh!" she retorted. "*You're* sore! Haven't you been watching me? Or did you just think I took up a new way of walking?" They laughed, and hugged once more.

John dropped his bombshell over breakfast. He had proposed, and Hannah had said yes. The wedding would be about this time next year. Meanwhile, Hannah would get her degree, and John was due to sit for his Mate's ticket two months before the wedding. Hannah was sure her father would then employ John on one of his small ships, while she worked in the shipyard design office.

They shook hands and hugged, and celebrated with the last bottle of wine - at eight o'clock in the morning. Once the wine was finished, they had to rush to reach the ship ahead of the Mate's deadline. Kerstin told the others of their own plans for the future as they drove to the docks. Then they held each other tight, dreading the final parting.

On arrival at the ship, they left the girls at the bottom of the gangplank. But the Mate's wife had other ideas. She was on the boat deck, and waved for the girls to come on board and have a cup of coffee with her. John and Inglis changed into their working clothes, then had time to sit down with them for a while. Long enough to tell the Mate's wife all the good news. The girls had been remarkably patient in not telling her before they got there. She was delighted, and for the next fifteen minutes John and Inglis couldn't get a word in sideways.

Finally it really was time for the last hugs and kisses, and they saw the girls to the gangplank, before taking up their positions for leaving port. They stayed on the dock, waving as the crew singled up the ropes. The ship was facing upriver, and the current was flowing downriver, as high tide had just passed.

The pilot wanted to swing the ship's stern out and round, before letting go the last bow rope. There was only one tug, pulling the stern round with the help of the ship's own engine going slow astern, and the helm hard over. On the forecastle they eased out the last rope from the main winch drum, a little at a time, on the Mate's orders.

By the time the ship was at right angles to the dock, the massive rope was bar tight. They had four turns on the big winch drum - which was all it would take - and three of them hanging onto the tail rope to keep it feeding out slowly. Then it happened!

A passenger ship was coming downstream, and would pass close astern of them. Her whistle blared out its warning, and the Skipper shouted at the forecastle through his bullhorn

"Secure the rope!"

Aussie quickly looped a chain strop round the tail rope, as the rest of them held on with all their strength. But still the heavy rope crept round the winch drum. A second strop was put on the rope, and secured to the second lot of heavy cleats set in the deck. The strops took over the strain, and the head rope began to sing.

Oh, my God! If that massive rope broke, it would mow down everything on the dock - and the girls were still there! Inglis ran to the rail and waved his hat frantically, shouting at the girls to get back out of the way. But they couldn't hear his words, and simply waved back at him. He nearly cried or wet his pants in frustration. He waved, and shouted at the top of his voice, straining his vocal chords - but it was useless; they just couldn't hear, and carried on waving.

Inglis could release one of the strops, and ease the rope. Maybe they would hit the passenger ship, maybe not. His career would be finished, but he didn't care a damn. If that rope broke and hit the girls, he didn't want to live any more, never mind have a career. He made up his mind to do it, and the hell with all else. He turned and ran towards the strops, just as the pilot shouted at the dock through the loudhailer, in Swedish. Inglis looked over his shoulder. The two dockies at the bollard turned, waved at the girls, and they all started running - thank God!

The rope was humming and creaking, the strops were threatening to pull the cleats out of the deck, and the winch drum started to smoke as Aussie put it in reverse, and poured sand on the rope from a fire bucket.

"Everybody down!" screamed the Mate, as the whole forecastle began to tremble. There were sounds of cracking, tearing and ripping from the dock, and the rope went suddenly loose. Inglis risked a look, just in time to see the bollard, ripped right out of the solid timber of the dock, spring into the air, and describe an arc into the water - all two tons or so of it. Twenty feet of dockside collapsed and followed it into the river.

It had held just long enough for the danger to pass. The white passenger ship was passing astern of them. The tanker's bow started to swing downstream, and they winched in the rope as fast as it would come. The bollard was left somewhere at the bottom of the river. Inglis waved his hat once more in the direction of the dock, and they were on their way to Oslo.

A moment later Paddy deliberately tripped Inglis as he moved away from the rail, and he landed on his backside. He jumped up and turned on Paddy.

"Fuck you Paddy! What the hell's the matter with you?"

"Sorry Mister McAndrew, SIR. An accident - SO sorry."

There was a grim smile on his face as he stared straight at Inglis. The Mate came hurrying over and glared at them both.

"What the hell's going on here?" he demanded.

For a moment Inglis was tempted to tell him what had really happened, but decided this still wasn't the time.

"Nothing sir. I just tripped and lost my temper."

"Well, watch what you're doing in future then," he said. "And see me in my cabin in ten minutes."

"Aye aye sir," Inglis answered, catching the smirk on Paddy's face, and wishing he had told the Mate the truth. The Mate's wife was leaving the cabin as Inglis got there.

"Have you been a naughty boy, Inglis? I've just been told to take a walk so you can be lectured in private."

"I'm afraid so ma'am. Sorry to disturb."

The Mate made him stand in front of the desk while he glared. The silence lasted for minutes, and Inglis felt more and more guilty, as the Mate continued to glare at him without saying a word. After an eternity, it was almost a relief when he finally spoke.

"Just who the hell d'you think you are, McAndrew?'

That had Inglis stumped, and he didn't know what to say - so he said nothing.

"Well! Answer me - BOY!" That *really* hurt Inglis.

"I'm sorry sir, I don't know what you mean."

"I'll tell you what I mean then. You pranced around on the forecastle like some kind of an idiotic freak just now. What the HELL did you think you were doing?"

"I thought the rope might break sir, and I was worried about the people on the dock. I was trying to warn them sir."

"Is that so?" asked the Mate ominously. "I take it therefore that you consider yourself the only person on this ship capable of perceiving a dangerous situation. No doubt as a result of your long and VAST experience - would that be right?"

"No sir," Inglis whispered.

"Speak UP! I can't hear you. Your voice was perfectly okay for shouting ten minutes ago, wasn't it?"

"Yes sir...I mean, no sir....I mean my voice is okay sir, apart from a slight strain - but I don't think I meant to imply that anyone else wasn't aware of the danger. I was just scared silly for the girls sir."

"SILLY is exactly the right bloody word - thank you. You know, sometimes I don't think you know *what* you think, Inglis. Just after I told everybody to get down, you stuck your SILLY head up to see what was happening. You could have had your bloody head chopped off if the bollard hadn't given way instead of the rope, couldn't you?"

"Yes sir, I suppose I could have sir."

"There's no bloody suppose about it. One day, when and *if* you're ever a *real* officer, you'll make decisions, and give orders, and you'll expect them to be carried out. In the meantime you will do exactly as I tell you - to the letter - or life will become very unpleasant for you, I promise. Do you understand?"

"Yes sir, I understand, and I'm sorry sir. I really appreciate what you have done for me sir, and I'm truly sorry I've let you down. I'll try my best to make up for it."

Inglis meant what he said. He was mortified at having to be told off by this man who had just stood his watches so he could be with his girlfriend. A man he almost worshipped for his decency, and his abilities, and his humanity. If this man said he was wrong, then there was no doubt about it; he *was* wrong, whatever he himself might have thought. The Mate was peering at him.

"You know, I do believe you actually mean that....Right, that's that then. I won't punish you this time, due to extenuating circumstances. But if you step out of line again, I'll come down on you like a ton of bricks. Meanwhile, some time in the very near future, you'd better make up your mind to tell someone what the hell is going on between you and Paddy. That's all, you can go now."

The trip to Oslo was scheduled to take twelve hours, so they should be tying up there by ten o'clock in the evening. They were actually going to a place called Drammen, about twenty-five miles south west of the city, at the head of a long fjord leading off the main Oslofjord.

Inglis was now officially a watchkeeper, so he was free until noon, when he would join Big John on the bridge. But actually, he still had a heap to do besides his watch. He sat in the cabin, trying to read a chapter of the Admiralty Manual of Seamanship, Volume Two. But none of it would sink in. He was brooding over his lecture from the Mate, and moping about leaving Kerstin; and he was working up a hate for Paddy.

At 11.30 Inglis made up his mind, and went aft looking for a showdown. He found Paddy in the crew's recreation room, playing darts with Elvis. A few other sailors were playing cards at a table. Inglis walked over to Paddy.

"I want to talk to you Paddy. You owe me an explanation, and I want to know what the hell's on your mind."

Paddy looked at him casually, with a smirk on his face.

"You're a smartarse, McAndrew. Been at sea a couple of months and think you know it all. Take a man's job, and ponce around like a fancy man with the women. You make me sick. Now piss off, I'm playing darts."

The men at the table had stopped playing cards, and everyone in the room was watching to see what happened. A couple of men grinned as if agreeing with Paddy's words.

"That's not good enough!" Inglis shouted. "I'm not going to piss off. I want to have it out right here and now!"

"What?" said Paddy."You want me to hit you, so you can go running to the Skipper and report me for hitting a superior officer, is that the game? What kind of a bloody fool d'you take me for? Superior! That's a bloody laugh for a start. But I'm not as stupid as you think. One day I'll show you how superior you are, you snotty bastard, if I ever catch you ashore on your own!"

He turned to throw a dart. Inglis was angry, frustrated, and looking for trouble. He shouted at Paddy.

"Okay, you've got it! Tonight in Drammen, outside the dock gates, half an hour after we dock - bloody be there!"

He turned and stormed from the room, shaking with anger. As he stepped onto the catwalk, Elvis caught up with him and grabbed him by the arm.

"For Christ's sake Inglis, don't be so bloody stupid. You've just given him exactly what he wants. The bastard will kill you!"

"It's on, Elvis. Even if he does kill me, he won't get away scot free. I'll get in a few of my own - bloody hard!"

"You don't bloody understand, do you?" he said urgently. "It's not just that he's bigger and older than you. He's a boxer. He was in line for the amateur title in Northern Ireland, and nearly turned professional. You won't even know what's hit you. Have some bloody sense - call it off!"

"No!" Inglis shouted. "It's on tonight. I've got to settle this one way or the other, and I can't back down now. I don't want to back down anyway. You can pick up the pieces if you like."

"Oh shit!" cursed Elvis. "He'll kill you - oh SHIT!"

He turned away, and Inglis went to the cabin to prepare for his watch. He was beginning to regret his rash impulse. But there was just no honorable way out now, so he would have to go through with it. Better a beating than shame.

They tied up in Drammen half an hour ahead of schedule - the ship seemed to consistently make half a knot more than design cruise, whatever loaded state she was in.

A few minutes after ten o'clock Inglis went down the gangplank. Elvis had made one more plea for him to call off the fight, but he was adamant. Inglis was also scared! Who the hell did he think he was, taking on this boxer?

At least Elvis had gone ahead with a few of the hands, and would probably ensure he didn't actually die! It was stupid and arrogant of him, but there was just no way he could back down, and still keep his own self-respect. So, he just had to face the music and make the best of it. Maybe if he could get in a few lucky punches. *That's it, think positive*, he told himself as he left the docks. *Hit him first, and hit him hard.*

Paddy arrived a few minutes after him. Inglis took off his hat and gave it to Elvis, along with his uniform jacket. Now he was just anybody, as they shaped up to each other, in true Marquis of Queensbury fashion. Well, Inglis did. While he was shaping up, Paddy moved like lightning, and Inglis' eyes were already watering before he realized Paddy had hit him! By that time the blows were coming thick and fast, and furious, and Inglis was reeling, unable even to see them coming.

How could anyone hit so hard and so fast? Inglis jabbed his fists out at empty air. Still the blows rained in on his face and chest. He tried to keep Paddy out with fists and elbows while he spotted him. But he might as well have held up a paper bag. Paddy was everywhere and nowhere. Before Inglis could make up his mind to punch him in one position, he wasn't there any more. *Some fight this, you bloody stupid hero*, Inglis thought, just before a piledriver hit him on the side of the head. He went sideways, tripped and fell to the ground. Looking up from his ignominious position, he saw Paddy standing, hands on hips, growling.

"Get up, you snivelling bastard. I haven't started yet."

Oh my God, Inglis thought, *what now? If I stay down here where it's comfortable, I'm a coward. If I get up, he'll execute me. Elvis was right, I AM a bloody idiot. I'm not even a hint of a match for him. Some bloody hero I turned out to be.*

He pushed himself up, and made a quick lunge at Paddy. *One good punch, just one good hard punch is all I need, just to slow him down enough to see.* His right fist went out like a thunderbolt - and hit empty air! As Inglis reeled off balance, another piledriver caught him behind the left ear, bringing an instant galaxy of stars. The ground came up to meet him again, and all he could think was that he hadn't even remotely seen the punch starting, never mind avoid it.

Oh God, oh mother, somebody help me out of this mess. He shook the fog from his mind and rolled over. There was blood in his mouth, blood on his arms; his face and neck were numb. And he hadn't even hit Paddy yet. He dearly wanted to stay down, and have somebody tuck him in and kiss him goodnight. *Please mum, let me sleep. Please mum, wake me up and tell me it's only a nightmare. Coward, coward, coward.* The word sounded noiselessly in his brain. Then he remembered Mum being thrown out by Dad for supposedly playing up with the Polish guitar-playing refugee when he was a child, still on his hands and knees - like now, on hands and knees.

Only now he was supposed to be a man. He groaned and pushed himself back onto his feet. Where the hell was Paddy? Inglis realized he was facing the wrong way, and Paddy was behind him. He tried to turn quickly, but as he turned, the blows rained in on his kidneys, then his stomach and ribs, before the numbing impacts to his face and head once more.

Inglis couldn't see where Paddy was; the scene was dim and blurred. Even with his eyes wide open, he was looking through clouded stippled glass. He lurched forward as his knees buckled. His hands touched Paddy's legs. He grabbed and pulled himself forward. Another terrible blow exploded above his left ear, and the strength went out of his arms; as he heard someone in the distance shouting.

"Let go you bastard, let go!"
Inglis let go. He had no choice. His hands wouldn't do as they were told anyway. He was on the ground again, senses reeling, hardly knowing which way was up any more; but knowing that was the way he had to go, as long as he had any strength left. Somehow, he managed to push himself up on his knees, peering around for Paddy. Paddy found him first - after all, he knew where Inglis was.

More blows rained down on him, and he had another close encounter with the ground. He could hear that voice in the distance again, this time shouting a different message.
"Stay down, you stupid bastard, for God's sake stay down."

Then Paddy started to kick him. The kicks came like machine gun bullets, and at first they hurt. Inglis curled up with his arms over his face, as the kicks began to lose their impact. It didn't matter any more. It didn't hurt any more. He didn't care any more. The faraway voice rose to a scream, repeating itself over and over.
"Stay down...bastard...stay down...bastard...stay down."

Well, I must still be conscious, if I can still hear him, was the inane thought creeping through Inglis' mind, as he relaxed, no longer caring what happened. Somehow, as he relaxed, instead of fading away, he became more aware. The kicking had stopped. The voice went on, but now it seemed closer, and Inglis thought he heard a note of pleading in it.
"Stay down....bastard....stay down....bastard."

Now it sounded breathless, almost sobbing. Inglis opened his aching eyes and saw Paddy quite clearly. The fog was gone, the stippled glass no longer there. Paddy stood with arms hanging loosely by his sides, chest heaving. The words were still coming from his lips, short and clipped between gasps. Saliva ran down from the corner of his mouth, and he wiped it away with the back of his hand, which was covered with blood - his or Inglis'? Not that it mattered a damn.

Slowly, like an old man, Inglis managed to push himself up onto his knees. He stared at Paddy, as his voice rose in pitch, and lowered in volume while he stared back at Inglis.

"Stay down, dear God, stay down, you stupid bastard."

That's when Inglis saw the fear in Paddy's eyes. For a moment he couldn't believe it. He was scared. Inglis knew it, he could *feel* it, though he could feel nothing else. Much later he realized Paddy was just scared he might really kill him; but at the time, the knowledge sent one last surge of adrenalin through Inglis' veins. He tucked his toes forward under his backside, and adjusted his weight, not taking his eyes from Paddy's for a second. Paddy took half a pace forward, his eyes widening almost in horror. Then he stopped.

"No, no...stay down...for pity's sake...stay down."

The hell with the Marquis of Queensbury - what the hell did he know anyway, Inglis thought vaguely. He dug his toes in and surged upward, aiming his head for Paddy's stomach. Paddy didn't move, his eyes widening even further, before Inglis' head hit him just below the ribs, forcing an explosion of breath from his mouth. Inglis felt himself losing balance again, just before the lights went out completely, as Paddy clobbered him on the back of the neck. At least he thought that was what happened - Inglis didn't feel a thing any more...........

He was on his back when he regained consciousness. Elvis and the other sailors were there, looking down at him.

"Jesus Christ!" growled Elvis. "We should have stopped it. Damn you Paddy, you bullying bastard. The Old Man'll kill the whole bloody lot of us now!"

Others nodded and mumbled in agreement. Elvis and Ginger supported Inglis between them. They staggered back to the ship, with Inglis gradually recovering his senses and his breath on the way. A hundred yards short of the gangplank, Inglis had gathered his thoughts enough to mutter

"Hold it......wait a minute." The words sounded slurred and distant, but they all stopped walking.

219

"Listen," Inglis said. "Don't want trouble...Paddy and I....walking along.....minding own business ....gang of toughs.....five of them.....rest of you....came along....broke up....just in time...okay?"

He peered around their faces with his half closed right eye - the left one was closed all the way! They looked at each other, then back at Inglis, and Elvis spoke.

"Okay Inglis, if that's what you want - and thanks."

Paddy leaned over towards him, and Inglis swerved instinctively.

"Shit, hold still man" he said. "The fight's over, and you have to be the dumbest fighter I ever met. But at least you've got some guts. If you keep fighting like that, I'm just gonna have to teach you a bit about *how* to fight. Or that stupid pigheaded stubborn streak'll get you killed. A good fighter knows when he's beat, at least. I'll teach you if you keep your word on the story - okay?"

"Okay Paddy," Inglis mumbled. "I sure as hell need it."

With that they all headed for the gangplank, Elvis still supporting Inglis on one side, Paddy taking over the other.

"Stupid dumb bastard you are," muttered Paddy. "Maybe now you've learned being an officer doesn't make you God. And just because I'm helping you doesn't mean I've fallen in love with you either. You've got plenty humble pie to eat yet."

"Yes, darling," Inglis mumbled, managing to crack a weak grin. Then he nodded to himself - and the pain seared into his brain from the back of his neck. It had been one hell of a painful lesson. Talk about pride coming before a fall - this was the ultimate!

CHAPTER 21

Somehow or other they managed to get on board that night without attracting the attention of the ship's whole complement. Big John - who was still on watch - stacked on a turn with the sailors, but they stuck to the story Inglis had given them. John finally helped him to his cabin, and got him into his bunk. If he found out the truth too soon, he would probably kill Paddy. Jimmy helped with his undressing, muttering softly.

"Oh ma God, whit a mess. We should git the Steward."

In the end Inglis convinced them he would survive until morning, and he didn't want anyone waking the Chief Steward or the Old Man.

The next morning was a whole new ball game. When Inglis woke up he couldn't see! Both eyes were closed right up, and for a while he panicked in silence. Then he found that if he held his head a certain way, he could just see a chink of light through his right eye. Thank God, at least he wasn't blind after all. But when he tried to move, his whole body felt as if it was on fire. He was in a terrible, horrible mess.

His nose was blocked solid, and swollen to twice its normal size. His ears were in a mess, and his mouth felt as though it had been stuffed with cotton wool. There were pains in his chest, stomach, kidneys, back, legs, and just about everywhere imaginable. Except his hands - they were okay, because he hadn't landed a single punch!

Inglis tried to talk, and made a croaking noise. He made it louder, and a few moments later he heard Jimmy getting down from the top bunk. Then the words stumbled from him.

"Oh Jesus...oh ma God...Ah'll git the Steward...dinna move!"

The last bit was more than a little superfluous - Inglis doubted his ability to move right then if his life depended on it. He found out later it was only 6.30am. Meanwhile the Chief Steward arrived, and poked around, and bathed his eyes, and muttered oaths and blasphemies. Finally he told Jimmy to fetch the Skipper. That was a good one, fetch the Skipper. Nobody *fetches* the Skipper! But he came, and the Chief told him they had to get a doctor to come and see Inglis straight away.

The Skipper questioned him, but his answers were hopeless. His words were slurred, and every one was painful to pronounce. The

221

doctor came and caused him pain. He put bandages on his eyes, and gave the Chief instructions. The doctor wanted to take him to hospital, but the one word Inglis managed to get out loud and clear was "NO!"

There was a stream of visitors during the forenoon, and the Mate's wife took up residence in the cabin to keep an eye on him. Jimmy had to move his bedding into the spare stateroom across the corridor until further notice.   Inglis had never felt so helpless in all his life. The Mate's wife had to help him drink - he couldn't eat anything. When he needed to go to the toilet, he made a superhuman effort to walk there; with Jimmy holding and guiding him, and staying with him while he was on the throne. It was frightening to be blind and almost helpless.

Word got back to him that the story had stuck, and the Old Man had given up his investigation. Everyone at the scene of the crime had been marched into his day cabin and questioned separately, and it had been a nervous morning. After lunch the Mate called in, and he wasn't so dumb, as usual. He spoke to his wife, making sure Inglis could hear.

"It's all rubbish you know, about this gang of toughs. Paddy has been niggling Inglis for weeks. Inglis got tired of it, and was stupid enough to challenge Paddy to a fight. Which was just what Paddy wanted - Paddy's a boxer you know - away from the ship of course. Now they're all covering up, but they can't cover up without Inglis' help. You know what I think? *He* told them to cover up, because he didn't want any of them getting in trouble. As if they hadn't caused him enough trouble! But sailors are a funny lot my dear, as you well know. Don't be surprised if, after this, the lot of them look after him like their own kid brother. If not, I might mention my suspicions to Big John. I just hope it was worth all the pain, that's all. Are you awake Inglis?"

"No sir," croaked Inglis.
"That's what I thought" he said. "I'll see you again later, when you are!"
They were in Drammen for nearly forty-eight hours, with the doctor paying three more visits; removing the bandages from Inglis' eyes on the final one, two hours before they sailed.
The Mate had been standing Inglis' cargo watch, which distressed him, after what the Mate had already done for them in Goteborg. But there wasn't a thing Inglis could do about that, except resume his

duties as soon as he was physically capable of doing so. Not once did the Mate try to blackmail him into telling him the truth about the fight. He was a real man, a good man, and had been almost a father to him. Inglis would miss him very much when he left the ship, which would be soon.

It was a thirty-six hour trip to Bergen, where they unloaded half the remaining cargo in just over twenty-four hours. Inglis also insisted on standing his own cargo watch, since he could at least see again. His movements around the deck were still very geriatric, but he had only himself to blame for that, so he gritted his teeth and got on with it. His only real memory of Bergen was seeing the bottom of the harbor - fifty feet below the surface - as if there were almost nothing on it, so clear was the water. But he was on the mend, and when they left Bergen at noon on the second day, he went from cargo watch, to the forecastle for leaving port; then straight onto the wheel, which he took over from Elvis; who was always the helmsman when entering or leaving port, no matter whose turn it was.

Between Bergen and Trondheim they took the inshore route, which meant there was something to see all the way. It also meant that Inglis was busy with his practical navigation after his trick on the wheel. The weather was being kind, and visibility was excellent, so there was really no chance of not knowing exactly where they were.

Inglis therefore spent his time taking bearings on the monkey island, then rushing - like a snail rushes - down to the chartroom to take the readings from the Decca. Then he would plot the two different fixes, and see how close they came on the chart. He was getting good, because nearly every pair plotted inside three cables; which was about how far the ship traveled in the time it took him to scramble painfully from the monkey island to the chartroom.

There was no way Inglis was going to repeat his previous error of applying the variation the wrong way round - not *ever*! He was pleased with himself. His wounds were healing, and he no longer ached with *every* movement; and the world started to be quite a beautiful place again. The mountains and the snow, with the sea below them, were truly spectacular. Just think, he was being paid for a trip others forked out a fair chunk of their earnings to enjoy. In fact, things were going so well that he looked over his shoulder every now and then, to see if

Fate was creeping up on him again.

His watch at sea was now from twelve till four, both day and night. His trick at the wheel that night was really something to remember. They sailed through the fjords in the moonlight, between high mountains capped with snow, in waters that were almost dead calm in places. Twice Inglis felt he was steering the ship into a dead end, only to find a cleft opening up in the mountains, leading off in another direction, just as he thought they might have to turn round.

In one fjord they passed almost directly under a massive overhang of rock two thousand feet above, at the top of a vertical cliff face. John said it was called the Devil's Pulpit. The snow was streaming off the overhang in the wind, yet there wasn't even a breeze on the surface of the fjord. The whole of the next day comprised one scenic wonder after another, until they berthed in Trondheim after sunset.

Inglis didn't go ashore in Trondheim. Though his face was healing, it still wasn't a pretty sight. When he tried to shave, it was tender and painful - so he had decided to grow a beard. The combination of bruising and stubble was enough to give some kid nightmares, so he stayed on board. He stood the Second Mate's watch for him, in return for his favor in Goteborg. That meant he was on duty from midnight until four in the afternoon.

They sailed at eight o'clock in the evening, taking on ballast as they went. The North Sea was in benevolent mood for that time of the year, as they took the offshore route, on their way south to Rotterdam. The ship was to load a cargo for Le Havre and Gibraltar, before proceeding in ballast to the Persian Gulf. Deep sea at last! If he couldn't see Kerstin, he would rather be far away, than just out of reach. The bad news was that the Mate would be relieved at Rotterdam, along with the Second Mate and Second Engineer - and Sparks, the radio operator. All of the departing ship's officers were being promoted. Sparks was being replaced, as he actually worked for the radio company, and was on hire.

They took three days and six hours to reach Rotterdam, docking there at two o'clock in the morning. The trip south had been uneventful, with moderate seas, and winds that had not exceeded twenty knots - quiet for the North Sea.

Big John convinced Inglis they should go ashore together in the evening, having swapped watches with the Second Mate, who was making preparations for his relief. Inglis was reluctant at first, but as John said, he hadn't been ashore since Goteborg, and it was time he crawled back out of his shell. John was right of course. Inglis had been very introspective over the last couple of weeks, keeping to himself, frequently brooding, and not good company.

His face was now almost back to normal, with the beard starting to look like one, instead of a few forgotten shaves. It was time to get back into the world and have some fun. But he didn't want any women. Kerstin was still too close, and he wasn't ready to be good company to any girl other than her. This suited John just fine. He had his Hannah now, and couldn't give a damn for other women, even if he could get one to date him. He'd had his limited fling, and he was seven years older than Inglis.

They arranged to go ashore at six o'clock that evening. Meanwhile Inglis grabbed a few hours sleep before going on watch at eight in the morning. The new Mate came on board at ten o'clock, accompanied by the replacements for the Second Mate and Second Engineer. Straightaway, Inglis knew things were going to be very different from now on. He met them at the gangplank, and greeted the new Mate.

"Welcome aboard sir. The Mate is with the Skipper in his day cabin. They're expecting you sir. I'm Cadet McAndrew, Officer of the Watch."

The new Mate shot Inglis a look from his bleary eyes, and snapped at him.

"It's Captain to you, not Skipper. And it's First Mate, not Mate. Remember it in future. And you're not an Officer of the Watch, whatever you might think. You're a bloody cadet - and don't forget THAT either. One of the new over-educated cadets our masters have taken to inflicting on us too, by the look of you."

Oh boy! This Mate was going to be a real barrel of laughs, Inglis could see that. He was a short skinny man with ginger hair, and he obviously had a complex about his size for a start. Wait till he met Big John! The new Second Mate stood behind him, rubbing his hands

225

together; casting a feeble smile around him, and looking to the Mate for guidance. This pair would make *Forth Venturer* a very happy ship, Inglis didn't think. But at least the Second Engineer seemed a reasonable sort. He stood behind the other two with an honest grin on his face, and a shrug of the shoulders, before turning down the corners of his mouth at Inglis. The trio disappeared amidships while Inglis got on with his duties.

Their Mate Mr. Vickers, and his wife left the ship at two o'clock, after saying goodbye to them all, and wishing them luck for the future. Inglis knew he for one would miss Mr. Vickers even more than he had thought, and wished he was going with him. At six o'clock Big John and Inglis went ashore, discussing recent events in the first pub they came to.

"What d'you think of our new First and Second Mates, John?"

"Bloody First Misery and Second Misery more like, by the looks of them Inglis. I reckon we should get drunk to kill the pain. But from here on in, you and I better look after each other, and cover for each other - right?"

"Right, John, I'll drink to that," Inglis answered, and they got stuck into some serious drinking. Two hours later they were involved in the fringes of a fight, during which a fair amount of pub furniture was damaged. But they extricated themselves safely just before the police arrived, with no damage to either of them. John was on watch at midnight, so two pubs later it was time to make tracks for the ship.

They left Rotterdam for Le Havre at noon the next day. It was a twenty-hour trip, and they docked in Le Havre at eight o'clock the morning after; just in time for Inglis to have a whole cargo watch ahead of him.

On the way from Rotterdam, the new Mate had made his presence felt. He pranced around on the forecastle, giving out unnecessary orders as they left Rotterdam, and again as they entered Le Havre.

During the trip he had Inglis put back on day work, without giving any reason. The Skipper agreed, but only on condition Inglis still did his time on the wheel; so the Mate barked at him on the slightest provocation. Word went round the ship that his cabin was full of gin, and he was a heavy secret drinker. There didn't seem to be much secret about it to Inglis - one look in his bloodshot eyes was enough!

Every time someone spoke to him, he seemed to accept it as a challenge of some kind; and altogether, he had the whole ship in a state of nervous tension within hours of stepping on board. It looked as if someone would have to provide a bit of light entertainment, if *Forth Venturer* was to remain a happy ship. And Inglis was just about at the point of becoming the voluntary court jester. There was no way this little Hitler was going to make his life a misery if he could help it.

When Harry asked Inglis to go ashore with him and the Third Engineer that evening, Inglis said yes straight away, much to his surprise - Harry was just getting used to him saying no all the time.
"New Mate getting under your skin, is he?" asked Harry.
"Bloody right he is!" Inglis answered.
"Well, you're in good company there," said Harry. "The engineers don't appreciate him one little bit either. He'll come a cropper sooner or later if he keeps it up - just a matter of time."

"Yeah, well at least we still have *some* decent officers left on board Harry. We'll just have to make the best of it, and be happy whether the Mate likes it or not, eh?"
"You got it Inglis. Le Havre, here we come. I know a good little place where we can sling our hooks for the whole night!"
Harry's 'good little place' was the De De Bar. It was small and noisy, and it sold good beer. There was a singer, and all the employees, including those behind the bar, were young and female - trust Harry! They got stuck straight into the beer, and listened to the singer for a while. By midnight all the other customers had left, and Inglis asked when the place closed. There were three girls left on duty for three customers.

"When the last customer leaves Inglis, that's when."
He turned to one of the girls who had spent a great deal of time talking to them.
"D'you want to close up shop and go upstairs, darling?" he asked her.
"Okay Harry. You and your friend, and the one with the funny name, bring your beers upstairs."

The three girls cleared the last of the glasses away and bolted the door. Then they took the men through a small door beside the stage, and up a flight of narrow stairs. Inglis wasn't at all sure of this turn of events, or tried to kid himself he wasn't. But he hadn't agreed to go with Harry because of his reputation as a monk, so who the hell did he think he was kidding? Himself, as things turned out.

Inglis was more than a little drunk, and in the girls' apartment he became even drunker. But when it came to the real point of the evening, he couldn't be in it - he couldn't even get it up, as the saying goes. The girl who was trying to get it up, even offered to get him a little boy! Then she gave up, and joined one of her friends with Harry, who ended up having another 'double'. Inglis was the life of the party as he sat and moped drunkenly over Kerstin.

They left Le Havre bound for Gibraltar at two in the morning of the day after. In mid morning they passed within half a mile of one of the true Monarchs of the Sea. The *Queen Mary* was on her way up the English Channel to Southampton - or maybe Le Havre. Inglis watched her passing, cruising through the water at twice their maximum speed. She looked magnificently regal, as she scornfully brushed aside the waves, which were causing the tanker crew some discomfort. Inglis gazed in awe as she disappeared astern of them.

CHAPTER 22

The Skipper strode into the Officers' Dining Saloon with the Chief Engineer, looking for all the world like the Merchant navy's version of Laurel and Hardie. Captain Evans was a small wiry Welshman, nine stones wringing wet, and with a polished hairless dome. Beside him Chief McIntosh looked gargantuan, though he wasn't much over six feet.

At first glance he appeared overweight; but Inglis had reason to know it was mostly muscle. He could remember Chief McIntosh pinning two stokers to the bulkhead - one with each hand - when they were rash enough to think his orders were to be followed casually in their own sweet time. That was before they came to know his little eccentricities. The Chief's shock of thick black wavy hair added inches to his already adequate height.

Inglis had been growing his beard for two and a half weeks now, and was starting to feel quite proud of its three-quarter inch length. Very impressive for a seventeen-year-old - nearer eighteen - Inglis thought. As the Skipper passed the table, he turned to the Chief, and spoke in a piercing whisper.

"Funny how some people will go to great lengths to cultivate on their face what grows wild on their backside, don't you think Chief?"

The Devil got a sudden grip on Inglis as he instantly thought of the rejoinder. The Chief's laughter was just subsiding when Inglis turned to Big John, who was sitting beside him.

"Why is it John, that some people find it impossible to grow on top of their head what grows wild on their backside?"

Big John nearly swallowed the soup spoon as he goggled at Inglis. Out of the corner of his eye, Inglis noticed the Skipper miss a pace and start to turn round. Then he changed his mind, and continued towards the top of his table, as the back of his neck glowed the shade of red preferred for port side navigation lights. Meanwhile, the Chief seemed in imminent danger of silently bursting the seams of his uniform jacket.

Silence reigned supreme as everyone held his breath; but Inglis noticed the Third Engineer struggling hard to keep his face straight.

His beard was less then a fortnight older.

The Skipper sat down at the head of his table with the Chief on his right, and the new Mate - who was glaring at Inglis' right ear - on his left. The old Man shook out his serviette in preparation for the forthcoming attack on the Steward's culinary offerings.

Everyone breathed out in unison, causing a distinct air current. Big John looked across the table.

"You've done it this time Inglis," he whispered. "He'll find a way to make you suffer for that bit of cheek."

Inglis looked at him and smiled at the expression of genuine concern on his face. He was still the tallest man Inglis had ever met, with a build that kept him well out of danger of appearing skinny. A broken nose, and hands the size of dinner plates completed the picture.

By nature he was the epitome of the gentle giant, and on at least one occasion he'd saved Inglis' skin ashore merely by appealing for calm. Nobody ever really cared to disagree with his quiet requests. Inglis distinctly remembered the Maltese sailor, in the bar on their recent visit to Rotterdam, whirling round with his fist raised. He looked straight at the top button of John's jacket, then slowly raised his eyes up the remaining eighteen inches or so; as his fist gradually subsided in sympathy with what his eyes registered. Inglis knew from experience that disconcerting feeling of having suddenly shrunk.

John's only real failing - which Inglis had discovered since taking up smoking - was that he constantly 'forgot' his cigarettes. As he was a heavy smoker, those closest to him were constantly suffering from an accelerated depletion rate in supplies. But for some reason none of them thought to argue about it.

It was an hour after dinner, and Inglis sat smoking a Woodbine Export in the cabin with Jimmy. He'd only been smoking for not much over a week, but was already a heavy puffer. Jimmy's small face was crinkled and creased as he laughed again at the recollection of this evening's little escapade.

"Come on Jimmy," Inglis said. "We'd better get these journals up to date, or the Second Mate will skin me alive. You know what he's turning out like."

"Aye, you're right Inglis. He'd be able to suck up to the Old Man jist fine if he caught ye oot wi' somethin' like that right noo."

Just then the cabin door burst open, and the Skipper himself bowled in, without prior invitation. They both jumped to their feet and faced him. He had never once called on them here before, except on the morning after Inglis' 'fight', when the Chief Steward had sent for him. He must have something pretty important on his mind. Thoughts of keelhauling and midnight paint chipping tumbled over each other in Inglis' disturbed brain.

"Good evening, Sunshine." Inglis squirmed at his recent nickname.
"Good evening sir."
"How good is your Morse code?" he demanded.
"Uh.......improving sir. I was about to go over it again with Jimmy." That was a lie!
"And your semaphore?"
"Well, it could probably do with some improvement sir." Inglis' brain was starting to whirl. What was the old bastard up to now?
"What about your International code flags?" he quizzed.
"Um...coming along sir, but probably needs more practice."

The Skipper peered closely at him, with an evil twinkle in his eyes.
"That's good, because you'll be getting plenty of practice in the near future. We're due in Gibraltar day after tomorrow; and as of right now, you're the ship's signals officer. Goodnight, and sweet dreams, Sunshine!"

He whirled around and made his exit - and Inglis could have sworn there was a gleeful glow emanating from the back of his neck this time.
"Oh Christ, Jimmy," Inglis moaned, looking across the cabin. "He knows bloody fine he's picked my Achilles Heel. How the hell am I going to swat up that lot in a day?"
"We'd jist better start practicin' right noo, I suppose," replied Jimmy. "He really got you, didn't he? But it took him more than an hour to think about it, if that's any consolation."
"It's no bloody consolation at all!" Inglis retorted. "Where the hell are all the books?"
"*I was about to go over it with Jimmy*," said the younger cadet, before dodging a flying shoe.

231

Next day, during Inglis' first trick on the wheel, he was very busy. At least he was now accepted as a good helmsman if nothing else. A copy of the *Oservers Book of Ships* lay balanced on the binnacle, where he could glance at it frequently between the compass repeater and the horizon. It wasn't quite as good as the *Admiralty Manual of Seamanship* - but that was too big to balance on the binnacle. Nevertheless, the pages on International Code Flags seemed packed with more and more unlearnable facts.

Inglis stood with eyes closed, trying to conjure up mental pictures of the alphabet flags. A piercing voice screamed in his ear.

"Watch your head McAndrew, you're five degrees off course!"

When Inglis opened his eyes he saw that Millie was exaggerating - it was only three degrees. The new Second Mate's name was Miller, which would normally have dubbed him 'Dusty'. But this Miller was a fussy, fastidious person, with a falsetto voice, particularly when upset, which was often. He was also the only noticeably religious officer on board.

The old Swedish bosun had christened him Millie within minutes of their first acquaintance, and the name had been adopted by the rest of the crew as a natural. It was now his responsibility to teach Inglis navigation, for which Inglis had a natural bent in any case. But Millie always seemed to make it much more complicated than it really was. During his watch at sea, he was constantly fiddling with his sextant, as though he had doubts about his last plot on the chart, which was probably all of ten minutes old. The rumor was that he had run a ship aground while Acting First Mate, and he was terrified of ever doing it again. No doubt having heard of their mishap in Copenhagen would have strengthened his resolve.

Millie had given Inglis a thorough dressing down for kinking the Trident log line on clearing Le Havre. This had resulted in a few extra minutes elapsing before it functioned properly. He had pranced up and down, waving his arms as if practicing semaphore, and drummed into Inglis' head the absolutely vital importance of the log being functional in time to coincide with his shore sighting and official starting time - which was all a load of poppycock. When he had quite finished, Inglis made what he thought to be a generous and conciliatory offer.

"If you'll just lend me your chronometer, I'll nip up to the monkey island, get a couple of quick cross bearings, and we can start from there, Second."

He obviously wasn't accustomed to first year cadets saying such things. His look reminded Inglis of the time he took a liberty with a new girlfriend - a second before her cute little hand made contact with his face!

Then of course, the Second Mate had started in on the prancing and waving act, and Inglis gazed at the horizon, resigned to a long unheard lecture. He hadn't forgotten to remind Inglis that he should 'address' him as SIR, and not Second.

At the end of his trick on the wheel, the First Mate collared him, with a glint in his eye. The glint was quite an achievement, as his eyes were usually dull and bloodshot from his first bottle of gin - which he seemed to need before facing the rest of them for the day.

"The pantry boy's sick," he blurted. "Report to the Chief Steward for the rest of the day. I'm sure he'll find enough to keep you out of mischief."

"AYE AYE, SIR!" Inglis boomed out, standing rigidly to attention, and glaring an inch above his red hair - which was separated from the deck by five feet five inches of scrawny freckles. It amused Inglis to do this with the new Mate, because it subjected him to no little embarrassment, about which he could do absolutely nothing by way of official reprimand. He had started off by gunning for Inglis, so Inglis was taking a few pot shots back, and they would see who gave in first. Being stubborn was one thing Inglis had had plenty of experience in.

As usual, the patches of skin between the freckles glowed the same color as his hair, and he glanced furtively around to see who was listening. Before he could think of anything more to say, Inglis broke away and slid down the handrails of the ladder from the wing of the bridge to the boat deck. This exercise usually gave him visions of being a paratrooper in a red beret, and was much more interesting than using your feet on the steps. Mind you, if you picked the wrong moment, especially in a rough sea, it could be a bone shaking experience to meet the deck coming up at you on the roll, just as you were in full flight.

"Come in!" boomed the voice from behind the door, and Inglis strode into the Chief Steward's lair. He sat in his swivel chair, looking like one of the witches from Macbeth. He had been christened Horatio Louden, but answered only to Chief. Inglis had often wondered how much ribbing he'd suffered as a young steward, and concluded that he *had* to make Chief just to get away from it.

He was another smallish man, but thickset and powerful. When he was angry, his brow furrowed, his chest puffed out like a pigeon, and the tip of his long curved nose quivered a fraction of an inch from his equally curved chin. Altogether a frightening vision to behold, especially as the little dark eyes seemed to bore right through you.

For his nose to come so close to his chin, it occurred to Inglis that at some time he got the wrong set of false teeth, liked the ferocious result, and decided to keep them! His hobby was playing the bagpipes, and since his cabin was next door, Inglis sometimes had to catnap at unusual hours when he was in the mood to practice. It's usual to use a chanter for bagpipe practice; but due no doubt to the restricted clearance between nose and chin, the Chief always practiced on the full pipes - which of course are blown from the corner of the mouth, clear of facial obstructions.

The piercing eyes glared at Inglis from their positions abeam of the heroic nose.
"Been annoying the Old man again, McAndrew? Some o' you young loons never seem to learn that life's a lot easier if ye keep yer heid doon."
"Ah well, Chief," Inglis rejoined. "I can't help it you see. It just seems to come natural like; and you have to admit it does make life more interesting."
"Aye, ye could be right," says he. "Now you jist nip doon and see the Second Steward in the officers' pantry. I'm sure he'll manage to make life more interesting for you for a while. In fact, I've already taken the trouble to instruct him accordingly. 'Make life more interesting for Mister McAndrew' I told him, so off you go and see what he's got for you."

The Second Steward had quite obviously been adequately briefed,

234

and welcomed Inglis with open arms.

"Here's some soap. The bucket and scrubbing brush are in that cupboard. Let's have the deck in here scrubbed spotless. Then you can empty the slop bucket and scrub that out; and when you've finished that, the big refrigerator needs cleaning. I'll be back in an hour to see if you've done it all."

The utter indignity! Here he was, the company's Senior Cadet on an oceangoing tanker, deputizing for the pantry boy. The humiliation, and shattered dreams of greatness. What was he being trained as - Superior Char Lady Number One? S.C. = Senior Cadet or Superior Char - *you can cut THAT out*! Still, where there's life, there's hope.

Inglis was nearly finished his floor scrubbing when the idea began to form in his mind. The Bosses wanted to play silly buggers with him, why not play silly buggers with them? Gradually the idea took definite shape.......

Every evening at dinner, the same ceremony was enacted towards the conclusion of the meal. The Old Man would ease himself in his chair, look towards the pantry serving hatch, and in would march the Second Steward with the Skipper's special cheese dish. With an impressive flourish, the Steward would whisk off the lid under the Old Man's nose, and the ritual nibbling and savoring would begin. The big slab of soap Inglis was using on the floor looked remarkably like Captain Evans' favorite Cheddar cheese.......

He nipped across to the refrigerator, opened the door, and peered at the mixed delicacies within. There, in pride of place on the middle shelf, was the magnificent cheese dish, quietly awaiting its daily moment of glory. Lifting the lid, he noticed with soaring spirits, the large block of Cheddar in the middle, surrounded by smaller pieces of Danish Blue and other lesser Evans favorites; basking in the reflected glory from big brother in the middle.

Inglis shot across the pantry and bolted the door; grabbed the Cheddar, and cut a thin slice with the cheese knife. Then he repeated the process with the soap. Perfect, bloody perfect - they both cut almost exactly the same! In seconds he had the soap trimmed to shape and size, and ensconced in the place of honor.

Dinner that evening seemed to drag on forever. Half way through dessert, Big John looked at Inglis curiously.

"What the hell's the matter with you, Inglis? You've done nothing but fidget and brood for the last twenty minutes."

Inglis glanced anxiously at him, his brain whirling.

"Aw, you'd be fidgeting and brooding too, if you'd spent the day scrubbing the pantry, and had to act as Signals Officer from the morning. I suppose your signaling's perfect then, is it?'

John grinned down at him over the table.

"Is that all that's worrying you? As a matter of fact, my Morse is terrible. I was meaning to thank you for so selflessly volunteering to take on the job as you did. It was very thoughtful of you, and I really appreciate it."

"You big bloody mullock heap!" Inglis said. "It's a never-ending source of amazement to me why the Old man doesn't tie a chain round your neck, and use you for an anchor!"

Big John grinned at him with delight and relief.

"That's more like it - back to normal!" he whooped, prior to sinking another two-pound morsel of apple pie. But Inglis wasn't back to normal. He had begun regretting his rash impulse some time ago, and was trying to figure a way out of his predicament. It had seemed such a great joke at the time; now he wasn't nearly so sure. But there was just no way he could get to the cheese dish now - maybe if he tripped the Second Steward?

The big moment arrived, and Inglis missed his chance. In marched the Second Steward while he was still thinking about it. Off came the lid of the cheese dish with practiced perfection.

Slowly the Old man buttered a cracker, and carefully reached for the cheese knife. Inglis could barely watch from the corner of his eye - it definitely hadn't been such a great idea. He held his breath in anticipation. Captain Evans was taking some Danish Blue! Maybe he wouldn't have any Cheddar tonight? Inglis could surely re-switch them tomorrow. *And maybe pigs fly also*, he thought.

Five more minutes dragged past, during which he had some more Danish Blue, and a slice of Edam. Then horror of horrors, the knife was poised over the Cheddar. Inglis nearly shouted at him to leave it alone, but that wouldn't help much now.

Off came a thick slice, to be carried with reverence, and deposited on the large cracker biscuit. Delicately, between thumb and forefinger, the delicious morsel was conveyed to the Captain's mouth. His eyes were closed in sensuous anticipation. In slow motion he began chewing, eyes still closed.

Suddenly and simultaneously, the eyes popped open and bulged, bits of half chewed biscuit and soap sprayed indiscriminately around the table; the Skipper's chair flew back, and a great roar of rage and frustration filled the saloon.

The Steward cringed in terror, the Mate ducked to avoid flying debris, and the Chief Engineer sat stolidly, with a bemused expression on his face. The Old Man grabbed a carafe of water and filled his mouth. Showing a remarkably quick recovery time, the Chief Engineer's hand swooped on the cheese dish lid, and held it upside down in front of the Skipper's face for him to spit in.

Captain Evans strode down the room, carafe in one hand, cheese dish lid in the other, spitting as he came. He glared at Inglis as he passed, and choked as he spoke.

"Day cabin McAndrew - NOW!"

Inglis sat enthralled for a moment. He'd heard of people frothing at the mouth with anger, but this was the first time he'd seen it with his own eyes! Big John leaned across the table, eyes wide open in horror as he stared at Inglis in disbelief.

"Jesus, what have you done, Inglis? You'd better get up there at the double, or you'll be in even more trouble. Though I can't for the life of me imagine more trouble than you're in already. Christ man, you must have gone round the twist!"

Inglis bounded up the stairs two at a time, his heart in his mouth with trepidation. It had definitely been funny, but was it worth the consequences? Ah well, most great artistes had to suffer for their art at some time, and there was no way he was going to be a willing partner to M.V. Misery Venturer. *Somebody* had to be the jester!

The Skipper's day cabin door was open, so he walked straight in, rapping the door panel with his knuckles as he passed. Might as well get it over with. Captain Evans was struggling valiantly with his affliction - infliction? - now holding an opened bottle of wine in his hand - what a waste! - while spitting in the sink.

"You young bastard....you did this....*gasp*....I know you did......*cough*. I'll kill you....*gargle*......I'll have the Chief Engineer....*gasp*....lock you in the....*gulp*....forrard pumproom."

He choked, coughed and gasped for a few minutes, while Inglis wondered vaguely in which order these terrible fates were to apply. He started to open his mouth to plead his case - what case? It was open and shut, like his mouth!

"Shut up - *gasp* - shut up - *choke* - Don't say a word - *gulp* - I know you did it - *gargle* - what the hell - *sputter, spit* - has got into you?"

Inglis stood silently while he continued to gulp, spit, cough and splutter. The Skipper had ordered him not to say a word, hadn't he?

"Well - *gulp* - damn you - *cough, spit* - answer me!"

Inglis opened his mouth and closed it again twice before starting.

"Well, I suppose it must have been me sir. You see, I was scrubbing the pantry floor this afternoon - one of my important new duties under the new Mate - and then I had to clean out the refrigerator. The floor soap and the Cheddar do look very alike, sir. I must admit, I did take the lid off the cheese dish to have a look..."

"Can I help, sir?" came the voice of doom from behind Inglis. He turned and saw the Chief Steward standing in the doorway, casting an evil and ferocious glare in his direction. Oh my God, caught in the middle. Now they would just chop him into little pieces, and flush him down the Skipper's toilet; and nobody would ever know what brought an abrupt end to his potentially brilliant seafaring career. The *Queen Mary* would never enjoy the glory of his command!

Captain Evans' strangled voice brought Inglis back from his noxious reverie.

"Get out - *cough* - McAndrew - *choke* - I'll deal - *splutter* - with you later - *hack, spit*."

Inglis practically ran out of the cabin, neatly sidestepping the Chief Steward's solid glare. Free, free - temporarily at least. Now he could resume his rapid climb up the ladder of promotion to fame and fortune! Suddenly he stopped, with a jolt of memory. Looking at his watch he realized they were due in sight of Gibraltar tomorrow morning - in eleven hours from now to be precise - and he was now Signals Officer. He abruptly changed course, and climbed back up the stairs to the chartroom. Once there, he began sorting methodically through the pigeonholes in the forward bulkhead. Each flag was taken out, unfurled, and checked against the wall chart, then returned to its place, neatly furled. This took quite a time.

In addition to the ship's recognition flags - G,H,J,C - Inglis double checked the bright red B flag, which is flown by all tankers carrying, loading, or unloading petroleum - they had five spares of that one. Also the 'Red Duster' ensign, and finally the company House Flag - a huge ensign which flew from the top of the mainmast when entering and leaving port. And quite often at sea also, depending on somebody's whim. It comprised a St.Andrews Cross, with red lion rampant on yellow background at the intersection of the cross, plus the company shield logo next to the jack in the middle.

This latter was the largest flag Inglis ever saw, and always caused problems whenever it was hoisted. In the morning he intended enlisting Jimmy's help to get it out of the way first.

For his final check, he made sure that G, H, J and C were tightly furled, with their lanyards wrapped around and tucked in with the toggles free. The authorities in Gibraltar, being R N orientated - were notoriously severe with British ships in any way lax with their signaling.

At ten in the evening by his watch Inglis turned in, tired but happy, in the thought that the Old Man hadn't yet carried out any of his threats on his person.

CHAPTER 23

By first light Inglis was up and about. In the bathroom mirror he was admiring and trimming his beard, which looked tawny, with red glints in it. The contrast with his blond hair was startling. He decided he should really have taken up pirating, and looked closely in the mirror.

"What big blue eyes you have, Grandmama," he told himself.

"Aye, they're beautiful! But the Second Mate jist rushed intae the cabin and ordered me tae tell ye we'll be raisin' Gibraltar in under half an 'oor!"

Inglis spun round to stare at Jimmy standing in the doorway.

"But Christ man, we should have more than an hour yet!"

"No, I think Millie jist didna' estimate it right. Or we've been pushed by a current he disna' ken aboot. Or mair likely he jist worried himsel' into makin' anither mistake."

They both ran to the cabin. As Inglis struggled to retrieve his left leg from the right leg of his uniform trousers, he shouted at Jimmy.

"Soon as you're dressed, nip up to the chartroom and fetch the Red Duster, while I sort out the house flag. On your way aft, ask the bosun to send me a hand to the mainmast; then come back and join us. It'll take the three of us to get that pig of a thing up in under fifteen minutes in this wind."

'AYE AYE SIR!" yelled Jimmy, standing stiffly to attention, and throwing him a mock salute, before peeling off at a high rate of knots with a cheeky grin.

It was a dull gray early April morning, with a heavy swell from the starboard quarter, and a stiff following wind. The ship was rolling and pitching, and she was still well down in the water, having unloaded only twenty percent in Le Havre. The seas were frequently rushing across the low main deck.

That meant they would have to hoist the house flag from the catwalk instead of the deck. Which in turn meant there would be no room in which to maneuver. Inglis fetched the vast bulk of the house flag from the locker, and ran aft along the catwalk to the mainmast. There, he began to unlash the long bamboo pole from its position

240

along the catwalk rail. Just as he was undoing the final lashing, Aussie came running from aft - the first time Inglis ever saw him running - followed by Jimmy.

Together they started to lash the tailings of the house flag to the bamboo pole, while Jimmy freed the main halyard, and unclipped the toggles. Aussie and Inglis struggled to keep the house flag from unfurling prematurely in the stiff following wind, while Jimmy gazed up at the dizzying height of the mast. Inglis cursed the parent company for being renowned as having the tallest masts on the seas. Any decent tanker had masts as short as practicable, but their masters in their wisdom decided that their flag should fly more than a hundred feet above the sea. The two huge masts must have added thousands to the cost of the ship.

The flag's bamboo pole had a toggle at the bottom, and another one two thirds of the way up, with the flag itself being lashed to the top two thirds. This meant that, when hoisted aloft, half of the flag projected above the topmast truck. It also meant that, in any kind of a wind, the damned thing had a mind of its own, once clear of the deck. They toggled her onto the halyard, then Inglis told Aussie and Jimmy to steady her clear of the catwalk, while he began to hoist.

Once clear of the deck, Inglis got Aussie to help him with the halyard, as the wind was really pulling at her, and it was all he could do to hold her. Jimmy backed off a few paces for a better view, and called out as the flag neared the lower shrouds. Just below the shrouds they let her stream for a few moments, while they hung on and caught their breath.

"Right, let's have a quick run past the shrouds - Now!" Inglis shouted, and he and Aussie tugged in unison, hand-over-hand.

"Whoa!" screamed Jimmy, in most un-nautical style. "She's going between the shrouds!" Just as they felt the halyard stick.

"Pull her back on the other line Aussie, while I hang onto this one."

Four times they caught her in the shrouds, cursing and swearing all the time. At the fifth attempt they were past. But more than ten minutes had gone already, and they still had the upper shrouds and the fore-and-aft stay to circumvent. Whoever had the brilliant idea of doing things this way, should have been made to do it himself a few times in a gale, by way of discouragement.

There were no yardarms on the mainmast, so she had to fly from the truck, or not at all. The upper shrouds were almost at the topmasthead, and weren't usually too much of a problem. But first they had to get it past the mainstay; which ran from the mainmast to the foremast, high above the monkey island, and about twenty feet below the truck. They got her half way past at the first go, then she started to curl round the stay.

"DOWN!" Inglis screamed, and they pulled her clear.

At the third attempt they almost had her past, when Inglis glanced at his watch - they had been at it for nearly twenty minutes! A feeling of deep despair almost overcame him as he looked up again, just in time to see the lower corner of the flag catch up on the stay.

"KEEP PULLING!" he bellowed at Aussie, who was all of two feet away. But she stretched tight and refused to let go.

"Damnation and hell's teeth," Inglis cursed. "That bloody stay must be frayed, and she's caught up on the wire ends. One more good heave, Aussie."

They heaved as hard as they could, almost hoisting themselves in the air - and suddenly the flag ran the last few feet to the top. There she streamed, massive and beautiful - with a chunk torn out of the bottom corner! Inglis nearly wept as he looked from the flag to Aussie, who merely shrugged.

"She'll be right mate," he offered philosophically.

The Second Mate appeared at the after end of the boat deck, waving his arms, and Inglis turned back to Aussie and Jimmy.

"Lash the bastard on at that!" he shouted, starting forward at the run. By the time he climbed to the bridge, he was gasping for breath. The Second Mate dumped the recognition flags in his arms, shouting as if he was a mile away.

"At the double! Gibraltar's coming up now. I already toggled the flags together for you."

Inglis struggled down three decks to the catwalk, staggered along the forward catwalk to the forecastle, and undid the starboard yardarm halyard. At least here there were no obstructions, and he could hoist the flags right up to the yardarm, furled all the way, before breaking them out.

He quickly toggled the top flag to the halyard, then the bottom one. Hoisting away hand-over-hand, they rapidly climbed to the yardarm. He gave a fierce tug on the bottom halyard. Simultaneously, the four flags unfurled, streaming beautifully in the wind.

"Thank God for that," Inglis said out loud, lashing the halyard to the after forecastle rail. A movement on the bridge caught his eye as he turned. The Second Mate was jumping up and down, waving his arms and pointing at the flags. *What the hell's the matter with that stupid bloody ponce now*, Inglis wondered. Then Captain Evans appeared on the wing of the bridge with the bullhorn at his lips. This time Inglis had no trouble hearing the terrible words, booming out loud and clear.

"You silly bugger, you've got them upside down. Get them down, get them down, for Christ's sake *get them down!*"

Galvanized into action, Inglis ran the flags down as fast as he could - which wasn't as fast as it should have been. In his haste he tied himself in knots, before managing to run them back up again, the right way round.

Thanks a bloody million Millie, was Inglis' thought, *for being so thoughtful as to toggle the bastards together for me!*

By this time Inglis was absolutely mortified, and exhausted to boot. Meanwhile, a baleful eye of light began to wink at them from the Gibraltar Signal Station. Inglis could only guess at the rude, sarcastic message carried on that beam of light. He didn't even try to read what it said, though technically he should have been on the bridge writing it down. But even he couldn't make a bloody fool of himself in two places at once! He looked at the Signal Station, and something inside him suddenly rebelled.

"STUFF THE WHOLE BLOODY LOT OF YOU!" he shouted at the top of his lungs in the direction of Gibraltar. But of course, Gibraltar took no bloody notice! And just to make things worse, there was a whole fleet of warships in and outside the anchorage - including a bloody great American aircraft carrier. Talk about advertising. Here comes *Forth Venturer* to give them all a drink, with her flags flying upside down.

All British merchant ships have recognition signals beginning with the letter G. Also, each alphabet flag has a second meaning to convey a complete message. Having run up the flags in reverse order, and being obviously a British ship, the message could be read as:-

C – yes,

J - I am on fire and have dangerous cargo aboard, keep well clear of me.

H - I have a pilot on board

G - I require a pilot.

Unfortunately, all four of these flags look exactly the same upside down as they do the right way up - which is true of nineteen of the alphabet flags. From that day forward nobody had to struggle with the pronunciation of Inglis' given name. He became known as Flag McAndrew, very quickly shortened to Flagmac, then simply Flag. Some smart character even suggested printing Flag T shirts!

As soon as they docked in Gibraltar, Inglis was summoned to the Captain's cabin. He didn't mince words, and he didn't waste too many either. He repeated - just in case Inglis hadn't clearly understood the first rendering - that he was a silly bugger. Not only was he a silly bugger, but he hadn't yet been dealt with for the cheese dish episode. And if he thought Captain Evans had forgotten *that*, he could bloody well think again. He asked Inglis if he had anything to say for himself, and this time he shut up. There was no point in telling him it might have been okay if Millie hadn't toggled the flags together. That would only get him into trouble, without getting Inglis out of it.

The Ship's Log was on the Captain's desk, massive and threatening. The Skipper's fountain pen lay alongside, ready and willing to make an entry, and wasn't disappointed. In went Inglis' name, together with the punishment for screwing up his duties as newly appointed Signals Officer. Fined two weeks wages, and not allowed ashore during the stay in Gibraltar.

The second bit Inglis didn't mind in the least. Who wants to wander round Gibraltar with no money, and everybody's finger pointing at the Silly Bugger!

"As for your brilliant soapy cheese idea," said Captain Evans. "It's up to you whether it goes in the book or not. What I *want* to do, is make you scrub decks, chip and paint, and clean the whistle for eight hours a day. In addition to a two-hour trick on the wheel each day, *plus* two hours navigation training, *and* an hour's ropework, *and* an hour's *Signals* study. *Plus* keeping your journal up to date. This to continue every day, including Sunday, until we reach Port Said. Where a review will be made; but not necessarily a favorable one."

Christ, he was really getting tough now. Inglis would have hardly enough time left to sleep!

"Of course," he added. "You may think that's a bit too harsh of me. In which case, we can just enter your little lark in the Log - and fine you another month's wages. But without the extra scrubbing and cleaning. Which will it be?"

Inglis stood up straight, his brain churning like a tin of live worms. There really wasn't much choice to be made. A month's wages, and a second entry in the Log on the one hand. On the other, a bit of extra work for a week or so - off the record. He made up his mind on the spot.

"I'll do the scrubbing and cleaning sir. And I appreciate being given the choice. I'll try not to make any more stupid mistakes in future sir, and....."

"ENOUGH!" shouted the Skipper. "I asked for an answer, not a bloody speech. Report to the Mate - NOW!"

"Aye aye sir." Inglis spun round and departed.

The Mate loved every moment of it, his bloodshot eyes almost shedding alcoholic tears of joy as he got his turn to have a shout at Inglis.

"Right! While we're here in Gibraltar, your cargo watch takes up eight hours. That leaves six hours for the good bits. From six to seven thirty tomorrow you'll scrub the wheelhouse. From four thirty till seven tomorrow you can start cleaning the whistle. The bosun will give you what you need for that. Then from seven to nine each day you can sand the bridge rails. Now you're on watch, so MOVE IT!"

Generous of him - he was giving Inglis half an hour for breakfast, and *another* half hour for tea. He'd thought maybe Jimmy would have to sneak him some sandwiches. He hurried off to the deck office, where Big John had been standing in for him during his lecture.

The shore pipes were coupled up, and pumping had begun when Inglis took over the watch. For the first hour he was too busy for contemplation. Later he had time to think about how his career was progressing. A bit like the ship, he thought - up and down with the wind, waves, and weather.

How would the Middle East treat him he wondered? Maybe things would pick up with the temperature. Already they had sailed from winter to summer in a couple of weeks.

Inglis had been at sea for exactly three months, so he could hardly expect to be an old salt yet, but no harm trying?

On the other hand - Land of the Arabian Nights, here comes Flag; so, lock up your daughters, and start shaking with fear – or..........?

Lightning Source UK Ltd.
Milton Keynes UK
UKOW02f2307180515

251808UK00001B/28/P

9 781908 481931